SHIRLEY CONRAN

TIGER EYES

M

MACMILLAN

LONDON

First published 1994 by Macmillan London

a division of Pan Macmillan Publishers Limited
Cavaye Place London SW10 9PG
and Basingstoke

Associated companies throughout the world

ISBN 0-333-61935-8

1 3 5 7 9 8 6 4 2

A CIP catalogue record for this book is available from
the British Library

Typeset by CentraCet Limited, Cambridge
Printed and bound in Great Britain by
Mackays of Chatham PLC, Chatham, Kent

This book is dedicated to
Mary Haft
who knows what the most important thing in life is.

CHAPTER ONE

INSIDE the Russian Tea Room there was a sudden ominous silence. Waiters paused in mid-swoop; the small Cossack orchestra stopped playing abruptly; elegantly dressed diners jerked up their heads and listened.

Outside, the sky exploded.

Within the restaurant, they all heard the rockets whoosh, then the frantic shrieks of people on the snow-piled street, followed by the peremptory scream of police sirens, and the urgent, hoarse hooting of foghorns.

Then a carillon of bells, pre-recorded and amplified, trilled over 57th Street. 'Happy New Year,' everyone cried, as New York slid noisily into 1992.

A waiter, wearing dark green Cossack tunic and pants tucked into crimson boots, poured more champagne into Plum's glass. As she lifted it, one of the shoestring straps of her bronze chiffon baby-doll dress slid from her shoulder. From across the table, Breeze Russell's clear blue eyes sent a warning look to his wife as, imperceptibly, he shook his blond head. The mere sniff of a cork made Plum giggle: it was a family joke.

Over a festive litter of silver confetti and six half-finished desserts, Breeze looked into his wife's big, hyacinth blue eyes, double-fringed with long black lashes, beneath a cap of red curls. Although she was thirty-six years old, her face still had an innocent, child-like quality. Breeze winked lovingly at her. For once, Plum had made an effort; she looked great tonight. When she felt like it, Plum could switch on an inner energy that lit up the delicate cream complexion, the appealingly uptilted nose and the generous, beautifully modelled pink mouth that still bewitched him.

Defiantly Plum lifted her glass, tossed her boyishly short red curls and smiled across the table at her husband. 'Happy New Year, darling,' she said, thankful that it would soon be over. She always felt uneasy on New Year's Eve, which had proven unlucky for her; whenever her life seemed truly wonderful, something seemed to change it for the worse, and particularly so on New Year's Eve. Too late, Plum would realize that given a little foresight, she might have avoided the disaster, but she lacked this magic power to foresee the future and twist it away from disaster.

However, tonight's New Year's Eve had nearly slid into the past – and nothing sinister had happened, Plum told herself: on the contrary, her immediate future looked particularly lustrous. Plum was *en route* from London to Australia, where an exhibition of her paintings was to be held in Sydney. Breeze, who was also her agent, had suggested that she break her journey at New York for a meeting with gallery owner Pevensky, who had expressed interest in giving her a New York show. They had decided to make it a family Christmas treat, so Plum's two sons (currently whooping it up in the Village) had also journeyed to New York.

Breeze looked around the table to catch the attention of his four guests: Jenny who was Plum's closest friend since their art college days, an effervescent woman with a carefully tangled mass of honey-coloured hair; Leo, a design journalist who wrote for *New Perspective* magazine and charmed women, although men never understood why or how. Leo had a slightly chubby, fresh complexion, wore gold granny spectacles, and might be Jenny's lover before the evening was over. Although only thirty-four, his fine sandy hair had already started to recede in a Kevin Costner peak; he wasn't vain and didn't trouble much about his appearance, but Leo had an agreeable expression, a friendly smile and an abundance of the journalist's second weapon, sympathy, so women did not feel threatened by him, and were often surprised to find him in their bed.

Breeze caught Leo's eye, then raised his glass and voice. 'I'd like to propose a toast to my favourite American clients – Suzannah and Victor!'

Prettily reticent, Suzannah smiled graciously across the table at Breeze; she had been flirting with him in her fake Southern-belle manner for the entire evening. Plum had surreptitiously watched the blue eyes dance and the flaxen curls shake prettily at Breeze, who had responded only with the gallantry due to the wife of a very good client, or so it seemed. Plum was used to women flirting with Breeze: they were fascinated by those Nordic cheekbones above sunken cheeks, a wide lean mouth, and the pale complexion that often accompanies very fair hair. Straight, sandy eyebrows met above a big nose, giving the impression that Breeze had a penetrating stare.

Breeze's nickname dated from his schooldays when, as captain of the cricket team, he had always belittled the opposition before a match. 'It's a breeze,' he used to say. 'We'll walk all over them!' This casual, comforting confidence was later to be an asset to his career, and smoothly reassured débutant art collectors such as Victor Marsh.

Breeze and Victor had met at a London party, where each had been impressed by the other's suavity. When Victor, who cheerfully admitted that he knew little about it, subsequently decided to invest in art, he had relied on Breeze to put him in the European picture.

Plum switched her gaze to the indulgently beaming, glossily vulpine Victor, who was also covertly watching his wife flirt with Breeze. About fifteen years older than Suzannah, Victor was still good-looking in his immaculate-Armani Wall-Street way, but he had to work to retain that big-shouldered, tapering silhouette. Suzannah had told Plum that a trainer came to their Manhattan apartment at six every morning.

Apart from this dawn discipline, Victor seemed to enjoy his life with good-humoured ferocity. An ex-football player who had been a minor hero at college, he had not had to endure the subtle disappointment and humiliating inadequacy of so many of his team-mates, whose subsequent lives had failed to match their gloriously carefree youthful success. Victor sometimes said that he was one of the lucky hunks who could face himself in the mirror every morning and not see a failure; clearly he did not consider this a lucky accident: he was fast, competitive and prepared to flatten anyone who stood in his way.

Victor's father had owned a small chain of cheap jewellers' shops, which specialized in engagement rings. Their cynical motto was: 'A diamond also lasts for ever.' After college, Victor had been apprenticed to Van Heyden & Stein, the leading Antwerp gem cutters. He had been deeply bored, and when he returned to New York had refused to work under his father. Instead, he finagled himself into the sales force of Bear Sterns, the brokerage firm, where he leapfrogged nimbly from job to job and deal to deal; before he was thirty, Victor owned his own brokerage firm.

He had made his fortune in the eighties, when he had purchased companies by using their own assets as capital. All day he had bought and sold businesses, like a small boy swapping video games. Then at night, with equal enjoyment, ferocity and determination, Victor had converted a scrap of his fortune into a prominent social position.

It used to take two generations before the *nouveau riche* became socially acceptable, but in the age of Fast Everything, acceptance has also speeded up, and new money now becomes old as soon as you have *lots*. To achieve the Marshes' smooth social transformation during the early eighties, Suzannah had sat on charity committees to raise money for many good causes, ranging from the Bronx zoo to the Daughters of America, and she was currently lobbying to get on the Board of the Metropolitan Museum of Art – more prestigious than that of the opera, or any political organization. She entertained lavishly: four times a week her Manhattan chef catered to thirty-two for lunch and forty-eight for dinner, while her country weekend parties were equally ambitious.

Breeze and Plum had spent a snow-smothered weekend before Christmas at the Marsh farmhouse in Cornwall Bridge, Connecticut. It was there that Suzannah Marsh had briskly and cleverly made her own fortune from an activity which is a daily thankless survival job that nobody ever notices, unless a woman stops doing it: running a home.

* * * *

Together, Suzannah and Victor epitomized the successful Manhattan couple, proving what Breeze so often said: 'You can't stand still on the escalator of life; you either keep going up – or you go down.' And, of course, it was true. You couldn't be a *bit* of a success, no matter what work you chose. Whether you were a nuclear physicist, a film star or an acrobat, it was an all-or-nothing world today.

So Breeze was pushing Plum up the escalator as hard as he could, which was, after all, his job as her agent. But Plum had discovered that success is bad for your health, and that nobody can have everything; if you want A then you have to sacrifice B, which is often your home life and leisure, if you are struggling up the escalator.

Breeze, who was tall and lean, strong and tough, was *never* ill and so could not understand Plum's tension, exhaustion and longing to hop off the escalator. Shocked, he would point out that Plum could not *pend* whatever exhibition she was working towards.

In the Russian Tea Room, the brittle hum of false jollity grew even louder, as the Queen of the Hearth lifted her champagne glass to propose a second toast. Demurely wrapped in a white lace Christian Lacroix gown, Suzannah wore her famous-person face; exquisitely made-up, this public face was more gentle, more open and honest than her private face, upon which her expression was sharply alert and slightly anxious.

Suzannah raised her voice above the forced carnival buzz of the restaurant and spoke in the butter-wouldn't-melt voice that she used when men were present. 'To Plum – such a *fun* person.'

Bitch, thought Plum, recognizing the put-down. She might have said 'successful painter', or even 'doting mother'. And at the precise moment that she smiled at Suzannah, in gracious acknowledgement of her contemptuous toast, Plum realized grimly that fun was one of the things that was missing from her life, particularly during that weekend spent in Connecticut, which had felt as if she had suddenly been plunked into the middle of some old MGM jingle-bells movie, with Suzannah taking the cash at the box-office.

Suzannah had the ferocious energy and equally impressive self-discipline of a woman who had not only made her own wedding-dress but also her own wedding-cake. She always looked immaculate; and her carefully casual, long blonde bob was shampooed twice a week, at Saks at 7 a.m., in the company of New York's most powerful women. Like them, Suzannah never stopped dictating instructions into her pocket tape recorder, except to use her cellular phone.

Before her marriage, Suzannah had been an assistant to the food editor of *House Beautiful* magazine, then had founded a one-man-band catering firm in New York which served private and corporate clients, of whom Victor had been one. Now, as well as the big catering business, Suzannah had her own cookery school and every Christmas saw the publication of another fat home-improvement book, complete with recipes: when accused of pinching her recipes, Suzannah frostily retorted that you couldn't copyright a recipe. She also had her own TV show and radio show, and the 'Suzannah' line of country clothes was sold through J. C. Penney. Suzannah how-to-do-it-like-me videos sold by the truckload not only to the average mom but also to college graduates, who ought to have known better than wistfully long to lead a life which would rightly require the entire staff of *Upstairs Downstairs*.

Plum had often wondered why Suzannah, prime mover and role model of the expensive, escapist world of the New Traditionalist Woman, drove herself (and everyone else) so hard, when she had all the money she could possibly need. Naïvely, she had asked her, during that Connecticut weekend.

'I'm just a *homebody* at heart,' Suzannah had smiled. 'I just like *my* home to look *nice*, and I want to *help other women* to enjoy *their* home life as I do.' This might have sounded genuine had Plum not recognized it as the opening sequence of Suzannah's video.

The gall, remembered Plum; she looked across the festive litter of silver hats and coloured streamers at Suzannah, who had refused to upset her coiffure by wearing a paper hat: she idly wondered whether her own mild contempt masked envy of the socially adroit Suzannah.

Plum found her social life far more of a strain than her painting, whether it involved being polite to clients, being interviewed by the press or dealing with the other numerous facets of her public persona. She always felt uneasy at this evening's type of occasion, supposedly fun, but firmly based on work. She found it difficult to reconcile the disparate worlds that the wife of a successful art-gallery owner inhabits: the world of the patron and the world of the artist.

Plum knew that one of the reasons for artistic prickliness was

that most modern painters never have any money – unlike the days
of Renaissance Italy, when there was a patronage system to commission the Sistine chapel or the bronze doors of the Basilica in Florence.
Then, successful painters were rich and grand. Raphael had several
palaces, Giotto's popularity was like that of a modern rock star, and
when the Pope wanted Michelangelo to paint in the Sistine chapel he
had to strike a deal with Lorenzo the Magnificent, which was like
Warner Brothers leasing one of their major stars to Paramount.

Of course, during the art boom of the eighties there had been a
handful of painters with super-star status and prices. Then, almost
overnight, in November 1990 it had all stopped. The consequent dive
in the art market had been worse than that of the 1920s depression.
There were still a few million-per-picture painters, such as Jasper
Johns or Brice Marden, around today, but not many. After the art
boom of the eighties, the atmosphere of the art market was like the
Titanic just after she struck the iceberg: deeply depressed.

       *   *   *   *

Leo grinned at Plum as he raised his glass. 'To Plum – the girl who
has everything!'

If I've got everything, Plum thought as she smiled dutifully back
at Leo, how is it that I'm spending New Year's Eve – the New
Beginning, the most important night of the year – entertaining two
near-strangers? Why wasn't she at home, roasting chestnuts in front
of the fire with the kids and making the usual jokes about New Year
resolutions, which always led into a serious discussion of what they
were all going to do the following year. If I truly have it all, Plum
asked herself, why can't I do what I want? And why do I feel this
nagging uneasiness?

To make himself heard above the Cossack orchestra, the benev-
olently beaming Victor raised his voice as he raised his glass. 'To our
hostess and my favourite painter, Plum Russell, the Madonna of the
art world! May she win the Biennale!'

Plum winced. Then she caught Breeze's warning look and
obediently smiled.

The Biennale exhibition, held every other year in Venice, Italy, is
the Olympics of the art world. The oldest and most distinguished

7

international art festival, it is the most important showcase and launching pad for contemporary artists. To represent your country at the Biennale is an achievement, and a passport to an important future. When exhibited in a gallery or photographed in an art magazine, a young artist's work generally reaches few people, but if he or she shows at the Biennale, that artist instantly has a world-wide specialist audience. Everyone of importance in the modern art world attends this showcase of the best international talent, and 2,000 art critics descend on Venice to see the latest work of both new and established artists. Both Jasper Johns and Robert Rauschenberg had won international recognition there, and Picasso, Matisse and Miró were all prizewinners. Over forty of the British artists who had shown at the Biennale since the Second World War had gone on to make international reputations and command high prices: Breeze intended that Plum should stand among them.

Seated beside Jenny, Leo squeezed her hand affectionately and said in a voice that did not quite ring true, 'And may Jenny have equal success with her painting!'

Jenny, Plum's best friend, was embarrassed; she pushed her thick, caramel-coloured hair behind one ear, in the characteristic gawky gesture of a large-boned woman; she flushed and quickly looked at her plate. Breeze hurriedly lifted his glass again. 'To the year ahead, may it bring all of us exactly what we want!'

'I've already got what I want!' Suzannah purred, as she held up her hand and spread her fingers so that they could all see the marquise-cut diamond; in the candlelight it flashed rainbow-coloured lances of light across the table. 'Twenty-carat D Flawless,' Suzannah purred. 'My Christmas gift.' With the tips of her shell-pink fingers, Suzannah blew a kiss to her husband. Once again, the other guests all gazed at the scintillating source of magic light and wondered what it had cost.

From behind Suzannah, a woman in a gold-sequinned jacket materialized. Smiling in playful half-apology, she firmly held out a menu and said, 'Do you mind? You *are* Suzannah Marsh, aren't you? May I have your autograph? You're my *heroine, wait* till I tell the kids . . .'

Smiling, Suzannah scribbled, then looked up and said in her

pussy-cat voice, 'You'd better also ask my friend to sign – this is *Plum Russell*, the famous abstract *painter!*'

The woman in sequins looked blank.

Plum blushed, from shyness, humiliation and rage. The seemingly generous Suzannah was well aware that Plum, although recognized in the art world and photographed occasionally by the tabloids, meant nothing to the average Britisher, let alone an American.

Facing Plum across the table, Jenny, unnoticed by the others, sympathetically mouthed: 'Bitch.'

Breeze, sitting next to Suzannah, leaned towards her, patted the hand adorned with the diamond ring and smiled flirtatiously. 'If Plum wins the Biennale, her name will be a part of art history for ever. She'll have real fame, not the ephemeral fame of some TV performer—' He broke off to call a waiter.

Remembering that Oscar Wilde's definition of a gentleman was 'one who is never unintentionally rude', Plum grinned appreciatively at her husband, which wasn't difficult. Breeze was tall, lean, muscular, well dressed, and he didn't look the slightest bit arty. His suits came from Savile Row; his shirts, his ties – even his underpants – came from Jermyn Street.

'Let's be realistic,' Plum said firmly. 'I have *no* chance of winning the Biennale. I wouldn't have been chosen by the British Council if the Italians hadn't decided on that theme.' Italy, who hosted the famous art festival, had chosen as their theme for 1992, 'A View of Woman', and the British Art Establishment, which in a hundred years had only once nominated a woman, Bridget Riley, had prudently decided to do so again.

'Nevertheless, the woman they chose was *you*,' Breeze emphasized. His salesman's optimism, which soared beyond the possible, added to the anxious responsibility that Plum felt: she had been given only a year to produce a body of good, fresh work to exhibit.

'If she won, Plum's price would quadruple overnight,' Victor said speculatively. He leaned across the litter of silver streamers towards Breeze. 'I'd like to have first option on the next work Plum shows in New York – after the Biennale.'

Breeze nodded approvingly at him. Photo-realism, hard-edged paintings were what the galleries currently wanted from young painters, not abstract impressionism. But Plum's work was very good, and there was never enough good work to go round. As soon as the news of the Biennale nomination had been announced, Breeze had started a discreet lobbying campaign. Although he usually handled such things himself, he had hired a publicity person, who quickly despaired of Plum, as she was both unwilling to meet the press and was rendered inarticulate by fright when she did. A modern artist couldn't be successful if she hid in a garret, ignored the press and excused her non-appearances by saying that she was painting.

Breeze knew that Plum appeared guarded and wary when she was merely shy, unsure of herself. She was humbly aware of great gulfs of knowledge in her social and scholastic background, especially when being interviewed by some intellectual about her painting. The only serious critic who did not intimidate her was the amiable, bear-like Robert Hughes. She felt diffident in the company of other successful painters, and only stuttered banal sentences. Despite the acclaim she had received and the art-circle bitchiness that proved her merit, Plum had little self-confidence.

This exasperated Breeze almost as much as it did Plum. He complained that she talked to interviewers as if her IQ were smaller than her shoe size and her vocabulary monosyllabic. Why this idiot act? 'Even your voice changes,' Breeze had once said. 'If you're not struck dumb in public, you sound tentative, hesitant and unsure of yourself. But you can express yourself perfectly well when you're not thinking about it – you can be just as uninhibited as you are when painting.'

'That's because I think about nothing but the painting when I'm painting.'

'Exactly. You aren't distracted by silly, childish thoughts of inferiority.'

'I swear I try, darling – but if I were a talker then I'd talk, not paint. If I liked being on TV I'd have been an actor. When I'm being interviewed, I feel like the rabbit in the headlights – brain paralysed by fright. I feel they're trying to catch me out.'

'They're only puzzled – surprised – that a small, shy woman could have produced these powerful paintings.'

'I know. *I* can see the disbelief in their faces. One day I'm going to say: "OK. I'll own up. I *don't* paint them: they're done by a gang of teenage dwarfs that I keep chained in the cellar. Satisfied?"'

'Perhaps a psychiatrist . . .' Breeze had mused.

Plum had refused to keep the appointment.

* * * *

In the cloakroom of the Russian Tea Room, as she watched Suzannah tug off her enormous diamond ring in order to wash her hands, Plum couldn't help wishing that she had Suzannah's enviable self-assurance: the most irritating thing about Suzannah was that nothing ever disturbed her serenity. So Plum, slightly tipsy, gave it a try. 'Aren't you frightened to wear that ring, Suzannah? Aren't you afraid that even here – uptown – some mugger'll chop your finger off to get it?'

'Of *course* not. When I'm outdoors I just twist the ring around, so that it faces my palm.' In the mirror, Suzannah's complacent eyes met those of Plum. 'And in this weather obviously I wear gloves. Anyway, my New Year resolution is to feel no fear. What's your resolution, Plum?'

Briskly, Plum said, 'My New Year resolution? No more blow jobs.'

In the mirror, Suzannah stared as if she couldn't believe what she had heard.

Recklessly, Plum continued. 'We've all been brainwashed about blow jobs, don't you think? If you don't want to do it, then you're not a tiger in the sack, you're considered a sexual failure.'

Beside Plum, Jenny solemnly nodded in agreement. 'In steamy novels, women who don't give blow jobs always lose their husbands.'

'I think we'd better rejoin the men,' Suzannah said frostily, and swept out of the tiny cloakroom.

Plum laughed in the mirror at Jenny's wide, generous smile, which made you feel that the sun was shining, even at midnight. Jenny was the perfect best friend: warm, sympathetic – and immediately supportive.

Jenny's mischievous golden eyes glinted as she combed her thick, untidy hair. 'If Suzannah hadn't gone off in a huff I was going to add that I *like* blow jobs. I love the power. I love to feel a man squirm with pleasure and know *he's* hoping that I won't stop.'

'Lucky Leo.'

'We haven't done it yet, but I think maybe tonight . . . If not, I'll have to consult Lulu.'

Jenny had a problem with men: plenty of short-term relationships but never one that endured. This was much discussed between her, Plum and Lulu, who was their authority on sex, partly because she always sounded so authoritative about it. Jenny had known Lulu since kindergarten days, Plum since art college, when the three girls had instinctively formed a protective little gang: loyal and supportive of each other, it had been them against the world, and twenty years later it still was.

Jenny refused to consider Lulu's theory about her man problem, which was that Jenny wanted too much too soon. Men sensed her anxiety, her clinging need for a permanent relationship, and this scared them off.

Jenny only saw the disadvantages that she chose to see, and preferred to blame her height. Nearly six feet tall, she would say, gloomily, 'Anatomy is destiny. Men want doll-size women like Plum who make them feel big and strong by contrast.'

Plum always retorted, 'Rubbish! You look like one of those glamorous, heroic women with streaming hair, on French stamps.'

'But you're small and pretty, like the doll on top of the Christmas tree. When men look down at you, they're hooked. Men don't want a woman their own size. Men's eyes slide past me because I'm *big*. They don't even notice I'm *there*.'

'Some men *love* Amazons,' Lulu would say loyally. 'And *we* don't care what size you are.'

It had taken years for Plum and Lulu to persuade Jenny to stop wearing frills and bows like the doll on top of the Christmas tree, and dress to suit her large frame. Now she wore tailored pants suits with belted, Greta Garbo trenchcoats and she crammed her long, honey-gold hair under big, theatrical felt hats from Herbert Johnson. Men still found her threatening.

Now as Jenny wrestled with her hair before the cloakroom mirror, Plum offered, 'We're going back to Suzannah's place for a nightcap. Want to come?'

'No, thanks. Leo's taking me to dance at Nell's.'

'Sounds more fun than seeing Victor's New Year present for Suzannah.'

'I thought that huge rock . . .'

'No, that was her *Christmas* gift. Her New Year gift is a painting.'

'One of yours?'

'You must be joking. Modern stuff wouldn't mix with the Sunny-bank Farm ambience. Victor has to keep my paintings in his office . . . No, Suzannah's New Year gift is an early Dutch flowerpiece.'

* * * *

The Lincoln Continental glided uptown. As Victor smoothly slid a small package into Breeze's hand, he asked casually, 'What's the art market like at the moment?'

Breeze carefully tucked the package inside his coat. 'Disastrous in Scandinavia, worse in Britain, not bad in Germany, fair in the rest of Europe and terrific in Hong Kong . . . overall, we're still seeing a market correction to the eighties.'

During the late eighties, when stock markets dived, art prices had soared. Having noticed the high auction reserves, many businessmen decided that good art was good business and so became instant collectors, buying art for resale as they bought pork bellies, grain or oil in commodity trading. As the cost of art went up and up, a few crafty international auctioneers further fuelled this boom by lending money to clients. Easy credit enabled them to bid record prices . . . Then the world seemed to run out of money, art prices dived, dealers started to go broke. So, because nearly everyone in the art business became greedy during the eighties, they had to pay for it in the nineties. Now every dealer was having an anxious time.

'The diamond market's also down – nobody buys diamonds in a depression,' Victor grumbled. 'And it might get worse. The Russian diamond stockpile is now worth over three billion dollars, and the market would collapse like a pack of cards if the Russians were forced to sell it in order to buy food and fuel for their starving millions. Inside Russia there's now rising political pressure to sell those diamonds – and not through de Beers.'

Breeze looked perplexed. 'I thought de Beers have a world

monopoly of diamonds; and as everyone's obliged to sell through de Beers, they're able to keep the price artificially high.'

Victor nodded. 'And if de Beers were to lose control – *wham*! Prices would dive.' He explained, 'In order to keep supply lower than demand, some countries aren't allowed to produce the amount of diamonds that they could: for years de Beers have kept Russian output twenty-five per cent lower than it could be. But now unauthorized, cheap diamonds – thought to be Russian – have started to appear on the Amsterdam market. In order to keep the market price up, de Beers are forced to buy these stones – but we all wonder how long they can afford to do so.'

'What would happen if de Beers ran out of money?' Suzannah asked sharply.

'The sale of a large stockpile of diamonds, uncontrolled by de Beers, would destroy the confidence of the market, and prices would dive,' Victor said gloomily. 'And should the Russians publicly sell outside de Beers, other diamond-producing countries would also want to do it, so they'd leave de Beers, who would then no longer control world diamond prices.'

'So prices would dive further?' asked Breeze.

Victor nodded. 'And once the public lost confidence in diamonds as a valuable investment, the market would plummet further still – perhaps even collapse, if there's a panic.'

'So now you tell me!' Suzannah said, in mock fury.

Victor laughed quietly. 'I'm not really worried, or I wouldn't be talking about it. Russia has de Beers by the balls. They'll be forced to sell the Russian stones and stockpile those of everyone else.'

'You're such a tease,' Suzannah said crossly. She knew that her moment of anxiety was Victor's controlling method of telling her not to go too far with Breeze. She gave a light laugh to get the conversation back on a convivial base. 'I thought diamonds were safe. I thought that's why they're a girl's best friend.'

'There's no such thing as safe,' Victor said seriously, 'and over-confidence is always a mistake.' He leaned towards Breeze. 'But there are always opportunities. I'm told that for someone with a steady nerve, there are terrific art bargains to be had at the moment.'

Breeze nodded. 'It sounds as if you've just acquired one. Of course it's not my field, but I know that Balthazar van der Ast was one of the most important flower painters of his period. Old Master paintings are still undervalued, particularly the Dutch and Flemish seventeenth-century painters: Jan van Kessel, Thomas Heeremans, Jan Brueghel, that lot . . .'

'Why's that?' Suzannah cheered up.

'Because of their rarity,' Breeze told her. 'And because they're not fashionable, compared to the Impressionists. And because people feel safe when buying authenticated Old Masters. "Old money buys old art" is a cliché that's true: art needs half a century for the scholarly community to evaluate it.'

Breeze did not add that Leo Castelli, granddaddy of modern art dealers, was one of the few people who could evaluate art in its own time. But why send his clients to his competitor? Instead, Breeze said, 'It's certainly a good time to buy Old Masters, although you need to be careful with seventeenth-century Dutch, because there's not much detailed documentation – especially for the early periods – and attribution is notoriously slippery.'

The Lincoln stopped beside a scalloped awning. A doorman dressed as a nineteenth-century hussar dashed out to open the door. As Plum ducked her head and stepped out on the red carpet, stained at the edges by snow slush, again she felt an undefined threat; a vague feeling of dread; that something unpleasant was about to crash on her head. This fear of a thunderbolt from on high always came on occasions when she was feeling particularly happy. From somewhere, Plum had acquired the idea that happiness had to be paid for, and that the price was always high. Again she wondered what nasty surprises this New Year held in store for her. Things were going much too well.

CHAPTER TWO

A HERBAL fragrance scented the air of Suzannah's apartment, which was an upmarket version of Sunnybank Farm: George Washington might have sat on the little upright couches and chairs. Suzannah's invisible staff had prepared midnight fare: dozens of mince pies had been kept hot in what looked like silver warming pans: geometrically-precise mountains of smoked salmon cartwheels had been carefully arranged beneath big silver domes; waiting in silver buckets were two dozen bottles of vintage Krug, standing beside fresh orange juice, hot spiced rum punch and Napoleon brandy. As there was enough for at least fifty people, Plum realized that Suzannah had expected the Russells' New Year's Eve party to be far larger than it was.

In the sitting-room, spotlit in a prominent position on the wall to the left of the fireplace, hung Suzannah's Dutch flower painting. It was small – the panel measured only about twenty-one inches high by fourteen inches wide – and it was beautiful. A colour scheme of bronze, ochre and cadmium yellows contained a few soft hues of orange: the entire picture seemed to radiate a golden glow. A central greenish glass vase contained spring flowers, daffodils, tulips and iris, delicately surrounded by green foliage. A fly – so life-like that you were tempted to brush it off – clung to the brightest yellow tulip. Around the base of the vase to the left were scattered sea-shells, a tiny yellow-green lizard and a few fallen petals. To the right, a Painted Lady butterfly hovered in the air.

'Look, he's signed it.' Suzannah proudly pointed to the signature – *Balthazar.*

Plum moved closer. Carefully, she examined the painting. She looked particularly at the fly, which had a flick of orange highlight on one transparent wing.

'Schneiders on Fifty-Seventh have a flower picture of the same period, but it's three times the price,' said Victor, 'and not so good, in my opinion.' He winked at Breeze. 'We were told that you can't go wrong with this sort of painting.'

'No wonder. These early Dutch painters are famous for their precision: look at that detail and clarity,' Breeze said respectfully.

'Look, you can even see the reflection in that drop of water on the table!' Suzannah said. 'And isn't the fly great? It's my favourite bit.'

Plum peered closer. 'It isn't a fly, it's a bluebottle . . . Where did you get this?'

'At Maltby's on Bond Street,' Suzannah replied, as she poured rum punch for everyone. 'My decorator located it.'

Looking at the painting with her back to the others, Plum whipped her emergency safety pin from her evening purse and carefully pressed the point into two areas of the painting. Then, before she had time to think, she said earnestly, 'Suzannah, you must get Maltby's to take this back. *It's a fake.*'

There was a moment of silent consternation. Plum had just breached the protocol of hospitality by challenging the discernment, both aesthetic and financial, of her hostess.

Suzannah gave an accusatory yelp. 'Of all the *nerve*! Plum's just jealous of me, like all the rest! She just wants to make me feel bad!'

Hastily, Breeze shot a man-to-man look at Victor, the wary, trouble-ahead look which means 'probably PMT'. Apologetically he said, 'I expect Plum's mistaken. She doesn't know much about old pictures. And it's fairly late, she must be very tired . . . and we've been drinking champagne all night . . .'

'It took my decorator *months* to track that picture down, when I said I wanted one like hers.' Suzannah grew angrier. 'If this picture was a fake, Cynthia would have been able to get it much quicker than she did.'

Defensively Plum said, 'I've told you only because you might be able to get your money back if you move fast enough. Mightn't they, Breeze?'

Victor looked questioningly at Breeze, who was extremely embarrassed.

'I'm sure there's no question of that picture being a fake,' Breeze soothed. 'Maltby's are a reputable firm. But if you like, Victor, when I get back to London I can visit them and make inquiries.'

'I'll make my own inquiries,' Victor said shortly.

'How *can* Plum know it's a fake?' Suzannah demanded, still furious. 'She only looked at it for two minutes. How can she possibly tell? It isn't even daylight.'

'I don't need daylight for this picture,' Plum answered firmly. 'I can see it has no spirit. The spirit of a painting can't be faked.'

'What's this *rubbish* about *spirit*?' Suzannah shrilled. 'This picture has been authenticated by *experts*. Plum's not an expert!'

Plum looked levelly at her hostess. 'You can't describe the spirit of a painting, you can only recognize it – or see that it's missing.' It was like having a musical ear, but much more rare. Breeze sometimes teased her about her good eye, saying it was the result of being visually uninhibited and unprejudiced by previous judgements: in other words – uneducated.

But Breeze wasn't going to be drawn into a discussion of Plum's natural aesthetic discernment at two in the morning. In a final attempt to pull the evening together, he gave a short laugh. 'I'm afraid that the art world's answer to Madonna isn't an expert on seventeenth-century Dutch painting as well.'

Incensed because Breeze had deliberately used the hated nickname given her by the British press to cheapen the sexual content of her paintings, Plum snapped, 'You don't have to be an expert to spot a fake. You know the dealer's old saying: Corot painted two thousand pictures, four thousand of which are in the States. Remember that all the museums of the world have been fooled by fakes – often very crude work. I sometimes stand in the Metropolitan or the Louvre or the British Museum and gaze up at spotlit things on plinths, and I'm amazed that anyone had the nerve to sell them as originals.' Angrily she turned to her husband. 'What you need to spot a fake is a good eye, and *I've* got a good eye, and Breeze *knows* it.'

'What's your eyesight got to do with it?' Suzannah demanded.

Breeze sighed. Like other good dealers, he might not know much about the subject of a painting – say, whether the style of dress was accurate for the supposed date of the painting – because he didn't have that sort of training, but any good dealer trusted his own judgement, by which he meant his eye. Breeze knew that a good eye needed constant development, training and exercise, which meant looking with alertness at everything. A dealer needed a good eye to spot talent, to build up a fine collection, to nose out a treasure in a junk shop or a bargain at a provincial auction: in other words, to be a dealer.

Most art historians didn't have a good eye, because they didn't trust such a personal judgement, they only trusted the intellectual and historical basis of a work of art. And because of this, many dealers had reservations about the judgements of art historians.

As always, when talking about painting, Plum's normally quiet, hesitant voice became strong and confident as she continued. 'Almost every famous artist has been faked, even living ones, like David Hockney. Some painters are easier to fake than others. Rubens had such great anatomical knowledge that he's almost impossible to copy. But flower painting . . .'

Angrily Breeze interrupted. 'You've had too much to drink! I'm taking you back to the hotel. I must apologize, Suzannah.'

'Wait a minute.' Victor had been mildly amused by Plum's rebellion and the discomfiture of the normally suave Breeze. He said, 'I've got an idea. If Plum is so sure of her artistic eye, how about a little bet on this picture?'

'*No!*' Breeze guessed roughly what Victor was about to propose. 'Plum, I forbid it!'

Plum glared at her husband. Thinking in terms of a hundred-dollar bet, she nodded at Victor. 'Done!'

'OK,' said Victor. 'If I win, let's say I get one of your paintings – my choice – free. If I lose, I pay you the gallery price less fifty per cent.' He held his hand out to Plum. 'But you must *prove* that this picture is a fake.'

Plum grabbed Victor's hand and shook it.

Breeze gave a tight smile. If Plum won, then Breeze would probably lose a good client. If Plum lost, then Victor would get a free picture by the British Biennale entrant. And Victor was using Plum to do the groundwork to give him evidence with which he could confront Maltby's; a shrewd operator, Victor knew how to use a bad card to his advantage.

*　*　*　*

'I realize you don't like her, but just because Suzannah thinks she shits violets is no need to insult the poor woman,' Breeze growled, as he shut the door of their hotel suite.

Plum undid her garnet satin evening cloak and stamped to the bedroom. 'Poor, she isn't! I admit she irritates me – I suppose it's because she has everything that any woman could want – but she has no reason to be such a bitch.'

'Look who's talking!'

'So I did the right thing in the wrong way!' Plum kicked off her violet satin evening shoes.

'It was *not* the right thing! You upset and embarrassed them! They're our clients, our friends, our *guests*!' Angrily, Breeze prowled up and down the bedroom.

'All the more reason to tell them they'd been stuck with a fake. Probably they can still get Maltby's to take it back, such a short time after sale.' Plum felt beneath her bronze chiffon skirts and yanked down her tights.

'I wouldn't be too sure. Maltby's will dispute it because they can't afford to do otherwise. And *you* can't afford to antagonize one of the few remaining big buyers in New York. Even if you're right – which I doubt – messengers who bring bad news tend to be beheaded.'

'*I'm right!*' Plum peeled off her tights.

'How can you be so bloody sure? As Suzannah said, you were seeing the picture in bad light, and you only looked for a minute or two . . .'

'You know as well as I do that the first look is the most important.' In that instant, a good eye puts together a quick, instinctive series of associations from a mental store of images and an internal computer translates them into gut feeling.

'Yes, but you have *no* knowledge, *no* experience, *no* training and *no* scholastic credentials. Maltby's will line up an impressive row of expert contradictory arguments against your one year's experience at a provincial art school!' Breeze spun round angrily and glared at Plum. 'They're going to do their best to make you look a fool! At best, this will be yet another of the art world's disputed attributions and at worst, you'll get dragged into a public dispute – which will mean a lot of undesirable publicity at the worst possible time for you!'

'I *know* it's a fake,' Plum persisted. 'I did the pin test, when no one was looking.' Old-time dealers kept a pin behind their jacket lapel. If a painting is old, the varnish has become as hard as glass. If you push a pin into a suspect area and the paint yields at all – that area isn't old.

'Thank God Suzannah didn't notice!' said Breeze.

'Breeze, I think *you* noticed something wrong with that picture. You were uneasy about it. You were embarrassed.'

'You're damn right! And I'll spell out why. Next week I'm hoping to fix a New York show with Pevensky to start immediately after the Biennale, which'll give it good lift-off. Pevensky can see you have great potential, you don't cost outrageous money and you're prepared to strut your stuff. But he won't like scandal.'

'Pevensky has one of the best modern galleries on Lower Broadway. Why should he care if a seventeenth-century Dutch flowerpiece is disputed?'

Breeze glared.

'So I shouldn't antagonize Maltby's!' Plum yanked at the zipper of her bronze chiffon baby-doll dress.

'You shouldn't antagonize the art world.'

'Aha! The conspiracy of silence!' The art world hated any whisper of fakery – a taboo subject. Public confidence dropped, sales dropped, the entire financial structure of the art world was thereby undermined.

Breeze shrugged his shoulders.

'Surely Maltby's would buy that flowerpiece back, if it were proven false?' Plum tried to sound placatory. She knew that sometimes scandals are hushed up, a picture is returned and the gallery takes a tax-deductible loss. Everyone wants to protect their position and nobody wants to look foolish. Everyone in the art world needs to avoid damaging the prestige of the great galleries, museums, and public institutions – their best customers – who have huge budgets and priceless collections bought for millions of dollars, sometimes with public money. Everyone wants to protect their own investment.

'*If* is a big, big word in the art world,' Breeze warned. 'Even if that picture's wrong, you'll be in shit up to your neck.' The art world's phrases for fake are 'something's wrong', or 'I don't like it', which means the same thing.

'I realize that.' Plum knew that art experts – dealers, auctioneers and art historians – generally try to be as vague as possible when confronted with a dubious picture, both in order to protect themselves legally and also to be tactful and kind: collectors are proud of their pictures. A dealer doesn't even tell another dealer if he thinks that he has been fooled by a fake. Such allegations are met with resentful fury, as an insult to eye and intelligence. Although few dealers have never been landed with a fake, few will admit it because it damages their reputation. Few dealers or auctioneers will even discuss the possibility that fakes might be circulating in the art market – although they all know that this is so.

'You might at least have agreed I have a good eye,' Plum added reproachfully. 'You might have backed me up that much.'

They both knew that a painterly eye – known as visual acuity – is very rare; dealers, connoisseurs, artists and art historians spend their lives cultivating this indefinable and mysterious skill.

'I'm surprised *you* never noticed anything,' Plum said again in a puzzled voice. 'That flowerpiece lacked spirit, it had a dull, lifeless quality . . . it lacked what those old boys put into their work – serenity.'

Breeze sighed. 'Thank God you didn't tell Suzannah her painting lacked serenity . . . OK, since you're so sure of yourself – what sort of fake do you reckon it is?'

'Not a changed signature. A new painting – a composite: someone's taken bits of other van der Asts and reassembled them – copied them all in one picture.'

'You mean a pastiche?' Breeze thought for a moment, then said decisively, 'Whether or not you're right about it, you simply can't afford the time to get involved in this potential scandal, Plum, and I can't allow your attention to be diverted. This time-wasting trip next week to Australia is bad enough . . . I'd never have agreed had I known about the Biennale . . . Right now you should be concentrating on those new paintings that the British Council expects, and we'll also need more new stuff for your New York show, because there'll never be a better time to pitch you. Unless you *win* the Biennale, of course.'

'For God's sake, stop hoping for *that!*' yelled Plum. 'You ought to know better! You know who I'll be up against! You know that you never even expected me to be *nominated* – and neither did anyone else!' She pleaded with Breeze. 'Won't you please stop setting me up for disappointment? Just being *selected* is an honour, as it is for the Olympics. Can't you see that it'll take the edge off that, if people are led to believe I might win, when we both know that it isn't possible?'

'You're over-reacting to that article in the *Post* last week!'

'*Of course I am!* Cinderella of the art world! How can you expect people to take me seriously when trash like that appears? . . . Damn, this zipper's stuck. Help me.' She lifted her arm.

'You know I hate that sort of rubbish as much as you do.' Breeze bent and fiddled with the dress zipper. 'But if you don't talk to these gossip writers, they just invent something. It's really more sensible to seem to be friendly . . . Don't forget your interview with the *New York Telegraph* tomorrow.'

'One minute you tell me I haven't a moment to waste, the next minute you tell me to talk to the press!'

'I don't know what's got into you this evening! I've never known you be so aggressive!' Breeze gave a sharp tug to the zipper.

'Ow! You've nicked my skin!' Plum's face flushed red with the effort to control her angry tears.

'Stop wriggling . . .'

Plum shouted, 'You put so much emphasis on my public persona that sometimes I feel I no longer know who I am! *Or* who I'm supposed to be! *Or* what I really think! I feel I'm living a false life in a world of false values! *I* feel a fake!'

'You're just reacting to the charm of New York,' said Breeze wearily. 'Look, let's drop this. Let's get to bed. We can discuss things more calmly in the morning.' He bent once again to fiddle with the zipper. 'I'm going to yank it hard or you'll have to sleep in this thing . . . There!'

'Thanks.' Plum shrugged off the bronze shoestring straps and her dress fell to the floor. She stepped out of the circle of crumpled chiffon and continued her attack. 'You humiliate me in public, Breeze! You say I'm drunk when I'm not! You belittle my education, my artistic intelligence and my judgement! You treat me like a child! And then when you're bored, you suggest we go to bed!'

'I meant to sleep!' But as he stared at her creamy little body, Breeze felt his penis stir.

'I've had enough!'

'Enough of what?' Breeze moved closer.

'Enough of your Svengali act! Enough of your domination or guidance, or whatever you call it! Whatever it is that makes you assume that *you* always know what's best for me and that I'll always do as *you* say!'

'Well, I do,' Breeze said reasonably, reaching for her beige nipples. 'Look where you were before you met me – just another grubby little art student. You know as well as I do that you'd have got nowhere without me. And if you hadn't . . .' Breeze stopped himself. Gently he bent his head to her breasts.

Angrily, Plum pulled away.

'Plum, this isn't a good way to start the New Year . . .'

'I'm not so sure. Perhaps it's time I faced facts.'

Breeze made a huge effort. 'Plum, I'm sorry. I shouldn't have handled that situation at Suzannah's the way I did. But please understand, darling – I couldn't believe my ears! You calmly sauntered up to that picture, and before we'd had time to drink Suzannah's cinnamon-soused concoction, you calmly told her that her new, prize possession was worthless, and if she couldn't see it, well, she was insensitive. I could see my best client walking – she'll never again let Victor buy anything of yours. I could see that bitch spreading filth about you through the length and breadth of Long Island.' He caught hold of Plum's hand and kissed it; he looked shame-faced. 'And at this point I have to admit – perhaps *I'd* had too much to drink.'

'Just as well we never drank Suzannah's cinnamon-soused, witches' brew.' Plum kissed Breeze's knuckles.

'What if her painting *is* a fake? How can *you* prove it?' Breeze slid his left shoulder around her body and pressed her firm little buttocks against his thigh. His right hand parted her soft hair.

'I'll prove it somehow – because it's a fake! *I know it's a fake!* . . . Oh, Breeze.'

'Happy New Year, darling.'

CHAPTER THREE

Wednesday, 1 January 1992

PLUM LAY sprawled on her back, flushed and languid, not yet
fully awake on the first day of 1992. The hermetically sealed,
quiet warmth of the Ritz Carlton had subtly altered, she noticed
drowsily, slowly reclaiming her senses as she woke. Her nightdress had ridden up and the soft, goosedown quilt must have fallen
to the floor: the warmth felt lighter than it usually did when she
woke.

She also felt a gentle but scratchy warm pressure against her
naked, inner thigh. Puzzled at first, she slowly realized what it was.

Breeze's unshaven cheek.

Her body flooded with indolent warmth.

'You smell so erotic,' he whispered. 'Someone should bottle it
and make a fortune.'

'You've been spending too much time with Victor the money
machine,' Plum whispered back, sleepily thinking that one of the
great pleasures of marriage was being able to make jokes in bed; to
know that you had all the time in the world to be together, to be
close in every way.

Breeze's long, graceful hands prised her legs further apart.

Sleepily acquiescent, she shifted her position slightly. She felt
delicately languorous, incapable of moving, her muscles had lost all
power: it was as if her limp body melted under some sun god's
heated gaze. She felt his warm lips and her own arousal. Breeze's
probing tongue – nimble as his fingers – found the little bump it
sought; gently he licked with deliberate slowness, his even, steady

26

strokes insisting on her body's response. She felt the force of her passion mount from his mouth and slowly flood her body.

Plum started to gasp, to make little bird-like noises. Her sharp moans increased in tempo and grew louder, then eventually blurred into one long moan of pleasure.

Breeze looked up from the damp, silken red hair. 'Encore?'

Plum made a sleepy, satisfied sound, half purr, half growl.

Breeze bent his head.

Shortly afterwards, Plum started to gasp again. Arching her back, she thrust herself towards his mouth.

Breeze stopped, looked up and grinned.

She grasped his blond hair and tugged it. 'You brute,' she whispered, 'you teasing bastard.'

'I can't do a thing unless you let go of my hair . . . Why, yes, I can . . .' Breeze pushed her cream voile nightgown further up her body and she felt his hands on her breasts. He fondled them, squeezing her nipples until she could no longer bear the pleasurable tension, but could not bear to stop him.

'Don't stop, darling Breeze, don't stop,' Plum's hands fell away from the blond hair and clutched at the rumpled sheets beneath her.

'I don't intend to.' He pulled himself upwards and started to kiss her breasts, softly at first and then more roughly as his own passion threatened to pass beyond control. His breathing became harsh. His body thrust at hers. Abruptly he stopped thinking so unselfishly of Plum's pleasure.

He pulled himself up on his elbows and she gasped again as she felt his flesh hard against hers. Strong hands slid beneath her buttocks, as he raised her slightly. He felt to join them. Their bodies joined. Slowly he twisted himself within her. Happily trapped beneath him, Plum felt the strength of Breeze's hard body as it plunged into hers. She flung herself against him with equal passion. Hungrily, wordlessly, they thrust against each other, their indolent eroticism now replaced by a mutual and tempestuous appetite. Their bodies moved wordlessly, rhythmically, faster and faster, more and more urgently . . .

Later, lying back against a tangle of sheets, Plum smelled the familiar warm, almond odour of his sated appetite.

'What a wonderful way to wake up,' she murmured, knowing that Breeze had just apologized for his lack of support on the previous night.

*　*　*　*

Plum opened languid eyes when she heard a tap at the door.

'That'll be breakfast,' Breeze said. 'I ordered it for eleven.' He grabbed his white towelling bathrobe and went to the door.

Plum heard muttered words, then a trolley table was wheeled in by two blue-uniformed waiters and Plum sniffed the delicious aroma of Columbian coffee. One waiter pulled the window curtains apart and Plum saw frosted Central Park spread before her. The other waiter clicked up the sides of the now-large circular table. From the hot cupboard beneath, he produced silver serving dishes. Plum looked with pleasure at the butter-coloured linen cloth, the silver cutlery, the fine china and the vase of snowdrops on the table.

'I hope you're hungry,' Breeze said, as the waiters left. He lifted the silver cover of a serving dish. 'We have scrambled eggs, bacon, mushrooms, sausages – a real British breakfast.' He lifted the other cover. 'Plus waffles and maple syrup. And here's sliced bananas and cream because I know you love that.' He shook a pale blue napkin from a basket and added, 'We have toast and honey, or croissants with strawberry preserve. Also fresh orange juice and a bowl of cherries. That should stop you fainting from hunger before lunch.'

'I feel faint just hearing you talk about it. Just coffee for me, please.'

'A few cherries?'

'No, just coffee with cream.'

'I'm sure you'd love a few cherries . . . shiny, rosy cherries.'

'If you think the cherries are so wonderful, have them yourself, darling.'

'But you *love* cherries in winter.'

Plum looked up at Breeze's face. 'Why this insistence? Own up! You've bought an orchard? . . . Or a fruit import business? . . . OK, I'll have a couple of cherries, to please you, but only to hang from my ears.'

Carefully Breeze handed the white porcelain bowl to Plum. She pushed her short red hair away from her ears and dipped a hand into the cherry bowl. 'Hey, what's in here?'

'Happy New Year, darling.' Breeze leaned over and kissed her on the side of her almond-white neck.

Plum laughed. 'You really surprised me . . .' She groped beneath the cherries and produced a small scarlet and gold leather jeweller's box. She looked astonished. 'Breeze, *what have we here?*'

'Nothing you don't deserve,' Breeze said fondly.

Plum opened the box, 'I don't believe this!' She held up a diamond ring. The stone seemed to catch the dim light that filtered through the net curtains, to imprison and magnify it. Blue flashes shot from the ring, then orange-yellow ones.

Plum slid the ring on her finger and held out her hand to admire it. 'It's *blinding*! And for once my fingernails are clean!' Usually the unvarnished, short fingernails of her small, square hands were ingrained with paint, even after surgeon-like scrubbing.

'It's to celebrate the Biennale. I'm so proud of you.' Breeze kissed the top of her head. 'I know it isn't as big as Suzannah's . . .'

'Suzannah's ring is vulgarly, ostentatiously enormous: it isn't a ring, it's start-up capital!' Plum threw her arms around Breeze's neck.

Smiling, Breeze disentangled her arms and looked at the ring on her finger. 'We never got around to getting an engagement ring . . .'

'I said I'd rather have a jeep, and you gave me one,' Plum reminded him.

'Yes. You're just a simple, practical, down-to-earth sexpot.'

'In that case, maybe after breakfast I'll break my New Year resolution.' She explained how she had scandalized Suzannah. Breeze laughed fondly. By tacit consent, neither of them mentioned Suzannah's Dutch flowerpiece: that could wait, they weren't going to let it spoil their private start to the New Year.

Once again, Plum flashed her hand admiringly. Then, hesitantly, she turned to Breeze, 'Darling, are you sure that you can afford this . . . at the moment?'

'Yes. Cleo Brigstall gave me a good tip.' Breeze had also invited the Brigstalls to the Russian Tea Room on New Year's Eve, but Cleo's sinusitis had been so bad that she'd cancelled. A self-contained woman in her early thirties who worked in the City trading gold futures, Cleo was married – apparently happily – to a rising copyright lawyer who didn't yet earn much but would one day be made a partner in his firm. Breeze reported that Cleo never spent a penny over her budget and would never buy large pictures, because they were more difficult to resell.

Breeze added, 'And as a matter of fact, Victor got me a good deal on the diamond.'

'So that was what was going on in the back of the limo. But this must have cost *something*.' As Plum spoke, the diamond flashed blue-green then yellow. Anxiously she persisted. 'And I know you're anxious about Steinert . . . whether he'll pull out.'

Geoffrey Steinert was Breeze's backer. He was also Breeze's ex-father-in-law. In 1972, when Breeze had been a twenty-seven-year-old assistant working for the Pilkington Gallery, he had eloped with nineteen-year-old Geraldine-Ann, Mr Steinert's only daughter, against her family's wishes. After the eventual reconciliation, Geraldine-Ann's father, who owned a property empire, had been cajoled by his daughter into providing the capital for Breeze to open his own gallery in Cork Street, both sides of which are lined with London's best art galleries.

In 1976 young Geraldine-Ann eloped again, with her lover, Eileen, to join a lesbian New Age colony in Ibiza. Mr Steinert and Breeze were united in their shame and fury. Breeze provided fake grounds for divorce in order to avert a scandal, and Mr Steinert agreed to leave his investment in place. It proved a sound investment as art prices soared during the late seventies and eighties, but after the nineties crash, Mr Steinert had asked to withdraw his capital as soon as possible without incurring serious financial problems for Breeze. They met regularly to discuss Mr Steinert's definition of 'serious'.

'And you know what you're like about money, Breeze,' Plum added timidly.

'I don't know what you mean by that,' Breeze said stiffly. He stood up and paced the room, hands pushed deep into the pockets of his bathrobe.

'Yes, you do.' Breeze always became angry if she mentioned it, but he was secretly terrified of being without money: his waking nightmare was to be old, ill, penniless, in debt, and unable to support himself, with starvation and hypothermia looming before him. Plum knew why.

After Breeze's grandfather, a tenant farmer, became crippled by arthritis, he and his wife had had to be financially supported by Breeze's father, which had been a continuous financial strain upon him. As a child, when Breeze was naughty, his pocket money was taken away. Grimly, his father would say, 'You'd better learn that because you've got a bit of money, it doesn't follow that you'll be able to keep it.'

Breeze learned. Consequently, in money matters he veered mercurially from over-confidence to anxiety, if not panic. He carefully hid this from the world, but Plum knew of his nervous pacing up and down the bedroom at dawn, after a sleepless night. She had shaken him awake from Kafkaesque dreams, a wasteland of bills, debts, tax officials tapping him on the shoulder and screaming bank managers pointing to prison. Sometimes when this happened Breeze would abruptly bend over and clutch his stomach, feeling physical pains that only a reassuring call to his accountant could cure.

Plum had first met Breeze's accountant after one of these anxiety attacks. Sidney was a big man with a small, quiet voice like a lull in the centre of a storm. 'Poverty thought patterns, that's all,' he explained laconically, in a mild, precise voice. 'There's no reason for alarm. Breeze is in debt because if you've no capital, then borrowing money is the only way to start a business.' But privately he thought that if Breeze couldn't stand the heat, he'd better get out of the kitchen.

In the hushed splendour of the Ritz Carlton, Plum hopefully recalled Sidney's words as she looked at Breeze. He sat on the edge of the bed, angrily biting cherries with the menace, speed and precision of a Venus fly-trap. 'Don't worry, Plum. I can afford it.'

'Then it's a wonderful gift from a wonderful man,' Plum said gently. 'And now I'm definitely going to break my New Year resolution.'

✻   ✻   ✻   ✻

At midday, Breeze decided to face the cold and jog in Central Park.

Plum lay back against the pillows, stretched her arms and yawned. 'Don't go near that underpass bridge where everybody gets mugged in the movies. Every time I see that bridge on a screen I react like a Victorian audience watching the heroine walk into a trap. I shout, *'No! Don't do it! Danger ahead!'*

Breeze laughed, then noticed that a message had been pushed beneath the door.

He picked it up and read aloud, 'Ma, don't call us, we'll call you. We didn't get back till six a.m. – no cabs so had to walk miles from Spring Street.'

'In this snow! With Max's bronchitis! Oh, God, I should have organized a limo for them . . .'

'No, you shouldn't, Plum. Whoever heard of teenagers turning up at a Greenwich Village rave in a limo? Stop being a mother hen: you're not the type, too vague.' At the door, Breeze grinned over his shoulder. 'And it's too late to start: in case you'd forgotten, Toby is nineteen and Max is sixteen.'

'No, seventeen.'

'Old enough to look after himself, even in New York.' Whistling, Breeze disappeared.

Plum immediately dived into the working mother's swimming pool of guilt. Not the type? . . . Too vague? . . . Certainly she didn't think about her kids twenty-four hours a day, but she wasn't a bad mother. Come to think of it, what modern mother *wasn't* a bad mother, according to the previous generation, who'd all stayed home and knitted cakes? What had everyone expected? Some Mary Poppins update? She had done her best, Plum told herself defensively, which was all that anyone could do. And a mother's place was always in the wrong.

But if a father wasn't there, he wasn't there, and you couldn't run a family as if he were there. When the boys had been little, discipline had been definitely lax; Plum had decided that the fewer the rules, the fewer the rows and the fewer the punishments awarded that she would never administer anyway. A single mother couldn't use the weak threat: 'wait till your dad gets home'.

Plum started to worry the skin at the sides of her nails. But if a

mother had to work, then she had to work. This involved perpetual
guilt feelings, especially if she enjoyed her work, but it needn't affect
kids *that* much – unless they realized how much it worried her. Then
they had a wonderful weapon, because most children were callous
and they quite enjoyed hurting you: it proved they had power over
you. Which they did.

Plum had always consoled herself with the thought that quiet,
obedient, well-behaved children grew up into wimps, while high-
spirited children grew into interesting get-up-and-goers . . . didn't
they? And if you want a good man, grow your own.

She glanced at her wristwatch, then peered closer because the
watch – a plastic, all-black watch that Max had given her for
Christmas – had no numerals: Plum had already discovered that it
was easy for her to misread it and be an hour early, or an hour late.

It was nearly time to phone her mother. Allowing for the five-
hour time difference between the American east coast and Britain, it
was seven in the morning in Portsmouth. Her mother would be
preparing the morning tea tray in the kitchen, which smelled of stale
breadcrumbs and was still exactly the same as she'd always known it,
since babyhood.

*   *   *   *

'Mum! Open up! It's us!'

Plum jumped out of bed, grabbed a cream lace négligée, and ran
to open the door of the hotel bedroom.

'When you see a mother, kiss it!' Max leaped forward, wound
his arms around her and hugged Plum until she was breathless.

Behind him, Toby yawned, 'Happy New Year, Gorgeous!'

Like most teenagers, they were not interested in their mother;
they had nothing in common. They *loved* her dearly, of course, but
since they had grown up, there'd been something slightly forced
about their relationship. Plum, no longer leader-of-the-gang, sensed
a tolerant, instinctive, undiscussed plot to pretend that nothing had
altered: when nobody else was around they were still her boys. But
they weren't. They had separated from her. They were men. They
no longer told her their secrets, and yet they expected her to know
their fears and soothe them away.

Neither boy had noticed Plum's new diamond ring. So she held out her small, short-fingered craftsman's hand. As Suzannah had done, she spread her fingers. 'Look what Breeze just gave me!'

Both boys looked at the ring. Politely, Toby said, 'Great!' and drifted towards the television.

Max also simulated enthusiasm. 'Extra!'

It was clear to Plum that her sons thought her single flashing diamond of no interest: it was mumsy, boring, old-fashioned, uncool. Well, what had she expected? If she wanted their interest, she should have acquired a silver Hell's Angel's skull-and-crossbones ring.

Toby fiddled with the TV set. Not yet fully awake, his eyelids drooped and dark hair stuck up in spikes around his thin, sensitive face. He looked very like his father, Plum thought, before Jim's features had acquired that disagreeable, fault-finding, petulant expression. Or had that always been there, unnoticed when she was in love with him and seeing only what she wished to see?

Toby rubbed his clear grey eyes, shook his head violently, then punched a button on the TV remote control. Madonna, the wanton Queen of Pop, burst into the room. Wearing a strapless red satin gown, loaded with diamonds and surrounded by male dancers in tuxedos, she hollered, 'We are living in a *material* world, and *I* am a material girl!'

Max threw himself across the untidy bed, propped his chin on his elbows and gazed at the TV. He looked like his mother, with a long neck and a small head, the same huge, dark blue eyes and fiery red hair.

Plum watched the Material Girl try to shock. Unlike the shrewdly manipulated and coldly exploited Marilyn, this modern sex queen shrewdly exploited *herself*. Historically, the profits of female sexual exploitation had always been kept by men: Madonna was the first sex queen to keep it all for herself. Plum wondered whether that was why grown men hysterically denounced Madonna's mild porn, although they didn't raise a finger to close the hard porn industry.

'Time to phone Gran. Switch that off,' Plum said, wondering whether Madonna was happy. Or did her gruelling success schedule leave no time for that?

Both boys absent-mindedly grunted assent but did not take their eyes off the screen.

'Switch it off, guys,' Plum insisted. 'You know the oldies get upset if they expect something and it doesn't happen.'

Her sons gave two more grunts but did not move. Madonna was now being interviewed. The unctuous TV host said, 'Men get very intimidated by powerful women, don't they?'

'That's their problem,' Madonna said briskly. 'I take the risks, so I want to be in control.'

Plum switched the TV off and dialled Portsmouth, thinking how excited her mother would be about the diamond ring. Her mother loved jewellery, and wore as much as possible as often as possible. Plum decided that tomorrow she would get something from Tiffany for her mother; she loved those duck-egg-blue boxes.

Max grabbed the phone. 'Hi, Gran, I've got a joke for you. What's the difference between Heaven and Hell? . . . It's no fun if you don't try . . . No . . . No . . . Then I'll tell you. In Heaven all of the policemen are English, all of the chefs are French, all of the accountants are Swiss, all of the army is German and all of the lovers are Italian . . . *It isn't very funny because I haven't got to the joke yet, Gran* . . . and now you've made me forget it . . .'

Toby grabbed the telephone. 'In Hell, all the policemen are German, all the chefs are English, all the army is Italian, all the accountants are French and all the lovers are Swiss . . . Well, *we* do. We remembered it especially for you.'

Plum giggled, and grabbed the receiver. She finished her call by asking her father, hesitantly, if he knew anything about tracing the source of a faked picture.

Without asking for further information, Mr Phillips, a former customs officer, cleared his throat and spoke with a touch of pomposity. 'To track a criminal, follow the money backwards to source.'

'Easier said than done,' Plum thought. She'd better discuss it with Jenny.

*   *   *   *

Jenny was drinking coffee in bed. She stretched her arms and yawned. 'Breakfast in bed! At the Ritz Carlton! You're so generous to me, Plum. I love the occasional glamorous dollop of high-life! Speaking of which, have you phoned poor Lulu yet?'

'Not yet. I'm rather dreading it – you know what Lulu's like around New Year.' Plum bent to the floor and picked up a once-grey stuffed toy donkey, about the size of a cat. 'Doesn't this spoil the glamorous high-life image?' She tossed the decrepit creature back to Jenny. 'How was Nell's?' What Plum really meant was: how did things end up with Leo?

'More fun than most nightclubs. A crazy crowd: Eurotrash, with names like Italian racing cars. Cartier-encrusted girls who've done the Sotheby's course and know Steph of Monaco, wearing big black shades and blonde manes – ditto the men, who all met as boys at Le Rosey.'

'So you enjoyed bitching the night away.' Clearly Jenny hadn't scored with Leo.

'I like to exercise an occasional waspish sting of envy. Leo seems to know them all. They only talked about where they'd come from, where they were going, and what they were going to wear when they got there. The women wore insanely expensive, indecently short skirts, and no bra – if they need it, they simply get a tits lift, Leo says ...' Jenny stopped her chatter as Plum waved her hand under her nose. 'Plum, have you stolen that thing from Suzannah,' she asked, 'or did you get it out of a cracker? I mean, is it *real*?'

'Better ask Breeze. He gave it to me this morning.'

Jenny caught hold of Plum's hand. 'How much is a rock like that worth?'

'Don't know. Breeze said it's an eight-carat FVVS: what d'you suppose that means?'

'For Vivacious, Voluptuous Swingers?'

'Free with Vestal Virgins' Socks?'

'From a Very Virile Stud?' Jenny lifted the coffee pot. 'For a Very Valuable Star? Shouldn't there be another all-purpose category – SUTW: Shut-Up Toys for Wives? ... So have I forgotten your anniversary?'

'No, it's just for being good in bed, Breeze said.'

'Wow! Pity *I* don't get much practice!'

'Are you surprised?' Plum joked. 'That decrepit donkey would scare off any red-blooded man. What a dumb thing to bring to New York!'

'Where I go, Muffin goes, you know that.' Only half in jest, Jenny defiantly clutched the sagging toy to her breasts. 'But Muffin can't have scared off Leo, because he didn't come up. Said he was too tired. And he hasn't phoned this morning . . . Oh, *what* is it I do wrong, Plum? I *swear* I didn't come on too strong last night.'

'Isn't Leo staying in the Village with friends? They're probably still asleep. Don't fret about it – and don't phone him. *I'll* phone him. I need to ask his advice, then I'll find out how he feels about you.' To distract Jenny, Plum added, 'Listen, I need *your* advice. I got myself into trouble last night.' She giggled. 'I told Suzannah her Dutch flower painting's a fake.'

Jenny did not laugh, as Plum had expected, but listened carefully to what had happened the previous evening. 'So I've committed myself to finding the forger,' Plum concluded, 'but I don't know where to start! I thought I'd ask Leo. Journalists know how to do that sort of research, don't they? They know how to track down people.'

'Do you really want to get side-tracked on some needle-in-a-haystack chase for a forger who might be anywhere in the world when you only have five months before the Biennale?'

'Look, Breeze did his best to belittle me last night, he did his best to humiliate me, and this time I'm not going to forget it. I'm tired of being treated like a child by Breeze and more or less told not to be disobedient if I don't want to do what *he* decides should be done. For Breeze, when we're out of bed, I'm part painter, part obedient child – and that's all.'

'And you're *complaining*? You're not usually this stubborn.'

'That's what Breeze said. Maybe what you call stubborn is what I call not being pushed around any more.'

Jenny tried to dissuade Plum, but succeeded only in cementing Plum's determination to pursue her search, for Jenny produced all the arguments that Breeze had used, although she denied having talked to him. 'Listen, Plum, do you want me to give you my opinion – or just agree with you? Any sane person *would* agree with Breeze, and why pick a fight when he's just given you that sensational sparkler?'

'I won't be stopped by a diamond. I won't be seduced by an expensive shut-up toy!'

After Plum left, banging the door, Jenny huddled under the bedclothes and cuddled her worn, stuffed donkey. If racing drivers and tennis stars travelled with mascots, why shouldn't she? Muffin had comforted her for as long as she could remember. Plum had had two husbands and two children, while Jenny had had none. Plum didn't understand what it was like to be thirty-six years old and wonder why the hell nobody wanted to marry you.

* * * *

Beyond the panoramic hotel window, the snowy afternoon glittered and sparkled invitingly. Plum decided to follow Breeze's example and walk in Central Park. Leaving her sons glued to MTV, she trudged beneath gaunt, witch-fingered trees and snow-laden conifers, crunching fresh footprints in the newly fallen snow.

Around her, people walked with coat collars upturned and hands in pockets, their breath visible in mist-grey puffs. Joggers thumped past, and kids whizzed on roller-skates, dexterously dodging the head-down, determined cyclists, who looked like French carnival performers in striped tops over tight black cycling shorts.

Although it was still daylight, electric necklaces of light looped from the black boughs of the skeletal trees that surrounded the frozen lake in Central Park. It was as charmingly busy as an old Dutch skating painting, Plum thought, as she watched the hot-chestnut vendor and dancing couples waltzing to music.

Nevertheless, Plum wondered why Jenny, usually so sympathetic, so gently supportive, so good-natured and soothing, had sided with Breeze in a situation which for Plum had now escalated to a matter of honour. She regretted having yelled at Jenny because for once she hadn't agreed with her. She'd ask Jenny to lunch at La Grenouille tomorrow; according to Breeze, that was where smart New York women ate lunch.

The afternoon suddenly grew colder. Plum banged her gloved

hands together for warmth, then turned back towards Central Park South. On frozen feet she trudged towards the black trees that edged the park, where a line of dejected carriage horses waited patiently for tourists.

Back at the hotel, Plum telephoned Leo and fixed a lunch date. Then she dialled Lulu's number. As she listened to the constipated wheeze of the British telephone bell, she felt apprehensive, and half hoped that Lulu would not reply.

Chapter Four

P LUM'S breakfast interview with Sol Schweitzer of the *New York Telegraph* took place at 8 a.m. in the Jockey Club restaurant on the ground floor of the Ritz Carlton.

Sol Schweitzer, a small, thin, sharp-faced man with a deceptively soothing manner, had been briefed to keep away from Plum's painting. A more general article was required for the features section. This was just as well, because Sol was the paper's theatre critic, standing in for someone who had influenza.

He started with standard dull questions, deliberately designed to calm the subject's anxieties. Whereabouts in Britain do you come from? What's your family background? How many times have you been married? How closely do you work with your current husband? How much money do you make?

Nervously, Plum replied. Portsmouth, that's a naval town in the south of England . . . My dad was a customs officer and we lived an ordinary life like everyone else in our road . . . At school I was good at art and nothing else, so when I was sixteen I went to Hampshire Art College . . . Breeze is my second husband and he's also my agent . . . We live in London and I've no idea how much money I make. Yes, Breeze looks after that sort of thing.

Plum knew how dull her monosyllabic answers sounded. But to her surprise, the journalist's questions honed her view of the past, and as she gave her guarded answers her thinking seemed to sharpen into focus. Today she could see more clearly what she had been groping for yesterday as she had tried to put her finger on what had gone wrong with her life, to pinpoint and analyse the dissatisfaction that was bubbling uneasily beneath her seemingly envious existence like a head of steam in a pressure-cooker. Today, Plum realized that the only way she could come to terms with the present was by working out what in the past had led to it – and why. So in her head, Plum interviewed herself. *Why* did she do that? *Why* had that happened? *Why* had she allowed it to happen?

As Plum remembered the reasons for her actions, she knew that no matter how much she wished she had thought or behaved differently, at the time there had never seemed any alternative. Looking back with the benefit of hindsight could not change what had already happened. But perhaps that was the kernel of her problem: her life had simply happened to her, and she had allowed it to happen. She had passively accepted the demands of other people and of situations. It had never occurred to the obedient little girl, which Plum still was at heart, to swim against the tide of other people's approval.

*   *   *   *

Plum, christened Sheila, had been an only child. The Phillipses lived an uneventful, lower-middle-class life in a small, bow-fronted ter-raced house that was spotlessly clean and furnished with as many frills as possible. Mrs Phillips believed in keeping up appearances, which covered many activities and possibilities. You always wore knickers in case you had a street accident; you never answered the door with curlers in your hair; you washed the empty milk-bottles before you put them on the doorstep for the milkman to collect in the morning; you never allowed your family in the front room, so that it was tidy if anyone called unexpectedly. But if anyone called, you kept them waiting in the passage. Mrs Phillips's favourite phrases were: 'What will the neighbours think?' and 'We like to keep ourselves to ourselves,' which meant that the neighbours were kept at bay.

In all minor matters, from her opinion of the Royal Family (which she discussed knowledgeably, as if they were related) to her choice of colour for the toilet cover, Patricia Phillips was supported by her husband, Don. He was a small man with a bland expression that concealed an obstinate streak and a tough disposition. Like all petty bureaucrats he did things by the book, hated to make decisions, and enjoyed seeing the guilty-until-proven-innocent tremble before him. At home, where he was the complacent king of his castle, his wife endlessly repeated his platitudinous opinions, which she only wished the government could hear. This domestic martinet never bothered to be tactful, for he thought of himself as an honest man who spoke the plain truth and believed in plain speaking, so his statements were often hurtful.

In particular, Plum remembered one Christmas dinner spent at her Aunt Harriet's home, with her dentist uncle and their four huge, silent sons. After the first bottle of South African sherry had been emptied, her father had playfully told Aunt Harriet he could see she'd put on weight. As usual, when her dad put his foot in it, her mum had tried to soften his words by explaining that Don was only being cruel to be kind.

But Aunt Harriet had said, 'No, he's being cruel to be cruel. Don's high standards are the reason for his fault-finding, but they're never used to measure his own behaviour – because he sees himself as bloody perfect. But Don's only perfect in one way: he's a perfect pain in the ass.'

Plum's mum had quickly said, 'Don, she knows no better. Don't let her spoil your Christmas.'

At the end of the meal, after they'd all congratulated Aunt Harriet on it, Plum's dad had quietly said that in his honest opinion, the turkey had been too dry and the stuffing too moist, but the cranberry sauce had been quite good. Aunt Harriet had said, 'Then let me give you some more,' and poured the remnants in the sauceboat over her brother-in-law's head. After the uproar that followed, the Phillipses had hurried home.

Little Plum, an observant child, did not only notice the strange and often contradictory behaviour of adults. She was interested in the oddest things: she would hold something close to her eye and peer at it. She would kneel on the grass, staining her socks, to stare into the heart of a dandelion, and she would lift a strawberry close to her eye before eating it. Twice, needlessly, her mother had Plum's eyes tested.

Although affectionate, the quiet child learned to be wary; a good girl never hurled herself into her mother's lap, lest she crumple her clothes. Although naturally exuberant, Plum learned to be unobtrusive, mouse-quiet, and never naughty – with one exception. When she was three years old, Plum filched a knife and a bar of Lux soap; hidden beneath the kitchen table, she carved a Scottie dog, like the one that advertised canned pet food on TV. This crude, cream canine stood on the shelf above the fireplace for months, while its legs slowly melted. After that it was understood that little Sheila was artistic: her mother didn't know where she got it from, although Aunt Harriet – who also had the red hair – was considered to have an artistic temperament. On her niece's tenth birthday, Aunt Harriet wickedly gave her an adult's box of oil-paints. Ignoring her other gifts, Plum spent a day of wild delight, but smeared paint over the furniture, and stained her best dress with streaks of chrome yellow. Couldn't have her making that mess again, said her mother, and locked the paints in a cupboard.

The highlight of Plum's uneventful school career came when she was fifteen, when her school arranged summer holiday exchanges with French girls living in Bordeaux. Plum fell in love with France, with the sun, the garlic-scented food and the sensual atmosphere. Her French exchange girl had hated the rain, the food and the prim respectability of Portsmouth, so the visits were never repeated.

A year later – on 27 May 1971 – her sixteenth birthday – Plum nervously announced that she wanted to study art. To her astonishment, her parents made no objections. They looked at each other and nodded – the soap Scottie dog had been a clear indication of artistic talent, and Sheila, as her parents still called her, hadn't shone in any other school subject. The Hampshire Art College fashion department, her mother decided. Mrs Phillips, who was always planning an outfit, imagined herself admired at parties in gorgeous gowns run up by Sheila over the weekend. Mrs Phillips always remembered events by the clothes she wore to them ('We met them at that wedding where I wore my brown lace' . . . 'It was the day I first wore my blue satin . . .').

The girls in the fashion department designed wedding-dresses on pale blue paper with much white paint slashed on, to indicate voluminous net skirts. Plum had quickly transferred to the painting department, where immediately she knew that her future was settled. Here, among the easels under the skylight, Plum felt sure of herself, and reached confidently towards her own standards of perfection. Here, the seemingly quiet, neat orderliness of Plum's character was immediately contradicted by the irrational passion of her powerful, sometimes chaotic canvases.

'Trying to run before you can walk,' commented Mr Davis, her favourite teacher. 'You'd do better to spend more time in life class; plenty of time later for this abstract stuff. You've got to understand structure before you can decide what to abstract *from*.' In the staff-room it was agreed that the new girl, the little redhead, had an astonishing colour sense; she was a natural. She had what it took to be a real corker. Pity she was a girl.

Mrs Phillips was not so enthusiastic about her daughter's change of subject. Puzzled, she peered at a canvas that Plum was painting in her bedroom.

'Is that brown splodge on the green bit supposed to be a cow?'

'No, Mum, it's just a balanced pattern of colour.'

Mrs Phillips, thinking of her knitting patterns, peered again at the canvas. 'How can it be a pattern when it doesn't repeat? What does it *mean*, dear?'

Plum shrugged. 'A piece of music doesn't *mean* anything; it conveys a mood; people don't complain that Beethoven's Ninth doesn't *mean* anything. I'm painting how I feel.'

'Well, you haven't finished it yet, dear, have you?'

'As a matter of fact, yes, I have.'

'*How do you know?*'

*   *   *   *

Plum and Jenny met in the first hour of their first day at college, in the cracked, white tiled cloakroom which stank of turps because it was here that everyone cleaned their brushes.

'Why don't you wear lipstick?' Jenny asked. 'Wanna try mine?' Mary Quant's 'Shocker Pink' changed hands. The two girls then sat next to each other in classes and were inseparable outside them. Together, they experimented with make-up, went on the banana diet and exchanged inaccurate sex information. As little girls they had wondered where you put the noses and how you breathed when you kissed; now they argued whether you both pushed at once, or when he pushed, did you pull back? Or vice versa? Despite the ludicrous difference in height – Jenny was the taller by almost a foot – they wore identical clothes, the obligatory art-student uniform of dead-white make-up, black jeans and skinny black sweater stretched tight over bra-less breasts.

Plum's first, timidly rebellious step was to change her name – she had never liked it, and there were two other Sheilas in the first year.

Jenny encouraged her. 'Why *should* we be stuck with names our parents like? Why *shouldn't* we choose our own name? Let's think of something more original for you: how about Mercedes? Petronella? Persephone? Delilah?'

These suggestions were turned down; too long, too stuffy, impossible to spell, nothing classical or biblical – yuck!

Eventually Jenny said, 'I know what would suit you – and that dark red hair. Plum!'

Her parents were appalled; their Sheila had never before gone against their wishes. And this awful name sounded like one of those new boutiques – Biba, Shiva, and suchlike. 'We'd never have sent you to art college if we'd known,' her mother said once again. Mrs Phillips's accusations and lamentations, like Hokusai's *Hundred Views of Mount Fuji*, were always basically the same, with only slight variations.

* * * *

The just-vanished sixties had been an exciting period in art. Op art dazzled. Pop art exploded into the media with nauseous Oldenburg hamburgers, irreverent Jasper Johns flags, Lichtenstein's comic-strip people with mouth bubbles, Rauschenberg's naughty goat, and Warhol's repetitious Marilyns, baleful parody of advertising. At Hampshire Art College nobody wanted to sit, evening after evening, drawing stolid models in life class, especially not the first-year students. Together Plum and Jenny complained as loudly as they dared about the old-fashioned classic teaching methods employed at the art college. They longed to ride bicycles through pools of paint, then over sheets stretched taut on the floor, which is what they thought happened at the hip London schools. The entire first-year class spurned all attempts to study the Old Masters, preferring to emulate the moderns. But geometric abstraction, ready-mades, minimalist art, kinetic art and all other efforts to be trendy were dismissed with relish by Mr Davis as basically either Russian Constructivist or Early Bauhaus, and forty years out of date. Also foolishly pretentious in anyone who was skipping the evening life classes, he added over his spectacles.

Eventually all the first-years did as old Davis wanted, and so they learned to draw. In many other British art schools, pupils were being taught by the casualties of the sixties, a time when figurative painting was scornfully denigrated and discarded. Thus many of *their* pupils – the following generation of painters and teachers – were never taught how to draw, or other classic disciplines.

Out of class, the first-years were equally obedient, as they enthusiastically accepted the often unrealistic aims and attitudes of the student leaders. They all became normally rebellious, conforming nonconformists.

*　*　*　*

The week after they had become friends, Jenny introduced Plum to Lulu, whom Jenny had known since kindergarten. A year younger than the other two, Lulu Frazer was still at school, but due to enter the art college the following year, when she would be sixteen. Impatiently, Lulu waited to join Jenny, to wear democratic black and splash paint around all day.

Lulu was a beauty; her skin was cream and pink; her mischievous clear grey eyes scorned rules, and she shook her mass of tightly curled, dark hair at convention. She was a tall girl – five foot eight, which tiny Plum thought the perfect height. She longed to walk with a lanky lope, like long-legged Lulu.

Lulu didn't behave like the youngest of the trio. Headstrong and rebellious, she made a habit of jumping out of the frying-pan into another hotter frying-pan; and she had a bad habit of getting found out. 'Good practice for Mummy,' she said scornfully, when caught red-handed. Lulu's parents were both doctors – they had met at medical school. Lulu's mother, a child psychologist, and her father, a paediatrician, both worked at Portsmouth General.

Lulu had been adopted, which her two friends found romantic. However, Lulu was not the by-blow of some royal prince and a beautiful, fiery gypsy, although she often behaved dramatically, as if this ought to have been the case. Lulu was the result of a liaison between a married Jewish doctor and a Catholic nurse. Her adoptive father had delivered her: that had been the last time her natural mother had seen her.

Unlike her elder brother, Dennis (also adopted), who was academic and decided to be a brain surgeon at the age when most boys long to be astronauts, Lulu cheerfully failed every exam she sat at the local state school where her aggressively democratic parents had sent her.

Her life changed radically when she won a local art competition, organized by Portsmouth Civic Art Workshop. The family attic was immediately transformed into a real studio. Her mother proudly bought her a little portable easel and a box of oil-paints, while her father explained with relief to relatives that Lulu was artistic, and they were often late developers.

* * * *

At the end of her first term, having produced twice as much work as anyone else, Jenny won the Best Student's Portfolio prize. The other first-year students didn't think she deserved to win the prize – even if it *was* only a book token. Neither did many of the masters, but Jenny worked hard, whereas her fellow-students – no longer grimly supervised as at school – had used their new-found freedom to have fun. And where Jenny lacked talent she compensated with effort and determination that the other students did not understand.

Jenny's ambition stemmed from the subconscious knowledge – never confronted – that she did not possess much original talent. Unlike her, Plum was not so much focused on a career as she was on the act of painting: she lived with her inexplicable urge to paint, but she didn't yet know how good a painter she was – and neither did the other students.

Plum won the History of Art prize, which was a bit like winning the scripture prize at school in that it was the prize that nobody tried for. After a class day-trip to the National Gallery, Plum became fascinated by the precision and techniques of the early painters. She found recent history of art far more difficult to study, until Mr Davis, finding Plum bent over a library book entitled, *The Institutional Culture of Late Modernism*, advised her not to puzzle over any period labelled 'neo', 'nouveau', 'post' or 'trans'. 'These are the labels of artists desperately pretending to be different from their predecessors,' he told her. 'For instance, expressionism is constantly being repitched under an updated label.'

*   *   *   *

Just before the end of the Christmas term, Jenny reluctantly took Plum back to her home for tea, having run out of excuses for not returning hospitality. When Jenny's dad arrived back unexpectedly early, Plum immediately smelled the reason for Jenny's reluctance. Tom Black worked as a salesman for a central heating firm that provided systems for hospitals, schools and other municipal buildings. His convivial drinking when entertaining clients had long escalated from before-and-during-lunch and a-quick-one-after-work, to steady drinking from mid-morning to bedtime.

Jenny, his youngest child and only daughter, had inherited her father's looks. She had his big frame, his amber eyes and amber hair; and like him, she had a laughing conviviality that attracted people.

Fiercely proud of his daughter, Tom Black, when sober, frequently said that Jenny was the apple of his eye. However, when drunk – and after Jenny's fourth birthday he was rarely completely sober – he became unpredictable and aggressive. He then frequently lectured Jenny on how to succeed in life. His motto was: *success at any price*. Slurring his words, he would say, 'If you aren't a success, d'y'know what you are, Jenny? *A failure!* ... Your dad won the Best Southern Region Salesman award *three times running*. So you must be a success, Jenny ...' If she wasn't top of her class, then the apple of his eye was beaten with her dad's leather belt – for her own good. Unsurprisingly, Jenny's self-worth became dependent on her father's approval.

At night, when Jenny heard her father shouting, her mother screaming or sobbing, she buried her head under the bedclothes and tightly hugged her toy donkey. Muffin understood how desperately she wished that she knew how to stop her dad doing these awful things to her mum, whatever they were – things that men did in the dark.

Jenny's mother – like so many of her generation – dealt with her problem by pretending, even to herself, that it did not exist. Shamed by her husband's behaviour, she ignored her miserably chaotic life and pretended that she lived the sort of comfortable, comforting existence enjoyed by Mrs Dale, the Doctor's wife. She pretended even to her little daughter that everything was normal. From her, Jenny learned to hide her fear and shame and to live a permanent lie.

The adult Jenny's outwardly cheerful exterior still concealed a bewildered child whose values had been permanently confused, and whose aim in life was to hide her vulnerability, and her mistrust of men.

By the end of her first term at art college, it had become clear that Jenny couldn't keep a man: she was always too anxious to establish a relationship, she wanted commitment on the first date: men found her claustrophobic; her angst-ridden relationships were off almost before they were on.

One evening, Lulu's mother unexpectedly explained why (she was breathtakingly broad-minded and had painstakingly instructed Lulu about sex: at the age of twelve, Lulu could spell 'fallopian tubes'). Plum was at Lulu's home, helping make a costume for Lulu's mother to wear at a charity Christmas play. As the two girls knelt to pin up the hem of the Wicked Witch of the West, they discussed the latest man to flee from Jenny – a pleasant Royal Marine who felt that at nineteen he was too young to marry.

Standing in her stockinged feet, Lulu's mother absent-mindedly said that Jenny's problem stemmed back to her father. An alcoholic father made a little girl feel that men were frightening, unpredictable and unreliable. When such girls grew up, they resented the insecurity of their childhood and became desperately anxious never to feel so vulnerable again, nor let a man get close enough to have the trusting, safe relationship that paradoxically they longed for.

'Acrobats and dancers trust their partners to catch them,' Lulu's mother had said, as if thinking aloud, 'but an insecure woman never has that trust. And because she doesn't trust her sexual partner and fears her own vulnerability, she'll never let herself go sexually. She'll hang on, and won't yield to the experience. So I expect Jenny is non-orgasmic.'

Astonished and fascinated, Plum listened as Lulu's mother dreamily continued: 'And if an insecure woman feels that her only possible happiness depends on one man, then she's terrified of losing him. Sensing this, he feels trapped – so he runs for freedom. That's how Jenny will always sabotage herself.'

'So that's why Jenny's such a clinger!' Lulu had cried. 'Mummy, you should be an agony aunt on the *Portsmouth Evening News*.'

'No, darling, they'd never print words like "orgasm".'

*   *   *   *

Between classes, the art students converged in the noisy, shabby, smoke-filled café on the corner. At the central table, reserved for older students, the college dances, stunts and protests were quietly planned amid the noisy arguments of surrounding tables. Often these concerned the lackadaisical Portsmouth football team, but there was also a running battle to decide who was *the* major influence on modern art. All students pushed the claims of their artist-favourite-of-the-moment, with far more passion than they did for the football players – especially the newly expert first-years.

'Picasso *must* be the biggest influence, because he invented collage,' Jenny argued one morning.

Plum agreed. 'Picasso's metal guitar sculpture led directly to Russian Constructivism and assembled, welded sculpture in the West.'

'But Duchamp demystified art by inventing Readymades,' another student objected. 'And he attacked pseudo-religious art, *and* he was the first person to use ordinary objects as art components.'

'What about Dada?' The girl next to Plum demanded. 'Dada provided freedom to experiment at all levels . . .'

Jenny sniffed. 'Dadaists were influenced by Futurists and *they* were influenced by the Cubists – so there you are, back at Picasso . . . Ooh, look, *here comes Jim* . . .' Their argument stopped abruptly

50

as the college hero swaggered into the café with the stiff-legged strut
of a man whose jeans are too tight.

Well over six feet tall, Jim Slade was a graphic designer who had
just started his third year. He was lean and taut as a greyhound, with
long legs and arms. The female students all gazed longingly at the
sharply modelled features of his pale face. Above a wide thin mouth,
Jim's nose was straight and narrow; his clear grey eyes in blue-white
sclerae shone beneath long straight black eyebrows. This blend of
sharp good looks and tough delicacy gave Jim a sensitive but don't-
mess-with-me macho charm that sent shivers down those girlish
spines. Jim's attraction did not only depend on his visual impact but
also his glamour status in college: he was Vice-President of the
Students' Union and organizer of the annual Rag Week and every
other protest.

Jenny turned pale. She leaned towards Plum and whispered,
'He's coming over to us! . . . I can't *stand* it!'

Jim slowly sauntered over to their little table. To the scruffy
first-years, it was as if a golden god in a glittering chariot had
descended slowly from heaven to their feet. Plum and Jenny felt faint
from joy as they meekly looked up into Jim's self-confident grey
eyes. Gorgeous was the only word.

'You two girls doing anything tonight?' Jim asked, in his
deliberately-stressed, working-class accent.

Both shook their heads, instantly deciding to cut the evening life
class.

'Care to help me stuff some . . . envelopes?' Jim was known for
his bawdy sense of humour.

They giggled their assent. Jim sauntered back to his table.

* * * *

On the surface, Jim was bright and clever with mesmeric charm, but
beneath this power to enchant ran a dark, cruel streak: to love Jim
meant that you let down your guard, and Jim, who never let down
his, could not resist a lowered guard. He had to check his power –
to cause pain.

Why did Jim fall for Plum? Jim's predatory instincts were
attracted by Plum's innocence and youthful bloom, as seductive as

the fine mauve mist on a freshly plucked plum that you can't resist smearing, to see if it disappears, which it always does. And although she didn't realize it, Plum was the prettiest girl of her year.

Why did Plum immediately fall in love – in lust – with Jim? Having timidly emerged from her father's domination as King of the Castle, the virginal Plum was attracted by another superbly self-confident man who appeared to have all the answers to Life's questions. Everything in Plum's world – her talent, her hopes and her urge to paint – were immediately sublimated to Jim's possession not only of her body but of her brain. All her senses were focused on him, so that her present and her future were obscured by the dazzling golden image that Jim projected. And Plum was the envy of the college as she became Jim's handmaiden in his major project: a scale model for a ton of iron from the local car dump, destined to be crushed and entitled *Los Angeles Freeway 16.5*. Because Plum's own self-image was not strong and clear, she had been mesmerized by a man who was as confidently self-assured as he was selfish.

*   *   *   *

Plum couldn't remember much about the New Year's Eve art college fancy-dress ball – a swirl of balloons, beer and bonhomie – but she remembered every minute of the drive home, through the snow, in Jim's old Ford Cortina, crammed with other students who needed a lift. When only Jim, Jenny and Plum remained in the car, Jim rattled past Plum's road in order to drop Jenny off first. As she buttoned up her tweed coat, Jenny said goodnight with barely concealed disappointment; she hurried up the path, lifting her net skirts clear of the new fallen snow, then turned to wave good-night.

Jim scrunched to a halt by the churchyard and switched off the lights, so he and Plum could only see each other dimly, silhouetted by the light of a distant street lamp. He grabbed her shoulders, his tongue firmly forcing her lips apart. Plum did not realize that she was kissing her future goodbye.

Slowly, Jim unwound the college scarf from her head. Slowly, he unbuttoned her winter coat. He groped through pink chiffon (a Zandra Rhodes knock-off, bought at Handley's pre-Christmas sale), then swiftly plunged his hands down the front and pulled Plum's breasts out.

Jim's head bent to each small, pale nipple in turn. He fondled and kissed her breasts until they ached but yearned for more, and then his hand stealthily snaked beneath the pink chiffon skirt. Plum felt his finger hook over the top of her tights and was alarmed: she had never let him go that far. Everyone else might be doing it in daisy chains – as Jim assured her was the case – but Plum was scared that . . . something . . . might happen. 'Something' was pregnancy.

As Plum tried to stop Jim she heard chiffon rip, and found it very exciting. Then she felt Jim's hand plunge down inside her tights, sliding over her belly, then between her thighs. He stroked her silky pubic mound and murmured, 'You see? There's nothing to be frightened of . . .' Plum's firm resolution melted, as her body felt increasingly dreamily erotic . . .

With cunning expertise, Jim's hand suddenly twisted lower, diving between her split. Plum heard a pleased grunt as he felt her wetness. He pulled his hand back to just above her split and tentatively felt around with his forefinger until she bucked beneath his finger and he knew that he had located the magic spot. He started to rub . . . and it was as if he had ignited a firework touch-paper. Plum soared straight up into the stratosphere.

She shrieked with disbelief as she felt her first orgasm ripple through her body. 'I'd no idea . . . I thought it hurt . . . Oh, darling Jim, *do it again!*'

Swiftly, Jim hitched his thumb under the elastic waistband of Plum's tights and yanked them off.

By the time the windows had steamed up and the front seat of the old Cortina was a whirl of arms and legs half-entrapped by clothes, Jim had unzipped and shoved her hand firmly on his *thing*, which seemed to have a life of its own as it reared and jumped in her hand. She was uncertain what to do with it: did you squeeze, pump or stir? There was no time to wonder. As they panted towards a climax Plum felt the rhythm of her life speed up, like a Charlie Chaplin movie: *it* was about to happen.

One of Jim's hands pushed her legs further apart as the other felt between them. His middle finger pushed insistently against resistance. Her little hips thrust towards him. Jim's pelvis jerked upwards against her soft, naked stomach . . . it *was* going to happen . . .

They both ignored the firm tap at the window and continued their frenzied pursuit of each other's flesh.

A further, sharper tap was followed by a male voice. 'Police, open up!'

'Aaaaaagh, don't you dare open the door, Jim!' Plum tried unsuccessfully to disentangle her leg from the steering-wheel, as they struggled in a constricting morass of half-discarded clothing. She groped for her coat but couldn't locate it. She tried to hide her breasts with her crossed hands.

Jim muttered, 'If this is someone's idea of a joke, I swear I'll break his bloody neck!'

'Open up, please, sir. You can't park here without your lights on. And I'll have to ask you to move on.'

It was no joke.

Later, they did it, uninterrupted. It wasn't as painful as Plum had expected, but going the whole way was disappointing: not nearly as exciting as what he'd done before.

Partly because doing it proved such an anti-climax, Plum was too bashful to talk of her disappointment to Lulu and Jenny, who were still hopeful, highly imaginative virgins. So she adopted a superior air when her friends pestered her to know what it was like. Smugly she said she couldn't possibly describe the rapture, they'd find out soon enough, and she refused to be drawn further.

Sworn to secrecy, Lulu and Jenny thought Plum had better get on the Pill fast, before it happened again – as it would, they told each other, writhing and groaning with envy. But Plum was too embarrassed to visit the family doctor.

At first she was too frightened to do it again, but Jim could not keep his hands off her. And like every couple in love, they felt themselves beneath the protection of a benevolent, magic star, immune to the mundane: it couldn't happen to them.

Eventually, Lulu asked her mother what Lulu's (anonymous) friend should do. Lulu's mother, believing that the anonymous friend was Lulu, put her on the Pill immediately. Lulu gave the pills to Plum. Plum relaxed; now she felt completely safe. But it was too late, although for some weeks Plum did not realize that she was pregnant. Dirty Dame Nature had snapped the trap on Plum before she realized that it existed. She was now responsible for somebody else's life before she'd started a life of her own.

Later, Plum wondered whether she had unconsciously put off her decision to go on the Pill, whether she had dithered and prevaricated because she wanted the baby that would tie her to Jim.

She didn't dare tell her mum. Eventually, when she could no longer hide her shape, she asked Aunt Harriet to break the news. This turned out to be a worse move than the conception.

'How could you tell *that woman*? The shame and humiliation of it!' Mr Phillips roared among the autumnal tints of the small back room where they read, ate, watched TV and – very occasionally – argued.

'Don, Harriet *is* family,' Plum's mum said. 'And soon everyone'll know.'

'Can't you . . . can't something be done?'

But it was too late for an abortion.

Although not the sort of man to be forced into marriage, to everyone's surprise, Jim (a traditionally rebellious non-conformist) decided to do the unexpected thing. Why not mate in the heady, sexual intensity of their youth, as Nature intended? Everything would work out, somehow. Jim had the arrogant self-confidence of youth: rash, brash and false because it had never been tested.

So Mrs Phillips escorted the bride-to-be, then six months pregnant, to Handley's maternity department to buy a cream silk dress. Before they entered the department store, Mrs Phillips tugged off her gold wedding band. 'You'd better wear this.'

Throughout the Register Office ceremony, Jim's mother looked reproachfully at the bride from behind elaborate, pale blue spectacles. Occasionally she snivelled daintily into an embroidered handkerchief. She had been widowed when Jim was eight years old. Her husband, Edgar, a piano-tuner and a chain-smoker, had died of lung cancer: in those days they never knew it killed you.

Looking back later, Plum was astonished at the speed with which her life had altered. One minute she was dancing in the snow in pink chiffon . . . and then . . . trepidation, calendar consultations, tears, dread, confession, hysteria, now let's all keep calm, a wedding cake that glistened like the Guildhall after rain, emotional speeches, the Isle of Wight ferry, the honeymoon in a boarding-house with cardboard walls, then back to her own bedroom in Mafeking Road, which her mother had painted pale blue as a surprise: it now contained a brass double bed, Aunt Harriet's gift. Above this, Jim, who was heavily into the Russian Constructivists, pinned a powerful and gloomy Rodchenko reproduction poster of bottles of beer next to Lissitzky's *Beat the Whites with the Red Wedge*.

Downstairs, the rarely used front parlour was transformed into a nursery. Jim banned the Disney-animal wall frieze, bought by Mr Phillips: something visually stimulating was needed for Jim's baby. He worked on a sort-of-Fauve scheme in red and purple, but then decided that the de Stijl group were right about their ultimate style for a new world, right to restrict forms to the rectangle and use only the three primary colours. So Jim painted one entire nursery wall in the yellow, red and blue linear pattern of Mondrian's *Broadway Boogie-Woogie (1943)*. Smiling bravely, Mrs Phillips knitted small white sweaters, although Jim had asked for black.

* * * *

Sex in the brass double bed disappointed Plum. It was as inhibiting for Jim as it was for her to know that they were within a foot of her mother's head in the next room. They whispered as they fumbled for each other beneath the sheets. *Shhhhhhh*, each cautioned the other. Now Jim did it fairly fast. In and out. From the rear, when she swelled hard as a football in front. On the rare occasions when she climaxed, Jim swiftly clamped his hand over her mouth. 'You don't seem to be able to manage it unless even the bloody wind's in the right direction,' he complained. Any disappointment Plum felt was obviously due to some lack in her body's response, probably because she was pregnant. Was she sure that she should still be doing it? They didn't want to hurt the baby.

Plum felt far too timid and unsure of herself to insist on her own satisfaction. Once she had whispered, 'Let's do it like we did it that first time, in the Ford.'

'You mean, with clothes on?' Jim asked, rather intrigued, as he looked at her child-like face beneath tousled horse-chestnut hair.

'No. With your hand.'

'But you'd make such a noise.'

So eventually, secretly, she did it herself, after her afternoon nap. But this was not what she wanted. She wanted Jim to touch her: it was not only a physical yearning but also an emotional one. She wanted him to reach for her body with slow tenderness; she wanted to feel again the rising sensuality which had soared to swamp her senses when their bodies had first joined. Frequently, after her nap, she remembered the warmth of his flesh against hers as their bodies – fiercely clamped together – had climbed, dipped, hesitated and then soared again . . . finally to float back to earth in soft, warm contentment. She wanted eroticism again.

* * * *

Plum left college for ever at the end of the 1972 summer term, although she refused to stop painting and worked whenever she wasn't feeling nauseous. Her dad cleared out their old bicycle shed in the back yard. She planned to heat it with an oil stove in winter, although her mum warned that those things were dangerous.

To encourage Plum, Lulu's mother purchased one of her paintings. 'It's *not* because she feels sorry for you,' Lulu insisted. 'She *likes* abstracts: she says that obviously the unconscious can't be consciously directed.' As Lulu's mother was the only parent who understood the roots of abstract expressionism, it was not surprising that Lulu was destined to be the only pupil of the first year whose paintings were realistic and precise.

Exhausted and swollen during the last month of her pregnancy, Plum felt deeply undesirable. By contrast, when the autumn term started, Jim became even more of a glamorous figure at college. He was considered even more of a dishy hero for having done the right thing by that stupid bitch (not so stupid, as it turned out) after putting her in the family way. As a married man, Jim was now forbidden territory, but that only made him more attractive, and it deterred few, for it was obvious that the delectable Jim was quietly available. And no wonder: Plum was now a tired, bloated, dreary little creature. Serve her right.

* * * *

An eight-pound boy with his dad's long legs, Toby stared at his mother and yawned. But when the hospital nurse put him to his mother's breast, the tiny mouth immediately clamped on her nipple and sucked hard. Plum was astonished by the force and determination of the fragile little creature, who had been in the world for only a few minutes. As one miniature hand with perfect nails – more delicate than that of any doll – clutched at her breast, she felt she would burst with joy. She had just met her son and they had loved, accepted and trusted each other at first sight. Paradoxically, at the point where Toby left her body, she now felt joined to him for ever.

Right from the start, Jim felt left out; the atmosphere in Mafeking Road became even more strained when Plum's friends visited. Behind their back, Jim referred to Jenny as 'Miss Manhunt' and Lulu as 'The one with verbal diarrhoea'.

Jenny was now in the second year, having won the Best First-Year Student prize, and lost her virginity to the art history professor. Lulu had made a triumphant entry into the first year with a charity fund-raising stunt: dressed as Lady Godiva in a nude body-stocking, she had ridden up the wide college staircase on a white horse. Then she found that she couldn't get the terrified horse to take one step *down* the stairs. It took the fire brigade with ropes, the local RSPCA rep, and a dressage teacher from Petersfield to get the shaking animal back on the street.

Just before Christmas 1972, after Lulu and Jenny had spent a Sunday afternoon playing with Toby the living doll, Jim slammed the door behind them and announced that in future he would leave when *they* arrived.

'How can you expect me to stay home when *they're* always hanging round, giggling?'

'At least they keep me company,' Plum yelled, 'and I don't complain about *your* friends, not even that bitch who telephones twice a night.' Plum would not have dared to shout had her father been home, but that evening, for once, they were alone in the house.

Jim smirked. 'Oh, Jilly Thompson. She's in the first year, with your gabby friend, Lulu. She's helping me organize a protest against government cultural cuts. She's mad about me, of course. Jealous?'

Delighted to have finally provoked Plum, Jim felt an erotic urge. He grabbed her round the waist and pulled her to him. Knowing they were alone, he hurled her on to her father's favourite armchair, tore her sweater off, then fell upon her half-naked, almond-white body. He hadn't felt so randy in months. He bit her breasts, just hard enough to excite her.

They both heard a shriek from the nursery, followed by a terrifying series of yells.

Half-naked, Plum muttered, 'He *can't* be hungry yet . . .' She disentangled herself, dashed towards the nursery – and charged into her dad in the passage. They had not heard his key in the front door. The football match had been postponed, due to rain.

The next day, when Plum questioned Lulu about Jilly Thompson, Lulu had looked flustered. Eventually she said, 'She looks like any other scruffy, long-haired student – one of those pushy, left-wing types that's always protesting on behalf of the workers, but never does much work herself.'

'But is she pretty, Lulu?'

'No,' said Lulu loyally. 'Sallow face, eyebags, long black witchy hair. Don't worry.'

* * * *

Jim found the attention that he self-importantly sought by becoming further involved in college politics. He was disappointed and furious when he failed to be elected President of the Students' Union. The new President was a fiery rebel who snarled at the students and told them they were assholes; they loved it. Jim never argued against the majority and wouldn't stand up for his own convictions. He hungered for success – but he wouldn't take risks for it.

* * * *

In September 1973, having finished his course, Jim went to London to do a two-year MA postgraduate course at the Royal College of Art. He planned to be a weekend commuter – it was only a ninety-minute journey to Portsmouth. However, he immediately became involved in a series of protests against the death of President Allende of Chile, the world's first democratically elected Marxist head of state, who had been killed during a military coup. So Jim didn't see much of Portsmouth that term.

Quietly, the marriage started to crumble. Mr Phillips stopped being so friendly to Jim, but Mrs Phillips shared her generation's ostrich attitude to unhappiness: *Count your blessings*, she had been taught. This determination to look on the bright side meant that she shut her eyes to the perplexities and uncertainties, the doubts and anxieties, of those she loved: so she did not help to understand or resolve their troubles.

Mrs Phillips said defensively that Jim was the Clint Eastwood type, a loner who didn't say much, who felt confined by domesticity and needed wide open spaces. She told herself that as he was studying in London it was just as well that motherhood would keep Plum busy. It was a pity that whenever she had a spare moment she disappeared into that shed and messed about with her paints. She was now a grown woman and should put away childish things.

* * * *

On Christmas Eve, after they had briskly made love, Plum falteringly told Jim that she was pregnant again.

He sat up and snapped on the light. 'But you've always put your thing in!'

'Apparently a diaphragm isn't a hundred per cent safe.'

'Apparently not. I suppose you want to keep it or you wouldn't have told me.'

'Don't you think it will be nice, Jim, having them so close together?'

He rolled away from her and considered. 'Might as well, I suppose.' It would distract her, keep her off his back.

Feeling disappointed and isolated, Plum turned off the light.

* * * *

On New Year's Eve 1973, Jim and Plum went as usual to the Hampshire Art College dance.

'What's up with Lulu?' Plum yelled across the table to Jenny against the esoteric medley played by Brent Ford and the Nylons. 'She's talking as if someone wound her up with a key in her back. She can't seem to finish a sentence and I can't follow what she's talking about, it's so erratic. But she's only had one glass of wine, and she hasn't even finished it.'

Jenny jerked her head towards the cloakroom. Once there, she said tersely, 'Lulu's doing drugs. A girl-friend – from that snobby, horsey school she went to – introduced her to some Nigerians in London who ship the stuff in – diplomatic immunity. They take the girls to glamorous London parties, then they put them on the milk train back to Portsmouth.'

'But haven't Lulu's parents . . .'

'No, they don't realize what's up – they think Lulu's weird behaviour is just normal behaviour, plus art student eccentricity. But Lulu was only allowed into the second year on probation.'

'Why does she do it?'

'She says it makes her feel terrific, gives her self-confidence; dancing the night away at Annabel's makes her forget she's a fat girl from the provinces.'

'But Lulu isn't fat,' Plum protested.

'She thinks she is. She thinks her waist should be the same size as yours. I don't want to worry you when you're pregnant, but will you try and knock some sense into her?'

Plum tried, but Lulu was defiant. It was nothing serious, nothing she couldn't kick any time. It wasn't as though she was shooting heroin. And everybody did it. Now would Plum please shut up.

Two months later in April, Lulu's tutor took her aside and said, 'We know you're still taking drugs.'

'So what? I can handle it.'

'Then how do you explain that you were our star pupil and now you're doing barely mediocre work?' Mr Davis asked angrily. 'If you don't pull yourself together, you'll have to leave.'

In May, Lulu was suspended. Her distraught parents sent her to an expensive clinic. 'Addiction is an illness,' Lulu's mother told Plum. 'You wouldn't blame Lulu for having measles. She didn't *want* this to happen.'

* * * *

Max was born on 10 June 1974. He was two weeks early, arrived with great speed, and was delivered in the hospital corridor. Jim's mother missed the birth, by one day. While buying corn plasters, she keeled over in Boots the chemist and died on the spot. A merciful release for her daughter, Mrs Phillips had sniffed to her husband. Count your blessings.

*   *   *   *

In August, Lulu was discharged – clean, but clearly depressed. She stayed in her room and ate very little. Soon, it became obvious that Lulu now found food repulsive: she became increasingly gaunt.

Plum went round to Lulu's home as often as she could, pushing her two sons in a pram. But Max often cried and Toby needed constant attention and would try to stick his tiny starfish fingers into every electrical socket outlet, if not watched. The babies proved too much of a strain for Lulu's shredded nerves.

Jenny was supportive of Lulu, and even worked in her studio, hoping to persuade her to start painting again. But Lulu screamed that painting reminded her of therapy at the rehab clinic. Patient Jenny was never offended by her friend's violent abruptness, but 'Why must you be so horribly *understanding*?' Lulu yelled, in exasperation. 'Can't you see I just want to be left alone?'

Then to everyone's surprise, in September Lulu acquired a respectable boy-friend. Mo was one of the architectural students. Studious, reserved and non-convivial, he positively courted unpopularity: he didn't smoke or drink, in order to save money to buy books. Mo saw that Lulu never missed a Narc Anon meeting. Theirs was a serious, be-faithful relationship, and Lulu's parents nervously hoped it wasn't too good to last, as they listened to the thunderous crash of Beethoven symphonies from Lulu's attic studio, where she painted portraits of Mo, bent over his drawing-board.

Mo worked hard and he made Lulu work hard, and behind her back he talked to her tutor, who persuaded the authorities to accept her back and let her take her second year again.

*   *   *   *

At the end of that year Toby caught scarlet fever. Just before he came out of quarantine, little Max ran a temperature. Just as Max came out of quarantine, both boys caught chicken-pox, closely followed by measles. The doctor said that their mother was to be congratulated on getting it all over at once.

Mrs Phillips agreed that it was all for the best, despite her concern for her daughter. One cold May afternoon while the babies were asleep, she brought a mug of tea to Plum. 'Why don't you have a nap as well?' she suggested.

'Because this is my only quiet moment in the day, and I *must* do a sketch a day if I want to keep up,' Plum yawned. 'Now let me do you, Mum.' She picked up her sketch book and quickly sketched her mother sitting in her fireside armchair. 'A page every day,' Professor Davis had told Plum when she left college. 'Make it a habit, like breakfast. If there's no time to sketch, then go without breakfast. Daily sketching will keep your eye sharp, whether you're painting or not.'

*　*　*　*

The following month, Jim finished his graphics course and found to his humiliation and fury that he couldn't get a job. Pentagram had not begged him to join, Wolff Olins had not flung open their doors, neither had any less distinguished design firm. They knew that Royal College graduates like Jim were as arrogant as they were inexperienced. He had been talented enough to get into the college but his work was not original enough to stand out from the rest. Jim could not see this, hence his growing bitterness and resentment against what he now found to be an impassive and uncaring world.

So after two carefree years in London, Jim, now twenty-five, found himself back in Portsmouth with his in-laws, feeling stifled by his family ties, for which he blamed his wife.

He took his frustration out on the military in Portugal, who had imposed a constitution giving all essential power to the armed forces.

As well as organizing protest rallies, Jim now used Plum as a lightning rod to rid himself of his feelings of ineffectuality and frustration. Partly because she meekly accepted it, Plum became the butt of Jim's jokes. His crude wit was sharp and sure as a dentist's drill probing for a nerve, although he was careful never to ridicule her before her parents.

Plum was the most convenient and acquiescent target for his spiteful arrows. Jim criticized her intellect, her lack of poise, her dress sense, her childcare, and her sexual performance. Although Plum had the sense to realize that his verbal bullying resulted from his loss of self-esteem and freedom, Jim's disapproval was inescapable, as quietly persistent as a dripping tap. Eventually it eroded Plum's under-developed self-confidence.

The one area that Jim could not criticize was Plum's undoubted creative talent, which he was painfully aware he could not match. Subconsciously he realized that he would always trail behind her. This threat to Jim's potency was the hidden menace that threatened their marriage.

Plum and Jim now knew each other so well that any thoughtlessly phrased word could elicit an exasperated response. They knew exactly how to push each other's buttons, exactly how each would react to one swift look of rage, of accusation, of martyred resignation that would trigger a further provocative response from the other partner. Spats flared up over nothing, and this dangerous chain of action and reaction was repeated until it became almost a habit. Eventually they bickered without thinking or noticing it.

Tired and depressed after nursing the children, Plum tried to avoid quarrelling with Jim and spent as much time as possible in the garden shed – always too cold or too muggy. However, she found it difficult to focus her concentration on painting when she could only grab an occasional hour in which to work. The kids required her constant attention and there were always distractions – not wonderfully irresistible temptations, but the quiet treadmill of housework: it was endless, and you never got any praise for it, you never got promotion, you never got a rise; if you complained about being unappreciated, it was assumed that your period was due.

Plum found it increasingly difficult to keep in Perfect Wife and Mother mode. She charged around the supermarket as if the baby buggy were a tank. She realized something was wrong – but what? During the first part of her life she had been meekly obedient, pushed around at home and at school. For about six seconds she had enjoyed being a silly, frivolous teenager. She didn't regret having her kids. They might have been accidents, but they weren't mistakes: she wished only that she hadn't had them so early. But now – and this was the part she didn't understand – Plum had what every girl wanted: she had a handsome husband and two beautiful children whom she adored. She felt bewildered and ashamed that this didn't seem to be enough.

She tried, unsuccessfully, to talk to her mother about these feelings of quiet yearning that seemed to have no cause, but Mrs Phillips, frightened of discussing feelings, had the female tendency to rationalize a depressing situation. Every now and then, young kids got you down. Once Jim had a job he'd be a changed man. Count your blessings! again became her refrain. She took Plum to the doctor, who prescribed an iron tonic for her nerves.

By the autumn of 1975, Plum felt her life was leaking away, a drop at a time, with nothing to show for it: she felt trapped. In contrast, Lulu had enthusiastically started her third year at art college and Jenny, who had joyfully left Portsmouth for the freedom of London, was living in grant-assisted squalor in a basement back room in Westbourne Grove. Plum and Lulu had been surprised when Jenny was accepted by the Slade because (although they never confided this disloyal thought to each other) they both considered Jenny's figurative style, based on dream sequences and fantasies, to be static, dull, mannered and derivative – and anyone who tried to work figuratively was scorned by other students, who despised such unfashionable work, except in the life class.

Lulu, who had again become accustomed to hearing her talent praised by those who wanted to stop her squandering it, found it frustrating that she had only just completed her second year as a provincial student, while Jenny was at one of London's best painting schools. Even more depressing, Mo had also moved to London, having secured a place at the Architectural Association School. After quiet arguments with Plum and noisy rows with her teachers and parents (who feared that if Lulu were unhappy enough, she might again reach for drugs), Lulu dropped out of the third year and followed Mo to liberating London.

Over Mo's bed hung a reproduction of the Malevich *Project for an Airplane Pilot's House (1924)*. Pinned next to it was a fly-blown photograph of Tatlin's spiral model for the monument to the Third International, being carried in procession through the Leningrad streets in 1926. Under these symbols of triumphant aspiration, Mo and Lulu made love, planned updated agitprop and argued happily whether Bucky Fuller's geodesic domes or recycled plastic yurts might best solve the world's housing problem.

After a few heady weeks of going to bed at dawn and getting up at noon, Lulu tried to get into one of the London art colleges, but it was too late for that year: all places were taken. She didn't try very hard because she knew that to get in anywhere she would need a recommendation from Hampshire Art College, and she knew she wouldn't get it.

Having seen her two girl-friends drop out of college, Jenny developed tunnel vision: Plum and Lulu had clearly demonstrated why Shakespeare wasn't a woman. Feverishly, Jenny worked at her carefully detailed, representational pictures and vowed that she would not be distracted by men. Sourly, Jim told Plum that Jenny probably wouldn't get the chance to do otherwise. Jenny came on too strong – anyone could see she was desperate for it and a man didn't want to be wanted: a man wanted to pursue the elusive and feel triumph when he finally snared it.

* * * *

Just before Christmas 1975, after being unemployed for six interminable months, Jim was unexpectedly offered a job at Hampshire Art College – a vacancy had occurred due to illness. He could start the following month, in the department where he had been a student. He was delighted; he looked forward to resuming the carefree popularity of his youth, with an attractive added air of authority.

On the day that Jim received this offer, Plum slit an envelope and read to her astonishment and joy that she had won the Southern Artists' Most Promising Young Painter prize – and a cheque for £1,000. It was the first time she had entered herself in a competition, thinking she had as much chance of winning it as her dad had of winning a national lottery.

* * * *

The cheque was ceremoniously presented at Portsmouth Civic Centre, and the judges' comment read aloud: 'While clearly lacking technical experience, this painter is as spirited and original as she is talented.'

'I was painting my mood,' Plum explained to her puzzled parents. The colour scheme, different from any of her previous work, was a swirling mass of dark greens and blacks that conveyed all the hidden frustration and fury that Plum, the young mother, didn't realize she felt.

That evening, after Mr Phillips had hosted a celebration meal at the local Queen's Hotel, they returned to find Toby still playing in the sitting-room – no longer papered in autumnal shades but painted a moody shade of malachite by Jim. Toby hadn't been able to sleep, had tormented the baby-sitter, and the room was a mess of toys.

Quickly, Plum put Toby to bed. In the next cot lay his brother, also awake and alert, but quietly so. Red-headed Max, a solemn child who smiled trustingly at his mother, looked exactly like her. He had inherited her big hyacinth blue eyes and rose-petal complexion; he had her little nose, the same delicate line of her jaw and cheekbone, and his hair grew in the same elfin half-curl. But Max's eyes were troubled and wary, unlike Toby's eyes which were bold, confident and naughty, as his father's used to be. Now, Jim's once-scornful eyes had the slightly uneasy pleading look of a man who has been forced to beg – and been refused. As he grew older, his good looks were spoiled by his resentful expression. Nothing was ever his fault; someone else was always to blame, especially for his inability to make his mark in London. A disgruntled man who felt that the world owed him a living and had failed to provide it, Jim felt he had never been given the chance that he deserved, the chance to star.

As Plum bent to kiss Max goodnight, her mother tiptoed into the nursery, beckoned Plum aside and whispered that she didn't like to interfere, but they'd all had a drop or two to drink, so would Plum *please* be careful tonight, she couldn't cope with a third one underfoot.

Toby gazed up at his mother. His black-lashed grey eyes dominated his sharply modelled face: Toby looked like his dad.

'You needn't worry, Mum,' Plum whispered. It was months since they'd done it. She knew what that meant.

*   *   *   *

On the afternoon of 31 December 1975, Toby sneaked into the strictly forbidden garden shed and overturned the oil stove, which whooshed into flame. As the shed burned to the ground, those of Plum's paintings that were not incinerated were destroyed by water from the firemen's hoses. Plum, who had at first thought that Toby was in the shed, collapsed from shock and relief when little Max told her that Toby was hiding under the boys' bunks.

When Jim returned and heard what had happened, he turned white and pulled Plum upstairs to their bedroom. 'You stupid bitch! Toby might have been killed! If you hadn't made that place a bloody fire trap . . . Why don't you just *give up* painting? You know you haven't a hope in hell of getting anywhere! Just because you won some provincial art prize doesn't make you Leonardo da bloody Vinci!'

'I'm tired of being your scapegoat,' Plum shouted back. 'I can't stand your jealousy any more. Why blame *me* for your lack of success? When we married, I didn't expect this!'

'What did you *expect* of marriage?' Jim yelled. 'An endless round of compliments?'

'Not loneliness! I expected support. I didn't expect to be sabotaged by the one person in this house who doesn't think that if you gave a chimpanzee a brush, he'd paint like Picasso. *Why* shouldn't I go on with my painting? Why is it so wrong to want to do something else as well as be a mother? Aren't I allowed a life of my own? Why do I feel guilty even *thinking* about it?'

As she spoke Plum realized there would be no escape for the next twenty years. She would metamorphose into one of the mothers who wait for their kids outside the junior school at the end of the road. She would become a frantic one-man band in the day-to-day struggle to keep them fed and clean in matching socks with their sweaters darned. After they blocked the sink with toilet paper, she would battle with some plumber who couldn't unblock it but flooded the kitchen. She would worry that every

68

heat rash was the plague. She would hurry the kids to the dentist, the Christmas concert, the sports field, and make endless other arrangements. Plum had discovered what nobody tells a young girl: it isn't marriage but children that snatch away your personal life.

With an effort, Plum tried to control her anger and explain these frustrated feelings to Jim.

'I can't stand *any more* of your selfishness,' Jim growled.

'I don't have the *time* to be selfish,' Plum shrieked. 'What every mother needs is *more time*! Why *should* I feel guilty for thinking about my *own* happiness?'

'Selfish bitch! *And* you're no good in bed any more!'

'How would you know?' she flashed back, but it was probably true. She did not know whether now she put off going to bed every night because sex without fulfilment depressed her, or whether she was merely so tired that she hadn't the energy to get undressed, let alone pretend to be Playmate of the Month.

'I suppose Jilly Thompson's a tiger in the sack,' Plum spat.

'Leave Jilly out of this. What did *you* bloody well expect of life?'

'*Not this!*' Plum had vaguely expected to marry a painter; they would paint together in happy proximity and would raise three or four blond children in a Laura Ashley dream-setting of rustic simplicity, where they all wore straw hats and ran slowly through poppy-filled fields of corn at sunset; the corn was always ripe and it never rained. This perfect family all sat down together to eat around a huge pine kitchen table; everyone was nice to everyone else, nobody ever threw spinach and there were never any leftovers – naturally, she was a terrific cook.

'Divorce,' Jim screamed.

'Done,' snapped Plum. She slammed out of the bedroom.

As she couldn't go to the shed, the remains of which still smoked, Plum stormed into the kitchen. Her mother followed her. Unavoidably, Mrs Phillips had heard most of the quarrel, especially the word 'divorce'. As she reached for the tin of instant coffee, she anxiously tried to talk some sense into her daughter.

Knowing exactly what she was about to hear, Plum sipped her

coffee as her mother's words rolled over her head. 'Why can't you be grateful for what you've got? . . . Think yourself lucky you never had to slave in a factory like I did . . . Think yourself lucky that things aren't worse . . . *Why can't you count your blessings!* . . . You've got more than most, you know . . . Think of the kiddies . . . You won't be able to manage on your own . . . If you'd only forget this painting nonsense . . . If we'd known it was going to be an *obsession*, we'd never have let you go to college . . . Oh, you're as stubborn as your dad!'

Wearily, Plum put down her cup. 'Mum, there's something you don't understand. I'm a painter, whether I paint or not – and that dominates my entire life. It's the reason for decisions which may seem odd, eccentric or downright self-destructive to you.' She stared at her mother's uncomprehending face. 'I don't know what virtue there is in painting. I don't feel I made a decision to paint. I couldn't *not* paint. It's an urge, like giving birth – as inexorable as second-stage contractions.'

Her mother winced.

Plum sighed, and tried again. 'Mum, I wish I could describe to you how I love painting. I can't imagine life without it. It's the first thing I think of when I wake up and the last thing before I sleep. I am always thinking about it, whatever I'm doing: scrubbing a floor, wiping a nose or warming baked beans. If I couldn't paint – if God suddenly decided that Windsor & Newton was a blight upon the earth and removed all paint from the world – I would be terminally depressed, my heart would shrivel, I'd turn my face to the wall and die. So please never again ask me to give up painting, because I can't.'

As she spoke, Plum heard Jim slam out of the front door. He went alone to the New Year's Eve college hop, and he never returned. Plum's marriage was over.

* * * *

Now, sixteen years later, in the Jockey Club, the journalist leaned over the table towards Plum and repeated his question with growing impatience. 'And are you enjoying New York?'

Plum nodded, 'It's wonderful.'

Was she ill? Did she have a hangover? Did her monosyllabic vocabulary really include only ten words? Sol Schweitzer decided to try the one subject he'd been told to avoid.

'I've seen some of your paintings,' he said, 'and they reminded me of that bit in *Antony and Cleopatra*, where Eros tells Antony that Cleopatra is dead, and he says:

> Sometimes we see a cloud that's dragonish:
> A vapour sometime like a bear or lion,
> A towered citadel, a pendant rock,
> A forked mountain, or blue promontory
> With trees upon it . . .'

Plum's face lit up. '*Yes*, that's how it sometimes feels . . .'

'How do you start a painting? What do you think about?'

'Often, I feel a lot of nervous stimulation – free-floating energy that causes exaggerated, emotional ups-and-downs,' Plum said slowly. 'This nervous energy produces a diffused, distressed feeling in me: I need to create calm from my inner chaos. I feel that *something needs to be done* – but I never know what, until I'm standing in front of a canvas and staring at it.'

'And then?'

Plum smiled. 'And then, gradually, I realize what needs to be done. This unconscious, disorganized, chaotic part of me needs to be coaxed into one direction: I need to beam the energy until it is no longer incoherent, but a sharp, unmistakable explosive statement, with rhythm and balance, in front of me, on canvas.'

'And when you finish a canvas?'

'Then, sometimes I feel as I do when I hear the clear, joyful notes of a trumpet. Elation, *at last, I've done something wonderful*! Then suddenly it passes, and I feel exhausted. The next day I've recovered from this physical exhaustion, and I notice that my mind is skittering around – making notes, getting ideas, noticing things . . . planning the next picture. And so, once again, I find myself with my head on one side, staring at a canvas.'

'More coffee, sir?' The waiter waved a shining silver pot.

Sol Schweitzer shook his head, leaned forward and switched off his tape recorder with an air of finality. He had the angle he needed. Plum Russell seemed to be two people: an exuberant and animated painter, but a subdued and passive woman. Why?

CHAPTER FIVE

Thursday, 2 January 1992

AT TEN O'CLOCK, just before the doors closed, Plum and Jenny tumbled into Tiffany's elevator and found themselves riding up with a modern heroine. They gazed surreptitiously at the patron saint of the world's divorced women. Her hair was pulled back in a blonde braid under a stetson; she wore cowboy boots and an ankle-length dark mink. Hers was the perfect nineties Cinderella story, for Ivana had turned herself into her own Princess Charming, and there she was – just like any other sensible woman in a supermarket – shopping early in the morning, before the store became too crowded.

Surreptitiously staring, Plum remembered what it felt like to be dumped.

But, when Ivana's husband dumped her for another woman, Ivana had not said one vindictive word. She kept her dignity, she hired the best PR and plastic surgeon, and – like Madonna – reinvented herself. With a wave of her magic cheque book, she metamorphosed into a Lurex update of Brigitte Bardot. This new Ivana image, publicized worldwide, could now be used to sell things to other women: sportswear, lingerie, perfume, novels, gold-plated toilet seats – anything. So Ivana resurfaced triumphantly with everything she needed: children, status, a career as a logo, multi-millions in alimony, boxes dripping with jewels, closets full of clothes, yachts, cars and plenty of places to ski or lie in the sun.

Plum suddenly wanted to ask Ivana – who supposedly had everything that any woman could want – whether *she* was now happy. She guessed that Ivana would stare at her with the brilliant blue contact lenses that now covered her brown eyes, and say, 'Off coss.' Any other answer would be bad for business. But it was too late. The elevator sighed to a stop, and Ivana stepped out.

Later, after they had ordered lunch in La Grenouille, Plum asked Jenny, 'D'you think Ivana's happy?'

'She can spit in anyone's eye,' Jenny said cheerfully. 'She can do as she wants, and not many women can say that.'

'All the women here can,' said Plum, looking around the restaurant. 'Do you think *they're* happy?'

The smart and powerful ladies of New York perched among a fragrant abundance of spring flowers. Plum gazed at their stretched skin faces, their skulls visible through thin hair, worn away by tinting, heating and perming. She observed the iron wills in action as the ladies pushed expensive food around their plates rather than into their expensively dressed, starved bodies, and drank only designer water. These gaunt little carcasses contained some of the most powerful self-made women in the world.

'This isn't how I imagined the pinnacle of success,' Plum mused aloud. 'Not-having-lunch at La Grenouille.' She turned to Jenny. 'But I'll tell you something that depresses me – *they* look like *I* feel. Starved and empty. But I've got everything I ever wanted – the family, the fame, the money. So why don't I feel happy? Why do I feel that something's wrong – although I don't know what?'

'Perhaps you have too much,' Jenny said cheerfully. 'Perhaps you're a spoiled brat. Most women don't have time to wonder whether they're happy.'

After lunch they parted, Jenny to plunder Bloomingdale's and Plum for the final fitting of her Australian tour clothes. The yellow cab stopped with a jerk at a downtown office off Seventh Avenue. The driver, who spoke no English, argued noisily in Serbo-Croat about her generous tip. Flustered, Plum shoved another couple of dollars at him, whereupon he released the door locks and she was able to scramble out.

Small, chubby and Chinese, Anna Sui was as shy as Plum but equally headstrong and opinionated about her work. Plum loved the originality of Anna's clothes, an offbeat mixture of sophisticated nostalgia. Some of the Australian outfits were historically romantic, some were sixties-hippy, the dresses were Barbie-doll-demure, the suits were a combination of grown-up businesswoman and seductress. Ann also made huge Cavalier hats, jewel-coloured velvet pants and swashbuckler boots. Plum loved the wonderfully theatrical clothes and the extraordinary hats. She pulled on a chain-mail helmet, based on an antique, Japanese martial design, and pulled aggressive faces at herself in the mirror. Pity you couldn't wear a helmet to face the critics.

*   *   *   *

Plum, who had decided on an early night, pulled back the curtains to expose the clear, star-spangled New York sky before she climbed into bed. Breeze, who would be back late, was looking at Dick Smith's recent paintings, way downtown on Warren.

*   *   *   *

At about eleven o'clock, Plum woke suddenly. Her hotel bedroom was expensively silent, but she had a strong sense of foreboding. Her body was taut and trembled. Her mouth was dry and her tongue felt too big for it; she didn't want to swallow or breathe, in case she made a noise. Her heart seemed unnaturally loud – loud enough to betray her. In the darkened, hushed room, she could hear nothing, although her ears strained to catch the slightest sound. Was that a faint rustle, from beyond the half-open door to the vestibule? As quietly as possible, she reached out and switched on the bedside light, half expecting an invisible hand to shoot out and encircle hers, in a grip as damp and chill as an iron railing on a foggy night.

The room flooded with soft light. Plum looked around at the fragrant bowls of white narcissi, the careful blend of English antique-style furniture, standing solidly on deep green carpet; at the hunting prints that hung in orderly fashion on the walls. There was nobody in the silent room.

She must have had a nightmare, although she couldn't remember it.

Yet Plum sensed a heavy, malevolent presence. She felt that somebody was silently waiting for her to go back to sleep, when her unknown aggressor would step stealthily forward, a length of wire in his hand, emerging from . . . the sitting-room? The bathroom? The closet? The small vestibule?

Trembling, naked, Plum slid from her bed; with clammy hands, she locked the intercommunicating door between the bedroom and the sitting-room. Then she crept into the hall, checked the main door to the suite; the reassuring brass safety chain was in place. There was no reason for alarm.

Suddenly, Plum remembered all the movies she'd seen in which the heroine unthinkingly locks herself in a room with the hidden murderer. Her stomach plunged sickeningly.

Plum ran back to the bedroom, flung herself across the bed, grabbed the telephone, dropped it and retrieved it, dialled reception, then changed her mind and dialled room service, which rang and rang. She would look an idiot if she asked for the house detective because she'd had a bad dream. In a strained voice she ordered hot milk and honey – fast. She would ask the waiter to check the bathroom and the closets.

By the time the waiter arrived, Plum had calmed herself. She was getting hysterical for *no reason whatsoever*. But despite her hot milk and the waiter's reassurance that the hotel security system was first-class, Plum was unable to get back to sleep. She lay awake in the dark, still with a strong sense of foreboding. So she switched the light on, picked up *Lark Rise To Candleford*, with which she always travelled, and tried to read. The serene tranquillity of village life evaded her; her brain was unable to absorb the contents of the printed words. Eventually, she drifted to sleep . . . The book slowly collapsed on her breast . . .

Plum woke with a start. Again she trembled as she heard a muffled banging on the door. Was she imagining it? Her mouth went dry, and she breathed with difficulty. Her ribs felt constricted by iron bands.

Again, she heard the banging, then, 'Plum, are you OK?'

She had locked out Breeze!

Upon hearing his voice Plum felt safe again. She rushed from the bed to unbolt the door.

Friday, 3 January 1992

The following day was one of those bright, cerulean-sky, winter days when the city really looked as romantic and charming as it did on the cover of the *New Yorker*, Plum thought as she journeyed downtown to lunch with Leo.

As she paid the cab, she momentarily felt the biting chill of West Broadway, then she entered the friendly warmth of good food and cheerful hum of voices. The Odeon was a classic thirties French brasserie: you could eat an exquisite six-course meal with vintage Krug and *foie gras* flown in that morning from Strasbourg, or sit for hours over a cup of coffee to read the foreign newspapers and magazines provided by the management. The place had once been smart, but now the feverish set had moved on and the regular addicts had returned: painters, writers and the Wall Street crowd for lunches.

Leo was waiting at the thirties-style bar. He wore a crumpled ivory silk shirt from Turnbull & Asser, and a russet suede bomber jacket from Joseph that needed a good brush, as did his neglected snuff suede après-polo boots. Leo's expensive clothes always looked as if they came from a thrift shop.

He eyed Plum's tweed fishing hat, her mist-green tweed mini-skirt and demurely long tweed jacket. 'Nice blouse.' He touched a cream silk cuff that reached her knuckles. He said, 'I like the lavender lace tights and the purple boots. You look like a reincarnation of Twiggy, darling!'

'I'll never be that thin, but a girl can dream . . .'

Leo lifted his triangular cocktail in greeting. 'Here's to our dreams. I only ever drink these enormous Martinis in the Big Apple, I consider it the *vin du pays*.'

'I'll have lemon juice. What's your dream, Leo?'

'What every other architect's dream is.' Leo had trained and worked as an architect until the slump of '87. 'To build my own house in some idyllic setting, poised above a waterfall and surrounded by forest. Frank Lloyd Wright's Fallingwater is what I have in mind . . .' Suddenly he grabbed Plum's hand and stared at the diamond. '*Where* did you get *that*?'

'Woolworths.'

'You must tell me which branch.' Leo ordered fresh lemon juice for Plum and then said, 'I was sorry not to meet Cleo Brigstall the other night: I hear she has a terrific apartment somewhere around here – thought I might cover it for the magazine.'

'I don't think she'd want publicity,' Plum said. 'She's the highest-ranking woman they've ever had in Morgan Grenfell. Earns well over a million dollars a year, but keeps a low profile.'

'Nice to be able to choose!' After they had been seated by the window, Leo looked carefully at the menu. '*Wild* salmon. Does that mean it was ferocious, or that it doesn't come from a fish farm? How about oysters beforehand?'

Leo liked to live well, although he wrongly believed he had simple tastes, which was probably why he was always short of cash. He insisted that he didn't earn much but Plum had noticed that Leo travelled in style, had loads of expensive fun and knew plenty of smart girls. She rarely saw him with the same girl twice. Breeze considered Leo a hanger-on who would never snap a tendon leaping to snatch a bill. But Leo was sharply knowledgeable about the international art and design scene, and an entertaining and cheerful companion.

Leo had already heard that Plum thought Suzannah's Dutch flowerpiece was a fake and intended to prove it: the size of her bet with Victor had already been grossly inflated by telephonic gossip.

As they ate salmon poached in champagne, Plum said, 'I seem to remember you did a story about art fraud, a couple of years ago.'

Leo nodded. 'Had a girl-friend who worked for a big detective agency.'

'Your piece linked art fraud to organized crime.'

'That's right. Art fraud's now *very* big business. In terms of cash involved, it's the third biggest world crime problem. The drugs and arms boys are using the art business to launder money. Even the Ginza district in Tokyo – the top prestige art district – has been heavily infiltrated by Yakuzi – the Japanese mafia. It's so *easy*!'

He sipped his wine. 'If I were tracking a painting, Japan is the last place I'd want to search for it, because they only have a two-year Statute of Limitations. That means I'd have to find it, prove it was faked, and then pursue the lawsuit, all within two years – which is unlikely. *Any* criminal can simply stick a stolen art work in a Japanese bank vault for two years, then sell it there with impunity. And elsewhere, it's *still* easy, too. A crook doesn't pay duty on art when he crosses a border. If the art object is more than fifty years old, he merely scribbles a list of what he's carrying, states the value, gives the list to the border police and carries the loot across.'

'But what's that got to do with *fake* art?'

'When crooks discovered the huge sums of money involved in art sales, it seemed only logical and sensible to them to steal the art or paint their own.'

'Nothing new about fakes,' Plum pointed out. 'Dürer was actually faked during his lifetime, like David Hockney.'

Leo laughed. 'Between 1909 and 1951 over nine thousand Rembrandts were imported to the United States, according to Customs archives.' He shrugged, adding, 'Of course it's no crime to copy or imitate a painting – that happens in museums and art schools all the time.'

Plum grinned. 'Breeze says the only art galleries that aren't suffering in this recession are those which openly sell copies of paintings.'

'There are other legitimate industries that also fog the area of deceit.' Leo explained that some insurance companies make the owners of a painting secretly agree to exhibit the copy – and keep the original in a bank vault. And often the loss adjusters of an insurance company negotiate with thieves to ransom a stolen art work – often behind the back of the police. Understandably the insurance company prefers to pay 10 per cent of the value to the thieves, rather than 100 per cent to the owners.

Often European museums did not carry insurance because they could not afford to do so. They would then cover up a robbery, rather than reveal their own incompetence. They negotiated with the thieves if they could, otherwise the stolen goods just went on the underground market. And one ecclesiastical insurance company reckoned that every four hours an antique was stolen from some British church.

'What chutzpah!' Plum exclaimed.

Leo looked serious. 'Very little art crime is trackable, let alone recoverable. An added problem in proving fraud is that a crime has *only* been committed when someone implies that the work of art is an original in order to sell it.'

'So that's when you call in the cops, Leo?'

'You don't always want to call in the cops. Lots of cases don't get to the police because the greedy buyers didn't care that they were buying stolen goods. For instance, Fabergé is one of the most heavily forged items. Some fence tells a collector, "Hey, I've got a jewelled egg . . . but it's hot . . . stolen." This is an easy way to sell a fake to an enthusiastic and unscrupulous collector who thinks he's buying it cheaply.'

'Greed always makes a person vulnerable.'

Leo nodded. 'Just before the First World War, the *Mona Lisa* was stolen from the Louvre – typical lax museum security – and sold to an Italian, who hid it. But the thieves had a secondary motive: they had accumulated many copies of the *Mona Lisa* – at least fifteen copies were sold for huge sums. Two years later, the police found the original and returned it to the Louvre – but nobody who'd secretly bought the fakes dared complain to the police that they'd been screwed.'

He looked amused. '*You* can't call in the cops, Plum. The cops aren't going to listen to *you*.'

'Why not?'

He ticked the reasons off on his fingers. 'Suzannah's picture isn't your property. The owner insists no crime has been committed. And you haven't got one scrap of hard evidence.'

'Yet,' Plum said stubbornly.

'You probably need an international detective agency – Jules Kroll specializes in art crime, but they're expensive.'

'How expensive?'

'As much as a good lawyer – but what private person can afford *that*? . . . Maybe fifteen hundred dollars a day for each operator in the field . . .' Leo leaned across the table and patted Plum's hand.

'*You* can't pay that sort of money, Plum – and why should you? Suzannah's picture is none of your business. Your search could be dangerous ... No, Plum, I'm serious ... So why don't you visit Victor's office after lunch – and call this bet off.'

'Like a good girl, huh? No, I'm going to pursue this and I'm doing it on principle.'

'I've noticed that people only say *that* when they're about to do something bloody stupid – that they can't justify in any other way.' Leo sighed. 'But if you're determined ... you'd better check this picture hasn't been stolen, because if it has – and that's possible – then it's a police matter and they'll immediately take the problem off your hands. So check with Trace's art crime register.'

'What's that?'

'An international monthly magazine that lists art theft.'

'Does anyone keep a list of *fakes*?'

'Yes. IFAR – the International Foundation for Art Research. Their head office is uptown but they work mainly for museums, galleries and the insurance industry. Maybe they'd advise you of the current US and world experts on Dutch flowerpieces, but they're unlikely to help more than that.'

'Why not?'

'Because you aren't an academic and you're not from a big organization that can afford their consultancy fee.'

With a touch of belligerence, Plum said, 'You mean I *would* be taken seriously if I were prepared to pay for it? Then why wouldn't the police be interested?'

'You aren't some eccentric little old lady and we aren't eating lunch in an Agatha Christie novel. In real life the NYPD are busy fishing real bodies out of the Hudson, chasing real drug-dealers and trying to avoid real teenage-gang drive-by shootings. The police have no time to deal with art fraud: they find the art world frustrating, because they don't understand what the fuck it's about – apart from Joe Keenan and Vincent Sabo of the NYPD – but I doubt they'll have spare time to help *you*, Plum.'

He broke off as the waiter served arugula salad, then leaned forward. 'Almost all cops are useless for art crime. It's a question of money. How much can a government afford to pay to protect the art that brings in the tourists who account for one of the top three money-making industries in Europe? Those tourists don't go to Italy to inspect the Fiat factories, but no government has spare funds to train cops or customs officers to recognize an antique piece of art. And if art crooks can fool top art historians, who've been training for thirty years, as well as dealers who've been backing their eye since they started in the business, then what chance do the cops have?'

'Can't they follow the trail back to the forger?'

'Maybe – but the cops haven't the expertise in art that they have in normal crimes committed by normal criminals. Cops understand criminal motivation and they can plant informers in the criminal underworld – but they don't understand the art world, and trying to do so is like trying to hold water in their bare hands. They need to see, touch and understand something – such as a corpse – in order to come to grips with it.' Leo paused as the waiter offered a silver bowl of grated Parmesan cheese.

'Cops can't even spot an art crime when they're *looking* at one,' he continued earnestly, 'because they can't tell a genuine piece of art from a fake, and it's unreasonable to expect them to. And because they can't spot the difference, they can't understand how anyone else can be so positive that this particular brushstroke *wasn't* made by Picasso or whoever.'

'Leo, are you saying that the average cop can't help me because he can't tell a Guardi from a Canaletto?'

'That's about it – especially in the USA, because it's a huge country with comparatively few cops, almost none of whom are discerning art connoisseurs.'

'But if art fraud is the third biggest world crime problem in cash terms, what about the FBI and Interpol?'

'There's one specialist in the FBI and a few in Interpol. There are only three criminal art specialists in London, only two in New York and one in LA. The only other art cops who are any use are in the specially trained Italian art squad, but they're all needed in Italy.'

'Specially trained?' Plum wanted to know more.

'One in four men is colour blind to some degree, so trainees start with an eye test. They learn to paint, check materials for age, forgery techniques and the idiosyncrasies of famous painters, then finish with a basic chemistry course, so they can analyse pigments.'

'So they're virtually taught how to fake?'

'Yes. The Italians reckon you need to be a painter and a forger to recognize a fake.'

'If the cops are no use, and it takes a painter to spot a forgery – why, then I'm qualified,' Plum said firmly. 'So will you help me?'

Leo looked uncomfortable. 'I'd rather not.'

'Has Breeze been talking to you? Did he ask you to persuade me to drop this thing? Did he ask you to convince me it was stupid?'

'It's not *stupid* – it's bloody reckless! And that's *my* opinion.' Leo had a shrewd respect for the sharp, tough Breeze, who was one of his favourite contacts. Leo also had a certain sympathy for him; generous Breeze was a flash-cash man from the affluent eighties, uneasily adjusting to the lean, mean nineties. Why should Leo make that task more difficult? 'I like Breeze,' Leo added. 'I enjoy his company, and I admit I don't want to antagonize him.'

'Me, too. We haven't declared war,' Plum said sharply.

Leo leaned across the table and took her hands. 'Plum, the main reason I don't want to help you is because a search for this forger could be bloody dangerous. No one can mess around with organized crime. Don't let your stubbornness and a row with your husband put your life in danger.'

Plum remembered her panic on the previous night. But that had been imaginary fear, like a child's in the night. And probably Leo, with his talk of sinister gangsters, was also exaggerating the dangers. Leo had a tendency to dramatize situations: he was a writer.

Plum pulled her shoulders back. She wasn't going to let Leo frighten her into doing what he wanted, rather than what she wanted. But as she reached for the mist-green jacket on the back of her chair and pulled it around her shoulders, despite the warmth of the restaurant, she felt a chill.

CHAPTER SIX

As PLUM left the glowing warmth of the Odeon restaurant, she saw that the sky was clear and promising, the glorious blue of Italian church ceilings. She decided to walk to Wall Street, via the pretty eighteenth-century buildings of South Street Seaport, where the little houses always reminded her of Portsmouth and she could buy a pair of gloves to replace the pair she had left in that last cab.

She walked briskly along West Broadway. It reminded her of Edward Hopper's sooty, red-brick paintings, of the loneliness, anxiety and grimy menace of a big city that she had felt when she first lived in London.

She was surprised by the invisible violence of the wind as it tore up the street from the south. The day had begun warm and the snow had begun to melt, but now the sodden slush had started to freeze in hard, grey-brown lumps and ridges. The sidewalks were slippery and dangerous.

The few pedestrians wore heavy dark clothes and huddled forward as they struggled against the wind. Plum turned up the collar of her spinach-coloured tweed overcoat and stuck her bare hands deep in the pockets, remembering the days when she had walked because she couldn't afford bus fares.

Plum had refused Leo's offer to accompany her because she wanted – at last – to think quietly about a problem she had been avoiding for years. This was a feeling of inner loneliness that Plum found hard to explain – because she had a husband, children and plenty of friends. So she had always firmly dismissed this ridiculous feeling, but now, increasingly, she experienced that strange, sad wistfulness, as if in a dream that she couldn't quite remember; it was as if she had lost a part of herself, and this hidden, neglected part was calling to her, becoming increasingly insistent that she search for it, warning Plum that until she did so, she would feel stunted and unfulfilled, an incomplete person.

Now, as she stomped against the wind towards Wall Street, squelching in her unsuitably fragile suede boots, Plum felt that she was heading for trouble. The fact that she couldn't put her finger on her problem made it all the more ominous.

At the intersection of West Broadway and Chambers, Plum turned left. Almost immediately the wind eased, although it was still gusty. She hurried past the little speciality shops that sold nuts, coffee-beans, fudge and fingernails. Above them curved neon lines of eerie, glowing colour: 'Free delivery – Michelob Lite Beer' in searing orange, 'Tuxedos for hire' in X-ray pale blue, 'Instant psychic reading' offered in pale green.

Plum turned into the Korean deli on Chambers and hurried to the empty rear of the shop. Hidden behind a freezer of beer cans, she quickly tugged off her diamond ring and shoved it deep into her coat pocket. No longer was she mugger material. Should she put the ring in her purse? No, that was what the muggers always snatched, only idiots carried their valuables in their purse. She felt uneasy, knowing that the ring was lying in her coat pocket, not safely attached to anything, or stuck on a finger. Suddenly Plum recognized her strange and threatening feeling: it was insecurity. But why should she feel insecure?

At the intersection Plum turned right. On Broadway she immediately felt the wind blast into her face; keen as a knife blade, it snatched her breath. She gasped for air, opened her mouth – and the wind leaped down her throat. She could feel it chilling her lungs, attacking her body from inside. Plum clamped her mouth shut and clutched her chest; she had never felt so cold.

The sky was still a serene pale blue, broached by the Gothic spire of the Woolworth building. The sparse traffic limped along, moving slowly. On the far sidewalk, a few dazed-looking bag-ladies huddled close to the ventilators of the city's subterranean steam-heat system. In the little park that surrounded City Hall, shivering bums crowded miserably on benches. A few were already too drunk to shiver; their empty bottles lay in the slush.

Plum felt guilty for feeling unfulfilled. Poor little rich girl, she jeered at herself. But it was no use telling herself that she was lucky, that she had everything that any woman could want – far more than most. And Plum had been able to develop as a painter, unlike most people who, through no fault of their own, lived their life far below the level of their talent. *Some* women never realized what their talents were. But since when did a painter need a sports car and a jacuzzi? Her ambitious social life was merely another expensive way of keeping up with the Joneses – exactly what she hadn't liked about her mother's life: that inter-woman, domestic competitiveness that stemmed from insecurity; that destructive, chicken-pecking, dainty aggression, that ruthless defence.

At the far end of the narrow streets of South Street Seaport Plum now saw masts of nineteenth-century sailing barques, moored to the dock. The ancient, small-bricked buildings that clustered around the Fulton Street fish market, once warehouses and lodging-houses, were now chic boutiques and speciality food shops. At the Laura Ashley shop Plum bought some misty purple gloves and a matching woollen muffler, then went into a fitting-room where she slipped her diamond ring back on her finger. She'd be glad when she'd left this city and wouldn't feel obliged to hide it.

At Zabar's, tempted by the yeasty odour of newly baked bread, Plum bought a bag of cookies for the boys, then remembered that chubby Max was on a diet and health-freak Toby wouldn't touch anything that contained sugar. It often happened that she still thought of them as children, which exasperated them, but she couldn't help it. She had always thought of them as children and had not been able to stop overnight just because their voices had broken.

Plum halted. Suddenly she realized what her problem was. She felt incomplete, undeveloped as a person; that strong, firm sense of identity in Plum the painter and Plum the mother was missing in Plum the woman.

When had she last felt whole? Perhaps when she first started to carve out a life of her own, when she first went to London, when things were tough and life was a struggle – but she had her sons, her paintings and her friends. Somehow there was more time then for laughter and the other simple things that added meaning to a woman's experience. Plum wondered whether part of the price-tag of success was a loss of joy in these simple things of life, in apples, hugs and sunsets.

CHAPTER SEVEN

P LUM stepped out of Victor's private office elevator and found herself staring at one of her own paintings. Sizzling with chrome yellow, saffron and citron, it lifted her spirits. She remembered how happy she'd felt while working on that painting. It had been just before Toby cheerfully left home to live with four other students in a squat and she felt as if one of her arms had been wrenched off. After that, for many months, there had been only dark and sombre shades on her palette, and on the paint-encrusted table upon which she mixed her colours.

Jenny had tried to console her. 'Most women devote their life to their children, then when they leave home – Mum's left with nothing. *You've* got your painting, Plum.' And indeed that had been what consoled Plum.

In her paintings, Plum revealed herself, emotionally naked and defenceless. If a painting had to be explained in words, then it had not achieved what she had hoped; it had not made the viewer understand and share those emotions. Just as a composer uses sound, so Plum used paint to transmit her thoughts and feelings. Now in Victor's office, she wondered how to express her newly surfacing feelings of being emotionally numb, frozen and stunted.

She stared at the huge canvas and – as usual – immediately wanted to alter it. The hanging light was never the same as the clear, northern aspect of her London studio. In this soft January light, reflected off the water of New York harbour, some of the cadmium looked too harsh for the ochres, while the burnt sienna gashes should have been heavier and thicker: tonally, they weren't earning their keep.

Plum was shown into Victor's office, which did not look like that of a Hollywood tycoon, as Plum expected, but like a modern museum. One wall was a sheet of glass overlooking the harbour; another contained glass shelves upon which were a collection of New Guinea tribal masks. On the third wall hung another of Plum's paintings – one of her sombre black-and-purples. The office contained little furniture: three grey flannel couches grouped around a low, six-foot slab of slate, upon which was a slim orange file and a glass bowl containing Victor's business cards, which listed sixteen personal telephone numbers, including car phone and car fax.

Plum looked beyond the wall of glass at a vast, grey area of the East River, silent, ominous, implacably cold. The far shore was a dark, smudged charcoal line, the buildings on it a soft mauve-grey: a Monet scene.

The door opened. The whole room seemed filled with Victor's expansive presence as they exchanged greetings. 'Sixties Revivalist suit, huh? What happened to your boots? Better take 'em off, they're soaking . . . I'll send you back in the Rolls . . . Miss Ohrbach, I'll need the car in half an hour!' He lifted Plum's hand. 'You like it, huh?'

Plum waved her fingers, watching the diamond catch the light and throw it out again in dazzling streaks of blue, green, gold. 'It's fabulous, Victor! I feel like an old-fashioned movie queen!'

Victor shrugged and threw his hands apart. 'I told Breeze, now is a good time to buy.' He wandered to the window and stared across the water to the distant lavender smudge of coastline. 'You're going ahead with this . . . investigation?'

Plum nodded.

'I told Suzannah you wouldn't chicken out. Matter of fact, I had five thousand, said you wouldn't.' He smiled, 'She's not too thrilled by your suggestion, but I want the facts established. Naturally, I'll help you all I can, but I shouldn't bother Suzannah at the apartment. She's a very busy lady, as you know.'

'But, Victor, I really need to examine that picture *very carefully* – and in daylight!'

'I'm sorry, Plum. It's just not possible.'

Hearing the note of finality in Victor's voice, Plum realized that she was being told to keep away from the Marshes' apartment. She thought, 'He's had a colossal row with Suzannah. So now, blast it, I can't examine that Dutch painting in daylight – I can't check the weave of the back!' Any art dealer's wife knew that the important sequence of checking a suspect painting was to look at it and get the gut feeling that was the sum of your experience; then you did the pin test – and then you checked the back.

An old painting might be on wood, metal or canvas. If canvas, you checked the weave; Neapolitan canvases were coarse like sacking, old Venetian canvases had a herringbone pattern. The further north the source of a European canvas, the finer the weave became, because the painter had had access to the developing textile industry.

Often a collector's mark was stamped on the back of a frame – a monogram or owner's initial, plus a number that referred to his inventory. An old canvas might also have traces of an exhibition label glued to the back, or an auction-house stock number that would help track its history: Sotheby's uses a chalk mark or a sticky label, Phillips uses blue chalk, but Christie's is the only auction-house to record a permanent mark – two letters and three numbers, referring to the sale date and lot number recorded in Christie's library.

Plum felt frustrated. She had been hoping that the condition of the back would be a give-away, because it wasn't that good a fake.

Victor lifted the slim orange file from the slate table. 'Miss Ohrbach's made a copy of the provenance and included a copy transparency. I've added a photostat of my cheque in payment, and also a letter authorizing you to make any inquiries about the picture on my behalf. Is there anything else you need?'

Plum said, 'I'd like to break my journey in Los Angeles and see the decorator who found this Balthazar van der Ast for you.' As Victor leaned forward and buzzed for his secretary, Plum added, 'And you mentioned an uptown dealer who also has a similar picture. Which dealer?'

'Artur Schneider on Fifty-seventh. Sure, I'll arrange for you to meet with Cynthia Bly in LA. She's in shock. Told me Maltby's of Bond Street are a *very* reputable firm. Says, sure, our painting had some restoration work, but she said that's kosher, there's very little genuine old stuff that hasn't needed some attention.'

Plum nodded. 'There's a grey area in restoration, where imitation and repair . . . shade into deception. Some restoration work *can* mean ninety per cent new, but that's not the case with your picture.'

'Cynthia said you might mean the picture wasn't *totally* by van der Ast: maybe an assistant helped out.' She had explained to Victor that successful artists, from the Renaissance onwards, had often operated large studios to meet demand, and their pupils had certainly helped produce paintings. They started on the sky, then as they became proficient they were promoted to backgrounds, clothes, dogs, horses, then finally human flesh.

'That wasn't what I meant, Victor.'

'Cynthia also wondered if you meant the picture had been copied in van der Ast's studio, immediately after he had painted it. She says that was done a lot.' She had said that historically, after a picture was finished, copies were often made in the studio. For instance, up to forty copies were produced by Leonardo da Vinci's assistants, and such studio copies were always considered up to the Master's standard.

Plum shook her head.

'So you reckon our picture is a direct copy of another painting by van der Ast – something in some museum?'

'I suspect it's a composite of bits from other paintings by van der Ast, which means that it was newly painted by an experienced forger.'

'OK. Prove it.'

*   *   *   *

Plum leaned back against the magnolia leather upholstery of the maroon Rolls and opened Victor's orange file to look at the provenance. Ideally, this is a collection of documents that enables the purchaser of a painting to trace the work back clearly through various sales transactions to that of the original artist. It also chronicles any appearances in exhibitions or scholarly books. But a complete provenance is rare: owners forget to record such matters.

Without a clear provenance, there was always argument about authenticity. So Breeze, who kept a careful record of everything he sold, made Plum press a paint thumbprint on the back of each canvas as well as signing it on the front: her thumbprint was also attached to the bill of sale.

Victor's orange file contained two envelopes. In the first was a ten by eight-inch copy transparency of the charming flowerpiece and a full description of the painting, both signed by Mr Maltby. The second envelope contained a sparsely documented history of the painting, together with copies of various old bills of sale, and an expertise in Dutch, apparently written in 1922. The painting had never been exhibited. As the Rolls pulled on to East 57th, Plum closed the file. Provenances, as well as paintings, could be forged.

From the sidewalk, Plum peered through the discreetly protected window of Artur Schneider's art gallery. Before a bottle-green velvet curtain, spotlit on a small easel, was a Dutch still-life that measured about eighteen inches square. Upon a walnut table stood a blue-patterned, broad-rimmed Ming bowl, filled with strawberries and cherries; more cherries were strewn in the foreground, together with some strawberry leaves and carnation petals. A few gleaming droplets of water had fallen from the flowers on to the table; a bluebottle perched on one of the strawberries. According to the small card propped beside the easel, it had been painted on copper between 1615 and 1630 by Jacob van Hulsdonck.

When Plum rang the security bell, the door was opened by a large, middle-aged man with gold-rimmed, granny spectacles behind which were the pale eyes of a cod. There was nobody else in the shop, which reminded Plum of Suzannah's sitting-room: a few antiques were placed against dark green walls upon which hung several small oil paintings, mostly in ornate gilt frames, carefully spotlit.

The pictures – all slickly cleaned and shining – included three seventeenth-century paintings. One showed a fishing boat on a storm-tossed, snot-coloured sea; one was a tavern scene in which beery, stout peasants played cards, smoked long clay pipes or danced to the music of a pot-bellied fiddler; the third, a jolly winter landscape, showed people having fun on a frozen river. Among the skaters were a horse-drawn sleigh and a group of men with sticks playing a game on ice.

'School of Hendrick Avercamp. They're playing colf – the origin of golf and ice hockey, invented in the Low Countries around 1300,' Mr Schneider said, in a limp voice that was not quite a lisp.

Mr Schneider, who had noticed Plum step from the maroon Rolls, did not mind removing the picture from the window for her to examine after she explained that she was helping someone choose a special gift for his wife's birthday.

'A seventeenth-century Dutch still-life is *very* special,' he commented roguishly. 'As you are no doubt aware, it was the golden age of Dutch and Flemish painting. Look at that detail and clarity; note the serenity.'

'I feel that I've seen a similar painting of that blue and white bowl,' Plum mused. 'There's no doubt it was painted by van Hulsdonck?'

'No doubt,' Mr Schneider said, a faint chill in his voice. 'But as I'm sure you know' (meaning that he thought that she didn't), 'every painter of this period carefully kept all his sketch studies and these were used over and over again, by the artist, his pupils and sometimes even his colleagues, because they borrowed from each other – sketches were handed down for generations. As you probably know, there's a famous skating couple that first appears in a frozen river scene by Hendrick Avercamp, then reappears in several of his other paintings, and also in paintings by Barent Avercamp and Arent Arentsz.'

'And the price?'

'The asking price is one hundred eighty-five,' Mr Schneider said firmly. He noticed that Plum did not wince.

'Open to negotiation?'

Mr Schneider paused carefully, then said, 'To a certain extent. Might I know the name of the lucky birthday lady?'

'Mrs Victor Marsh.'

Mr Schneider blinked. He was clearly not a *Wall Street Journal* reader.

Plum added, 'Suzannah Marsh.'

Recognition lit up Mr Schneider's face. 'Sunnybank Farm? The mail order catalogue?' Almost all the flower-sprigged rustic luxury at Sunnybank Farm – with the exception of the white Persian cats and Suzannah's two apprehensively silent little daughters – could be purchased by mail order catalogue from 'Suzannah of Sunnybank Farm'.

'Of course, this painting would be *perfect* for that sort of ambiance,' he enthused. 'When would Mrs Marsh care to see the picture?'

'It's to be a surprise. Mr Marsh saw the painting in your window, and asked me to check the provenance.' Plum wasn't going to ask where Schneider had obtained the painting, for she knew he wouldn't tell her, but she might be able to find out from the provenance.

Mr Schneider's attitude changed very slightly, as he realized that Plum was neither mistress nor decorator (no business card, no discount negotiated), but probably the secretary of the owner of the Rolls.

As Plum carefully scrutinized the painting, then turned it over, Mr Schneider realized that she was not merely window-shopping. Half an hour later Plum knew that the pretty little Jacob van Hulsdonck was a fake, and Mr Schneider knew that she probably knew: however, they would both pretend not to know.

'I assume that there would be . . .' Plum said politely, 'that I would receive . . .'

'Of course. Ten per cent commission.' Whoever she was.

'I usually get a dealer's fifteen per cent . . . on something like this.' Plum knew that unless she haggled for a commission, he wouldn't think her a serious prospect and she'd never get a copy of the provenance. 'Thank you. Then might I have a copy of this provenance? . . . Mrs Russell . . . At the Ritz Carlton . . . Yes, of course, I'll return it tomorrow. Thank you *so* much . . .'

While Mr Schneider was bending over a filing cabinet with his back turned, Plum quietly took the hotel sewing kit from her purse and pulled out a pin. It sank into the unresisting paint.

Ten minutes later, Plum knew that Mr Schneider had purchased the painting from Lévi-Fontaine, a well-known second-division Paris auction-house. They would never sell a first-rate Matisse, but Lévi-Fontaine would be certain to get a good price for something like a half-finished Fantin-Latour sketch.

As she left, Mr Schneider said smoothly, 'Perhaps you should know that someone else is interested in that painting. One of your compatriots.'

'Then I'd better get Mr Marsh in here as quickly as possible. Is this compatriot a dealer?'

'I got the impression it was a private inquiry. The customer came in this morning and talked to my assistant, who's at the dentist this afternoon. Vernon just said a Britisher had looked at the painting for about half an hour and promised to return later. I don't think it was a trade inquiry or Vernon would have told me.'

CHAPTER EIGHT

STUCK in the Rolls in cross-town traffic, Plum opened the second provenance, which wasn't as detailed as the one Victor had given her. She would get it copied by the hotel, and return it to Schneider in the morning. Plum idly wondered if his British customer was really interested, or whether Schneider was merely trying to push the sale: perhaps both. It didn't matter: the other customer was welcome to the fake van Hulsdonck.

Plum settled back in her seat, behind the big shoulders and maroon uniform of Victor's driver; she enjoyed being so opulently protected from the cold weather.

She sneaked another look at her diamond ring, fascinated by the blue-white, shimmering stone. Thoughts of insecurity were far from her mind. Here was tangible proof that *she had made it*, despite Jim's sneers.

Monday, 1 March 1976

Exactly two months after Jim's departure on New Year's Eve, as her parents sat drinking tea before the sitting-room fire, Plum hesitantly told them what she intended to do.

The mutterings of never-had-a-divorce-in-our-family were as nothing to their horrified objections when, nervous but determined, Plum announced that she intended to move to London.

If she got a job, who would look after the kiddies, her mother fretted? If she didn't get a job, how would she feed them? That prize money wouldn't last forever. Plum must not be so selfish.

Plum pointed out that Jim had a job and would legally have to provide for the children from his salary. (She had not yet discovered that child support won't support a child.) She argued that she was more likely to get a well-paid job in London than in Portsmouth.

Plum's mother immediately guessed that, should she find nothing else (as was likely for someone with no training or job experience), Plum was going to try for a job as an artist's model. Hysteria. *Why, why* did she have to do this to her parents?

'I want *my* chance to develop my talent. Jim had his chance. Why shouldn't I?'

'That's as may be – but you needn't drag the kiddies off to London.'

Eventually Mrs Phillips demanded, 'What can you get in London that you can't get in Portsmouth?'

'I've told you – London's one of the world's leading art centres. I'll never get anywhere here, because I'll never sell anything here. You name me one – *just one* – international art dealer who operates out of Portsmouth!'

'I don't know what's got into you!' her mother stormed, accustomed to Plum's diffident timidity, not this fierce determination. 'You're a different person! This painting's become an obsession! It isn't healthy!'

'Yes, Mum, when I'm painting, I *am* a different person: I know what I'm doing and I know why I'm doing it. And now *I want to be that person all the time.*'

'That's enough nonsense from you, my girl!' her father said, lifting his newspaper again. 'We don't want to hear *one more word* about going to London! You've upset your mother enough. Isn't it time the kiddies had their supper?'

Two months later, on a sunny May morning, Plum's mother went to Handley's early summer sale. Plum ran to the pub at the end of the road and called a taxi. She and her two sons caught the 11.20 to Waterloo.

Jenny had found two attic rooms for them (one with an ancient Baby Belling stove and a sink) in raffish Kentish Town, north London. The soot-grimed terrace of down-at-heel houses had originally been built for big, prosperous Victorian families, who had fled when the new London railroads were routed through their gardens. Now each house held many families; like the rest, Plum's entrance hall was a depressing clutter of battered prams and bicycles that nobody would bother to steal.

Because of the strong paint odour and the mess involved, Plum painted in the smaller room and they all three slept and lived in the other. Toby, not yet four years old, and Max, not yet two, were too young to go to state school and of course a fee-paying nursery school was out of the question, so they were constantly under their mother's feet, except during their afternoon nap. Plum now found herself in a more exhausting and harassing position than before – but with no help. She quickly found out that you can't be a traditional mother if a traditional father isn't present, and turned into a combination of girl guide and gang-leader. However, she felt unquenchably optimistic. Something would turn up, she told herself, and at least she had managed to get to London, hadn't she?

But, like Lulu (currently proving with Mo that two could live as cheaply as one), Plum found that she couldn't get a grant or a place in a painting school. She grabbed a poorly paid job as an evening waitress. During the day – a lucky break – she looked after the baby of the woman who lived on the ground floor and worked in a bakery, who returned the favour by looking after Toby and Max in the evening. Shortly afterwards, Plum agreed to care for two other babies during the day. Ironically, she was now more tired and more chained to children than before, and she had even less time to paint.

Unsurprisingly, Plum's first London paintings were almost monochromatic in their gloom. She felt alienated from the city, which was full of lonely crowds and artificial distractions, a breeding ground for anxiety and anomie. From Camden library she borrowed a book on Edward Hopper, and felt a comforting affinity with the isolated people in his paintings.

One October night, Plum arrived home dead tired to find Lulu crouched on the doorstep, waiting for her. She had broken up with Mo.

'He's found another emotional cripple who appealed to his Salvation Army instincts,' Lulu said bitterly. 'I was pushed out this morning, and she's already moved in. I've got nowhere to sleep and nowhere to go, no money and no job. I've already been round to Jenny but she tried to persuade me to go back home. She wouldn't let me stay with her, although her place is so cheap that even *I* could afford half the rent!' Jenny, now starting her second year at the Slade, still lived in a lodging-house in Westbourne Grove, overstuffed with impoverished West Indians. She lived in the basement that overlooked the backyard, a mess of rusty iron and disintegrating old mattresses.

'I expect Jenny was afraid that if you moved in, you'd never move out. You can stay here.' Plum well understood how desperate Lulu was to keep in the art world – which meant London.

'Thanks,' Lulu said morosely. 'More likely Jenny's just starting an affair. She's getting fearfully secretive.'

Lulu stayed with Plum for a month, slept in the studio and woke up with a headache every morning. She vowed never to become a mother: bedlam.

Jenny found Lulu a poorly paid, three-day-a-week job in the Round House, at the office-skivvy end of experimental theatre. Surprisingly, Jenny persuaded Jim to get some official Hampshire Art College letterhead and write a letter of recommendation for Lulu.

'How the hell did you manage that?' Plum marvelled. 'He'd never have done it if I'd asked.'

'Easy. He's devoted to the kids, right? So I simply asked him if he wanted a junkie living with them.'

'But Lulu's kicked it.'

'How can Jim be sure?'

'Listen, I don't want any custody problems, Jenny . . .'

*　*　*　*

Once installed in London, Plum was sadly disappointed by the art scene. She had naïvely thought that – somehow – her life was going to fall into place at last. At last she would paint like crazy all day and then argue until five in the morning, over coffee and bottles of Abbot ale, with bearded people wearing black polo-neck sweaters, about the fundamentals of art and how they would change society with their brushes.

Not a bit of it. The art scene turned out to be extremely cynical and very competitive. The students of the Royal College and the Royal Academy Schools had the lion's share of the newcomers' market: their work was viewed by prospective buyers. The remainder of the British postgraduate students, with no Establishment strings to pull, were left wondering how they were ever going to get even a nibble at success.

Together, in Plum's attic rooms, the three provincial girls swapped stories and pooled their gloomy experiences. By now they had all encountered that depressing Catch 22 of the art world, the gallery game, when an artist's work is viewed only on recommendation, not on portfolio merit. Gallery owners and art-world potentates will *not* look at a young artist's work unless it has been specifically recommended by some fellow mover-or-shaker of the art world. This was as frustrating as being unable to get your first job without previous experience.

So a provincial student like Plum, who hadn't even finished her college course, although she had won a provincial award, had no hope of getting her portfolio inspected. Naturally, it was even more difficult to show your work if you claimed that most of it had been burned to cinders in a garden shed. Like her friends, Plum quickly saw that, for a woman, there were two clear routes to success. To be taken seriously you had to be very plain, wear paint-spattered overalls and Doc Martens and sulk in public until you were at least thirty-four years old. Or you could take the glamour route, and screw all the tutors, eminent officials, gallery owners and any important painters who weren't gay or agonizing with their miserable wives about this possibility. Such behaviour might get you on a few mailing lists, although it certainly could not get your work exhibited outside craft-based provincial galleries.

Once on the lists, you could start playing the gallery game because you received invitations to gallery openings. You hung around all the shows, did a great deal of gallery-posing, and learned to recognize the art journalists, some of whom might eventually recognize you, although only in a slow-and-distant-head-nod manner. Your aim was to be recognized (nobody was particularly interested in your work), and to do this, you had to be seen around:

you had to become a Recognized Face. You also went in for all the competitions: if you won any, the head-nods became almost imperceptibly warmer.

Lulu, who had phoned all the galleries from the Round House, pretending to be her own secretary, was on all the lists in no time. She decided to get to know the art crowd in the evenings and teach herself to type during the four days a week when she wasn't working, after which she would be able to temp three days a week, and, as God was her witness, she'd never eat turnips again.

At first everything went according to plan for Lulu. She lived on the wine and free bites to eat at the gallery openings, where she met loads of artists and useful contacts. Plum was less lucky. She was too tired to be disappointed by her London life. She was not free in the evenings and hardly ever during the day, although Jenny baby-sat on Saturday morning and Lulu every other Saturday afternoon, so that she could get out to buy food and visit the launderette.

Plum, whose divorce proceedings were creaking ahead on the grounds of irretrievable marriage breakdown, usually had plenty of warning before her mother or Jim called (as he did every Saturday afternoon to take the kids out). These visitors always saw a tidy place with no extra children, as they smelled the fragrant odour of the bakery lady's cinnamon buns warming in the Baby Belling.

However, one afternoon just before Christmas, Mrs Phillips arrived unexpectedly; this was deliberate.

The bakery lady's baby daughter, having filched some chocolate, had just vomited; the other two tots were bawling their heads off, and two-year-old Max had started up in sympathy. No wonder Plum didn't hear the bell ring.

Her mother sat on the (unmade) bed and dissolved in tears. Through her sobs, Plum heard, 'Never expected a child of mine . . . this squalor . . . those poor kiddies . . . my only grandchildren . . . we knew you were artistic when you carved that Scottie dog . . . and you did win that prize . . . I never had a chance, I was out of school and into the hosiery factory . . . Jim had his chance, why shouldn't you? . . . Sheila, if you want to paint this bad . . . I'll look after the kiddies, this isn't good for them or you . . . You can come down to Portsmouth Friday night, then go back to London on Monday morning . . . and that'll give me a chance to get a bit of flesh on your bones.'

Reluctantly, Plum agreed that should she be unable to support herself within two years, then she would face common sense and train in Portsmouth for a respectable job.

Humble and grateful, she flung her arms around her mother. 'Mum, I'll never forget this! You're a wonder!'

'No, I'm just a mum.'

* * * *

Jim had been delighted at the prospect of seeing more of his sons. Once again a big fish and glad to be back in his small pond, he now happily shared a bachelor pad with two other male teachers. They all drank beer straight from the can and there wasn't a lace mat in the place. Of Plum, he sourly said to his flatmates, 'She'll never survive. She hasn't got the talent.' His face tightened into a scowl. 'That Southern Artist prize was a one-off, flash-in-the-pan. The only way *she'll* make it is on her back. And she's not very good at that, either.'

* * * *

For the first time in her life, Plum had no one around to care for, or to tell her what to do. The day she travelled back, alone, from Portsmouth, she took the tube from Waterloo to Trafalgar Square, and spent the day with the Crivellis in the National Gallery, in a state of ecstatic intensity that had as much to do with her new freedom as with artistic uplift. This heady feeling of adventure and excitement lasted until bedtime; then, as she undressed, she felt a creeping apprehension, a psychic cold chill at the back of her neck, as though someone had left a window open. This slowly grew to mild fright, then escalated to cold, black fear: she was now on her own and she had what she wanted – *but what she wanted was her kids.* She felt homesick and lonely.

Finally, she got up, dressed and went to the pub at the end of the road, where there was a public phone.

Jenny's soothing voice reassured her. 'Plum, we all go through it . . .'

It took Plum a week to realize that occasional loneliness was the reverse side of freedom's gold coin: like everyone else, she developed a few techniques to counter the feeling of isolation that often enveloped her like clammy fog. This bleak desolation could generally be dispersed by a call to Lulu, who immediately turned life around into a crazy adventure, or to Jenny, who patiently comforted Plum and reminded her that feeling lonely was part of the transition to a new way of life, and would pass.

'You *can't* have it all. Don't believe what you read in women's magazines,' said Jenny repeatedly. 'And you've only got this one chance to earn your living by painting – so you mustn't blow it, Plum.' Then Jenny would always remind her that she 'd see her kids at the weekend, when she'd soon appreciate peace and tranquillity. 'And, Plum, you always say a mother's place is in the wrong . . .'

Jenny had experienced bad luck: her grant had been cancelled for some technical reason concerning her father's income tax ceiling, and she had been obliged to leave the Slade before finishing her final year. Undeterred, she worked as a waitress in a pub and stocked supermarket shelves in the evening – anything to stay in London.

In January 1977, a fortnight after first tasting these sweet-sour fruits of freedom twenty-one-year-old Plum was offered a job by a seedy middle-aged painter who smelled of stale beer. She was introduced to Bill Hobbs at a gallery opening to which Lulu had dragged her. Plum mistakenly thought that being a painter's assistant would be a substitute for art school, but the work was drudgery and disappointingly dull. She was almost relieved when she was abruptly fired after three winter months spent working in a freezing basement.

After that, she had various short-term, dead-end evening jobs: she waited at table, washed dishes, and conducted door-to-door market surveys, which simply involved ticking boxes in answer to questions but which angered people who had settled down to watch TV just before she rang the doorbell. During the day she painted, and because she started at dawn, as soon as it was light enough to see, lack of sleep became a serious problem. She often fell asleep when she didn't mean to, particularly on buses; she would pass her stop and be woken at the end of the line.

*   *   *   *

For two years Plum's life was as uneventful as it was tiring; paid work, painting and weekend childcare left her little spare time or energy, although she sometimes went to hectic student parties and had a few flirtations. Her London social life centred around the launderette and the local supermarket, where her trolley was never bumped into by a tall, dark, unattached stranger who loved cooking and other people's children.

It was during this period that Lulu, living on a small allowance from her parents, became their authority on sex.

'You're a promiscuous hussy,' yawned Plum one Sunday evening in her studio, after she and Jenny had listened to Lulu's latest experiments: Lulu said you still had to draw a map for some men, saying, '*Here be Clitoris.*'

'I'm a serious sexual explorer,' Lulu said firmly. 'Never again shall I place my bet for a lifetime's happiness on one man.' She still mourned Mo.

'Why are women never happy without a man?' Jenny asked, draining the bottle of cheap Algerian red into their glasses. 'Why can men be perfectly content by themselves, but women never are?'

'Women have low self-esteem and high expectations,' said Lulu, 'a fatal combination. We're not good enough for ourselves.'

*   *   *   *

In October 1978, Jenny showed six paintings at the Avant Avant gallery in Fulham Road. In November, Lulu had arranged for Plum to exhibit eight paintings in the Shoestring, a scruffy gallery in Camden Town.

After being on exhibition for a week, Jenny's greenish still-lifes, blackish landscapes and sombre, sallow portraits all remained embarrassingly unsold. Jim, who had arrived at the Avant Avant with a loyal little support group from Hampshire Art College, comforted her. 'Don't worry, it's just part of the job specification,' he said, throwing a reassuring arm around Jenny's shoulders. 'All the best painters starve because critics fail to recognize their genius. We all know that! Remember, Brendan Behan said a critic is like a eunuch in a harem: he *wants* to do it, he knows *how* to do it, all around him he can *see* other people doing it – but *he* can't do it.'

The following month, at the Shoestring Gallery, Plum remembered Jim's words. Dressed in a clinging, ankle-length T-shirt of plum velvet, she looked self-assured but was understandably nervous about exhibiting her first paintings; the two-year nursery-care deal that she'd made with her mother ran out at the end of the following month. She felt as frantic as Cinderella when the clock started to strike midnight.

The Shoestring Gallery, in Chalk Farm Road, Camden Town, smelled of sawdust and cheap white wine. Decoration was minimal: black floor tiles covered the long low room, the walls and ceiling were painted matt black, and black spotlights were directed on to the paintings. Lulu had compiled Plum's guest list – a string of important people, none of whom Plum knew and none of whom she expected to turn up. Lulu said you never knew.

'You can hardly see who's here,' complained Lulu, peering through the gloom. 'I should have brought a torch.' Then she gasped, and grabbed Plum's arm. '*Look!* Over there! By your biggest picture! The blond hunk!'

'Dishy,' Plum agreed. 'Who is he?'

'That's Breeze Russell! The Russell Gallery in Cork Street! I put him on your list! *See! You never know!* Who's the girl he's with, Miss Puss-in-Boots?'

Breeze was pursuing the Shoestring receptionist, a striking blonde in a black catsuit and high-heeled boots. After an art course at Sotheby's (the modern equivalent of finishing school), the smart job for a socially well-connected girl was in an art gallery; a gallery girl job did not interfere with one's social or weekend life, and it was understood that one needed time off for Ascot. The tartier the girls looked, the better connected they generally proved.

Half an hour after Lulu had spotted Breeze, Plum turned round and found the blond hunk smiling at her. He was better groomed and better dressed than any man she'd ever met: he smelled faintly of lemons, and rich living. She stared into his blue eyes – surely bluer than any she'd seen before – and at his high lean cheekbones and wide, lean mouth, and found it hard to believe that he was talking to her, talking business, truly interested in her work.

'This is good stuff,' he said to Plum, who could only think, God, he has perfect teeth as well. 'Abstract expressionism isn't popular at the moment, but your work is strong and has great impact.'

Noticing Plum's stricken face, he added, 'Don't worry. After seventy years of abstraction, everyone knows that it's one of the perennial forms of consciousness.'

'You mean it's here to stay?'

Breeze Russell nodded. 'And anyway, no painting is wholly abstract or wholly realist.' He smiled reassuringly. 'But try not to paint too big. Rooms are getting smaller, and while it's nice to sell to banks and museums, the right private sales mean that your stuff is constantly seen on the right walls. I hear you've signed up with the Shoestring for three years . . .'

'One of their standard display conditions,' Plum said, apologetically.

'How did I miss you? I check all the big London school shows.'

'I only did one year at college. I'm mostly self-taught.'

He looked surprised. 'How come there hasn't been any word out?' Art-world take-off is by word of mouth among other artists, which quickly reaches the dealers, then the collectors and critics.

'Only a few friends have seen my stuff: these canvases are too big to lug around.'

'Where can I get in touch with you?'

Shy, inarticulate, dazed by joy, Plum scribbled her phone number on the catalogue list. He smiled again and left.

By the end of the month, Plum had sold all her paintings except the biggest canvas, for a total of just under £3,000, after deduction of gallery commission.

Although her mother had offered to look after her grandsons for a third year, Plum had proved that she could earn her living by painting. She could afford to have her sons live with her again. And now Toby went to school all day, and so did Max, in the morning.

Lulu was thrilled, Jenny less so. Jenny could not help contrasting Plum's success with her lack of it.

Plum's joy was tinged with guilt (sad, uncomplaining, hard-working Jenny) and also apprehension. Surely this was too good to be true? She didn't deserve it. Fate would surely make her pay for it.

Fate did. Breeze did not telephone.

*   *   *   *

Three months later, in February 1979, Plum made one of her dreams come true. With part of the proceeds from the sale of her paintings, she flew to Bordeaux, remembering with affection her girlhood, school exchange visit. After a week spent viewing sheds and ruins, she purchased a crumbling cottage in Valvert, a village in Lot-et-Garonne. A magnolia tree grew by the kitchen door and a thicket of tall rhododendrons shielded the garden from the road.

Mrs Phillips, who had never set foot outside England, found Plum's purchase hard to understand.

'I want us to have – own – a home of our own,' Plum explained, after her trip to France. 'And I'll never be able to afford to buy a home in Britain. This French cottage only cost about two thousand pounds: you couldn't buy a British dog-kennel for that.'

That Easter, Lulu borrowed her parents' Volvo station wagon and she, Jenny, Plum and the boys caught the Southampton night ferry to France.

The roof of the cottage at Valvert had been repaired, and new shutters and doors had been fitted by Monsieur Laforge, the local carpenter and odd-job man. The house was not really habitable, but they camped in, using sleeping-bags and ignoring the lack of water, electricity and furniture. These, with the exterior repainting, would have to wait until Plum could afford them; meanwhile, they intended to paint the kitchen.

South-west France was sunny, charming and old-fashioned; the locally produced food and wine were delicious, the cost of living very low. The Britishers were quickly accepted into local village life, and Plum became particularly friendly with the family of the neighbouring farmer, Monsieur Merlin, who was also the village Mayor.

Max and Toby loved visiting the Merlin farm. They watched Madame Merlin crouched by cows to milk them; they helped her to feed the ducks, chickens, rabbits and goats; they helped the Merlin children to pick early vegetables (broccoli and Brussels sprouts, cabbages and carrots, radishes and rhubarb) and great bunches of narcissi from the orchard that sloped to the river. Every afternoon the Britishers swam in this chilly, cypress-fringed river that ran past the bottom of Plum's garden.

After watching Plum swim with her sons, Monsieur Merlin asked if she would teach his fourteen-year-old, Paul, to swim. Thin, tall and shy, Paul had nearly drowned in a boating accident as a child, and was consequently frightened of water. Plum succeeded in teaching him a slow, sedate breast-stroke.

It was almost a perfect holiday, except for one thing: it quickly became clear that Lulu was no longer clean. She was unreliable, erratic, often incoherent. Plum stopped her painting the kitchen, because clearing up after her slapdash work took more time than doing the job without her. Jenny filched the Volvo keys and hung on to them. Plum searched Lulu's duffel-bag but found nothing. They agreed that she was not to be left alone in the house or with the children. Eventually Lulu confessed that she had met the Nigerians again. Like Oscar Wilde, she explained, she could resist anything except temptation.

Shortly after their return to Britain, Lulu lost her job at the Round House. Out of her skull, she had scattered the office Rolodex address cards from a top-floor window over the roofs of Chalk Farm, while singing, 'I'm Dreaming of a White Christmas'.

Depressed and anxious, her parents once more asked each other where they had gone wrong. Lulu's father paid for her to return to the expensive clinic for another three-month rehab.

In July, without Lulu, Jenny, Plum and the boys drove to Valvert in Jenny's mother's Volkswagen – a tight squeeze. Just before sunset, the car breasted the summit of the valley. Below them lay the sluggish, olive curve of the poplar-lined river; beyond it, the houses of the village straggled on either side of a narrow road.

'Oh, my God,' shrieked Plum. 'Monsieur Laforge must have misunderstood me! Look!'

The crumbling exterior walls of the cottage had been repaired and painted cream; as the car drew nearer, they could see that the new wooden shutters had been painted pale lavender. 'I can't pay him!' Plum groaned, '*I haven't any money!*'

When they reached the cottage, Plum became more agitated. The entire interior had been painted cream, except for her bedroom walls, which were corset pink; pine fitments lined the kitchen; there was even a washing machine.

'This is awful! I mean it's wonderful, exactly what I want. Monsieur Laforge asked me how I wanted the interior, so I told him – but I also told him I couldn't afford it yet! God, he must have misunderstood my awful French!'

At that moment, there was a knock on the door. Monsieur Laforge had seen a strange car drive across the valley and to the cottage. 'You like your new house, yes?' he beamed.

'Yes, I love it, but . . . did I ask you to do this work?'

'No, Madame Plum.'

'Thank God for that! So why did you do it?'

'I run out of work between two big jobs. I know what you wish so I work on your house. For electrician I sought my cousin, Jacques, who has retired, but it displeases him to be without occupation.'

'But the washing machine!'

'Ah, yes, you will be obliged to pay for that. With young ones, such a machine is a necessity. It was cheap – from old stock, when Jacques sold his shop.'

'Then you've also had town water piped in?'

'Yes. And electricity; that too must be paid for.'

'*But I have no money!*'

'Apart from these things I mention, this is of no consequence. One cannot expect you to pay for work that you did not request.'

'But I . . . can't accept your work as a gift!'

'But certainly no! You may pay me when convenient.'

'Back home it's a major effort to get a plumber to turn up,' marvelled Jenny. 'Out here you've just had your house redecorated painlessly without paying for it.'

'But I have *no money*, Monsieur Laforge,' Plum repeated. 'How can I pay for the water, the electricity and the washing machine?' She was almost weeping. She did not want to get in trouble with the local power companies, or be branded an unreliable foreigner.

'Ah, I had the idea. You are a painter, no? Then you paint the houses in the area – you paint portraits of houses, instead of people. I know who has money. I show you which houses to paint.'

Jenny burst into laughter. 'He's suggesting we work like the eighteenth-century itinerant painters, who used to move from one country manor house to the next, painting portraits of the owner, his family, their dogs and their horses. He hasn't seen your painting, Plum! But it sounds as though my style's ideal!'

All that summer, Jenny painted portraits of houses. Within hours of setting up her easel, the house owner was breathing respectfully at her elbow, wondering to the sky what would be the cost of such a picture. Every single picture sold – at prices decided upon by Monsieur Laforge. Plum and Jenny decided to spend every school holiday in Valvert. They would buy camp beds on their next trip, and gradually furnish the house from local junk shops.

* * * *

That autumn, Lulu's father paid for a silent, nail-biting Lulu to take a one-year art administration course, which would enable her to earn her own living in the art world. He respected Lulu's wish to be independent of her parents, but he wanted her to train for a job with a future. She could then paint or not, as she pleased

* * * *

A year later, a still chastened Lulu managed to land an art admin job in Birmingham, promoting painters and organizing exhibitions. It was an exciting, creative job. She loved her work and proved very good at it.

* * * *

The following year, in October 1981, after two more shared shows, Jenny held her first one-man exhibition at the Avant Avant. Unfortunately her work was only slightly more successful than her previous exhibited paintings. Jenny suspected that her dad had arranged for a few friends to drop in and buy pictures: she recognized one of them, who had previously shown no interest in art.

When Plum had tried to comfort Jenny by reminding her of her success in France (they had now finished furnishing the cottage), Jenny had cried angrily that she wanted to be recognized as a *serious* painter – just as Plum did.

* * * *

The following month, on 3 November 1981, Plum's divorce became final. Two weeks later she held her own first one-man exhibition. The Shoestring Gallery was now a long, low white room with bare scrubbed floorboards and insufficient heat, but plenty of cheap white wine.

Plum had turned up early, wearing a black velvet dress from Fenwick's that looked as if it had cost more than it did. She was shaking with fright, and felt sick.

Siegfried, the gallery owner, also wore black velvet: tight black jeans and a hooded top that covered his shaven head and gave him a monkish appearance. 'Guess what, darling? Two pictures pre-sold!' He waved at two canvases, each with a red star stuck on. 'But there are two purchase conditions: firstly, you're to dine tonight with the purchaser . . .'

'Who's that?' Plum asked eagerly.

'Ah, that's the second condition: you're not to know.'

'How romantic! Or is it a *la belle et la bête* situation? You don't look at all pleased, Siegfried, considering that you've just sold two!'

'When you get to the Café Royal, you'll understand why I'm not pleased,' Siegfried said sourly, turning away.

'But I can't go! My sons are coming later, with my friend Jenny – I promised the boys they could come to my first show!'

'Why not take them to meet the mystery purchaser? He didn't say that you were to be alone. And he hasn't seen a white woman for at least two weeks.' Siegfried gave a malicious smile. 'Here comes a reporter from the *Ham and High*. For God's sake don't look frightened – *smile*.'

* * * *

In the mirrored, gilded rococo splendour of the Grill Room at the Café Royal where Augustus John and Arnold Bennett had once held court, Plum and her two sons were escorted by the head waiter to the central table. There sat Breeze. Plum's heart started to tap-dance.

When they were seated on crimson velvet chairs, Breeze waved aside the waiter's menu. 'Just bring me the biggest ice-cream in the world.' Unseen by the children, he winked at the waiter.

'Chocolate chip, chocolate mint, coffee crumble, caramel fudge, maple walnut, cream 'n' peaches, raspberry swirl, blackberry, blueberry, baby strawberry, passion fruit, or tutti frutti, Sir?'

Breeze nodded. 'All of those please.'

When the enormous ice-cream appeared Toby's mouth fell open and Max gasped. Nervously, they both looked at their mother, expecting her veto.

Breeze waved the ice-cream away. 'That can't possibly be the biggest ice-cream *in the world*. Please ask the chef to try again.'

Max's face crumpled with disappointment.

Shortly afterwards, a larger multi-coloured pyramid appeared upon a silver platter. Breeze nodded. 'We'll have two please.' He whispered to Plum, 'My mother says if you let a boy have what he wants, he'll never eat enough to make himself sick.'

'I hope your mother's right.' Plum looked apprehensive.

'My mother has four sons, so she's used to boys and so am I. Pete, the youngest, was born when I was seventeen; now he's seventeen. Shall we start with an omelette Arnold Bennett, filled with smoked haddock, cream and grated Parmesan? Waiter, more champagne, please.'

* * * *

After the meal, Breeze drove them back to Kentish Town in his silver Mercedes. 'Can I come in, Plum?' he asked casually. 'I'd like to see more of your work, then discuss what you do next.'

Her heart still tap-danced as she quickly put the torpid boys to bed and unlocked the door of her studio. 'I'm sorry it's such a mess . . .'

'What studio isn't?' Breeze prowled around the cold room. By the harsh light of the naked central bulb he peered at the sketches pinned to the wall. He pulled each canvas from the stack in the corner and examined it carefully. He even asked to look at her sketchbooks. Then he carefully examined Plum.

'I've got two front fillings and a back tooth missing,' she said tartly.

'Ah, but how do you go over distance? That's what has to be decided before I handle you. You have the talent, but do you have the tenacity and are you promotable? Are you prepared to strut your stuff for publicity?'

'And suppose I don't want you to handle me?' Plum was immediately on the defensive.

Breeze smiled slowly. 'We both know you do.'

He moved forwards and took her in his arms. She felt his warm breath on her ear as he murmured, 'You're such a delicate little thing.'

As she felt his warm hand on the thin black velvet that covered her breasts, she started to shake. She had already noticed that his hands were long and slim; now she was discovering how sensitive they were. With tantalizing slowness, Breeze explored her breasts.

Trembling with excitement, Plum longed to feel him. She unbuttoned his jacket and burrowed beneath it, tugging at the silk fabric of his shirt, eager to feel her hands upon his warm muscular flesh beneath.

Breeze bent his head. His mouth forced her lips apart; his big body pressed against hers. He reached for her hand and thrust it between them, so she felt his excitement. Behind her back, he grabbed the clinging velvet of her dress and tugged it upwards. His warm hands grasped her buttocks, and pressed her body even closer against his. Dovetailed against each other, they swayed and trembled with passion.

'Isn't there somewhere else we could go?' he whispered. The studio was bare except for the easel, the canvases and the battered, paint-spattered table on which lay Plum's palette and some twisted tubes of paint.

'No,' she whispered back. 'Anywhere else the boys might hear us.'

He lifted her, then took two steps forward, so that Plum was pressed against the wall. He leaned to one side and yanked the string that switched off the harsh light. He disengaged his body from hers just long enough to pull her dress over her head. Now she was naked, pressed against the cold, unyielding wall. She shivered, as much from cold as from passion. In the darkness, she felt him move away, and heard him rip his clothes off.

His lips were dry and firm. She felt his hands explore her body: as all strength left her, she thought she was going to fall. Then she felt his hand press her pudendum, find her clitoris, and rub it rhythmically until she groaned and clung to him as he coaxed from her body a response more rapid and intense than she had ever known. After some time he gently eased her thighs apart, and felt for her. She was pressed hard against the wall as he entered her, but she no longer felt the cold.

* * * *

The following afternoon, Plum took a bus to Piccadilly and floated on feet that hardly touched the pavement to Cork Street, the heart of the gallery world. Suddenly feeling shy, she loitered before the plate-glass window of the Russell Gallery, gazing at the lone painting of fishing boats by Christopher Wood. Eventually, she pushed open the door.

Breeze's office, at the back of the building, had no window. Unlike the spacious, pale grey serenity of the rest of the gallery, here paintings were propped in disorderly abandon against the walls. Two Jacobean wooden carvings of angels lay on the floor, and expensive art books lay in untidy piles on every flat surface except the desk. This was covered by letters, transparencies, photographs of paintings, press clippings and a pile of that morning's newspapers.

Breeze, wearing a pink silk shirt, was clamped to the telephone. He was on the track of an undocumented sketch for *The Isle of the*

Dead by the melancholic Swiss painter Arnold Böcklin, a major influence upon de Chirico.

He looked up as Plum entered. 'Hi! You've had a good review in the *Standard*, seen it? No?' He picked up the newspaper and read. '"Incandescent, vibrant paintings in which swirls, clots, clouds, shimmers of pigment suggest a natural landscape, sometimes romantic, sometimes sinister, always powerful . . . this free-hand lyricism produces sensuous paintings that are marvellously joyful."' Breeze smiled at Plum. 'You can't ask for better than "Marvellously joyful". He goes on to praise the two I bought.'

He tossed the newspaper to Plum and picked up another. 'Listen to this – today's *Times*: "Some of her pictures are delicately seductive, others splash upon your consciousness like an exploding grenade . . . this painter is not intellectually neat but creates in a thunderous burst . . . cerebratory sensuousness and euphoric intensity . . . wild, lurid, just-controlled excess . . ."'

Breeze laughed, 'And you've also had some praise from the *Express*, listen: "It is impossible to consider this exciting work without the sexual content; not only the sensual treatment of the paint but the frankly erotic shapes and images grasp the viewer's mind: I counted nineteen phallic symbols in one picture that scarcely measured one square yard" . . . I'm afraid that's exactly what the *Telegraph* critic *doesn't* like, so I won't read you what he says.'

'How *wonderful*! You're not making it up to tease me?' Plum dashed forward and snatched the cuttings from his hand. 'What the hell does he mean by phallic symbols – my paintings are *abstract*.'

'They are as unconsciously sexy as you are, darling.'

'Look, here's a photograph of me with Siegfried.'

'Ah, Siegfried. I'm afraid he's not happy. He's already telephoned, as he couldn't get a reply from your place.'

'But why is he unhappy? These are wonderful reviews!'

'Exactly. He hates to lose you. He knows he should have had you under retainer; Siegfried was too sharp for his own good. I told him you were now under contract to *me*, which is about to be the truth.' Breeze moved towards Plum and took her in his arms: she smelled his odour. Again she felt his body stir against hers.

'Have I slept my way to the top?' she murmured. 'Jim said the only way I'd make it was on my back.'

'I think Jim's right, whoever he is, but we'd better check.'

'At least this room has a carpet.'

* * * *

They ate lunch in Le Bahia, an old-fashioned Spanish restaurant, with wall tiles painted in ultramarine patterns, a good guitarist, a tart red wine and delicious paella.

'How could Jim bear to let you go?' Breeze asked fondly as coffee arrived.

'Now I think I know what went wrong,' Plum said. 'The problem was very simple – although neither of us could see it. Jim expected me to stay the same as the girl he married but – she wasn't me. When we started going out together, I longed for Jim to love me, so without realizing it, I pretended to be the sort of girl I thought he wanted. I watched football, I listened as he explained what the Prime Minister was doing wrong . . .' Reluctantly, she remembered her rapt, intent face which clearly showed Jim that she thought him the most intelligent man on earth, and was honoured and grateful just to be in his presence.

Plum sighed. 'When we married this false me pretended to be the sort of wife Jim wanted: I went into Perfect Wife Mode – a quietly adoring, distorting mirror that reflected him back to himself larger than life and twice as wonderful. But at some time I started to resent being in PWM and unable to be myself, so PWM gradually faded away – and I appeared in her place. One morning, Jim woke up and realized that he wasn't married to the woman he thought he was, and he felt cheated. I suppose he was.'

'That's your past. Now let's discuss your future.' Breeze dropped his fond smile and looked serious. 'You *do* realize what's going to happen? You have no illusions, I hope. There's just as much bullshit in the art world as there is in any other business area, Plum. It's all promotion, hype and hustle and it's ridiculously romantic idealism to expect anything else. You must understand that we all have to play the Art Game if we want to be successful: artists who refuse to do so never get anywhere – ever. If you don't play the Art Game, you won't make it.'

'I understand. What do you want me to do?'

'Start by losing your provincial accent: I'll arrange elocution lessons. I'm afraid you'll have to lose your adorable scruffy look: go to a top hairdresser, then we'll get you some good clothes. They must be distinctive, so you'll need styling. After that, I'll send you to interview coaching school, so you won't be intimidated by aggressive journalists and you'll feel okay on TV.'

'When do we start?'

Breeze glanced at his watch. 'In about ten minutes.'

Christina Viera was a beautifully lean Argentinian model, turned stylist. With narrowed eyes, she stared at Plum and said repeatedly, 'Turn around again, dolling,' until Plum felt like a slave at auction. 'We do not change her – we just make her stand out more – she's gotta *project*, gotta look a *star!*' Christina decided. 'The hair stays short but *groomed*: she's gotta go to John Michael twice a week. For each exhibition, we dress her in the colours of the best painting, the one on the catalogue cover.'

Plum felt a little ashamed by such shrewd commercialism, but it was a good idea: despicable but clever.

* * * *

While Breeze orchestrated Plum's career they continued their passionate love affair.

One evening, after making love before the log fire in his bedroom, Plum, dizzy with bliss, whispered, 'Breeze, you could have any girl in London. So why did you choose me? I'm a shy, suburban girl with nothing from nowhere.'

Breeze nibbled her ear. 'So was Cinderella.'

His self-confident air of utter certainty reassured Plum and boosted her wobbly self-confidence; he made her feel safe. Like many an ex-wife with low self-esteem and young children, Plum mistook gratitude for true love.

* * * *

Breeze ensured Plum's professional success in several ways. He saw that her work was exhibited in a fashionable gallery – his. She was carefully introduced to the gossip press as well as the art press – although of course the art press had its own gossip press. Breeze entertained a great deal, both at smart restaurants such as the Caprice and at his five-floor Regency house in Chester Terrace, the interior of which had been designed by architect Nigel Coates. Here, in the white reception rooms (even the floor boards were lacquered white), stood a line of Empire chairs upholstered in *eau-de-Nil*; spotlights focused all attention on the walls, where beautiful and impressive paintings hung – until they were sold.

To his clients, Breeze was charming and amiable, attentive and accommodating. As quietly persuasive as he was personable, he didn't mind lending a painting to a good client for as much as six months, while the client made up his mind whether or not he wanted to buy it. Fond of the grand gesture, Breeze knew how to dazzle his clientele with glamorous luncheon parties on a river boat, in a pretty little private marquee on the bank of the Serpentine in Hyde Park, or in the eighteenth-century, grey stone Orangerie at Holland Park. At elegant dinner parties, opera first nights and charity dances attended by royalty, Breeze knew how to turn one good contact into twenty.

There are those who think it heresy to mention art and money in the same breath; then there are others, like most people in the art business, who cannot separate the two. Breeze was one of the latter. The Russell Gallery supposedly championed young British artists: this generated much publicity but very little income. The real money came from blue chip dealing in modern painting – anything painted since 1900. You were a contemporary painter until you committed suicide, then you became a modern painter.

Breeze's deals were often conducted over the telephone; sometimes he never saw the art object that he bought and sold from a catalogue and transparencies. He would quietly disappear from a dinner party for half an hour, having apologetically explained to his hostess that the five-hour time difference between London and New York meant that he had to bid for an important Oldenberg at ten o'clock that night.

In February 1982, as they drove away from a dinner party during the course of which Breeze had acquired a small Braque oil sketch, Plum asked if it gave him a buzz to bid half a million dollars over the telephone for something that he would never see.

Breeze stared at her. 'Of course not, it's just a deal. What I enjoy is the creative side of the business: the thrill of discovering the next generation of artists before other people are aware of them – searching the studios to find an unknown who I reckon'll make it – that's my gamble, and also my thrill.'

'What do you do after that?'

'What I did with you. Once I've found the artist, I decide how to present him, I put the show together, I get the publicity – that's all exciting.' Breeze looked glum as he added, 'The other ninety per cent of my work is running the damn gallery, which is virtually running a shop. I hate *that* – it's boring and it's expensive. Premises in Cork Street cost a fortune, then there's rent, staff salaries, stock . . . the costs mount frighteningly fast. So that's why my commission is forty per cent of anything I sell. Some galleries charge a lot more.' Breeze braked at his front door. 'Artists grumble about paying commission – but they wouldn't get *any* money without the gallery to sell from. Contemporary art is made successful only by the gallery owners who can pay to present it: they back their own taste, put their money behind their own eye – and spend a fortune.' He kissed her on the nose. 'Talking of expense, I've something to show you.'

The tiny lift ascended to the top floor. When Plum stepped out, she saw that it had been converted from three small bedrooms into one big studio with a huge skylight facing north.

'Like it? Feel like moving in with me? Now that the boys are used to having me around . . . Nigel's converted the basement into an apartment for them: the bedrooms are like medieval tents, but there's a modern little carpentry workshop – want to see it?'

The boys were even more delighted than their mother: they could fly their kites in Regent's Park, they were close enough to Kentish Town to see their friends, they had their own TV and nobody would nag them about stereo noise in the basement.

Breeze's resident manservant promptly gave notice, but the daily who had been with Breeze for ten years saw no reason to leave.

Sandra was big and bony with scrawny legs and a heart of flint; she ran the house as efficiently as the barracks across the road to the rear, in Albany Street. Plum soon saw that she would be unable to establish a cosy relationship with Sandra, but as she had no idea how to run a big house she was glad of her presence.

Unused to home help, Plum rushed around tidying up after her menfolk before Sandra arrived in the morning. Breeze, like all his generation, had been raised a chauvinist. 'Put those things down! Let those boys pick up after themselves,' Breeze told her. 'Where are my clean socks?'

When Jim heard that Plum and the boys had moved in with Breeze, there was a major row. Jim didn't want his sons exposed to the influence of that Philistine. He didn't want his sons to acquire Yuppie values nor be endangered by the evil proximity of money; he didn't want them spoiled. When Plum started to remonstrate, he rang off without waiting for her to finish.

Plum, who was still in bed, slammed down the telephone.

Breeze shrugged his shoulders. 'What did you expect? After the reviews of your show, Jim's going to object to whatever you do. He's read every one of those newspaper articles about the Cinderella of Kentish Town. You're getting the success *he* hoped for, so he's jealous of you. Once he was in love with you, and now he's in – hate with you – and there's nothing you can do about it.'

'But why should Jim hate me?'

'He hates you because of what you now stand for: courage, determination in adversity, success, fame, money, the works.' Breeze gave a thin smile. 'Jim expected to take London by storm, then show New York a thing or two, but he's ended back where he started – and there's nothing wrong with that, except it wasn't part of his grand scheme. But now Jim's on a teacher's salary, while you're driving an Alfa Romeo. And what Jim *really* can't forgive is that he's famous only for having been married to you.'

'I haven't got an Alfa Romeo.'

'Yes, you have. Look out of the window. Toby insisted on a sports car. Max chose red.'

Breeze had been right about Jim's jealousy. Jim told the boys that their mother would probably break her bloody neck in that stupid sports car.

*   *   *   *

For a moment, Plum wished that Jim could see her sitting in the back of the maroon chauffeur-driven Rolls, as it glided through New York. Then, exasperated, she wondered why she still felt she needed to prove herself to him?

CHAPTER NINE

UPON returning to the Ritz Carlton, Plum checked her messages. Cynthia Bly had telephoned. Plum returned the call and was told Miss Bly would be delighted to see Plum Russell, any time. Plum called British Airways and arranged to break her journey to Australia at Los Angeles.

Next she telephoned *Trace* magazine in Plymouth, England, but was told that the magazine did not track forgeries unless they had been stolen, and no van der Ast had recently gone missing. The only similar item recently recorded on their computer was a cityscape by Jan van der Heyden, stolen the previous month from Atherton, Lancashire. Plum tried IFAR but – as Leo had predicted – the International Foundation for Art Research preferred only to be involved if the owner of the art object personally contacted them.

As she replaced the receiver, Plum heard the door to her suite slam. Breeze dashed in to collect some price lists before a meeting. As he stuffed papers into his briefcase, Plum told him about her visit to Artur Schneider and asked him if he would accompany her to have another look at the so-called Jacob van Hulsdonck.

'He's much forged,' Plum finished. 'I seem to remember he had four or five pupils, so the forgeries aren't easy to detect.'

Breeze halted. His long hands flew into the air in a gesture of exasperated despair. 'You'll be finding Reds under the bed next! No, I won't go back to this shop with you. For one thing, I haven't time to waste and for another, it's none of my business – any more than it is yours.' His voice rose. 'For God's sake, *drop* this! A painter, of all people, shouldn't be stirring up trouble and undermining public confidence in art in this idiotic way! Forget this bloody nonsense!'

He realized he was shouting, and made a visible effort to lower his voice. 'Be reasonable, darling. Right now you should be devoting a hundred and ten per cent of your time to your career! You can't *half* have a career, and only potential failures think otherwise – look at Lulu! Only heroines in beach-read books manage to have a successful career in their spare time. So forget this idiotic girl-detective stuff!'

'Why is it idiotic to track down a faker – someone who's exploiting people, deceiving them and robbing them?'

'*Caveat emptor* – let the buyer beware! Especially if he's as rich as Victor. So forget this nonsense, darling. Be a good girl and do as I say.'

'Can't you understand that I'm no longer going to do anything just because you say so?' yelled Plum. Their argument spotlit the rebellious feelings that had been building inside her head for many months. 'First you twist logic, Breeze, and then you use psychological pressure to make me do what *you* want!'

'You do what *I* want because *I* know what's best for you,' Breeze hollered back.

'You *think* you know what is best for me. But now *I* want to make my own decisions – even if they're the wrong ones. I'm no longer your good girl! I'm no longer obediently docile! I don't want to be a perfect wife – or a perfect person – *I just want to be myself*!'

Breeze opened his mouth, then looked at his watch and muttered, 'I've got no time for a row now.' He rushed out of the door and almost collided with a hotel messenger, bringing a letter for Plum.

Still angry, Plum tore open the envelope. Inside was a single sheet of cheap, white paper; some letters had been cut from a newspaper and pasted on the page. Plum stared at the sheet of paper:

FORGET duTCh pic OR you ARe DEAD.

Plum yanked the door open, but both Breeze and the messenger had disappeared. She ran to the telephone. 'Reception? Has my husband left the hotel? Mr Russell . . . Suite 105 . . . No, it doesn't matter. But you've just sent up a letter. I'd like to speak to whoever accepted it.'

Apparently the letter had been hand-delivered, but not by a

regular messenger. It had been handed in by a scruffy young white kid wearing jeans and a dark pea jacket . . . maybe thirteen years old. He just handed it over at the front desk, then disappeared. Was anything wrong?

Plum's hands shook as she picked up the envelope. PLUM RUSSELL RITZ CARLTON HOTEL was scrawled in childish capital letters in two lines on the envelope: that was all. She wondered if this was some prank, one of her sons perhaps . . . although Toby and Max were no longer children, and they didn't know anything about . . . But they did! They had heard Plum talk to her dad, when he advised her to trace the money back to source. So of course that must be the explanation – a stupid boyish prank! But another part of Plum's mind asked, why should either of her sons want to frighten her? And suppose it wasn't their prank?

She hurriedly dialled her sons' room number, but there was no reply.

An hour later, Breeze returned from a successful meeting to find his wife still staring at the envelope. She flew into his arms and, in a muffled voice, explained to his chest what had happened . . . 'And, Breeze, the most frightening thing of all is that *whoever sent that letter must be someone I know*!'

'Darling, this is some bloody silly idiot's idea of a joke!' Breeze stroked the back of her head and hugged her. 'But nobody who knows you would do anything so fucking stupid. Nobody who *knows* you wants to scare you, darling.'

Plum pulled her head back and stared up at him with frightened blue eyes. 'Then who sent it?'

'Manhattan is a village, so far as gossip goes,' said Breeze reassuringly. 'I'm surprised this story hasn't already made page six of the *Post*. But you can bet it will – they get hold of everything. Victor's probably told whoever he had lunch with about your ridiculous bet – and don't forget Suzannah is a *news item*. By now she'll have told all her friends what a bitch *you* are, plus any journalist with access to a telephone . . . And Leo's a one-man grapevine . . . This is the quiet season for gossip – everyone they're interested in is at Aspen or Palm Beach – some journalists will do anything for a story. So perhaps some mischievous – or drunken – idiot sent it just to start a hare.'

'But supposing it isn't a mischievous prank?' whispered Plum. 'Shouldn't I call the police?'

'Darling,' whispered Breeze soothingly, 'NYPD hasn't enough cops to handle the pile of murdered bodies they find every day in this city. Do you suppose they're going to pay much attention to a mischievous letter?'

For a few minutes, Plum allowed herself to be soothed, to believe what she wanted to believe. How had she expected Breeze to react? Call in the hotel detective, who wouldn't be able to give more information than the front desk? Order bodyguards with guns and Rottweilers? Send out for a little pearl-handled Smith & Wesson, for Plum to slip in her stocking top?

'I don't want cops posted outside my door every night,' she said uncertainly, 'but I don't like to automatically assume that this isn't a . . . serious threat.' She shivered.

'My poor darling.' Breeze hugged her. '*I'll* tell you what you're going to do about this letter.' He shoved the envelope into his jacket pocket. 'You're going to forget about it! I'll have a word with the hotel detective, and make sure they keep a special eye on our door tonight. You're leaving town tomorrow – and I'm not going to let you out of my sight until I see you're on that plane!' With one protective arm still hugging Plum, he picked up the phone and ordered a bottle of Dom Perignon to be sent up. Gently, he kissed Plum's forehead. 'Now just *forget* this! Don't think of it, don't mention it to anyone – just *put it out of your mind*! It was a nasty, malicious practical joke, but perhaps you now see that you ought to drop this forgery hunt – it's already caused enough trouble for us, hasn't it?'

CHAPTER TEN

Saturday, 4 January 1992

O N THE edge of Los Angeles airport, palm trees stirred as the light, warm breeze lifted the cotton skirts of long-legged girls; airport personnel wore short-sleeved shirts and no socks. Plum's spirits immediately lifted after the gothic gloom of London and the bitter chill of New York. She felt sinful, as if watching a movie in broad daylight, partly because, to avoid argument, she had not told Breeze that she was stopping in LA. Jenny knew, though – in case anything happened to Max or Toby.

Cynthia Bly, a small, slim blonde, waited at the barrier. Probably a few years younger than Plum, she wore cream linen pants with a matching front-thonged jacket (beneath which was clearly no under-wear) and crocodile loafers.

'Anna Sui, right?' Cynthia nodded approvingly at Plum's fifties Barbie-doll suit in a black-and-white striped denim with ankle-length skirt slit to the pelvis.

As Plum's luggage was loaded into the boot of a silver, open-top Mercedes, her tote bag spilled on the pavement, an embarrassing litter of airplane boiled sweets, crumpled tissues, make-up, a packet of tampons and . . .

'What's this?' Cynthia stooped to pick it up.

'That's an old sketchbook. I was drawing on the plane. I do something every day.'

'I know your work,' Cynthia said, as she crouched on the pavement and flipped through the pages. 'This is like Hockney's new stuff. He's now working with a darker palette, plus the usual playful slashes of colour.'

Cynthia turned her head, and her grey eyes, black-fringed by individual false eyelashes, smiled at Plum. 'I've booked you in the Four Seasons; it's drop-dead-gorgeous now they've redecorated. Your first trip to LA?'

Plum nodded. Breeze did not think much of the LA art scene. Basically, most of the buyers were cheapskate: if something cost less than their Porsche, they'd buy it. The market was based largely around West Coast artists, especially movie star painters: when Dennis Hopper had a show, it was always a sell-out. The serious LA buyers shopped in New York, London or Paris.

'Just dump your bags,' Cynthia advised, as they slid into the hotel forecourt. 'Tell them to unpack and press everything. We'll go have lunch in Venice – then I'll take you home and you can see if I've been screwed . . . no need to blush, that's what you're here for. Victor asked me to copy my provenance.'

'You also bought your painting from Maltby's?'

'Yes. Jaimie Lorimer recommended them. You know him, right? He's one of London's hottest dealers, right?'

Jaimie Lorimer was Breeze's hated rival. Plum made no comment, but asked when Cynthia had purchased her painting.

'Three years ago, in 1989. A birthday present to myself. Suzannah wanted to buy it off me but I kinda like it.'

The traffic was bad: Cynthia spent the journey rearranging appointments on her car telephone. 'There's zip in the way of public transport in LA, so you need a car and you spend your life in it.' She swerved to avoid a black teenager on roller-blades, adding, 'People love 'em as if they were pets. Here, all cars are clean – inside and out; a dirty car is like wearing dirty underwear.'

They drove through shopping areas and wide streets lined with tall Emperor palms; purple bougainvillaea drooped over the sun-baked backyard walls of low, pink stucco houses. Plum caught glimpses of tropical greenery, still pools and patios. The sharp, bright light gave them an air of menace.

'Yeah, that light means earthquake weather. Sorry, this is taking for ever. LA's now one endless city from Santa Barbara to the Mexican border.'

Venice was a seaside suburb on the edge of the Pacific. The streets were colonnaded, as in Italy: there were iron bars on the windows, graffiti on the pink and white walls, and wriggling pink neon signs that announced nightclubs, saloons and honky-tonks. Plum blinked at the carnival atmosphere.

'Sorry you're leaving tomorrow night, you'll miss the sword-swallowers and fortune-tellers on Sunday,' Cynthia said, pointing. 'Those wild-haired people with shades are the hip crowd – movie people, rock musicians, jazz musicians – come to watch the action on the beach: the gay weightlifters and wrestlers working out. Or maybe they're just counting the men with blond ponytails.'

The two women paused at an open-air beach gym, where beautiful men lifted weights, worked out on gleaming machinery, or lay on their backs to receive electronic muscle stimulation.

'Muscle Beach,' Cynthia sighed. 'All gay.'

They ate lunch in 72 Market Street: raw brick walls, waving palms and skilful indirect lighting – essential, Cynthia said, for the glamour showbiz crowd. Plum had never seen so many gorgeous women: perfect teeth, perfect hair, wrinkle-free clothes. The men were, or had been, handsome, slim, suntanned and relaxed. '*Every-one's* beautiful,' she marvelled.

'They don't dare not be,' Cynthia replied. She waved to some newcomers and picked at her Kick-Ass chili. 'Here, your body is your major asset. Every fifty-year-old in LA looks like me . . . Sure I am. I have my masseur visit once a week; my trainer twice a week – all women over forty with good bodies have trainers – and I get rolfed once a fortnight. Plus I have cosmetic surgery whenever I need it.' She sighed. 'I musta had the last *retroussée* nose job in the world – it's the only thing that dates me. And of course we all starve to stay thin. Here, it's a sin to be fat because it could cost you your job.'

Cynthia wrinkled her turned-up nose and laughed grimly. 'So we exercise. Everyone gets up at six but nobody – unless you're working on a movie – gets to work before ten because they're jogging while learning Japanese on a Walkman, or riding their exercise bikes in front of the TV, or doing aerobics or jazzercise, or practising some martial art, or cultivating a relationship with a machine at the gym.' Suddenly she beamed and stood up. 'Hey, there's Sly! I'm doing his new beach house. Mind if I just say hello?'

While Cynthia table-hopped, Plum idly listened to the conversation of the beautiful people at neighbouring tables.

'. . . She'd fuck a snake to get that part . . .'

'. . . We *all* know Cindy is *very* fuckable . . .'

'*Fan*-fucking-tastic!'

'. . . So I said, fuck you, mister, keep your hands in your own fucking pockets . . .'

'So there I was, having my massage, right? The guy reaches my ass and I'm half-asleep, right? Then I feel something odd so I look over my shoulder and I gotta tell ya, his putz is so small, no wonder he has to go rear entry. So I holler, '*Outta here!*' He just zippered up, packed up his table without looking at me and left muttering, "I thought you were Jewish" . . . I *am* Jewish, right?'

Plum nearly fell off her chair.

When Cynthia returned, Plum told her what she'd heard. Again, Cynthia laughed. 'LA is fuck city, in every way. Haven't you noticed yet? If you aren't terrific at sex, don't come here. Everybody lives, breathes and makes their living – either directly or indirectly – from sex. This city hasn't got a beating pulse, it's got a throbbing dick.' Not caring that the waiter was serving their shrimp with spinach salad, Cynthia leaned towards Plum. 'LA is about power through sex – and power is all that counts here. This city is about who has power *at this moment*. Your business and social position depend on one thing only – your last success. If you're important to them *at that instant*, people will do what you want and they'll tell you what you want to hear; but if not, they won't waste their time on you, and they have no intention of doing what they promise. LA stands for Lies Allowed.'

* * * *

From the road, Cynthia's house and four-car garage looked a bit like a top-security prison, but that was because it faced the almost deserted beach of Marina del Rey. Inside were pale woods, silver and dark green areas, restful as forest glades.

In the kitchen were two couches and a forty-five-inch TV. The dining-room was a small, square lake; the table, seating twenty, stood on a central wooden island.

Cynthia's bedroom suite included a bathroom furnished like a sitting-room, a gym and three walk-in closets: winter, summer and sportswear.

'You're obviously a very successful decorator, Cynthia.' Clearly, people kept their promises to her.

'Yeah. Two reasons.' Cynthia smiled as they took the lift down to street level. 'I never discuss my clients, and I let them take all the credit: all the best ideas – all the ideas – are theirs, I tell anyone who asks.'

Cynthia's silver-grey office also looked like a living-room, and like Victor, she had no desk. She only took meetings there, she explained, she was out nearly all day. While driving, she always used either her phone or her dictaphone.

On the wall to the left of the door hung a flower painting. In a bottle-green glass vase was a charming bouquet of rich black tulips; bunched before them were fatter, butter-coloured tulips feathered with flame, some lily of the valley and two pale pink primulae; to the left, a black butterfly with big yellow spots on the interior wings perched on an overblown pale pink rose that was shedding its petals. On the wooden table beneath it curled a tiny green lizard. The painting, dated 1627, was signed with the monogram of Ambrosius Bosschaert the Elder.

Plum took the painting to the kitchen, where there was a table and better light. She took out the magnifying-glass that she'd bought at a philatelist on West 57th and scrutinized the painting, inch by inch.

'Fairly rare to find such an early canvas,' she said. 'Most similar paintings were on copper, or fine-grained wood.' The finely carved gilt frame was certainly seventeenth-century: the back of the finely woven canvas looked as if it might also be as old, but revealed nothing else of interest. She pulled the hotel sewing kit from her purse and did the pin test: after minimal initial resistance, the pin sank into the paint.

Eventually Cynthia said impatiently, 'Well, whaddaya think?'

'Ambrosius was a terrific old boy,' Plum said slowly, as she stared at the little painting. 'His speciality was those short, hair-thin lines on the rounded edges of the tulip petals.'

Cynthia peered at the flower painting. 'Where? *I* can't see them.'

'No, they aren't there.'

Cynthia sighed. 'How can you be so sure? You've hardly looked at it.'

From her tote bag, Plum produced the copy provenance files of the two fakes she had seen in New York. She pulled out the two transparencies and handed them to Cynthia. 'Look at the bluebottle in Suzannah's picture and the one in the Schneider picture – they're identical.'

Cynthia examined the two transparencies. 'Hey! Here's my lizard, in Suzannah's picture.'

'Hadn't you noticed it before?'

'Of course, they're not the same colour. Suzannah's lizard is golden; mine's dark green.'

'But it *is* the same lizard – the same size and in almost the same position.'

Cynthia sighed again. 'So two bluebottles link Suzannah's picture and the Schneider painting, and two lizards link Suzannah's painting to mine. The three pictures are obviously connected.' She wrinkled the *retroussée* nose. 'But if they're fakes, how come the forger made such a clumsy error? It's so obvious to duplicate those components.'

'It isn't necessarily an error. Seventeenth-century painters shared their sketchbooks: they were like working capital, and handed down for generations. But this work is fairly recent.'

Plum's magnifying-glass hovered above the painting. 'However, the forger isn't as good as he thinks he is.' She explained that there was a certain lifelessness about an efficient copy. However skilful the painter, a forgery will be laboured. So a really good forger never made an exact copy of anything; instead, he made a careful study of his chosen painter and the techniques he used and then imagined that he *was* the Old Master.'

'Aha! Actors call that "creative imagery technique".'

Plum scribbled notes in her sketchbook. This was the first of the three fakes that she had been able to examine closely. She could see other hints of forgery: just as everyone has a characteristic hand-writing, every painter has his own style, so a forger cannot avoid leaving traces of his own personality on his forgery.

'So tell me the worst,' Cynthia said.

Plum turned back to the painting. Slowly, she said, 'The choice of palette colours is subtle, but not as sensitive as in genuine Dutch paintings of this period. This was the Golden Age of flower painting, remember.'

Cynthia smiled wryly, 'Sometimes you just have to say what the fuck.'

Suddenly Plum, astonished, burst out, '*I think I know who painted them!*'

Cynthia twisted around. 'You *know*?'

Plum wished she hadn't spoken aloud: it would be months before she could check on her hunch – and it was still only a guess.

'A definite maybe, Cynthia.'

'*Who?*'

'I can't tell you until I'm certain.'

Cynthia looked worried. 'You won't do anything risky?'

Plum thought back to her fear when she first read the anonymous letter. She shook her head.

Again, Cynthia looked at her flower painting. 'Before you arrived I decided if this thing *is* a fake, I'm going to do nothing about it. I don't want to get caught up in something that could be dangerous – some well-protected gang of forgers.'

She walked to a French provincial armoire opposite the fire-place, then fished down the front of her jacket for a tiny key on a gold chain around her neck. The big cupboard had been cleverly fitted as a filing cabinet. 'You don't want your secretary to see the sensitive stuff,' Cynthia explained. 'That way things get leaked to the press.'

'What things?'

'What some star has in his bedroom to promote his private fantasies.'

'*Such as?*'

'I never discuss my clients, remember?' Cynthia produced two large beige envelopes and handed one to Plum. 'Here's a copy of my provenance. I'll put the original back in the safe.' She walked to one of the bookcases that flanked the fireplace, pulled out a book and touched a hidden mechanism. Three shelves of books slid aside into the wall and revealed a standard Chubb office safe. She gazed at it doubtfully. 'I can never decide whether there's any point in hiding a safe; if you're burglarized, it's generally an inside-information job, so they know where it is. And if it isn't – they tear the place apart looking for it.' She twisted the combination, opened the safe and carefully placed the provenance envelope in it.

Plum quickly scanned the thin file. 'Here's an attestation on Maltby's letterhead that the painting was purchased by them in 1989 at auction from Borden & Plow in Sussex – that must be a small, out-of-town auction-house, because I've never heard of it. The painting must have been knocked down cheap, or Maltby's would have included the bill in the provenance.'

Cynthia grinned. 'Ah, the hell with it. Let's forget this forgery shit for a few hours. Let's hit the town.'

＊　＊　＊　＊

As she backed the silver Mercedes out of the garage, Cynthia said, 'I figure you'd like a look at the city; so I'm going to drive in a big, wobbly rectangle right around it.'

The car stereo system pumped out 'America' from *West Side Story*, while a warm breeze gently shirred Plum's hair. They drove up the Pacific Coast Highway, with the rugged Santa Monica mountains on the right. At concert-hall volume, Cynthia switched from track to track to match the mood of the changing landscape.

Cynthia said, 'I love the ocean and the endless sky, and the general sense that possibilities here are limitless. The rest of America laughs at LA experiments and trends – then sheepishly follows us. Here, people behave as if tomorrow were today: so they're accustomed to advanced technology and expect good organization, whether they're buying fast food or a Learjet.'

Cynthia turned right on Topanga and switched to Freddie Mercury and Queen strutting 'We Are the Champions'. At the interchange, she took a right on to the Hollywood Freeway and headed back towards the centre of town.

'Where's Hollywood?' Plum asked.

'We just passed it,' Cynthia said. 'No point in taking you there. Hollywood's sleazy: pimps, whores and druggies, disappointed tourists hung with cameras, dazed newcomers, looking for the myth.' She laughed. 'But Hollywood *doesn't exist* and never has: Hollywood is a state of mind, it's the biggest myth in Hollywood.'

Plum giggled. 'You sound so cynical.'

'You learn as you get older.' Cynthia looked rueful. 'I used to wonder why it took me fifty years to grow up. But any sane woman needs fifty years to figure out this insane world.' Abruptly, she switched off the music and pushed her blonde hair back from her face. 'Career women like me grope their way towards success. We screw up. Other women bitch about us. Men ambush us and we walk right into their traps. We feel the arrows in our backs, but we decide that the pain must in some way be our own fault: maybe we weren't standing up straight. So we limp along. We don't realize this is psychological warfare.'

The traffic halted because of an accident ahead. Cynthia swore quietly. 'We went after careers, so we could be independent and wouldn't need to rely on anyone else for anything. Some of us made it but it's been so tough and time-consuming; tunnel vision leaves no time to develop our other areas. I'm not talking sewing drapes, you understand, I'm talking about seeking meaning in my life.'

As always, Plum was taken by surprise. In Britain nobody talked about feelings, but in America strangers bared their souls to strangers without giving it a thought. Cautiously she said, 'That's what *I'm* starting to think about.' Ahead of them, the traffic was moving again. 'Are you happily married?' Cynthia asked idly.

After a long pause, Plum muttered, 'I'm not sure.'

'I was married – for about two minutes.'

'What went wrong?'

'Does it matter? It was one of those marriages that failed because the man felt increasingly unimportant alongside his successful wife. Not that I *felt* important, I might add.'

The breeze whipped their hair as Plum said defensively, 'It's not like that with us. Our problem is that Breeze and I are both successful; but he likes it and I don't, and he doesn't understand why.'

'So why don't you?'

Plum thought for a moment. 'It's exhausting and devouring. Satisfaction is what I get from my painting, but it's got to the point where one of the reasons I paint is to avoid the rest of my life: to escape reality. I don't even know what reality *is*. I'm afraid to stop and examine my life, because I don't want to see that I've turned into a money machine. The person who made it possible for me to paint is Breeze, but I now realize that the person who won't let me stop – is Breeze.'

'Honey, that's the catch. Success leaves no time to enjoy it, or even wonder why you aren't. I see it with all my movie star clients: they end up paying a fortune to get their heads screwed on again.'

After the Mercedes moved on to the Harbor Freeway, Plum timidly asked, 'Cynthia, have you ever felt sad without being able to pinpoint the reason?'

'You mean feeling like a wet fog's slowly settling around you and paralysing you, so any effort is too much? Who hasn't felt like that? Ah, what the hell! Only Cinderella was happy ever after.'

'Was she? We don't know what happened to Cinderella after she married. Who decided they were happy – him or her? What did she do that made her so happy? Did she have sixteen kids who never quarrelled or wore her out? Did she settle down to good works of a publicizable nature, like your presidents' wives?'

Cynthia laughed. 'Cinderella didn't have many inner resources that we know of. She was a meek little doormat with a depressive personality and no friends, who was pushed around by everybody.'

'Cinderella was a dependent, passive, exploited woman,' Plum agreed, as the Mercedes swerved north on to the San Diego Freeway.

'God only knows why she turned into the heroine of the entire female population of this planet,' Cynthia mused.

'She made no effort to change her life. But she still ended up top of the pile,' Plum pointed out.

'Which is why a lot of women think you can be a heroine without any effort. But I reckon it's better to be your own Prince

Charming, and choose your own shoes: they're less likely to be painful, along with your illusions.'

Eventually the Mercedes reached Venice Boulevard West and turned towards the ocean. Ahead of them burst a gloriously violent sunset, harsh streaks of fire and light.

Plum stretched her arms towards the sky and yelled, 'I want to stay!' She longed to start painting again.

'LA is tough but it sure is fun,' Cynthia said with pride.

* * * *

Two hours later, in her pale peach marble bathroom, Plum idly splashed in scented water.

Some things about Cynthia were puzzling her.

Cynthia had trained as a decorator at Parsons, New York. So she'd had an all-round visual training and was sharp enough to know a lot of background detail about her flower painting. So why wasn't she sharp enough to notice two almost identical lizards, in the two very expensive Dutch paintings she had purchased?

Cynthia had decided not to go to the police about her forged painting – and she had given almost the same reasons as Leo. That might merely be logic – but it could mean that Cynthia didn't want the police sniffing into her business. If so, why not?

Cynthia had said that art was priced, with cynicism and greed, in a rigged market – which was the forger's classic moral excuse. Plum had seen two of her hiding places – the safe and the French cupboard. Were there other, larger, hiding places?

Cynthia clearly wasn't short of money.

Might she be a member of a forgery gang – the distribution end?

CHAPTER ELEVEN

Tuesday, 7 January 1992

PLUM'S exhibition was to be held at Harry Salt's Sydney gallery. He was an old friend, tall, lean and bronzed, almost a caricature of the outdoor Australian, yet he was an urban creature who never left Sydney except to lie on a beach.

Which was what he immediately suggested on the drive back from Kingsford Smith airport. 'Have some fun on your first trip to Australia. We could drive to Wattamolla, Plum, after your interviews – the best beach you've ever seen: like something from *Coral Island*, stretches of white sand, quiet little coves and inlets where trees go right down to the water.'

'*What interviews?*' After the long overnight flight from Los Angeles, Plum desperately needed a bath and a sleep, to counteract the disorientation and exhaustion of jet-lag.

'The reporter from the *Bulletin* couldn't make it any other time – that's important coverage. And Cathie Perchwell wanted to get you before anyone else; she's a tough bitch, it was either that or no interview. Sorry. I warned you I'd arranged a busy schedule.'

The opening was six days ahead, on 13 January, but there was a lot to do before then. Hanging the pictures might take three days, and for Plum's first trip to Australia, Harry had arranged for her to meet potential buyers in a one-on-one situation before the big opening.

Awaiting her in the quiet luxury of the Regent Hotel was a basket of bath oils and lotions, flowers, champagne, newspapers and magazines. She saw that on the cover of *Vanity Fair* was a sweetly smiling photograph of Suzannah Marsh. Inside, Suzannah spoke briskly of her projects and lovingly of her Pops, a corporate lawyer who had taught her all she knew; there was hardly any mention of Victor or their two mouse-quiet daughters.

The article quietly dripped sarcasm and vitriol, but Suzannah shrugged off the interviewer's criticism and accusation that she encouraged unrealistic expectations in women. Plum flipped through the six-page pictorial account of pretend-life on the seventeen-acre stage set of Sunnybank Farm, where Suzannah pitched her carefully romantic, up-market update of rustic escapism.

Standing under the shower, Plum recalled Christmas, which had been organized from Suzannah's enormous kitchen noticeboard. Worklists as detailed as those of Stormin' Norman had been typed by Betsy, the overworked but ever-cheerful assistant, for Suzannah's three secretaries, two housekeepers, two maids, three gardeners and the odd-job man. In this kitchen, two maids had worn identical lavender-striped uniforms to execute little domestic tasks: wreaths of pine cones for the front door, holly-sprigged place settings for the dinner guests, the sort of pretty touches Plum never had time for in the chaotic countdown towards Christmas.

* * * *

After a lazy jasmine-scented bath, Plum wrapped herself in a bathrobe and went on to the balcony, where she gazed at the spectacular natural beauty of Sydney Harbour. The lush green shoreline meandered through dozens of craggy coves, bays and inlets. Far to her right was the narrow entrance to the harbour. To her left curved the sturdy steel Harbour Bridge. Below, on Bennelong Point, rose the soaring white curves of the Opera House. Beyond that, white sails flicked across the glassy dark blue water, and sturdy little ferries carried commuters across the harbour to the leafy suburbs of the North Shore and the grander residences of Rose Bay.

Beneath endless blue sky, the January morning was already hot and humid. It was almost too hot for her first-appearance outfit, a spectacular black body-stocking with snakeskin mini-skirt, but the *Bulletin* journalist arrived before she had time to change. He looked like a businessman, Plum thought, as they drank coffee on the balcony and she answered routine questions.

'Why do I paint? *I* sometimes wonder. I find it an anxious business. I'm always a bit worried when I'm working on a painting, and I'm always a bit miserable when I'm not. My husband knows when a painting isn't going well: I'm tetchy, grumpy, restless. Yes, I work six days a week at regular hours, otherwise I'd never get anything done. I paint from first light to dusk, with a short break for lunch. I don't leave the studio because it shatters my concentration.' Plum grinned, 'Painters aren't as rowdy as they're made out to be. We lead quiet lives and brood a lot. I've lived like this for the past ten years, although sometimes I feel shut off from real life.'

'Is this self-imposed isolation worth it?' the journalist asked.

'Is the work I've produced in that time any good? I hope so.' Plum again wondered whether she had fully used her life – or had she merely used her talent and wasted the last ten years?

'I can stop if I want,' she added defensively. But could she? She had once defied Breeze, absent on a business trip. Exhausted by the rigorous discipline he imposed, Plum went on strike, jumped on the first plane to Greece, booked in at a modest hotel, lay on the beach and thought, 'This is the life!' But two days later, she was tetchy, grumpy and restless. She had flown straight back to London and dashed into her studio.

'No, I've never had a problem with painting,' Plum patiently answered the next question. 'Of course, not every picture turns out right, first go. Some are quick and gleeful; others just won't come together so I destroy them. Some are laboured but eventually successful; I grope my way. Then I make a brush stroke, and realize that it's finished.'

'And then?'

Plum smiled. 'Suddenly I feel tired and content, my mind emptied and exhausted. I put down my palette and brushes. And then I realize I never want to look at that canvas again.'

'Never?'

'Never.'

* * * *

The next interview was very different.

Cathie Perchwell, one of the young punk stars of Australian journalism, slouched on the couch and stared at Plum. She was stick-thin and wore tight black pants, black shirt and bovver boots. Wild hair surrounded thick white make-up and a pouting purple mouth. She snapped on her tape recorder and started. 'Do you think brothels should be legalized?'

Wrong-footed, Plum stuttered, 'I've . . . I've never thought about it. Why?'

'The Queensland Criminal Justice Commission is trying to legalize brothels, to stamp out health risks; to stop organized crime exploiting prostitution. To cut the number of whores in prison!'

'I've never understood why the women go to prison but not their clients. If prostitution's an illegal act, then surely both partners act illegally?'

Cathie glowered, 'The male protection racket in action.' Her next question was as unexpected as her first, 'Are you happy?'

Defensive and bewildered, Plum stuttered, 'Why ask *that*?'

Cathie shrugged. 'You seem to have it all – husband, kids, career, money – while the rest of us struggle towards these goals, hoping they'll bring happiness. Do they?'

Playing for time, Plum said slowly, 'My happy moments have always come unexpectedly.' She wasn't going to open her heart to this nosy bitch. She remembered a night when Toby was two months old; she'd been sleepily propped up in bed, feeding him by the light of the moon. She had stroked Toby's flimsy hair, inhaled his milky, baby odour and had suddenly felt a moment of sudden, absurd happiness. This had been swiftly followed by the usual apprehension. Plum had firmly told herself that it was silly to feel she wasn't entitled to be happy, to feel guilty about feeling happy. But she did.

'Does sex make you as happy as you expected?' The question was deliberately offensive, swift and aggressive, meant to sting the listener into an unguarded response. Plum wondered how to deal with the belligerence.

Again, she parried. 'You mean being in love?' She thought of Jim. 'That euphoria dissolves, like morning mist, that's not real happiness.' Perhaps the way to deal with aggression was to wham it back. She looked at Cathie, 'Are *you* married, Cathie?'

'Yeah. He's a journalist; we'd lived together for three years.'

'And does sex make you as happy as you expected?'

'Let's get this straight. I'm the one asking the questions.' A long pause followed, then Cathie muttered, '*I don't know.*' She leaned forward and switched off the tape recorder. 'Life seems so flat, now we're married. So *undifferent*. I really love this guy, so I feel guilty when I catch myself thinking, "*Is that all there is* – for the rest of my life? Is that *it?*" '

'We've all been brought up to expect too much of marriage,' Plum said. Happiness was supposed to come, gift-wrapped, with the rest of the wedding presents.

'Marriage was just the latest disappointment. I'm bloody sick of feeling disillusioned after life's big moments.'

'Are you feeling OK?' Plum was suddenly worried by the white face.

Cathie gave a sharp laugh. 'Much as usual. Dissatisfied. Restless. Depressed.' She scowled, like a defiant, forlorn child, determined never to be snubbed or ignored again. 'I'm one of the highest paid journalists in Australia, you know, and I take no shit from anyone.' Then she looked weary. 'Sure, I'm a great success, but what's underneath that . . . isn't.' She gnawed her purple lower lip. 'I feel as if an important part of me has been anaesthetized or surgically removed – I don't know which is the missing part. *But I want it back.*'

Plum recognized the bewilderment and disorientation of yearning for something undefinable. She remembered the let-down feeling when she'd found that money, fame and being pampered like a film star didn't fill that void. Plum realized that Cathie had clearly expected marriage – becoming one of a pair – to fill this empty part of her. But it hadn't.

'That's enough about me.' With a sour, distancing smile, Cathie switched on the tape recorder and resumed her bad-girl act: she hurled a series of aggressive questions at Plum, hardly giving her time to reply, until the door opened and Harry appeared.

'Plum, you were due at the photographer ten minutes ago . . .'

Wednesday, 8 January 1992

On the following day, when Harry took Plum to his gallery, the weather had become hotter and more humid. Her paintings had travelled well, although one of them needed to be touched up. Harry, his assistant and Plum then settled down to the important business of deciding where to hang the paintings, a job that could never be plotted entirely on a paper plan.

By the end of the day, despite the air-conditioning, they were all sweaty, with arms aching after the strain of dragging big canvases. Harry opened a bottle of chilled white wine and mixed it with soda water; devitalized, they drank at first in silence. Then Plum told Harry about her pursuit of the forged seventeenth-century Dutch pictures; he was an old, trusted friend, and she hoped he might help her.

'There are plenty of fakes floating round *this* town,' said Harry. 'They find their way here because there are hardly any art historians and there was a lot of new money before this slump. People who knew piss-all about art bought it as an investment: sitting ducks.' He laughed. 'Perhaps the only Aussie collector who never got landed with a fake was Alan Bond, because Angela Nevill, his buyer, had a good eye. You heard Alan went bankrupt? The poor bastard's collection's being sold to pay off some of the bank loans that bought it. The poor bastard paid fifty-three million dollars for that Van Gogh *Irises*.'

Harry refilled Plum's glass. 'A lot of odd characters are starting to drift into town for the auction, including one that you might like to meet: a Yank art detective, Stephanie Brownlow. She's quietly shadowing a well-known thief who suddenly decided to visit Sydney. I'm helping her, so she might help you!'

Suddenly, Plum no longer felt tired. 'Harry, when could you fix a meeting?'

'Tomorrow?'

Thursday, 9 January 1992

The two women met for lunch at a smart, white marble vegetarian café. Stephanie Brownlow, who looked like an undernourished student, might have been nineteen or thirty-nine years old; pale and thin, she had a dull complexion that suggested too many lentil-based meals. She wore a beige mackintosh; some women can do this and look like Marlene Dietrich: others, like Stephanie, just look drab.

Plum had the feeling that Stephanie, who looked faintly amused, knew exactly what she was thinking, as they ordered salad with Roquefort dressing and iced coffee.

'I need to fade into the background,' Stephanie said in a flat, Boston accent. 'Forget all you've ever heard about detectives: the tough, hard-drinking thug, the other fictional stereotypes. A good detective tries to look boringly forgettable.'

Stephanie worked for a London firm and would say nothing about her visit to Australia, but she didn't mind talking generally – non-stop – about her work. 'Almost everyone gets to be a detective by accident,' she told Plum. 'My best subject at school was painting, so I did a degree in art history, and luckily I was a good all-round student, because a detective needs to know a lot about law, chemistry, physics, maths, forensic science and computer programming – just for starters.'

Stephanie briskly called for more hot rolls. 'One day someone asked my advice – I never realized he was a detective – and I gradually drifted into helping him.' She waved to the waiter for more iced coffee. 'As you probably know, since the eighties, art theft and fraud's become a serious problem, so my boss started to track paintings, realized that there were hardly any specialists in this area ... and now we're partners. I've just finished a Criminal Justice degree.'

Plum looked at her companion with respect, then told Stephanie about the forged flower paintings.

'Sounds as if they're pastiches,' Stephanie mused. 'When I get a piece that I think is a pastiche, I paint it *myself*: if you don't know how to do it, you won't be able to spot it. I find it relatively easy to produce a pastiche: I photocopy the relevant picture, cut out the items I want to use in my picture, assemble it and paste it on a backing, then photocopy it, using an overhead projector to throw my composition on canvas or wood. Then I sketch it – careful not to use lead pencil, because it wasn't invented until the nineteenth century: I use charcoal.'

'What do you think I should do next?' asked Plum, impressed.

'You can always hire me,' Stephanie said, calling for a second helping of salad. 'Except we're up to our necks in work at the moment . . . Seriously, you seem to be doing fine, so far. Your advantages are that you already have the specialist knowledge and you don't look tough and stubborn – you look fragile and easy to frighten: that's your cover. And you've been lucky to establish a connection between these paintings so fast.'

'I worry about that. Is it too much of a coincidence?'

Stephanie shook her head. 'You went to LA in pursuit of a fake and you found it, is all. Now look for more. If you're part of the art scene, it's not difficult to hear of a suspect painting being bragged about by some new owner. Have you heard of Lady Binger? Widow of one of these tough Aussie press tycoons. She collects flower paintings and has several wrong 'uns. While you're in Sydney, try to see her stuff.'

Stephanie called the waiter over and ordered double cheesecake with chocolate sauce, then added, 'You'll need much more detailed information. You have visual links – those bluebottles and the lizards – but now you need factual links from one picture to the other.' As the waiter served her, she added, 'Look for more of these fakes and don't be discouraged. In this game, rule one is patience, rule two is perseverance, and rule three is tenacity: a good detective hangs on like a Rottweiler, although we always play safe. No point getting killed for a client.' Stephanie poured chocolate sauce over an enormous slice of cheesecake. 'You also need some proof – technical proof – of forgery in the three paintings you've seen . . . D'you think your friend Cynthia would let her painting be examined by the Ashmolean Museum at Oxford? They invented a lot of tests, such as carbon dating and thermoluminescence, and their certificate of authenticity is an important one. Their testing charge is only around £200.'

'Cynthia might, provided it's insured,' Plum said. 'She could hardly refuse. Victor would expect her cooperation. And nothing should harm a well-packed painting.'

'Although it might disappear,' Stephanie said cheerfully, licking some cream from her thumb. 'Lots of art disappears at airports; the loading docks aren't part of the airport, you see. Sometimes art is stolen at a delivery airport as soon as it arrives, and the owners find they've collected an empty crate.'

'How do thieves know it's arriving?'

'There are crooked people in every area of commerce and through every level of the art trade; so there's always someone who can be bought, at a restorer or a customs office – anywhere.'

'Cynthia will just have to risk it,' Plum said. 'D'you know anyone I can ask for at the Ashmolean?'

Stephanie, with her mouth full, shook her head.

'D'you know anyone at the Courtauld?' The Courtauld Institute, a department of London University, is not only a famous art collection but also a school with an art history department and a famous restoration course. When the great museums of the world worry about attribution, they ask the Courtauld because of its emphasis on scientific as well as artistic authentication.

'Sorry, no. But I've a very good friend at the British Institute of Art – Professor Dame Enid Soames. Her field is Dutch and Flemish painting.' Stephanie broke off to ask for whipped cream, then turned back to Plum. 'If I wanted to authenticate a picture or prove a fake, I'd go straight to an academic for guidance. They have access to private collections, so they're up-to-date, and they know lots of useful esoteric stuff. A scholar might be able to tell you that a floral painting was a special gift for a special person, or to mark some special occasion – like a wedding ceremony – or incorporated the owner's crest. This sort of clue might lead to the original owner, and eventually establish the provenance of a painting.'

Stephanie reached for more cream. 'I believe Enid has access to the Witt Library at the Courtauld, which has a photographic archive.

Not many museums have that, and even fewer have computer catalogues. The one good thing about the Getty is their Art History Information Programme, which is compiling a comprehensive global record.'

Stephanie looked regretful as the last crumb of cheesecake disappeared. 'Plum, if you're serious about this search, you also need to know the difference between a civil case that's prosecuted by a private person and a criminal case that's prosecuted by the police. You need far more proof for a criminal case, but your strongest attack is to go for that. If it isn't successful, then start a civil case.'

'But I haven't any intention . . .'

'It sounds as though your friend Victor isn't going to let someone fleece him of ninety-five thousand dollars without trying to get it back.'

Stephanie called for more iced coffee. 'The problem is that most owners don't want to prosecute. If it's a civil case, they have to pay, and litigation is insanely expensive and difficult, especially in the States. Even if you're unquestionably in the right, you often lose your case. Because the law isn't about justice, it's just a game with crazy, illogical, elaborate rules called Law.'

As Plum called for the bill, Stephanie added, 'As well as being a possible waste of their money, it's undoubtedly a waste of an owner's time to prosecute. So they prefer to cut their losses and forget it, especially if they don't want publicity – and they won't, if they have any other valuables. If thieves read in the *Post* that you've paid a small fortune for a painting – especially if it's a fake – thieves assume (a) you are careless and (b) you live surrounded by valuable assets.'

As they said goodbye outside the restaurant, Stephanie threw a last crumb of information to Plum. 'The big London auction-houses have the best fake-detecting procedures,' she said, 'although that doesn't always prevent their selling something fake. But those old boys at the British Museum are very trusting – so don't go for help to any of the big London museums.'

* * * *

That evening, Plum went to bed early, to get a good rest before her exhibition. She switched on the television in the middle of the Margot Fonteyn story. Suddenly she heard the prima ballerina say that although she had been a star in her teens and an overnight international success, she had found it hard to come to terms with it. '. . . Gradually I came to accept that I was somebody,' explained the dancer. 'But it's funny to think that although I was thirty years old I had no real sense of my identity – unless I was in the ballet on the stage. So long as it was ballet *I knew who I was*.'

Plum knew exactly what the ballerina meant, because that was how Plum felt about her painting – and her own lack of identity when she wasn't working.

Monday, 13 January 1992

Looking around the crowded gallery, Plum wondered which hat belonged to Lady Binger. When Plum had asked that she be invited, Harry said, 'She's already on the list and has accepted. By the way, her name's Wilhelmina, but the irreverent call her Willie or Bingo.'

Gazing at the guests, Plum thought they seemed exactly the same sort of people that she might see at any European or American painting exhibition: basically buyers or sellers. Grand people were being introduced to rich people; bankers who backed gallery owners were being flattered by pretty girls; interior decorators and architects who might commission a canvas gossiped with designer friends.

The artists talked to each other, which was just as well. Plum knew the problems of inviting painters to gallery openings: often they were too anxious to make it clear they were Honest Visual Persons, unafraid of being rude to potential patrons. Psychological vulnerability often showed as contempt, aggression, or both, in artists struggling against the everyday professional hazards of fearing they were no good, or being depressed because they knew they were good but didn't have what it took to be acknowledged as good. To be famous, you needed the social instincts of a White House *chef de protocol* and skin as thick as grapefruit.

Harry worked his way through the smart crowd towards Plum and whispered, 'Old Bingo's just arrived. I'll take you over.' He steered Plum through the throng towards a dumpy matron wearing a Queen-Mother turquoise ensemble.

Harry flashed his sun-bronzed smile. '*Delighted* you could make it, Lady Binger. May I introduce you to the *other* star of the evening. I've told Plum here about your *wonderful* paintings and she's dying to hear about them from *you*.'

Lady Binger beamed. 'Then Mrs Russell must come to my next lunch.' She looked at Plum's hat. 'By the way . . . it isn't fancy dress.'

Plum's swashbuckler, Carnaby Street outfit was the sort of thing a fashion-conscious pirate captain might wear to rape 'n' pillage. The brim of the ruby sou'wester was pinned back with pheasant's feathers; under an unbuttoned ginger shirt, she wore a garnet suede *bustier*. Crimson canvas bell-bottom pants (flies laced in black suede) were worn with magenta canvas platform boots. Plum grabbed any excuse to wear platform shoes, and be at normal-people eye-level.

Ten minutes later, Harry steered her across the room towards a tall, striking blonde who was talking to Rex Irwin, a Sydney gallery owner and an old friend of Breeze.

Harry introduced her. 'This is Ita Buttrose, who runs her own magazine – it's called *Ita*, of course. Ita, what should Plum wear to one of Bingo's bashes?'

Big blue eyes looked thoughtful. 'It'll be smart but stuffy: think back ten years. I'll get my fashion editor to pick out a few outfits for you to choose from and send them to the Regent.'

Ten minutes later, Stephanie appeared at Plum's side, wearing a dull beige cotton dress. 'Heard the news? One of the smooth Italian art crime squad has been caught *in flagrante delicto* and arrested. He'd been a Mafia plant – for twelve years!' She added, '*Love* your outfit.'

Plum beamed, then whispered, 'Stephanie, there's something else I want to ask you. What sort of person becomes a forger? Does a forger do it only for money, or does he get a buzz out of it? Are forgers permanently terrified of being found out, or do they regard work simply as a routine day's chores, like a bank clerk?'

Stephanie laughed, showing little white teeth, pretty as seed pearls. 'Forgers do it for the money and they do it to show off. If they feel their talent has been neglected, they want to prove they're good artists; they want to prove that the art business which ignored them is stupid, ignorant and corrupt.' She scooped a glass of white wine from a passing tray. 'In a way, the forgers are right. Certainly experts can't always recognize a masterpiece. Some years ago, after an English country house robbery, wonderful pictures started to appear in sale-rooms: important stuff – Rubenses and Titians – were sold for next to nothing because they had no provenances and weren't authenticated by scholars, so nobody reckoned they were real.'

'I'm amazed that forgers seem to get away with it so easily,' Plum said.

Stephanie drained her glass. 'The con man's secret weapon is greed. The basis of every con trick is the victim's greed and gullibility, plus the expert's arrogance and everyone's fear of looking foolish.' As a waiter passed, she exchanged her empty glass for a full one. 'When a forgery is discovered, the owner, the gallery that sold it, *and* the scholar who's authenticated it don't want anyone to know: the forger relies on their fear of looking foolish: it's a powerful incentive to do nothing.'

'Not Victor,' Plum said. 'If he finds he's been cheated, he'll come out with both guns blazing, like John Wayne.'

CHAPTER TWELVE

Wednesday, 15 January 1992

FOR LADY Binger's luncheon, Plum picked an apricot linen sleeveless shift, black wrist-length gloves and a black straw halo. Having directed the cab, she wiped off her heavy make-up; like everything always did on a publicity schedule, the photographic session had over-run.

She settled back into her seat and opened the three envelopes that the Regency concierge handed to her. The first contained reviews. Anxiously, Plum read them: 'Plum Russell, one of the most highly regarded painters at work in Britain today . . . in the last ten years, with constancy and assurance, she has developed an abstract vocabulary both personal and profound . . . these new paintings range from delicate harmonies to turbulent discordance. Some are calmly tranquil, some are joyously seductive, others splash upon the consciousness like an exploding grenade.'

Couldn't complain about that! . . . Or this one . . . 'She is a painter's painter: perhaps *only* other painters can totally appreciate what Plum Russell does; she takes colour and bends it to her will: the colours dance or fight together at her command; they leap over the canvas with fiery force and delicate beauty . . . Her paintings, while lyrically romantic, have enormous strength: the turbulent force of her canvases assaults the eyes: they dazzle, they charm, they alarm, they hold you spellbound.'

Plum blew her cheeks out in a whew! of relief, then opened the second envelope. Immediately, she felt mutinous. Harry had again rearranged her schedule to slip in another interview.

*   *   *   *

Years ago, when Plum first moved in with Breeze, she had been surprised to find herself with so little free time. Although she no longer had the treadmill of housework, she found herself with a far more complicated life to organize. And Breeze expected the Cinderella of Kentish Town to spend most of her time in her new top-floor studio. If she was not painting, he wanted to know why. Was something wrong? Was she feeling ill? Lack of time, he had cheerily explained, was the downside of having a career instead of a job.

On the afternoon when Breeze found her helping Toby make a model tank in the basement workshop, he had spelt out his creed. 'In the real world, you have to work your ass off to get anywhere, and then you have to work harder to stay there.' He placed a reassuring arm around her shoulders. 'Out there are thousands of hungry painters, darling. They'd do *anything* to take your place – so don't throw away your place on the escalator – because someone else'll snap it up.'

In some ways, Breeze reminded Plum of her mother. Mrs Phillips could not stand what she called idleness; reading and thinking were considered 'doing nothing'. A woman should not have idle hands. Breeze had an updated, Filofax version of this guilt about wasting time; consequently, he packed his leisure time with activity, often something competitive, such as squash, and therefore almost another sort of work. His social diary was stuffed like a teenager's backpack. He never left himself a moment in which to wonder whether he enjoyed the projects with which he filled his so-called 'free' time.

*   *   *   *

Thinking of Hurricane Breeze and watching the busy Sydney street scenes outside her taxi reminded Plum of a couple of lines of poetry she had read at school:

> What is this life if, full of care,
> We have no time to stand and stare?

151

No time to stand beneath the boughs
And stare as long as sheep or cows.

Plum had hardly had a moment to herself since setting foot in
Australia, let alone getting to that beach at Wattamolla. She decided
to leave Lady Binger's lunch as early as possible and find some green
space in which to flop or walk.

The cab swung through Lady Binger's wide gates, then between
lush lawns towards a low cream house, surrounded by bougainvillaea. Plum opened the third envelope and pulled out a hotel message
slip. Lulu had telephoned twice, within the previous hour.

Plum shivered. Maybe it wasn't . . .

But maybe it was.

She wondered why Lulu had telephoned half-way round the
world twice in an hour? She felt increasingly apprehensive about her
friend, but had no time to call Lulu until she returned to the hotel. It
would have to wait until after lunch.

As Plum entered the cool dark hall, a manservant stepped
forward to take her gloves. Behind him, Plum noticed a Dufy
watercolour of a Mediterranean flower garden hanging on the wall.

'My late husband used to collect,' Lady Binger explained in the
drawing-room. 'The art turned out to be our best investment, even
better than property. So I still buy now for the collection, when I see
a picture Eric might have liked.'

In quick succession, far too fast for Plum to remember their
names, she was introduced to two dozen eminent people, including a
famous architect, a famous business tycoon's wife, a famous television company owner, a famous politician and his famous mistress.

Instead of the cheery, hospitable, hail-cobber-well-met Aussies
that Plum had encountered in Britain and Sydney, these middle-aged
people, who clearly considered themselves an Australian élite, seemed
caricatures of ancient English aristocrats. Like dreadful characters
from a Nancy Mitford novel, the women wore old-fashioned hair-
styles, over-elaborate dresses and too much jewellery. The men,
hewn from some reddish-purple rock, had even tougher faces than
the women; their stony, predatory eyes were wary, and their mean,

thin-lipped mouths hardly opened when they spoke. Clearly, every-one knew everyone else, and none of this incestuous little group was interested in allowing a stranger in – excepting international celebrities.

So Plum realized that the cheerful, grey-haired woman in the only inexpensive cotton dress must be a celebrity; Lady Binger introduced her as the famous Dinosaur Woman from New Zealand, Joan Whiffen. She was recovering from an early morning interview with Cathie Perchwell.

'Did she ask if you were happy?' Plum inquired.

'Yes,' the Dinosaur Woman nodded. 'She didn't look very happy herself, poor child. Great dark rings under her eyes.'

'What did you tell her?'

'I said yes, I'm happy. So she spat, "*Why?*" Because I have an outside interest, I told her. Being an ordinary housewife, led to believe the family was your duty, I was always busy when the kiddies were little. But I found it very boring. Then twenty years ago my husband retired. He went to night classes in geology. I started to help him. That's how I became an amateur palaeontologist. I still feel a bit uneducated, because I haven't been to university or got any letters after my name.'

'But that didn't matter,' said an over-tanned small man with short white hair that stuck up like toothbrush bristles. 'After ten years' work, Joan found proof that dinosaurs once lived in New Zealand.'

'Digging up dinosaurs sounds an expensive business,' Plum said.

'No, you don't need to spend much. We live very quietly on our national superannuation. But I do love lecturing abroad: there aren't many people in New Zealand who are interested in vertebrate palaeontology.'

The over-tanned man laughed, then turned to Plum. 'You don't remember me, do you? We met ten years ago, at your first West End show in 1982. I'm a dealer – Otto Talbot – and I came with Duggie Boman. You looked a lot more nervous then than you do today.'

* * * *

After hanging and rearranging paintings until three in the morning, Plum and Breeze had been exhausted. That evening, as they dressed they had squabbled over Lulu. Breeze, who suspected she hadn't kicked her habit, had not wanted to invite her.

'Don't be daft! Lulu couldn't have done that art admin course and got the promotional job in Birmingham if she hadn't been clean,' Plum cried. 'Anyway, I've already invited her, so *shut up*! There's no point arguing with me!' Nervous, she spilled her perfume. 'Lulu *will* be there and she *won't* let me down . . . Oh, Breeze, I know I smell like a brothel, but how do I look?'

She was having a last-minute attack of outfit-doubt. Christina, the fashion consultant, had taken her to Swanky Modes in Camden, where they had purchased a shocking pink *bustier*, tangerine hot pants, canary-yellow tights and cochineal Carmen Miranda shoes.

'You look wonderful.' Breeze sounded a bit too dutiful, so Plum rushed down to the hall, where her sons were waiting. Anxious for reassurance, she clattered down the stairs, crying, 'How do I look, boys?'

Toby and Max stared up.

Eventually, little Max said, 'You don't look like my mum, you look like a war . . . well, wars is how they spell them, Toby, how was I to know? . . . Well, you *did* ask, Mum! . . . You teach us to tell the troof, then you cry when we do . . .'

Plum burst into tears and dashed upstairs to change into something safer.

Breeze tried to explain to the two boys why their mother was upset. '*You've* both tried to look smart tonight, for Mum's opening, haven't you?'

Both boys nodded; they loved their outfits. Ten-year-old Toby looked like a miniature thug in zipped black leathers from the Great Portland Street motorbike shop; eight-year-old Max wore a khaki tunic and jodhpurs from Laurence Corner, the army surplus shop, where Plum bought the flying suits that she wore to paint.

'Mummy tried to look special,' Breeze explained. 'I think she looked terrific, but she won't listen to me now. When a woman's dressed to go out and asks, "How do I look?" you must *always* say wonderful!'

'You look wonderful,' the brothers dutifully chorused, when Plum appeared in a relatively safe tan leather battledress top and mini-skirt, with black stockings and pumps.

* * * *

Breeze had carefully lobbied all the important critics in advance of the opening, and Plum's paintings, mostly six-footers or bigger, were an immediate success. Above the approving buzz, Plum heard the harsh voice of a man who was clearly deaf but too vain to wear a hearing aid. He sat in an armchair that had been dragged to the middle of the gallery, where it was in everyone's way. His well-tailored, pale grey suit could not disguise his elephantine bulk.

The man jabbed his walking stick at Plum's favourite canvas. 'I'll buy the one Otto Talbot likes. What do you think of that one, Otto?' He jabbed his stick down on the foot of the harassed, amiable young man at his side. 'Charles! Hand me my other spectacles – these blasted things are making my eyes water! Don't tell me that you *haven't brought* my other spectacles! Check I'm getting my usual discount, Charles! And then tell Stanley to bring the car round in twenty minutes.'

'Twenty-five per cent museum discount and worth it,' Breeze muttered to Plum. 'That's Douglas Boman. Come and meet him.'

Plum shivered. Douglas Boman's affability to the fawning crowd around him could not conceal his air of menace: she sensed a bully's brutality as she watched him lean over and jab his elbow into the ribs of his young male companion, who was frantically searching his pockets for the missing spectacles.

Plum stared again at the grey strands slicked across a mottled bald head, at the pendulous grey cheeks on either side of the wet red mouth. So that odious creature was the world-renowned art critic: that unpleasant-looking man, with eyes like slimy oysters behind those pebble-thick lenses . . . *that* was one of the best Eyes of the twentieth century.

Like everyone in the art world, Plum knew that in the early thirties, when he was twenty-one, Douglas Boman had inherited a modest some of money from an aunt, with which he had purchased paintings from artists in Paris whom he knew personally: Picasso,

Matisse, Braque, Kandinsky, Léger, Gris. The Boman collection was equalled only by a few of the world's best museums. Since then, Douglas Boman was also known for his insolent tongue, and the vituperative letters he wrote to editors, writers and scholars who criticized the Cubist exhibitions that he organized all over the world.

'Who's his boy-friend?' Plum whispered to Breeze, looking at the harassed young man who had just been poked in the thigh and told to get a move on.

'That's his only son, Charley,' Breeze said. 'Also his unpaid assistant. Charley's a saint and a really nice guy, although he must be pretty weak, or he wouldn't allow himself to be so hen-pecked. Of course Charley knows he'll be a very *rich* saint, when his dad dies. I'll sneak the poor bugger away, while you charm Douglas.'

'Take Charley over to meet Jenny,' Plum suggested, as she switched on her smile and stepped forward.

The man with the white toothbrush-bristle hair kissed her hand; surreptitiously, Plum wiped it on her skirt. Later, Breeze had told her that Otto Talbot was Douglas Boman's lover.

᠅   ᠅   ᠅   ᠅

Lady Binger's meal was unexpected: on such a hot day Plum had hoped for local Sydney specialities, oysters and local fish. Instead, an over-cooked joint of beef and boiled vegetables followed by trifle reminded Plum of the traditional British roast that her mum had served on Sunday for nearly forty years.

After the meal, Lady Binger accompanied her guests on a tour of the dark and over-furnished house. She gave a more or less continuous guide-book recital about the elaborately framed paintings, which varied in size as much as in quality. All were flower pictures and many were beautiful.

Plum particularly liked a picture that faced the top of the stairs, a pastel by Odilon Redon, of a young girl in an orchard of apple blossom. Another good pastel, a Fantin-Latour sketch of yellow roses, hung in Lady Binger's bedroom, and in her boudoir hung a beautiful little Israel Isaacs basket of cornflowers.

'I found her that one,' Otto Talbot murmured to Plum.

Two seventeenth-century Dutch paintings hung in Sir Eric's study. 'Hendrick de Fromantiou,' Lady Binger announced. 'Note the monogram HDF. A passion-flower, tulips and African marigolds.'

Plum edged through the little group to get as close as she could to the first painting, which was exquisite, and undoubtedly genuine. Plum told herself that she shouldn't feel disappointed because her hostess hadn't been landed with a dud.

'These pictures are heavily symbolic, you know,' murmured Otto Talbot in his pedantic voice. 'That one offers a choice between virtue and vice, which is that maggot wriggling from the apple.'

Plum didn't like the man, there was something creepy about his voice: camp and silky, but also threatening, as he whispered, 'They're worth a bloody fortune.'

'Some of them,' Plum corrected as the little group moved before the final picture, a rectangular painting that measured about fifteen inches wide. In a pale brown vase, drooped a large tulip, with petals of strong yellow, edged with a salmon hue. It was surrounded by smaller tulips and other flowers – a daffodil, a few snowdrops, some sprigs of rosemary and forget-me-not. In the bottom left-hand corner, just above a fallen flower petal, was a date – 1629 – and a monogram: a Y that contained an A and a B – Ambrosius Bosschaert the Younger. Just above the monogram, a housefly crawled towards a large yellow caterpillar.

Plum stared, then caught her breath. She gazed in concentration, she subdued her other senses, yielding to her eye's decision.

'That caterpillar represents the earthly life of man,' Otto Talbot murmured, from behind Plum. 'You see, it's burdened with sin but destined to soar to Heaven, transformed into a butterfly.'

Plum was too excited to be irritated by Otto Talbot. Because all the senses that she used to judge a painting told Plum that she was staring at another fake.

＊　＊　＊　＊

All thought of a walk forgotten, Plum lingered after the other guests departed. She then told Lady Binger that she was working with an art historian on a history of Dutch flower painting, and would like to show her collaborator photographs of the two paintings in the Binger collection.

Lady Binger looked pleased, then asked if Plum would like to see the provenances. Plum couldn't believe her luck.

Lady Binger then caught her off-guard by asking the name of her fellow author, and the name of the publisher.

'I'm working with Professor Dame Enid Soames of the Courtauld,' Plum said firmly, hoping that her hostess wouldn't check. 'We have chosen Thames & Hudson as publishers.'

Looking even more pleased, Lady Binger ushered Plum into her gloomy, stuffy study, produced two beige files, and left Plum alone to read the provenances.

Plum looked perfunctorily at the de Fromantiou, then opened the other file. The Ambrosius Bosschaert the Younger had been purchased in 1988 – from Forrestière on the Avenue Matignon, just off the Faubourg St-Honoré, the smart Parisian gallery equivalent of Bond Street in London, or 57th and Madison in New York. Nothing in the provenance was dated later than 1962 – a convenient gap, as the most recent years were always the easiest ones to check on.

Plum turned to the list of exhibitions in which the picture had supposedly been shown. Eugene Bartot Gallery, London 1951. Dutch and Flemish Masters, Utrecht 1960, no.18 in the catalogue. Lorenz Gallery, Amsterdam 1964, no.7 in the catalogue. The painting had been mentioned in Sondheim's *Major Trends in Dutch Flower Painting*, pub. 1962, page 9.

Plum knew that the Bartot Gallery had closed at least thirty years beforehand. Sondheim's book – if it ever existed – was probably out of print, which is why the forger would have chosen it.

Now that she had more information, Plum tried to think of connecting links, as Stephanie had advised. The link between Suzannah's and Cynthia's paintings was Maltby's Gallery in Bond Street, London, from which they had both been purchased. Suzannah's picture had been acquired by Maltby's from an anonymous owner and had no previous sale documentation. Cynthia's picture came from an auction-house in Brighton – Borden & Plow – who had sold it on behalf of an anonymous owner, and there was no sale documentation prior to that.

The painting in the Schneider Gallery on 57th Street had been acquired from a French auction-house, Lévi-Fontaine, and likewise had little documentation, apart from a Belgian bill of sale in 1911. The connection between Artur Schneider's fake and that of Lady Binger was that they both came from Paris: a weak link.

Lady Binger reappeared. 'Otto Talbot's offered you a lift back to the Regent. And it's time for my afternoon rest . . .'

Plum closed the file. 'Would you mind if I had these copied?'

'Oh, I expect we've got copies in the archives. I'll ask the book-keeper to send you a set tomorrow.'

'Do you ever have any shipping problems?' Plum asked. 'One of my paintings was damaged on the journey here.'

'Sir Eric always used Colombe – in Paris – to ship our stuff from Europe, so I still do. Never had a moment's trouble. You might try them.'

☆　☆　☆　☆

Otto Talbot drove a black Jaguar Sovereign, a local status symbol which cost up to three times more in Australia than it did in Britain.

'Air-conditioning too much for you?' Otto Talbot adjusted it. They drove in silence until he said pointedly, 'You don't want to upset the old girl. What's the point? She's happy enough with her ragbag.'

'I agree they're ill-assorted, but some of her pictures are very good.'

'Old Bingo wants to think they're *all* good. I saw you giving that Ambrosius a look: you've got a good eye.' He turned momentarily to Plum. 'I expect you want to keep it.'

'*What do you mean?*' Immediately, Plum felt as she had done when the anonymous letter had arrived in New York: as if she had suddenly found herself alone, standing on the edge of a black chasm.

'I only mean that to keep a good eye takes constant practice, effort and discernment, my dear,' said the silky voice. 'We all have to take care of what we've got, don't we?'

'Did Lady Binger buy that Ambrosius from you?'

'No. But she buys a lot through me and I don't want her upset.' Otto Talbot's voice suddenly sounded almost dictatorial. As the Jaguar swung into the busy forecourt of the Regent, he glanced sideways at Plum. 'So don't do anything I wouldn't do.'

Plum shivered again. This man was in the business, and his reasons for not wanting her to upset any applecarts were the same as those of Breeze: they both sold apples. Nevertheless, there had been something chilling about that short trip in the Jaguar which had nothing to do with the air-conditioning.

Oh, the hell with Otto Talbot, she wasn't going to let him intimidate her. In fact . . . Plum marched across the Regent's elegant marble hall to the concierge and asked him to cancel her booking to London and rebook a flight via Paris.

CHAPTER THIRTEEN

Plum telephoned Lulu from the hotel lobby, but there was no reply. Why not, Plum anxiously wondered: it was three o'clock in the morning in London, and Lulu had a phone by her bed. Feeling drained after the formal luncheon and uneasy after her ride in Otto's Jaguar, she decided to go for a walk.

In Bridge Street, she stopped before the plate-glass window of an art gallery; inside, a woman wearing raw silk pants knelt to pull animal carvings from a packing case. Behind her hung a big, wonderful picture, an abstract of yellow and pink dots. The painting had lightness, joy, and carefree charm, but also assurance and authority. Plum could see that the design incorporated another hidden pattern beneath, which told a secret story; she felt this painting had been destined for her, was sending her some message. She pushed open the door.

'That's by Emily Kngwarreye. She's eighty years old and she only started to paint three years ago.' The woman in raw silk pants sat back on her heels. 'It's an aerial view of the desert in the Dream Time, when the Aboriginals believe Australia was created.'

'What's the underpainting?'

'Ah, you can see the songlines. They're a network of invisible paths that cover this country. Each path has a secret, sacred song which the Aboriginals sing when they walk to honour their ancestors and the land.' She stood and dusted her knees. 'I can't tell you more. You and I will never know what that painting's about.'

'I can see it was painted by a happy person. How much is it?'

'Ten thousand dollars.' The woman laughed. 'A lot of whites

who sneer at illiterate Aboriginals get mad as hell when they hear what museums are willing to pay for their paintings.'

'I'll buy it.' Plum knew that Breeze would have haggled over the price. 'And I'd like to meet the painter.'

'Not possible. Emily lives at Utopia, in the Northern Reservation.'

'I don't mind flying to the Northern Reservation.'

'You wouldn't be allowed in. The point of a reservation is to keep everyone out of it, so the Aboriginals can live as they lived before the whites arrived. They hunt, fish or gather food, then they paint, carve, or weave. And in the evenings they sing and dance.'

Well, thought Plum, hasn't Emily got the perfect life?

* * * *

With relief, Plum turned into the cool viridian Botanical Gardens. She took off her shoes and wandered among the subtropical trees and foliage: jade, malachite and sharp parrot-greens. Perhaps gamboge, and maybe a dash of sharp citrine to counter the green-gold? . . . But Plum's thoughts kept returning to Lulu: she couldn't help worrying about her.

* * * *

In 1984, shortly after Plum and Breeze had decided they might as well get married, Plum answered the doorbell and saw Lulu weeping on the doorstep. She grabbed a box of tissues, and hurried her to the elevator.

In Plum's studio mirror, Lulu peered at her dirty, dishevelled hair and white, blotchy face. 'The wreck of the Lulu,' she said. 'Coke certainly doesn't do much for the complexion.'

'How did it happen, Lulu?'

'I keep asking myself.' Lulu's voice wobbled, and she bit her underlip. 'At first things went well in Birmingham, but one day another girl told me that I hadn't a hope of promotion in art admin. You don't get to be Director of the Tate if you weren't at Oxford with the in-crowd and you don't even *hear* about the best jobs until they're taken.'

'But when I visited, everyone seemed to think you were a bright young newcomer with the energy to make things happen.'

'Oh yes, as a job it was exciting and I loved it.' Still staring at her ghost-white face in the mirror, Lulu started to cry. 'Then one day the Nigerians turned up at a show I'd organized; they'd brought a little coke.' She turned from the mirror. 'I was helpless, Plum. I knew it'd wreck my life again . . . but *I simply wasn't able to say no* . . . So one thing led to another and this morning – I was fired.'

Lulu looked again at her drooping reflection, at the crumpled, black coat covered in cat hairs. 'On the train to London all I could think was: *I've wasted nine years!* You're successful, Plum, and even Jenny's recognized as a painter – but *I'm nothing*! Where did my life go? How did I let it happen, Plum?'

This time, it took six months to get Lulu clean. Reluctantly, her parents refused her an allowance, hoping that this would bring her home where they could keep a careful eye on her. That was exactly what Lulu didn't want. Defiantly, she temped in assorted offices, served behind the counter at a fried chicken takeaway, and took other part-time, dead-end jobs. Finally she found a job that she enjoyed, with an employment agent's graphologist who checked the handwriting of all job applicants. But this was only a four-month stint while the regular secretary was away on maternity leave.

* * * *

Within a year of Plum's second wedding, Jim also remarried. His new wife was Sally, an eighteen-year-old student whom he described to Plum as a 'real woman'.

'So what are you? A chimpanzee?' Jenny had met Sally at a Portsmouth party. 'Jim wouldn't know what to do with a real woman. He'd be scared. Jim prefers Sally's permanent-little-girl act. She's small and unthreatening, with earnest, brown eyes and an anxious-to-please expression, like you used to have.'

'Jenny darling, you always say exactly what I want to hear.'

* * * *

Unfortunately, no matter how prettily Plum wheedled, Breeze refused to exhibit Jenny's work; neither would he help Jenny to get a show at some other gallery. He would not play the Gallery Game for Jenny. 'I'm glad Jenny's just started to sell a few,' he told Plum one night as he unbuttoned his shirt. 'But she'll never get good reviews and I'm *not* going to damage my professional reputation for her.'

Plum leaned back against antique French embroidered pillows and said persuasively, 'How could that possibly damage your . . .'

Breeze pulled off his shirt. 'You know as well as I do that Jenny's work is technically excellent, but it's derivative. Those sombre landscapes look like dirty, lumpy patchwork quilts, and the grey-faced, cardboard people she paints can't eat or shit, let alone love or hate: like Jenny, they're tight and over-anxious. Apart from that, she's the hottest thing since Botticelli.'

'Jenny works hard,' Plum pleaded. 'She has determination. You've told me often enough that talent needs determination to make success possible.'

'Yes, but determination without talent isn't enough in the long run.' Breeze threw his trousers on a chair.

'*Why* must you be so hard on her?'

'It took me two years of art school to realize I had everything going for me – except enough talent. So I decided on a peripheral career in the art world and now I'm a happy dealer instead of a resentful second-rate painter. Jenny should also do something peripheral. In the spotlight at the top isn't the only place that's fun.' He pulled off his underpants and jumped into bed.

* * * *

Lulu wobbled in and out of jobs and rehab clinics for two years, then at a 1986 Christmas party she met Ben. Skinny and dark, he was sardonically irresistible and they fell in love at first sight. 'He's a *wonderful* lover,' Lulu reported to Plum. 'I didn't have to train him.'

Ben finally got Lulu off drugs. Plum and Jenny wondered whether he had ever had a similar problem, as he seemed so knowledgeable. He encouraged Lulu to dump her job typing invoices in a fish cannery and start to paint. Ben earned good money as a pop-music recording engineer, so he would support her. He just wanted Lulu to be happy.

A year later, just before Lulu's thirty-first birthday, they were married. Her parents cried with happiness and relief as they waved them off on honeymoon to Jamaica. Ben was ten years older than Lulu, he had a steady job, he was even Jewish. Wolf was born five months later.

* * * *

The following year, it looked as if wedding bells were also about to ring for Jenny. She and Charley Hawtrey-Jones were having a passionate affair, which had to be concealed from Charley's father; it was London's best-kept secret. Everyone wondered why it hadn't happened before, for the two seemed ideally suited; Charley couldn't keep his hands off Jenny's Junoesque proportions and he seemed actually to enjoy her possessiveness: it decreased his low self-esteem. They seemed set on a steady course for the Register Office, until the summer of 1988, when Charley's father discovered one of Jenny's letters in the pocket of Charley's raincoat. After his father had roared every threat and jabbed every guilt button, Charley finally told Jenny he could no longer see her. It was not that Charley's father disapproved of Jenny, but that he had forced Charley to promise not to marry until after his father's death.

'*Forced?* You mean *bribed*,' Jenny said bitterly.

She was hurt, disappointed and disillusioned. For two years she was dejected and withdrawn. Plum and Lulu tried unsuccessfully to draw Jenny into their own lives, but their married happiness only emphasized Jenny's bleak loneliness. Once again she embarked on a series of high-tension, short-lived love affairs.

Then, in 1990, Jenny's grandmother died and left her enough money to purchase a sunny flat in an Edwardian house overlooking a garden square in Notting Hill. Once settled, Jenny became more cheerful. She now had a pretty home, although no man to share it with.

* * * *

Walking back to her hotel in the hot and humid Sydney afternoon, Plum decided that if she couldn't get Lulu by telephone, she would call Jenny, who would check on her.

At the Regent, another envelope awaited Plum. Plum tore it open, expecting a message from Lulu. But the call had been from her mother.

Plum raced to the elevator. Why should her mother telephone at five in the morning, British time? That could surely mean only one thing? *Toby or Max had had an accident!*

As she waited impatiently for the elevator, Plum remembered other accidents. When Toby fell off a ski-hoist and broke his collar bone; when Max nearly drowned in the Swiss Cottage swimming pool; when Toby asked for icing sugar and then blew up the kitchen; when Max fell from a first-floor window. The older they became, the worse the accidents. Her mother said it was the same with all children. You worried – they didn't: this was the invisible umbilical cord that tied you both for ever.

As she reached her door, Plum fumbled with shaking hands for her key, then dropped it. Then she jammed the key in the lock and couldn't turn it. Eventually, her hands still trembling, Plum punched her mother's Portsmouth number and counted the rings. Brrr . . . Brrr . . . Perhaps her mother had telephoned from somewhere else? *Some hospital?*

Plum was just about to ring off and phone the Portsmouth police when her mother answered. 'You caught me in the lav, dear, what's the matter? . . . Oh, so I did . . . No, nothing's happened to the boys . . . I had a touch of indigestion and couldn't sleep, and I knew it was daytime in Australia, so I gave the operator your card number, like you told me. I thought I'd give you a little surprise . . . No, dear, it *wasn't* only that . . . I wanted to tell you Jim's wife had another little girl yesterday morning, a sister for Melody and Harmony. Six pounds and both doing fine. Isn't that nice?'

Mrs Phillips was careful to keep in touch with Jim, the father of her grandchildren. Keeping in touch was now the done thing, she maintained. Lord Snowdon and Princess Margaret were divorced, but the Queen always included him at family functions; Princess Margaret just had to grin and bear it. So Mrs Phillips followed the royal example and had regular chats with Jim, not knowing that he crossly complained to Plum that her bloody mother couldn't keep off the phone.

'What name has Jim chosen for this one?' Plum said acidly. 'Rhapsody? Synthesis?'

'Norma. It would be nice if the boys sent flowers to their little half-sister. Jim would appreciate the thought.'

Plum dutifully scribbled the address of the hospital. She would order a garish arrangement: salmon pink gladioli with crimson roses and yellow lilies. Jim would appreciate the thought.

She then had a more constructive thought. 'Mum, is Aunt Harriet still in Paris? . . . Have you got her phone number?'

CHAPTER FOURTEEN

Saturday, 18 January 1992

PARIS WAS freezing. Plum climbed into an airport cab that smelt of unwashed armpits, Gauloises and Chanel No. 5; she touched the metal handle of the cab and her fingers stuck to it. Shivering, she decided to buy warm clothes. Thinking she wouldn't need it, Breeze had taken her suitcase of winter clothes back from New York to Britain.

Muffled in dark clothes, pedestrians hurried through the snowy streets of Paris. Plum decided that when she painted Paris, she'd do it in grey: dove breast to charcoal, plus the pale garter-blue of this sky and maybe gas-jet lavender with mauve and El Greco dark purples.

She spotted a boutique, told the cab to wait, and rushed inside, where she bought a black ankle-length Andalusian shepherd's cloak and two pairs of leggings with matching sweaters, one in cypress green and one in amethyst. She wriggled into the amethyst outfit, then directed the taxi to the Left Bank.

Aunt Harriet lived in a crumbling building off the Rue de l'Université, in two rooms at the top of a black curlicued central staircase which looked as if it were about to collapse.

Before Plum reached the top floor, a big woman with dark hair cut like a dishmop leaned over the stairs and shouted, 'Hi, Plum, you're the only one of my family who doesn't behave as if I've nicked the baby's piggy bank.' Aunt Harriet lifted her long purple skirt and clattered down the stairs. Her square, capable hands grabbed the largest suitcase.

'Why this unexpected visit? Have *you* run away as well?' Leading the way, Aunt Harriet twisted her long neck to look back; amused brown eyes looked down at Plum. 'Hope you don't mind sleeping on a camp bed in the kitchen.'

The small overheated apartment was piled with books. 'I think the radiators are about to explode, the concierge can't turn them down,' said Aunt Harriet. 'You haven't been here since I got this place, have you? ... I couldn't cook in a cupboard, so I turned the sitting-room into a kitchen: now that I'm not obliged to do it three times a day, endlessly, I quite enjoy cooking ... I've made you a *cassoulet toulousaine*, the ideal dish on a cold day ... You'd better put your suitcases under my bed, there's no space anywhere else ... The bedroom was so small, I turned it into a green-striped tent ... that's a genuine Napoleonic campaign bed, I got it at the flea market.'

'A single bed?'

'Yes. To make my intentions clear. No Frenchman could endure making love in a single bed: they're very spoiled.'

Exhausted after her long flight, Plum ate three portions of cassoulet – Aunt Harriet fished out extra pieces of goose and sausage for her – then fell asleep at the table. Her aunt steered her to the Napoleonic bed.

Sunday, 19 January 1992

Finding herself alone when she woke, Plum made herself a cup of tea and watched the blue-hued dusk settle over a classic chimney-pots view of Paris.

Aunt Harriet returned with a bag of roasted chestnuts, which she offered to Plum. 'You used to love these when you were little. Who'd have thought that little creature would turn out to be a successful painter ... D'you remember that nasty little Scottie dog you carved in soap? D'you remember that box of paints I gave you for – was it your tenth birthday?' Aunt Harriet had always egged her on: Plum remembered the crossbow, the frilly bra and other birthday gifts considered unsuitable for a young girl. Aunt Harriet and Plum were both outsiders from the same family; Aunt Harriet was as comforting as her mother but encouraged Plum in a way that her mum could not.

Aunt Harriet poured two generous glasses of red wine, offered one to Plum and peered at the hand that took it. 'That ring, Plum, is it real?'

'Don't I look the sort of person who'd own a real diamond ring, Aunt Harriet?'

'Not such a dull one. I expect someone gave it to you.' Aunt Harriet lit a pungent Gitane and inhaled with sensual relish. 'Diamonds aren't a girl's best friend – they're a *man's* best friend: they get men off the hook, and keep their women quiet.' She propped her elbows on the wooden kitchen table. 'You don't sound very happy, dear girl, despite all this success. So perhaps you'd better tell me why you've come.'

Plum described her pursuit of the fake paintings. Aunt Harriet blew a rather unsuccessful smoke ring, which wobbled up to the ceiling.

'But why stay here, Plum, instead of the Lancaster? Isn't that where you usually stay?'

'Yes, Breeze likes it.' The Hotel Lancaster was a small version of the London Connaught. Artists didn't feel as uneasy there as they might in the splendour of the Ritz, or the opulent George V.

'How *is* Breeze?' Aunt Harriet asked cautiously.

Plum laughed. 'I'm very busy and he's very busy. I stay at home while he rushes all over the world – New York, Cologne, Milan, Zurich, Madrid – although he tries not to be in more than two time zones a week. Breeze's life is his work and vice versa. He's always on the track of something or someone; he's always planning, planning, planning, or selling, selling, selling.'

'That's not a life, that's a frenzy.'

'Breeze likes excitement.'

Aunt Harriet shook her head. 'But it isn't what *you* want. Don't you talk about that?'

'We talk, but we don't say anything. That's what I wanted to discuss with you.'

Silently her aunt peeled the blackened skin from a chestnut. 'So, you're not only searching for these fake paintings?'

'No, I'm trying to work out what's wrong in my life.'

'You're too close to see what's wrong. Step back and view it from a distance.'

'How?'

'Simply decide what you like doing and what you don't – and why. Work out what it would cost you to do what you want, in terms of money, time and aggravation. Then decide whether to do it. If you don't like your life, you can always change it – although everyone thinks they can't, especially women of my generation, who only changed their life if they were forced to. *Now*, young women won't put up with what their mothers did. They've discovered that human beings always have choices, they aren't rooted to the spot.'

'I remember a line in some play: "The world was our oyster – and we chose Ruislip." I've always wondered why you chose Paris.' The family wouldn't have been so scandalized by Aunt Harriet's sudden divorce and departure had she run away to Bournemouth.

Aunt Harriet leaned back in her chair and clasped her hands behind her neck. 'My life really began in Paris, when I dumped those youthful spoon-fed ideas that hadn't worked, forgot what other people wanted me to be, and ignored all accusations of selfishness.'

'I often wonder if I'm being selfish,' Plum said, hesitantly.

'There's an easy test. If someone accuses you of being selfish and you feel guilty – then you aren't a selfish person: selfish people never feel guilty.' Aunt Harriet poured herself another glass of wine. 'I was fifty-four years old, married to a dentist, with four children and two grandchildren, but I'd never had an orgasm during intercourse. Len would never face the fact that what brought him to climax didn't bring me to climax, and one night I realized this summed up the rest of our marriage . . . Have you noticed how *controlling* some men are? Len kept *me* on a tight rein by keeping me short of cash. Have you noticed that some men might pay a woman's credit card bill or buy presents for her – but *they never give her cash*? Why not? Because cash is power. And what is power? Getting your own way. And *that's* why men hang on to their cash.'

Aunt Harriet lit a Gitane and stared beyond the window at the indigo sky, which had a dramatic, underlit, stage quality. 'So I decided to leave Len and study French at the Sorbonne, then become a translator. I also decided to find out what really made me happy.'

'And what did?'

'The oddest things. Playing Sibelius all night. Eating chocolate cake in bed at two in the morning. Going to jazz clubs. Getting up late. Doing what the hell I wanted without having to think about anyone else. To my surprise, within a short time I felt free. Then slowly I found out . . . who I really was.' Aunt Harriet tilted her chair backwards and removed the lid from an earthenware pot on the ancient stove. 'This onion soup's almost ready.' She reached behind her to lift a cheese-grater from a hook on the blue-tiled kitchen wall. 'Pass me that cheese, it's just behind you, dear girl.'

'And have you been happy without a permanent man? Aren't you lonely?' Plum pushed the hunk of Gruyère across the scrubbed wooden table.

'Not a bit. Now that I've found myself I don't want to risk losing myself again. And I was lonely when I was married. You can feel very lonely when you're lying next to the man who's supposed to care for you but doesn't.' Briskly, Aunt Harriet rubbed the cheese against the grater. 'Before I left, I cleaned the toilets with Len's toothbrush, then replaced it in his glass. I haven't told him – yet.'

Both women laughed. For a long time, they continued to discuss the pursuit of happiness.

✳   ✳   ✳   ✳

On Monday, as was usual in France, the shops were shut. Unde- terred, Aunt Harriet took Plum window-shopping. 'The Left Bank is the area I know best,' she said. 'Like most Parisians, I don't like to wander too far from home.' She hurried Plum to Debauve et Gallais. 'That's the best chocolate shop in Paris. Every month, when I get paid, I buy a small bag of rum truffles.'

On the Boulevard St-Germain, Aunt Harriet stopped in front of Madeleine Gély and looked longingly into the crowded interior. 'This tiny place sells the best umbrellas in the world. See that emerald one with the carved parrot head? And the adorable blue-striped one with the carved cat head? They all cost a king's ransom.'

Not all the shops were shut. At Hédiard, the speciality grocer, Aunt Harriet sniffed appreciatively. 'This place still smells like a grocer: supermarkets smell of nothing.'

Plum purchased everything recommended by Aunt Harriet, including a kilo of chocolate coffee beans, the *specialité de la maison*.

'Plum, how are you going to take all that back by air? . . . Oh, it's for *me*? . . . Dear child, you are so generous.'

* * * *

On Tuesday morning at ten o'clock, Plum, wrapped in her black cloak, shivered before the window of Forrestière in the Avenue Matignon. Inside, a young ginger-haired assistant struggled with the lock mechanism. He shrugged his shoulders with a look of humorous despair – then suddenly the lock yielded.

Most of the sculpture and paintings in the art gallery were late nineteenth-century. Clearly the prize of the collection was a Berthe Morisot self-portrait: under a wide-brimmed straw hat trimmed with violets, the lively young woman's face was simultaneously wistful and impudent. Good, flashy brushwork on the high, lace collar, Plum thought.

As she studied the picture, a thin, dark man in a well-tailored navy suit silently appeared at her side. He might have been Levantine or Greek; his face was lean and sharp, his hair silver grey, and his eyes shone black as olives.

'Yes?' the man asked haughtily in English.

Plum, who had been practising a few French phrases, felt unreasonably irritated. Did she have a sign on her back? Furthermore, he seemed to know before she opened her mouth that she was not here to buy.

Flustered, she said, 'I've come for information. An Australian friend, Lady Binger . . . er . . . sent me here.'

'We know Lady Binger. How can we help you?'

'Do you recall the flower painting by Ambrosius Bosschaert the Younger that you sold her in 1988?'

'I remember it well. My colleague Monsieur Maurice handled the sale.'

Plum suddenly lost her nerve, and told the truth. 'I'd like to know where you bought it,' she said with a nervous smile. 'Lady Binger gave me a copy of the provenance – see, I have it with me. But that information isn't in it.'

Suddenly the temperature inside the gallery seemed lower than that of the street outside. In a glacial voice, the man said, 'It is our policy to protect our clients at all times – both those who buy and those who sell. So we find it best to divulge no information.'

'That policy also protects *you*,' Plum pointed out. She knew that in the event of any trouble about a painting, a gallery could stop inquiries by saying anonymity was necessary to protect the client. And often it was. Galleries purchased important paintings from each other, from private dealers or at auctions; but sometimes they bought from collectors who wanted to avoid publicity and perhaps the consequent attention of the tax authorities, or some other legal confiscator. An anonymous client – noted as 'private collection' or 'private owner' – made it difficult to trace the recent history of a painting – although the more distant history might be impeccably clear in the provenance.

The shiny black eyes stared coldly at Plum. 'And why do you need this information?'

'I need to check the provenance.'

'Madame, at Forrestière we take weeks – sometimes months – to evaluate our paintings before buying them.' His chill was increasing every minute.

Plum nodded. She knew that a seller was often asked to leave a work of art with a reputable dealer, so that he could check the painting and its history. If a dealer doubted authenticity, he checked with a museum or sent a colour transparency of the painting with its history to a recognized expert on the artist.

Two hundred years ago, museums did not exist, and neither did art dealers. People bought their pictures directly from a painter or an owner, and they often listed their new acquisitions in a catalogue or in their normal household inventory, which included linen, glass and furniture. So the art descriptions were often sketchy and inaccurate, although such references are often the only old ones available.

But searching through such old records can take months; consequently, it is tempting for a dealer to take a risk if a painting seems a bargain – and is about to be offered to a rival.

'Why do you need to check our evaluation, Madame?'

'Because I think that painting may be wrong.' She might as well be hung for a sheep as a lamb.

The olive eyes flashed. 'At Forrestière we do not handle wrong paintings. Henri, please show this lady *out!*'

Again, the ginger-haired lad struggled with the mechanism which unlocked the plate-glass door. Again, there was a struggle. The lad apologized. Plum smiled. '*Pas de problème.*'

As the lock eventually turned, the lad turned his back to the gallery and muttered, 'Try Monfumat in the Rue Jacob.'

*   *   *   *

A gusty wind blew sparse snow across the classical grey buildings; it swirled beneath Plum's cloak and chilled her within seconds as she turned the corner into the Rue Faubourg St-Honoré. Hurrying past beguiling clothes shops and fur-coated, richly scented shoppers, she wondered whether all the cab drivers had emigrated. Then she stopped.

Immediately in front of her a blonde woman stepped out of Hermès. She wore an ankle-length crimson coat with matching boots and sable-edged gauntlet gloves. She was preceded by a uniformed commissionaire and followed by two sales assistants loaded with expensively wrapped packages, which were swiftly stowed by the chauffeur in the waiting limousine.

Plum hurriedly pulled up her cloak so it covered the lower part of her face. Swiftly she turned away, seemingly engrossed by a window display of insanely expensive smoking accessories. The last person Plum wanted to meet in Paris was Suzannah Marsh.

*   *   *   *

The Rue Jacob, which was on Plum's route back to the Rue de l'Université, contained many chic antique shops such as Monfumat.

An old-fashioned shop bell rang as Plum entered. The interior of the small shop smelled of beeswax. From the dark interior hurried a tall, fair young salesman with the fashionable bull neck of one who did weight-training. He, too, wore an expensive navy double-breasted suit: it must have passed some reassuring-to-customers test, Plum thought, as she smiled. 'I hope you speak a little English . . . Good . . . I'm trade. Here's my card.' She handed him a Russell Gallery card. 'I like that jug in your window – the one with the man sitting astride. What's the price?'

'That is a Jacqueline – it dates from the Revolution. This man is a revolutionary – see his tricolour cap? Quite rare. Two thousand francs. And the trade discount – ten percentage.' As he pushed a limp blond lock of hair away from his good-humoured face, Plum imagined him being told by his mother to dance with the wallflowers.

'I am used to a dealer's discount of twenty-five per cent.'

'Then we say fifteen percentage?'

Plum nodded. As the young man removed the jug from the window and wrapped it, they chatted with the bright smiles that show goodwill despite language problems.

Having established a cordial atmosphere, Plum lied winningly. 'There is also another matter. An English friend – an art historian, Professor Enid Soames – asked me to show you this transparency and check that you supplied the painting to Forrestière – it's now the property of an Australian. Your name is mentioned, but misspelt, in the provenance.'

The young man held Lady Binger's transparency before a table lamp. He looked uncertain. 'It is possible. Monsieur Monfumat himself is at the skiing in these moments . . . If you will return to here after the lunch, it will be possible to inquire of Simon, who occupies himself of the pictures.'

'I'm leaving Paris after lunch. So I'd be grateful if you'd look in your records *now*.' Plum also produced the Artur Schneider transparency. 'This is the other picture that the Professor wished to confirm came from you.'

'You have the dates of acquisition? . . . I can help you perhaps . . .'

It was nearly an hour, close to midday, before the young man found what Plum needed. He emerged from the back office with two file cards in his hand. 'It is written here,' he handed the two cards to Plum. 'You see, the Bosschaert was sold to Forrestière in March 1988. You understand it is not permitted to divulge the price . . . The van Hulsdonck was auctioned at Lévi-Fontaine in February 1990. Also, I am not permitted to relinquish the price, but an auction price is no secret. Lévi-Fontaine will tell you.'

'And where did you acquire these paintings?'

'Ah, that I am assuredly not permitted to divulge. The provider is always in confidence, you understand.'

'No matter. Professor Soames did not request such particulars.' His syntax was catching. Hurrying through a fresh dusting of snow, Plum gleefully thought, one failure, but one whopping success. Talk about linking the facts!

* * * *

After hurriedly eating a cheese omelette in Pam Pam, Plum set off for the Colombe warehouse, which was the other side of Paris, well beyond Montparnasse. The cab driver seemed uncertain of the route and stopped twice to ask.

Shortly after two o'clock, Plum arrived at the art storage and shipping firm which was housed in a large warehouse. Several grimy, slush-spattered lorries were at the loading bay; beyond a row of fork-lift trucks stood a reception hut, erected within the building. Behind it, Plum saw big, pale wooden crates, piled in orderly avenues, raying out as far as she could see.

A fat French warehouse assistant waddled out. '*Je peux vous aider?*' A grubby T-shirt stretched tightly over his big belly above sagging jeans and dirty trainers. His wild, shoulder-length dark hair was stuffed under a red baseball cap, above a luxuriant and drooping moustache; his small, dark eyes looked warily at Plum.

Plum produced Breeze's business card once more. 'Normally we use Momart for shipping, but my husband asked me to call on you to check your storage facilities.'

The fat man gave an all-purpose French shrug, with hands outspread. 'What do you want to know?' He spoke perfect English in a flat, South London accent. Seeing Plum's surprise, he gave a pleased, shy smile. 'My wife's from Lambeth.'

'I'd like to discuss prices for shipping and storage.'

'We quote per job. There's no set price for transport, although we quote set rates for storage and insurance. I can let you have a rate sheet.'

'When you collect a load that's going to – say, Australia – where is it stored?'

'Here. Unless it's Van Gogh's *Sunflowers*. An owner usually brings in an outside specialist security force for something valuable.'

'I'd like to see your crating facilities.'

Plum could hear the whine of the circular saw long before they reached the crate room, which smelled agreeably of fresh sawdust. A staple gun started to bang monotonously as she asked, 'When a valuable painting is delivered to you – what happens to it?'

'We have a careful security routine. Obviously I can't give you details, but a valuable painting is overseen from the moment it gets here until the moment it leaves. That painting will never be alone with anyone – it's always accompanied by its security nursemaid – and each department it goes into has to give a receipt for it. The security man has his receipts checked before he's allowed to leave the building.'

'And at night?'

'We have the usual professional security, with dogs, telephone checks throughout the night, direct line alarm to the *gendarmerie*, plus smoke and water detectors.'

'There's no possibility that a painting might be . . . substituted . . . for another?'

'Not a chance. The boss uses ex-police security consultants. This isn't an amateur outfit.'

That was what Plum had come to check. She continued to behave like a potential client for twenty minutes, then thanked her escort.

'By the way, I like your stuff,' he replied. 'Saw some in your London gallery last year. Good luck at the Biennale.'

Plum smiled as she stepped out into the pale, wintery light of the street. As she stood, blinking in the stronger light of day, a familiar face hurried past her. She immediately recognized the slightly chubby face, the fine blond hair that was just starting to recede in a widow's peak. She knew those dark grey eyes behind rimless glasses and the cheerful, about-to-smile expression.

Plum turned and shouted, '*Leo!*'

As Leo often did, the man wore a navy pea jacket, jeans and sneakers: one of his socks was electric green and the other dayglo pink. He did not stop, but seemed to be heading for the reception area. Plum stared, then hurried after him, certain she had not been mistaken. Clearly, Leo had been lost in thought, and hadn't heard her call to him.

The man dodged behind a big dirty red truck with British number plates. Plum heard the van's engine wrenched into life.

Suddenly suspicious, Plum stopped abruptly and fumbled in her tote bag for pen and paper. The bag slipped, and fell to the ground.

'The Jacqueline!' Her gift for Breeze was Plum's first thought. Momentarily distracted, she hardly dared hope it had survived its fall, but it had been carefully packed, and the box seemed undamaged. She lifted her head and crossly watched the dirty red truck lumber out of the parking bay, now too distant for her to read the number plate. She ran towards the door of the reception hut. But her fan had left.

Plum spoke slowly in French to the two clerks in the office. 'Who was the driver of that red van? The English one?'

'Don't know,' one of them muttered. 'First time we've seen him.'

Vexed with herself, Plum hailed a cab and directed it to the umbrella shop in the Rue du Bac, where she bought a Chinese yellow umbrella with a fuchsia lizard handle for Aunt Harriet. Why had Leo avoided her? Why did he have the keys of that shabby red truck? And why was a British design journalist behaving so furtively in a Paris art shipper's warehouse?

CHAPTER FIFTEEN

Thursday, 23 January 1992

BREEZE flung open the white front door as the taxi stopped in Chester Terrace. 'Where the hell have you been? I've been worried sick.' Glaring, he stood on the white marble steps, flanked by conical clipped yews in terracotta pots.

'Can't you wait until I've paid the cab?' Plum counted out the notes. 'Didn't you get my fax?'

'Your fax simply said, "Stopping in Paris for a few days." You didn't say *why*. You hadn't booked in at the Lancaster. For all I knew you were bonking yourself silly with some international playboy you met on the plane.'

'No such luck. I stopped off to see Aunt Harriet.' In Paris, Plum had felt defiantly disobedient. Playing truant from school – which she had never done – must feel like this: challenging authority, wicked, thrilling, free.

'Why this sudden urge to see your bloody aunt, when she's been in bloody Paris for three bloody years?' With ill grace, Breeze picked up the suitcases. 'I bet that's not the only reason you stopped in Paris!'

'It's five years since I've been there,' Plum said winningly. 'I'd forgotten what a magical city it is. The fountains in the Place de la Concorde were frozen; the Tuileries gardens were frosted with snow: I felt as if I were in a Hans Andersen fairy tale.'

'Spare me the travelogue. I'm pissed off and you can't charm me out of it!' Breeze dumped the suitcases on the white marble floor and slammed the front door. 'Okay, so I didn't really think you were screwing around – I'd have heard quick enough . . .' Exasperated, he burst out, 'It was something to do with Suzannah's fake flower painting, wasn't it?'

Plum hesitated.

'You stupid bitch!' Breeze roared. 'Don't you realize it takes only twenty-four hours for gossip to reach London from Australia? You know what a small world the art business is! Otto Oz was on the phone before you'd caught the plane!'

'Is Otto Oz the nasty little bastard's nickname? He gave me the creeps. I told him nothing!'

'You didn't have to – he sniffed it. He's a cunning, crooked operator and probably runs the odd fake himself.'

'So that's why he warned me not to meddle in matters that didn't concern me. I thought he'd been watching too many late-night Bogart re-runs on TV.'

Breeze's anger turned to rage. 'Art crooks are *crooks*, and crooks are ruthless! I don't want you wandering around seedy parts of Paris!'

So Leo had sneaked to Breeze. Plum snapped. 'I don't want *you* to treat me like a child!'

'You're bloody lucky to have someone do all the worrying for you! God, you're so bloody selfish!'

Suddenly thinking of Aunt Harriet, Plum bit back laughter. Behind Breeze's back, she saw Sandra come out of the kitchen with a welcoming smile, then quickly withdraw.

At Plum's smile, Breeze turned red with fury. 'I don't understand what's got into you. What do you *want*, for God's sake?'

Plum looked at the calm opulence of the marble hall. 'I'm surrounded by things *you* want. Sometimes *I* feel like one of your *things*. The golden goose in a gilded cage.' She turned to face him, 'Breeze, what I want is some time to myself.'

'You've just been round the bloody world by yourself!'

Plum looked mutinous. 'For eight years I've pursued career success with tunnel vision. You gave me my chance and I didn't let you down. I worked non-stop.'

Breeze roared, 'Because even you could see it was the smart thing to do!'

'Now I want time to think. There's more to life than working, making money and being successful.'

'There is?'

'Please take me seriously,' Plum pleaded.

'I don't know what's got into you, you don't seem the same person!'

'I don't want to be the same person!' Forgetting her planned speech, Plum burst out, 'I want to feel a complete, balanced person, Breeze, not a lopsided one – swollen one side and shrivelled on the other. I want to get to know my real self.' To work out which parts comprised the compliant mask Plum hid behind when she wanted people to like her. When she recognized and dumped those parts, she would be able to see who she really was, and who she wanted to be. Then she could work out what she wanted to do and why, and how she wanted to spend the rest of her life.

'Take all the time you need to sort out your identity crisis – but only *after* the Biennale. The British Council's been waiting for weeks to talk to you.'

'After the Biennale, I'm going to stop doing what other people want and start doing what *I* want.'

'I'd like to see you try! You've never taken any decisions!' Breeze roared, still furious.

'Time I had a bit of practice.'

They glared at each other.

'What are you complaining about?' sighed Breeze. 'What's *wrong* with doing what I want? Where were *you* before you met me? *I* know what's best for you.'

'I've been doing what *you* want for years, Breeze. Now, why can't *you* do what *I* want? Why don't *you* help me find these forgers?'

Breeze was silent. Eventually, making an effort to control his voice, he said, 'I don't want you to have anything to do with forgers, because I love you, and I want to look after you. But I give in. You can have whatever time you want, whenever you want it.' He hunched his shoulders and his long, graceful hands flew into the air, expressing fury, despair and resignation.

Plum couldn't help laughing. 'When you do that, you look quite

French.' She was relieved to lighten the atmosphere: she hated to step off the plane and straight into a row. She added, 'You know I won't let you down at the Biennale.'

Breeze forced a smile. 'I'm sorry, Plum. I really was worried sick. *You* don't know what you might be getting into – you've led a protected life. Outside, in the great big world, they play dirty.' He pulled her to him and kissed her hard. He whispered, 'I've missed you.' Theatrically, he threw his head back, flaring his nostrils.

'Oh, Rhett,' Plum murmured.

Breeze swept Plum into his arms and carried her up the beautiful staircase.

*   *   *   *

An hour later, Plum opened her eyes, yawned, stretched her arms and lazily looked around her bedroom. Outside, barren tree branches spread an abstract black pattern over the long windows. On the wall opposite them hung –

'Emily's painting!' Plum sat up, delighted. 'That's exactly where I wanted to hang it!'

'There's a coincidence,' Breeze murmured drowsily. 'It arrived three days ago. Came back from the stretcher this morning. You must admit that *sometimes* I'm wonderful ... Hey, you clearly weren't bonking in Paris. Can't a man have ten minutes' rest?'

Friday, 24 January 1992

On the following morning, Plum lay in the bath and Breeze updated his life while he shaved with a traditional razor. He was stalking an unknown sketch in oils by Richard Diebenkorn; it was one of his *Ocean Park* series and had supposedly been given in the early seventies to a British friend. Breeze had been unconvinced of its authenticity until his first sight of the small, aqueous-tinted Southern California seascape; it was a painting of delicately sensuous pleasure, as the owner unfortunately knew only too well.

Plum half-listened as she worked out her next move to trace the forger. She dared not phone Bill Hobbs until Breeze had left the house.

Breeze carefully scraped the lather from beneath his chin, then looked at Plum in the mirror. 'Oh, one other thing. We might be able to get a new rose named after you ... Good press coverage there ... Have to be careful about the colour, of course – can't call a yellow rose "Plum" ...'

Almost to herself, Plum muttered, 'Am I really good – or is it all hype?'

Razor in hand, Breeze turned to her. 'Hype doesn't work long-term, unless you're good,' he said sharply. 'Hype just saves time. Unlike most women, you've been able to get to the top without wasting time on the way. Look at Gillian Ayres – two kids meant she couldn't afford to stop teaching and start painting full-time until she was *fifty*!' Breeze turned back to the mirror and reached for his odourless after-shave from Trumpers, the royal hairdresser.

Plum shuddered. She loved to paint with an inexplicable passion. She remembered that when Breeze had first suggested they marry, she had said, 'Darling Breeze – before I say yes, yes, *yes*! – you'd better know ... and I feel guilty even thinking this, let alone saying it ... *I don't want any more kids.* I love Toby and Max more than anything in the world, but never again am I going to be torn between kids and painting.' She had been grateful when he immediately agreed.

Now, she wasn't so fervently grateful to Fate for sending Breeze and to Breeze for clearing everything out of her way so she could paint. For the first time – and even though the consequences frightened her – Plum disentangled gratitude and loyalty from love, and asked herself the question that for months she had been avoiding with agility. Did she still love Breeze? Had she ever?

Plum knew she didn't love him with the fierce, tiger-protective love that she felt for her kids: but she'd never loved anyone else that way – not even herself.

So did she love him? How could she tell? Never had she needed to do or sacrifice anything to test or prove her love for Breeze. But Plum knew what the big test would be – for it always was in fairy stories: would you sacrifice the thing you most cherished for your beloved? Would she give up painting for Breeze? That this was the last thing Breeze would want, was not the point: the point was, would she do it?

No. She wouldn't give up painting for anything – or anyone.

As the phone rang, Plum reached out a sudsy arm. 'Hello ... Richard Stepman ... The British Council ... Of course I remember you ... Breeze told me you want to update your plans ... How about this afternoon? Three o'clock? ... In my studio – that's where I keep my work records.'

As Breeze reached for his Philippe Starck toothbrush, he smiled to himself.

Plum replaced the phone and idly blew the suds from her hand into the air. 'I know I've met him at parties, but tell me more about Richard Stepman.'

'He's a close friend of Charley Boman. They met at Cambridge. Richard got an art history scholarship from Marlborough. He's the British Council's blue-eyed boy. Typical upper-class, impoverished Englishman. Dad, now deceased, was a general in the Grenadiers. Mum's a godsend to the gossip columns – Diana Stepman.'

'Of course. Deb of her year and fifties heartbreaker. She's a semi-invalid now, isn't she?'

'Yes, arthritis. Doesn't let it stand in her way, she's as popular as ever. Holds a bottle party every Thursday. Richard took me to one while you were in Oz.' Breeze poured Chypre cologne over himself. 'They live in a large mansion flat off the Gloucester Road, rent-controlled, I imagine. Richard has a struggle to pay for her nursing.'

* * * *

As always when meeting new men, Plum automatically checked Richard Stepman out on Jenny's behalf. As he stepped from the elevator outside her studio she saw a big, tanned, athletic-looking man with a good-natured face, smiling blue eyes and dark, floppy hair worn a little longer than was usual for an ambitious civil servant.

'I'm glad you'll be looking after me at the Biennale,' Plum said.

Richard laughed. 'The Italians are charming and enthusiastic, but not over-efficient: you'll need someone who knows what might go wrong, and who doesn't mind being screamed at. I've brought a rough schedule to discuss: we're expecting a lot of work from you and we need some of it quickly.' He followed Plum through the studio door and stopped abruptly.

Plum's visitor stared around the room at the fantastical landscapes. Pastoral, undulating fields lay between dark forests and misted mountains. Turreted towers and palaces stood among tufted trees. Onion-topped minarets were striped in canary and green, peacock-blue and purple, candy-pink and crimson. All these delicate buildings were surrounded by gardens in shimmering colours, in which brilliant flowers grew beneath astonishing trees, heavy with blossom or fruit, heedless of season. Beneath the architectural fantasies stretched lakes and shadowed caves. Above them, meteors shot through midnight skies.

'I've introduced a feeling of perspective,' Plum explained. 'An optional third dimension. All my new pictures are spatial abstractions, although basically they're still my internal moods, my states of mind.'

'They're terrific.' Richard sat on a paint-spattered Windsor chair and slowly opened his briefcase. But his attention was not on his schedule; his eyes were constantly drawn to the paintings.

*   *   *   *

After Richard had left, Plum checked her paint supplies. It was satisfying to be back in her studio, with nothing on her mind except her current painting: luxuriantly she sniffed the odour of turps and linseed oil, then eyed the canvas on which she was working. That blue patch, top left, looked flat; it needed more mauve and green scumble; which meant the area of emerald polka dots on melon needed to be more acid – the green sharpened with lemon . . . That north-east pink section was too recessive, and she wasn't sure she liked the shape. Someone had counted twelve phallic symbols in Plum's first canvas to hang in the Academy – although the Hanging Committee hadn't seemed to notice. Definitely reduce that pink area, the hue was a bit Miss Piggy, try ochre scumble . . .

When Plum heard the front door slam, she ran to the window and watched Breeze corkscrew into his Lamborghini. Then she telephoned Bill Hobbs. There was no reply, which meant that she'd have to go round to Bill's studio this afternoon and leave a note. She hoped that he still lived in Armada Road. *If* he was still in the business. Bill must be about seventy by now, and had frequently mumbled and grumbled about retiring when Plum had worked for him – fifteen years beforehand.

Plum's reverie was interrupted by a telephone call from Max. Yes, he was enjoying his foundation course at the Central and had *definitely* decided to become a potter when he'd finished the course. At Easter could he install a potter's wheel in the old basement workshop at Chester Terrace? Great Ma, thanks, must run . . .

Plum was just about to place an order with her paint supplier when the door bell pealed frantically and she heard her name yodelled. Lulu had arrived. As Sandra was shopping, Plum jumped into the lift.

Lulu fell into her arms. 'I didn't bring Wolf, he's got a cold . . . Oh, what a lovely cloak, may I try?' She picked up Plum's new black cloak from the hall chair.

On Lulu, the cloak reached only mid-calf. 'Hasn't it a glorious swirl?' Lulu twirled, as youthfully radiant and excited as a girl before her first ball.

Plum looked at Lulu's wild black hair, her violet skirt and bottle-green boots. 'That cloak makes you look like Augustus John's Dorelia: that romantic, half-tamed gypsy look. Keep it.'

'Plum, you angel! . . . It's years since I've had any decent clothes . . . I certainly never thought I'd fit into anything of yours . . . You're *sure* you don't want to keep it?'

'No,' Plum lied. Lulu rushed to the hall mirror and pulled the black hood up over her thick, dark curls. Her excited, eager face was once again cream and pink, her mouth a generous, tremulous line of cherry, her clear grey eyes smudged into sockets below flaring dark eyebrows. Above her delicately moulded, square jawline the beautifully modelled, high, wide cheekbones were no longer gaunt. There had been no lapse since Lulu married Ben, although the relieved Plum now knew enough about drug cures never to assume they were permanent.

'I'm falling in love with myself all over again,' Lulu sang as she

187

danced around the white hall, a tall, gracefully swirling dark shape beneath the chandelier. Suddenly, she stopped. 'Oh my God, I haven't told you! How could I have forgotten? I tried to phone you in Australia but the time was upside down and you weren't there.'

'I tried to call you back. No answer. Where were you?'

'With Jenny. Her father died.'

'*Poor Jenny!* Where is she now?'

'Still with her mother, in Portsmouth. But she's travelling back to London tonight.'

'How did it happen?'

'He was watching football on TV, fell asleep and never woke up. A better way to go than he deserved.'

'Don't let Jenny hear you say that.'

Lulu clutched her new Parisian cloak around her neck and looked defiant. 'I'm not going to be hypocritical,' she continued. 'I can't pretend I'm sorry Jenny's dad is dead, although I'm sorry to see Jenny so upset. Mummy said it was a psychologically unhealthy dependency. I went down to Portsmouth to be with her – I think Wolf picked up his cold on the train – but Jenny doesn't want to talk about it. You'll see.'

As Plum picked up the telephone to ring Jenny, Lulu noticed her diamond ring. She shrieked and pointed. 'My God, that's blindingly beautiful! From the slavedriver?'

Plum grinned. 'Who else?'

'It must have cost a king's ransom – enough to clear our mortgage anyway,' Lulu said wistfully.

As Lulu predicted, Jenny's mother had left the receiver off the hook.

Lulu refused to remove her new cloak for tea. 'No, I'm even going to wear it to bed, Plum. Ben's in for a wild night.' Disdaining the lift, she jumped up the wide stairs, two at a time, strode with her lanky, long-legged lope into Plum's sitting-room, and threw herself on to a cream silk couch. 'Oops, sorry. Shouldn't have put my boots on these cushions.' She kicked them off.

Over cinnamon buns and ginger biscuits, Plum told Lulu about her pursuit of the fake flower paintings. Lulu listened intently, and immediately agreed to accompany Plum to Maltby's on the following morning – provided her regular baby-sitter was available. Mrs Barton was a long-winded hypochondriac but Lulu didn't like to leave Wolf with unknown agency sitters, and she assumed an old age pensioner wouldn't smuggle in boyfriends.

* * * *

The following morning, Plum opened the *International Herald Tribune* to see a photograph of Suzannah Marsh, looking unusually harried. Two laconic paragraphs reported a suicide attempt by the business star's younger daughter. After disappointing examination results, she had jumped off the roof of her boarding school and fractured her pelvis.

Plum remembered Suzannah's two unnaturally quiet daughters. Outwardly the epitome of graceful motherhood, the soft-spoken Suzannah in her Ralph Lauren frills, lace and sprigged muslin was in fact a Home Hitler: ambitious, hardworking and demanding, she expected the same high standard of performance from her children.

After reading of such a disaster, it seemed only a minor inconvenience when Lulu apologetically reported that Mrs Barton had an ingrowing toenail; white-hot agony, and she couldn't break her appointment with the social services chiropodist.

* * * *

Wearing a shaggy orange fake fur, over indigo leggings and sweater, Plum travelled alone to Bond Street. Outside Maltby's, she hung around, scruffing the thin snow with Madonna blue leather boots, staring into the bow-fronted window, screwing up her courage. It had been far easier to be brazen in Paris, where nobody knew who she was.

When she finally pushed open the door, Plum found herself in a cosily Dickensian atmosphere. Gas-powered flames flickered beneath a carved pine fireplace, comfortable wing armchairs stood on either side of it. Plum half-expected Mr Pickwick to appear with a silver bowl of steaming punch. From a door at the rear, she could hear the ruptured murmur of a telephone conversation, as she wandered around the snug showroom. She beckoned to a flabby, ageing assistant, gave her name, and asked to speak to Mr Maltby.

The man who came from the rear room was a smaller version of Alfred Hitchcock. His well-cut, silver-grey suit could not disguise portliness; his egg-shaped head was almost bald and his neck spilled over his shirt collar.

Plum produced two files from her tote bag and explained that Victor Marsh had asked her to call to discuss his recent purchase. She added that Cynthia Bly was also concerned about her painting. Mr Maltby, quietly polite, suggested they talk in his office. They sat opposite each other at a large, scarred mahogany table piled high with box files and letters. Mr Maltby produced gold-rimmed glasses, carefully hooked them over his ears, then read Plum's two letters of authority, from Victor and Cynthia. Politely, he raised his eyebrows and looked over his spectacles at Plum. 'Do I understand that you wish to challenge the authenticity of these pictures?'

'Not exactly . . . that is . . . not yet,' Plum stammered. 'I've come here to find where these paintings came from. The provenance gives no details of your sources.'

Mr Maltby looked politely remote. 'We know the previous owner of both these paintings and have guaranteed to preserve anonymity. The paintings were sold on those implicit conditions. But I can assure you that I know more than the information contained in both provenances, and I have absolutely no doubt whatsoever as to their authenticity.'

'You know the previous owner of both of these pictures?'

Mr Maltby gave a brief nod, and stood up. 'Sorry I can't be of further assistance to you, Mrs Russell. Should you wish to buy or sell a property and ask for anonymity, we would respect your wishes: we never divulge private information about somebody else's property.'

*   *   *   *

What should she have done, Plum wondered in a taxi bound for Bayswater? Offer her body to that flabby old assistant in return for two addresses? Burgle the place, hoping that something in one of those piles of box files would reveal the original owners? As she paid the driver, Plum remembered that in Sydney, Stephanie had told her not to be surprised when she reached a dead end.

'Ah, it's you.' Over the intercom Jenny's voice sounded tired and drained. 'I suppose Lulu's told you about Dad. Come on up.'

Unkempt and white-faced, Jenny huddled in one corner of a sunflower-spattered couch, cuddling her toy donkey. The sunny, yellow living-room was furnished with good modern furniture and a Georgian tallboy with gleaming brass handles. Jenny was proud of her home and kept it spotless: no one would guess that a painter lived there.

'No need to look like that,' Jenny scowled. '*You've* got a husband to cuddle when you feel sad; Muffin's shared *my* bad times ever since I can remember. Don't tell me I'm being childish – because I know and I don't care.'

Plum flew to the couch. 'You've got me as well. Always. I promise.'

Much later, when Plum had heard about the funeral, about Jenny's regrets and misery, and Jenny had heard about the Australian exhibition, Plum told her of her progress in the pursuit of the fake paintings.

Jenny, who was making instant coffee in the kitchenette, turned around and stared through the doorway. She pushed back tangled hair from her red-rimmed, amber eyes and sighed. 'Plum, I can't believe it matters to you if a few rich ignorant people are fooled by some forger.' She turned on the tap and filled the kettle. 'What's in this trail for you? Nothing!' She spooned coffee grains into blue-striped mugs. 'Of course I'll help you if I can – which I doubt. But why bother?'

'That's more or less what Breeze says. But he *yells* it. I can't understand why he's so upset about my search. I don't believe he's just worried I might upset the trade.'

'So why *are* you doing this?'

'I'm not sure,' Plum tried to be honest with herself. 'Of course it's partly because Breeze treated me like a naughty child in front of Suzannah and Victor. That made me hopping mad. I felt aggressive and mutinous. Something snapped. I'd had *enough*! So the worm turned . . . Now *you* tell me I'm being childish.'

'No, just the opposite.' Jenny turned away to grope in the

refrigerator for cream. 'Suddenly, Plum, the good little girl isn't behaving to type.'

'You mean, I'm being disobedient?'

'That's it.' Jenny poured cream into both mugs. 'You were a shy, obedient child who became a shy, obedient adult who produced strong and powerful paintings – but still did as she was told. I thought you were building up to a show-down with Breeze – but why now?'

'I'm tired of being treated as a child,' Plum burst out. 'I want Breeze to understand that there are parts of my life that he isn't going to control. I want to prove to *myself* that I have the right to be taken seriously.'

'And that's the only reason you want to upset Breeze? This isn't some sort of subconscious retaliation?' Jenny came into the sitting-room and handed a mug to Plum, who was now striding up and down before the windows.

'Subconscious retaliation for what?'

'We've never discussed it, but I can't believe you don't know. So if you're going to pick a row with Breeze – why not pick a situation where you can hold the winning card?'

Plum stared at Jenny. 'What do you mean?'

'The wife is always the last to know, Plum.' Wearily Jenny pushed her tawny hair back from her puffy, white face.

'*What are you hinting at, Jenny?*'

'Lulu wouldn't let me tell you. She never let me tell you about Jim's girls either – she didn't want to hurt you.' Jenny looked into Plum's eyes. 'But if it were me I'd want to know. And I've always felt you knew, but didn't want to face it. So if you really want to be an adult, perhaps it's time you admitted to yourself what the rest of us have known for years.'

Plum turned white and carefully put her mug on the window-sill.

'Nobody will tell you if *I* don't.'

'OK, tell me.'

Jenny looked straight into Plum's staring blue eyes. 'Breeze is having an affair. Breeze is *always* having an affair. The entire London art world could give you a list. The latest is that South American woman I met at your place before Christmas. Miranda. Horsey-looking, bad legs. Rich husband who buys from Breeze.'

'Miranda de la Fuente? I don't believe it!'

'They lunch together every day, then pop back to her suite at Claridges.'

'I've got to check this out.' Plum grabbed her tote bag, fumbled with shaking hands for her address book, and stumbled to the telephone on Jenny's desk.

Breeze's secretary told her that he'd already left for lunch – she didn't know where – and wasn't expected back until late that afternoon.

Breeze was a man of set habits. Plum telephoned the restaurants where art dealers entertain important clients: the Caprice, Mark's Club and Harry's Bar. Then she tried Odins and the Ivy.

Finally, she realized where Breeze would be.

* * * *

A guitar played softly as Plum walked inside the doorway of Le Bahia. She blinked to accustom herself to the dim light, then moved slowly past the blue-tiled walls of the Spanish restaurant towards the secluded back booth, almost hidden from the rest of the room, where Breeze used to take her when first they met. She smelled saffron-flavoured paella and the enticing aroma of roasted sucking-pig. She hoped she wouldn't throw up.

* * * *

The small gilt carriage clock on the bedroom fireplace chimed eight as Breeze, standing astride before the log fire, stared at his wife. He couldn't remember Plum ever contradicting him, let alone shouting at him. Sure, they'd argued, like every other married couple, but nothing serious.

Plum stamped up and down their bedroom. 'Of course you didn't see me, Breeze! Nobody can see anything in that place – that's why people go there! And anyway, I wasn't going to give you the chance of virtuously protesting you were only having lunch with the wife of a client!' She turned to face her husband. 'So after I'd spotted you, I waited outside in a cab – then I followed you to Claridges. I sat in the hall, pretending to read a newspaper – and waited. *You didn't come downstairs until five o'clock!* When you walked back to Cork Street – I was behind you.'

'Playing the girl detective has clearly gone to your head!' Breeze growled. 'It isn't proof of adultery to take a client's wife to lunch . . .'

'Already played that line, two minutes ago! . . . No, I *won't* keep my voice down! I don't *care* if the staff hear!'

Breeze pulled at his left ear-lobe, a sure sign of anxiety. There was no point in continued denials that would only protract this scene, which had already lasted two hours. 'Look, it was nothing serious . . .'

'*I'm* the one who decides if it's serious – and I decide that it is!'

'I'm sorry, Plum,' Breeze sounded genuinely contrite. 'It won't happen again, darling, I promise.' He moved towards her. 'I truly, truly am sorry. I've behaved thoughtlessly.' He held out his arms. 'I've been a bloody fool, I admit. I'll make it up to you, darling, I'll . . .'

'*Stop* talking like a thirties movie!' Plum glared.

In a quick movement, Breeze grabbed Plum and pulled her hard against his chest. Swiftly he whispered of his love, his respect for her, his confidence that they could forget this and start again. He bent and kissed her red curls; he bent lower and kissed the top of her ear, then licked it, his secret invitation.

Plum's small fist punched him in the stomach. Breeze grunted and released his hold on her. She sprang backwards towards the fireplace. 'Be glad I didn't knee you!' She'd thought of it, but didn't quite dare.

'Look, Plum, how long is this going to go on? I mean, couldn't we take a break for a drink, like at the theatre?' Breeze ducked as the little carriage clock hit the wall behind his head. 'Hey! You could *really have hurt me* with that thing, Plum!'

'*You aren't taking this thing seriously!*'

'I am! I am!' How was he supposed to convince her of his seriousness?

As Plum grabbed a silver candlestick on the mantelpiece, she caught sight of the diamond on her finger, which sparkled in the firelit glow. She put down the candlestick and, weeping, tugged to remove her ring.

Breeze, who was hovering between the windows, ready to dodge the candlestick, pleaded with her. 'Don't do anything silly with that ring. No bloody stupid girlish gesture, please.'

Her face running with tears, Plum glared at him.'Don't worry. I only want to give it back to you.'

'Christ, Plum, I'm truly sorry. Please, please, darling, don't cry. Oh, Christ, I'm sorry.'

Sobbing, Plum put her hands up to her face.

Cautiously, Breeze moved forward.

Cautiously, he took her in his arms and pressed her face against his tweed jacket and murmured soothing reassurance, interspersed with bitter self-accusation.

Plum snuffled against the scratchy tweed. For who – except Breeze – could understand how she felt about such treachery?

But how many others had there been? She saw Breeze's wide, strong mouth bending to anonymously perfect, tip-tilted breasts; she saw his long, graceful hands reach between the knees of an anonymous pair of perfect legs; she saw his lean naked buttocks undulating rhythmically above anonymous white flesh; she saw their excitement grow to a frenzy as Breeze thrust, long and hard, again and again, into a beautiful, anonymous ivory body.

Plum kneed him.

＊　＊　＊　＊

Five days later, Plum and Breeze were still not speaking to each other, and Breeze was sleeping in a guest bedroom in the basement. Sandra the housekeeper had noticed the mood of black fury between them and decided on an attitude of ostentatiously formal non-involvement, as in United Nations observers. Plum gloomily suspected that Sandra, in her mind, once again ruled a bachelor establishment.

As she set out for lunch with Leo, Plum once again wondered how long Breeze had been unfaithful, and how often, and with how many women? She alternated between tears and fury. She was almost glad they weren't speaking, because his infidelity was the only thing she wanted to discuss, and she did not trust him to tell her the truth. Could she ever trust Breeze again to tell her the truth about *anything*? Had he ever? As if pushing her tongue into an aching tooth, to see if it still hurt, she nagged herself, repeatedly asking the same questions.

But as her taxi swung into Charlotte Street, Plum realized that she must push Breeze completely out of her mind if she were to accomplish anything at lunch. Once she started to cry on Leo's shoulder, they'd never get the conversation back on the track she wanted. So to hell with Breeze. And incidentally, to hell with Bill Hobbs, wherever he was. She had tucked a second note into his letter-box, but he had not yet replied: perhaps he still did those winter sales trips to Scandinavia, where everyone was so tired of winter that he found eager buyers . . .

Leo was already waiting at l'Étoile. Plum had known he would be unable to resist the traditional favourite Soho haunt of successful actors, writers and artists.

The ancient waiter recommended marinated herring followed by *escalope de veau à la Zingara*, while the equally ancient sommelier recommended a Château Larose-Trintaudon 1979. After eating their way through these delicious dishes, an enticingly sticky *baba au rhum* was served to Leo. Plum was back on her post-Christmas diet.

As brandy and coffee were placed before them, Plum asked Leo why he had avoided her in Paris.

'Haven't been to Paris for ages. You must have been mistaken,' he replied airily.

'Leo, I know it was you, you daft idiot. You were wearing odd socks, one pink, one green.' This affectation, started years ago by David Hockney, had become Leo's jokey visual signature: his odd socks were always carefully colour-coordinated.

After a long silence, Leo sighed. 'OK. I was there. I knew that was why you asked me to lunch, but I can't avoid you for ever. However, my reason for my trip to Paris was a love affair with a married woman. So I must be discreet, I can't talk about it.'

'A warehouse is hardly the place for a lovers' assignation.'

Plum nodded to the waiter for more brandy.

After further flimsy excuses, Leo reluctantly explained. 'A high-profile job at *New Perspective* doesn't pay very well. I haven't been able to get a better-paid job – there's not much demand for an architectural correspondent, especially not when what used to be Fleet Street is cutting back on staff. Ah, fuck it, Plum, if you must know, I drive for Colombe when someone's sick. Your average trucker won't do: they need men used to handling valuable paintings and antiques.' Leo sipped his brandy. 'The work's surprisingly well paid, with good expenses – and I get free trips to France.'

He stared at his untouched coffee cup. 'The first time I did it as a lark, but I still really enjoy it. It's fun on the road. I've a bunk bed behind my head, I'm self-contained, surprising things happen on each trip.' He smiled to himself.

'So why keep quiet about it, Leo?'

'Plum, you're married to Breeze. Surely you know the importance of a good façade?'

Plum was not convinced by Leo's explanation. He was not the Jack Kerouac type, he was far too fond of comfort. On the other hand, Leo's job probably didn't pay well, or he wouldn't live in that seedy, short-lease condemned building on the corner of Maddox Square. He always seemed to be short of cash, despite his smart, if crumpled clothes. And he drove a cheap little green Citroën *deux chevaux*. So if Leo were making a fortune out of forgery, where was he spending it?

Slightly belligerent, Leo said, 'I've told you the truth, Plum. You can easily check with Colombe's London office. I'll tell you something else. If your curiosity is connected to your damned search for fake paintings, then you're a bloody idiot. I told you it was dangerous! I wouldn't risk *my* neck having anything to do with the fake trade.'

Leo swirled the brandy in his balloon glass, then added crossly, 'If you're going to suspect everyone who takes a trip to Paris of smuggling fake paintings, why not ask that rich layabout Charley Boman what *he* was doing in France, last week? I spotted him on the Channel ferry – and why go to Paris by ferry if you aren't smuggling?'

Was Leo speaking the truth or trying to confuse her, Plum wondered?

'Listen, I'm telling you the truth, Plum, and it's not a wild guess. Later, when I made my delivery to Lévi-Fontaine, I saw Charley again in those rabbit-warren offices. He was nervous and jumpy, not his usual cheery self. Naturally I was glad he didn't notice me, despite the way he kept furtively looking around. Very suspicious, Plum – you'd have pulled out your magnifying-glass.'

Plum stared at Leo. 'Why would Charley smuggle?'

Leo shrugged his shoulders. 'No idea. But I know why Charley didn't spot me, when I was under his nose. Because it wouldn't occur to upper-crust, Old Etonian Charley to notice a simple truck driver.'

CHAPTER SIXTEEN

FOR THE next three weeks, to fulfil the British Council schedule, Plum painted during every minute of daylight. She attacked her canvases with an obsession that blotted out the fury and pain she felt at Breeze's treachery: she transferred it all to canvas.

Plum had telephoned Victor at the end of January. He had sounded deflated and worried. 'I suppose you've heard about Felicity's accident. She's getting the best medical care of course. I wish the press would drop it.'

Understandably, Victor had been hardly interested in Plum's progress. Although courteous, he had firmly made it clear that he didn't care if Plum were able to prove that the entire contents of the Louvre were fake – he was only interested in his own investment. He had added wearily that he reckoned they ought to settle their bet, one way or the other, by the end of March.

This gave Plum six weeks to solve her self-appointed conundrum, she thought, as she drummed her fingers impatiently on the paint-stained table in her studio and waited for the British Institute of Art to answer its telephone. She had telephoned on her return from Paris, and been told that Dame Enid would be in Rajasthan until the tenth of February. Plum had waited a day to allow Stephanie's scholarly contact to clear her desk after her six-week holiday.

'Good morning.' Unexpectedly, Dame Enid's voice was low, ringing, seductive. Plum imagined young Enid, star of her college amateur dramatic society, training her voice to reach imperiously, effortlessly to the back of some theatre.

After Plum had introduced herself and told of her search for the source of the forged paintings, Dame Enid said thoughtfully, 'Normally, to check a painting, I'd suggest you go straight to the catalogue résumés of the artists concerned, which are formed from original antique documentation. In this case, however, it isn't necessarily going to help, because if a forger can get his hands on such descriptions, he paints to fit them. Of course,' she added, 'if you can get the actual paintings to London, we can check them scientifically. You're familiar with test procedures?'

She explained that scientific forgery detection methods are similar to the forensic methods used to track criminals: a forger is tracked in the same way as a murderer. Then Dame Enid rattled off examples of detection. '. . . Magnification shows when age cracks were really painted . . . under ultra-violet radiation, certain chemicals fluoresce and so reveal false patinas . . . X-rays and infra-red reflectography reveal the painter's preliminary work and changes of mind: lack of it indicates forgery.'

'What about paint analysis?' Plum asked, trying to keep up.

'Microchemical analysis can sometimes prove that the pigments used were invented after the date on the painting. For instance, the first synthetic paint – Prussian blue – was invented in 1704, so any Renaissance picture containing it would be suspect.'

'But modern pigments in a painting might be a permissible restoration repair.'

'Yes. And scientific methods aren't infallible. There are easy ways to fool the scientific analysis. For instance, you can still buy eighteenth-century paintboxes at auctions – restorers often buy them.'

'So if a forger obtains old artists' materials then the newly forged painting will pass your scientific tests?'

'Exactly. Despite science, the most powerful detector is still the human brain and eye, helped by a microscope. So I think we'd better meet . . .'

*   *   *   *

Half an hour later, Plum drove nervously to Jaimie Lorimer's gallery off Jermyn Street. She needed to see Jaimie – recently returned from his winter holiday in Mustique – because it was he who had recommended Cynthia Bly to Maltby's. Plum knew that should Breeze hear about her visit, he would regard it as seriously disloyal, but she was still too angry to care. She had never discovered the reason why Jaimie and Breeze were such ferocious rivals, although – like anyone who reads a gossip column – she knew a lot of other things about Jaimie. He was American, from the West Coast, and because his mother's career had consisted of stormy marriages, Jaimie had been raised by his maternal grandmother, a once-wealthy Californian land-heiress. She paid for his schooling at a smart co-ed boarding school in the Ojai Valley, much favoured by movie stars, where each child had his own horse and psychiatric counsellor. Jaimie's Spanish blood was blamed for his theatrical, violent temper, which had occasionally led him to whack playmates over the head with a baseball bat or a coke bottle.

When Jaimie was thirteen, his grandmother could no longer afford her Bel Air mansion and moved to an apartment in San Francisco, taking her art collection – sentimental shepherdesses, school of Watteau – under the delusion that it would provide her with a comfortable old age.

When he was sixteen, Jaimie left school suddenly, after a childish tennis court dispute ended in a broken racquet and an ambulance for his opponent. His grandmother hurriedly apprenticed him to her Los Angeles art dealer, whose taste Jaimie deplored as much as he admired his sales skills.

Jaimie accompanied his boss on frequent buying trips to Europe, and finally helped him to open a gallery in London's Mayfair. Left to run this business, Jaimie quickly established a close relationship with the clients, whom he persuaded to follow him when he left to start his own business. Curious London dealers, whom Jaimie outbid at auction after auction, were unable to discover the identity of his financial backer.

When she arrived at the Lorimer Gallery, Plum was directed through the lofty cream rooms, past an exhibition of Matisse etchings, to Jaimie's office in the basement. It was bare but luxurious. Naturally, the walls were white, but (unusual in an art dealer's office) the carpet was burnt orange and guests sat on elegantly quirky 'Bull' chairs designed by Tom Dixon.

Jaimie sat behind a dark Spanish antique desk, in the sort of elaborate chair the Pope might use for audiences. Jaimie, talking on the telephone, waved Plum to a chair. She perched on the metal seat and watched him. Jaimie was about forty, tall and thin, and although he was dressed like a prim English businessman, he had a sexually self-confident, amoral air which attracted Plum against her will.

Theatrically different expressions crossed Jaimie's sun-tanned face as he spoke quickly and crossly in Spanish. Then he crashed the telephone back in its cradle and smiled warily at Plum. The telephone rang again. Jaimie's voice changed to one of quiet assurance. 'A Matisse drawing? A nude? I'm sure you realize that *everyone* wants a Matisse nude . . . Not at the moment, but I'm expecting one in tomorrow . . . Of *course*.' He slammed the phone down again, then pressed the intercom. 'Helga? . . . We need a Matisse nude . . . Yes, might as well ask for the Queen Mother nude, but we can try . . . Phone Waddington and Lumley Cazalet, will you? And take my calls.'

Jaimie turned to look at Plum. 'An unexpected pleasure,' he said, and waited. Although he smiled, his black eyes were sharp and wary.

Plum felt like a wren in front of a tom-cat. Her voice was higher than normal, almost breathless. 'Cynthia Bly said you recommended Maltby's to her . . . ?'

'Sure. For the sort of stuff she wanted.' Jaimie rubbed his attractively broken nose. 'They're reliable. So why not recommend them?'

Plum told him, then waited.

Reflectively, Jaimie rubbed the dimple in his chin. 'No need to tell you what might have happened. Cynthia was insistent . . . So Maltby's put the word out . . . and not surprisingly, they found what they wanted. Galleries generally do, if a client's naïve enough to be over-precise in his specification.' He shrugged. 'Plenty of dealers have a "restorer" who can supply to order.'

'Do you know any of these restorers?' Plum was thinking of Bill Hobbs.

'If I did, I wouldn't admit it.' He looked at Plum thoughtfully.

'But I can tell you where to get a genuine flower picture. Old van Soder in Amsterdam. And he'd know if any wrong 'uns were coming on the market. I can't help you further.' He smiled slightly. 'Does Breeze know you're here?'

Plum hesitated. Whatever she said, he'd gossip. If she said no, and asked him not to tell anyone, he'd add that to his story. She shrugged her shoulders and stood up.

＊　＊　＊　＊

Within minutes of dialling International Inquiries, Plum was speaking to Mr van Soder, who sounded tired. Although he swallowed his g's as if he were drinking, he spoke good English. Yes, he handled Dutch and Flemish paintings of the seventeenth century, but had recently decided to close his business until the current recession was over.

When Plum hesitantly asked if he had ever seen . . . sold . . . an *over-restored* painting, Mr van Soder chuckled. He would always buy back, for his sale price, any picture he had sold, so confident was he that his paintings were genuine. If it had been restored, he always mentioned that specifically in the provenance.

＊　＊　＊　＊

Three days later, on Valentine's Day, Breeze angrily burst into their bedroom, now occupied by Plum alone.

'Why the hell did you have to involve that prick Jaimie Lorimer in your ridiculous adventure? The vicious bitch had the news round town as soon as you left his office.'

Plum poked her towel-turbaned head out of the bathroom. 'Can't this wait till I've finished dressing?'

'No, it bloody can't! For God's sake stop this nonsense! You're making me the laughing stock of the art world, and you're in danger of discrediting yourself, just before the bloody Biennale!'

Wrapped in a towel, Plum hurried past him to her dressing-room. 'Breeze, can't we call a truce just for today?' She wriggled into Vandyke brown tights. 'Have you forgotten Ben and Lulu are coming to supper?'

'What's so special about Lulu? Except she had a fistful of talent and let it trickle through her fingers.'

'All the more reason to be nice to her. Haven't *you* ever screwed up – and realized afterwards that the entire thing was your fault and could have been avoided?' Plum pulled on a short flippy dress in damson velvet.

Breeze, who regretted his grumpy attack on Lulu, remained silent.

'Please be nice this evening, Breeze,' Plum pleaded, as she pushed her feet into cigar-brown velvet shoes embroidered with gold coronets. 'Ben only got back last week from a Toronto recording session; he's been away nearly five months; and you know what a treat it is for those two to get out together.'

Buttoning her cuffs, Plum returned to the bathroom and brushed her hair. She shouted through the door to Breeze, still fuming in their bedroom. 'Let's agree on a truce, Breeze, or else you can stay here by yourself this evening: I'll take Lulu and Ben to a restaurant.'

'Sure I'll agree to a truce,' Breeze said hastily. 'Anything to make you happy.' He'd been planning to make a move after an evening of warmth and intimacy with her old friends. God knew somebody had to be adult about this stupid situation. And he hated sleeping alone.

'I wish you really meant that you'd do anything to make me happy, you stubborn bastard,' Plum muttered to herself. She remembered her long conversation with Aunt Harriet about happiness.

'The age-old problem that's perplexed men for centuries,' Aunt Harriet had said, 'is: *what do women want from life?* And the answer is: more than they're getting.'

'And time to enjoy it,' Plum added.

'Ah, that's the catch,' Aunt Harriet said. 'Women with young children can't have a successful career because they get no help. Motherhood may be the most important job in the world, but politicians don't think so.'

'I'll tell you what women really want,' Plum replied. 'They want to do some of the things that men can do because they don't have a rushed life, because they get back-up from women.'

Aunt Harriet was pensive. 'And women want some money of their own. By keeping the cash, a man controls his woman. So the only way a woman can get real power to do as she pleases, is by earning her own money – and controlling the way it's spent.'

'Aunt Harriet, are you a feminist?'

'I do believe in fair play, whatever the battlefield. And didn't somebody say that the opposite of a feminist is a masochist?'

* * * *

At four o'clock that afternoon, Plum drove her black Porsche across the River Thames to meet Professor Dame Enid Soames, who left her office early on Fridays.

Dame Enid's apartment was in Prince of Wales Drive, a clump of Edwardian red brick buildings in Battersea. The Bengal-red front door was flung open by a tall, commanding woman who wore dusky pink velvet knickerbockers and short jacket over a gunmetal silk blouse. Her elegant long legs were clad in pale grey tights and matching suede pumps. Silver hair, cut in the asymmetrically androgynous style of the Princess of Wales, fell over one large blue eye; her lipstick matched her knickerbockers.

'*Do* come in!' Plum recognized the low ringing voice.

Clutching a large vodka Martini, Plum sat on a comfortable Voltaire chair in a butter-coloured, spacious sitting-room, scented by purple-blue hyacinths growing in Chinese blue-and-white porcelain bowls. Carefully she described her search and, one by one, handed her transparencies to Dame Enid.

Dame Enid knocked back her drink. 'You're lucky to have these photographs. If you'd had to dig in archives, your search might take months – perhaps years.' She drifted across the room to a filing cabinet, artfully disguised as a lamp table. 'Knowing what you wanted to discuss, I brought a few things home.' She riffled through a file and pulled out a transparency. 'This painting's supposed to be a previously unknown Jan van Kessel the Elder; it was purchased in Paris in 1989 from Tonon, a small dealer in the Marais.'

She handed the transparency to Plum. 'A Swedish industrialist purchased it for only forty-eight thousand dollars – about half the price it might fetch at auction. At first he thought he had a bargain – people are so easy to fool if they're greedy – but then he felt uneasy, so he sent it to us.' She flipped her silver forelock out of her eye and looked at Plum. 'Of course the Swede wishes to remain anonymous – owners always do. They don't want anyone to know they've been fooled – and they hope to unload the dud painting on somebody else. So if it's proven a fake, they want to hide the fact.'

Plum held the transparency to the light. The small, rectangular painting was painted in bright clear colours, with plenty of strong reds. Against a dark background, a pale wooden table was scattered with pewter cutlery and china plates of fruit; to the rear stood an earthenware wine jug, a bowl of flowers with a butterfly hovering above it and a few scattered flower petals beneath. On the right were a yellow caterpillar and two mice, nibbling at a walnut, by a silver spoon on the handle of which were red initials, 'JVK'.

'That yellow caterpillar!' Plum pointed excitedly. 'There's one in Lady Binger's picture too!' Another link, Plum thought excitedly. 'The bluebottle in Suzannah's painting also appears in the Artur Schneider picture. And the lizard in Cynthia's picture appears in Suzannah's – although he's a different colour.'

Dame Enid shook her head in warning. 'Remember painters often shared sketchbooks – although perhaps some small item was deliberately repeated in all pictures, as a witty signature: maybe a beetle or a snail.'

'Just as Alfred Hitchcock appeared briefly in all his movies.'

'Exactly.' Dame Enid extracted another file and offered a transparency to Plum. She smiled. 'I think this will interest you. It's another dubious painting by Jan van Kessel the Elder which has also been traced back to this dealer, Tonon.'

Plum held the transparency against the lamp, then blinked. 'But this *is* Lady Binger's painting!' She grabbed Lady Binger's transparency and compared the two.

'Exactly. Let's go to my study where there's a proper light-box.' They hurried to a book-lined room with a large central table and two adjustable typing chairs. When the two transparencies lay side by side, illuminated from below, on the light-box, Dame Enid nodded. 'They certainly seem to be the same picture.' She checked her file. 'Cotton's, the Bury Street art dealer, asked us to check this painting; the price Tonon was asking seemed suspiciously cheap.'

'So Tonon must have sold it to Monfumat,' Plum said excitedly, 'who sold it to Forrestière, who sold it to Lady Binger. Although none of that's recorded on Lady Binger's provenance.

Dame Enid reminded, 'Like a career résumé, anything that isn't impressive gets left out.' She picked a clip of reports from her file. 'Now let's check our chemical test results on the picture sent to us by Cotton's.' She scanned her notes and murmured, '. . . painted on a genuine seventeenth-century copper panel . . . but paint analysis showed traces of titanium oxide in the rutile form – that's a white pigment which didn't exist before 1920 and was only produced commercially from 1941 . . .'

Long, pink-polished fingernails flipped through further pages of notes. 'After checking the picture with Sotheby's, the Ashmolean and the Fitzwilliam – I say, they *were* being thorough – Cotton's refused to purchase. This should make Lady Binger have her painting checked!' Dame Enid returned to the filing cabinet. 'I've plenty of wrong paintings detailed in here, but I'm looking for one like that Bosschaert purchased at Maltby's. Was it this one?' She placed a transparency on the light-box. 'Ah, I thought so!'

Triumphant, Plum looked up from the light-box. 'That's Cynthia's painting!'

Dame Enid's big, blue eyes looked thoughtful. 'Maltby's illustrated that Bosschaert in their autumn 1989 catalogue, so I went along to look at it. Arnold Maltby told me more than he might have told anyone else about the provenance, because he was convinced of its authenticity and wanted me to be similarly convinced – for obvious reasons.'

Plum nodded. She knew the good opinion of an academic art historian could alter the value of a picture by thousands of pounds. She also knew that art scholars hate to commit themselves, because if they don't put themselves in the firing line, they can't be shot down.

'I was unconvinced that the Bosschaert was genuine,' Dame Enid continued, 'but it was none of my business. However, on the following Sunday the *Tribune* printed a photograph of it. On the subsequent Sunday they were obliged to publish a letter from one of my colleagues; here it is.'

Plum read the crumpled newspaper clipping. Professor Nicolaus Cunnington wrote that this hitherto unrecorded painting, which he had examined at Maltby's, contained ingredients from known paintings by Ambrosius Bosschaert – but of widely differing dates. So Professor Cunnington believed that the newly acquired Maltby picture was a pastiche.

'As you no doubt know,' Dame Enid tactfully explained, 'a painter's often fascinated by one subject – a woman or a vase – so he paints that one subject again and again during one period of his life: Picasso painted his mistresses, Matisse painted goldfish, Hockney painted water patterns. But eventually the fascination is exhausted; and after he's become bored, a painter rarely returns to that subject.'

Below the Cunnington letter was a defensive letter from Arnold Maltby, who disagreed with Professor Cunnington's verdict, especially in view of the condition of the mount and frame, which were clearly of the period. More important, the degree of residue on the picture was what one would expect after 300 years.

'Of course,' said Dame Enid, 'the residue is the layer of dust and dirt that darkens a picture over hundreds of years; when it's scraped away, you can see the original, lighter colours. Old Maltby meant he'd examined a scraping – and found the colour was lighter beneath. As far as I'm concerned, that proved an intelligent forger.'

'Why didn't Maltby's ask the Institute to give an opinion?' Plum asked.

'There hadn't been time to do so before it came up at auction – which is what a forger often relies on.'

'So Maltby's took a risk?'

Dame Enid nodded. 'Exactly. And when the painting was publicly questioned, so was Arnold Maltby's judgement and integrity: his reputation was at stake. Many dealers in his situation would defend their purchase, even if they thought it wrong. And Maltby was defending *two* paintings – because by that time he'd bought another one from the same source.'

Dame Enid sat back, stretched her arms and yawned. 'But Maltby had a trump card. Most old pictures have been holed and repaired or re-lined, but a forger can't work well on a bad canvas. So when an old painting is examined under ultraviolet, if there are no dark patches to indicate repairs, that painting is suspect. The Maltby painting sold to your friend Cynthia clearly showed signs of restoration in the bottom left-hand section, when examined under X-ray. Our examination of the painting purchased by the Swede showed that it also had restoration work of a similar size in a similar place.'

Plum stared. 'You're *sure*? Because Lady Binger's provenance notes that her painting had been holed and repaired.' She longed to discuss this with Bill Hobbs.

Plum added, 'Suzannah Marsh's picture – which also came from Maltby's – also mentions restoration. In fact it hardly mentions anything else.'

For the next hour, Dame Enid examined Plum's transparencies. Eventually, she looked up. 'I can't be certain until I've checked with our library, but I suspect all five of these paintings are pastiches – and related. I'll get these trannies enlarged and duplicated for you, then we'll do a microscope check on idiosyncrasies of the painter: that'll show whether any of them were painted by the same person.' She smiled. 'A forger who's copying another painter's idiosyncrasies doesn't realize that he also has little give-away habits: length of brush-stroke, thickness of paint, mixture of colours chosen and so on.'

'Painted by the same person?' Plum felt a surge of excitement, followed by doubt. 'Surely that would be too much of a coincidence?'

'Nevertheless, it's possible. I'm surprised you were able to locate so many in so short a time, but you followed a trail, didn't you?'

'Except with the Binger picture. I more or less walked straight into that. Sheer luck.'

'You're entitled to some good luck, and I expect you'll have some bad luck. What counts is capitalizing your good luck. You had the sense to come straight to the Institute, realizing that we might give you an overall view. Listen, I've plenty of records of other fakes that I haven't bothered to show you because they don't fit your facts. However, you'd better check my files, in case you recognize anything else – but I can't make it today.'

'Neither can I. I'm having friends over for supper.'

*   *   *   *

When Plum reached Chester Terrace, she saw a black-cloaked figure standing on her doorstep. Lulu turned and grinned. Under her cloak she wore a violet velvet catsuit which enhanced her creamy Irish skin and wild black hair. 'Ben's coming straight here from the recording studio, so he might be late,' she said apologetically. 'We can't afford to do without his overtime – our mortgage interest is crippling.'

Plum pushed the door open. 'I think most people are feeling short of money at the moment.'

Lulu laughed ruefully. 'Ben can't decide whether it's best to share a bank account so he can see what I'm spending, or have separate ones so I can't squander the mortgage money on what he calls luxuries and I call necessities – such as a new overcoat for Wolf; his old one's been let out twice.'

'Doesn't matter if Ben's late,' Plum said as they moved to the kitchen. 'I'm doing the cooking this evening; Sandra's gone to bingo. So we can talk till the others arrive – I've asked Cleo and Sandy Brigstall. Cleo buys from Breeze – or she used to. They've just returned from New York.' Briefly Plum filled Lulu in. In Manhattan, Cleo was under tough pressure at work, and increasingly troubled by bronchitis and sinusitis, and almost permanently on antibiotics: when she became resistant to one brand, she was simply switched to another. The ninth specialist she consulted, a homeopath, had warned her she was in danger of being permanently damaged and leaving her system defenceless. He had guaranteed to cure her, but only if she were prepared totally to change her life-style, for her body was telling her that she was allergic to New York.

So Cleo had dumped her million-dollars-a-year job, returned to England, and bought herself a market garden in Essex. David now commuted from Great Barfield to Lincoln's Inn.

Breeze returned home as Plum was finishing her story. 'The question is,' he said as he deftly opened a bottle of champagne, 'was Cleo right to drop out?'

'Of course,' Lulu said. 'She used big business to make her nest-egg and retired, aged thirty-four, to get on with her life.'

'Yeah, and she's made it more difficult for other women to do likewise,' Breeze said. 'Her firm invested a lot of money in Cleo, and now they've lost it – because she can't stand pressure at the top.'

'Naturally,' snapped Plum, 'rather than stop competing, the other City male chauvinists in Cleo's firm choose to neglect their wives, their families, their social lives and outside interests – and then drop dead after a heart attack at forty-five.'

'Don't be so simplistic,' Breeze snapped back, but he looked uneasy: he found it hard to resist the seductive, hard-edged excitement of business.

Hastily, Lulu said, 'A driven life-style's a killer for anyone.'

'Perhaps lots of people work too hard to get qualifications, or pay off the card or the mortgage,' Plum suggested. 'They put off living until they've done this or got that. But preparing for life can gobble it up: you run out of time.'

'To mortgage or not to mortgage, that is the question,' Lulu said. 'And either choice is tough. You can't bring up a child in the open air.'

Plum agreed. 'Sure, everyone needs a roof over their head, but too many people want things they *don't* need – too many clothes for instance.'

Lulu added firmly, 'Cleo dumped her excess baggage.'

Somewhere in the back of her head, Plum heard a warning bell.

Having prepared the meal, the two women left Breeze and went up to the studio, where Lulu lolled on the couch with a glass of champagne in hand and listened as Plum told of her discoveries concerning the fakes.

'But I really hate doing this checking work on my own,' Plum concluded. 'So I want to persuade you to come to Sussex with me next Tuesday – I'm going to visit an auction-house in Brighton.'

'Sure! This search is so exciting! Mrs Barton'll look after Wolf.'

'It's not the least bit exciting,' Plum warned. 'So far it's mostly been embarrassing, although Dame Enid was fun. And it's lonely work: I can see why Sherlock Holmes needed Doctor Watson – moral support.'

'Surely you don't need moral support just to go to Brighton and ask a few questions! If only Plum the person could be as bold and brave as Plum the painter.' Lulu remembered her mother saying that Plum's lack of self-confidence stemmed from an overbearing father.

Plum responded acerbically, 'If only Lulu the painter could be as bold and brave as Lulu the person.'

'Ouch – nasty! It's *so* hard to snatch time to paint. Ben's away so much I sometimes feel like a single parent – trapped. We can't afford a full-time nanny, and I won't leave Wolf with an inexperienced au pair who can't speak English properly.'

Plum understood. 'Do you remember when I was first pregnant and determined that I wasn't going to let a baby change my life – not like it changed everyone else's life? When I planned for the baby to snooze in a papoose-type back-sling while I painted!'

'I'm not sure you remember how depressing it is, not to have any time to paint,' Lulu said earnestly. 'Now, I don't care whether or not anyone sees my work, *I just want to paint.* Ben doesn't understand what it feels like for a painter not to paint. *He* can just disappear for five months leaving Wolf and me on our own – but he'd have a fit if *I* went away to paint for so long.'

They both laughed, then Lulu said, 'My book-keeping job on Thursday pays for two days' shared baby-sitting, so I've been able to paint one day a week – only enough time to get started: people don't understand that a painting isn't like a damned patchwork quilt – you can't pick it up for half an hour, here and there.'

'No, once you've painted full-time, you have to give it your all or nothing,' Plum agreed. 'You can't be an amateur Sunday painter.'

'I wish Ben understood that! This morning he started the same old argument: it's been fifteen years since I painted full-time, so why can't I stop struggling and wait another two years, until Wolf goes to school? When I yelled that painting was my way to communicate, Ben looked puzzled and said he didn't see I *had* anything to communicate.' Lulu was close to tears. 'Plum can you understand how angry I felt? I have *fifteen years of life* to communicate in my painting. Fifteen years of love, jealousy, regret, resentment, anger, laziness, passion and housework.'

Plum put down her glass. 'You don't have to tell me. I know it's hard for a mother to be a person. Which reminds me, we'd better get down to the kitchen while we can still stand. We're having carpaccio, baked salmon with all the trimmings, then a salad, followed by a spectacular cheese soufflé. Tonight, I'm showing off. Oh God, I forgot, Cleo's allergic to flour.'

* * * *

Downstairs, in the small library off the dining-room, Ben and Breeze were drinking pure malt whisky: between them lay the comfortably unspoken, shared male experience of females.

'Plum's being bloody difficult,' said Breeze glumly. '*I* don't know what she wants.'

'Lulu's being fucking impossible.' His dark, lean face perplexed, Ben slouched in a tan leather club chair with his long legs crossed, gazing into the flames of the fire. 'I know what *she* wants – a full-time nanny – but it costs more to run a nanny than it does to run a Rolls-Royce. Lulu can see I can't afford to run a Roller – but she *won't* see that I can't afford to run a nanny. It'd mean working even longer hours than I do now; she already complains I'm never at home and don't do my share of baby-care.'

He scratched his black curls. 'I married a secretary, not a thwarted Picasso. Naturally I didn't mind her painting when I could afford it – before we had Wolf – but now her fucking obsession is wrecking our marriage.'

'Same here.' Breeze pushed the decanter towards his fellow sufferer. 'They're all trying to work out how they can have it all – but women simply can't, if they have kids. Plum only managed because her mother was an unpaid nanny while she got started – and she'd never have got to the top without me to free her path *and* see that she stuck to it. Although I get precious little thanks.'

'At least your wife's a genuine painter, making genuine money.' Ben's black eyebrows met in a worried frown. 'But I can't help suspecting Lulu's painting obsession is as genuine as a tart's orgasm.' He sipped his drink. 'In fact, I think she's secretly afraid she's just a normal person like the rest of us, and that's why she's unconsciously setting up this situation where it's my fault she's not a genius, because I'm withholding the money she needs to be a genius.'

Breeze leaned forward for the decanter. 'The question is – is Lulu prepared to work or does she, like the rest of them, want to stir a spoonful of effortless, instant fame into her cup of life?'

Ben looked sharply at Breeze. 'Do you think Lulu's got any talent?'

'I've always seen great potential in Lulu,' Breeze said thoughtfully. 'Pity she was side-tracked. Pity she got in with the wrong crowd – but drugs can happen to any kid today.'

Ben nodded. 'Lulu dashes in to be part of the fun without thinking of the consequences. And her dad spoiled her rotten, so she picked up the idea she could always wriggle out of any trouble.'

'Of course, technically, Lulu's still ragged and unsure, still at art-school level,' said Breeze.

They drank in sympathetic silence until Ben said hesitantly, 'I don't even *like* Lulu's paintings: they're so fucking depressing. Of course, I don't dare say so.'

'Like Plum, Lulu paints her moods, but in a more representational way. Realistic revival. She's clearly influenced by Avigdor Arikha – but that's no bad thing.'

'Don't you see a lot of self-pity? Woman gazing into broom cupboard. Woman surveying table piled with dirty dishes. Early morning study of bathroom, just as family left it.'

Breeze looked thoughtful. 'Lulu's subject matter is women in their domestic setting: housewife clutches child, vacuum cleaner or cup of coffee. No, I don't see self-pity, I see honesty, anxiety and hope. Lulu's work has a wistfulness, a yearning quality that's appealing.'

Ben put his glass down. 'What do you think I should do about it?'

'Encourage her. Draw up a schedule, to get . . . say twenty paintings completed. Peg her to dates. Keep her morale up.' Breeze hesitated, then said, 'Tell you what, I'll help her get a show – on the understanding that you tell this to *no one* – especially not Lulu.'

A scream came from the kitchen. Both men leaped to their feet.

In the kitchen, Plum was trying to open the door of Europe's most expensive oven, installed as a home-coming surprise for her. 'Breeze, the oven door seems to have locked itself. I can't get the salmon out.'

'Turn the heat down.' The kitchen was not Breeze's domain.

'Can't, it's thermostatically controlled.'

'Here, let me do it.' Breeze picked up the instruction book from the table, but he was unable to discover how to turn off the oven. Eventually, exasperated, he exclaimed, 'If Sandra can operate the thing, then so can we.'

'Sandra won't use it,' Plum said, trying not to giggle. 'Haven't you noticed she's been serving only grills and hob-cooked dishes?'

At that moment, the Brigstalls arrived. Cleo looked much older and thinner than the last time Plum had seen her, but she seemed in good spirits and both she and Sandy burst into laughter as they heard of Plum's culinary problem. The six of them spent an hour arguing over the instruction book before Breeze decided to call the emergency engineer. As they had to let the engineer in, they couldn't go to a restaurant, so they ate cheese and salad, and occasionally peered through the glass-fronted panel as, slowly, the baked salmon turned black then incinerated.

Despite open windows, the kitchen was clouded with smoke when the engineer arrived. 'Did you follow the instruction book?' he said cheerily. 'Ah, then *that's* your problem! It's wrong.'

The instruction book gave the correct sequence of buttons to press in order to unlock the door, but neglected to explain that this had to be accomplished within six seconds, or it wouldn't budge. Breeze was furious. 'Even if I'd known that, I couldn't have done it in that time. I'm not a concert pianist.'

'At least you had something else to eat,' said the irritatingly cheery engineer, and told how he had been called out on Christmas Day by an unfortunate woman with eighteen guests to Christmas dinner, who couldn't unlock her turkey.

Plum thought of the old-fashioned gas stove that had stood in her mother's kitchen for as long as she could remember. She asked, 'Why would anyone *want* to lock an oven door?'

'To stop the turkey getting out?' Breeze suggested as he wrote a cheque to pay the engineer.

*   *   *   *

On the following morning, Lulu telephoned Plum. 'Oh, Plum, it's B – B – Ben . . .' Lulu was weeping.

Plum's heart sank. 'What's wrong?'

'Nu – nu – *nothing*! Last night on the way home, Ben stopped at the late-night flower stall near Piccadilly . . . and he gave me this bunch of red roses . . .'

'So you hate red roses, but there's no need to cry about it.'

'T – T – Tucked into the red roses was a cheque for five hundred pounds – that's practically all our spare cash,' Lulu sobbed. 'But the best part is – the cheque wasn't made out to me . . .'

'And that's *good*?'

'It was made out to Windsor & Newton! Which means Ben wants me to spend it all on paint.'

*   *   *   *

That night, Breeze again shared Plum's bed.

*   *   *   *

Leo reluctantly agreed to accompany Plum on her second visit to Maltby's. The shop was even warmer than on Plum's previous visit, and as if waiting for them, Mr Maltby stood in Dickensian pose, legs apart, toasting his backside before the elaborate carved fireplace.

As Plum entered, she saw Mr Maltby stiffen. He looked warily at Leo, who flashed his press card. *New Perspective* was a serious visual magazine; Leo could not be dismissed like some gossip columnist trying to whip up trouble.

Eventually, politely and smoothly pressured by Leo, Mr Maltby agreed to talk to them off the record, which meant that Leo would not report their conversation. Tensely, he recalled that an Ambrosius Bosschaert sold by Maltby's had been queried in the *Tribune*. Maltby's had then obliged the auction-house from which they had acquired the painting to disclose the name of the anonymous previous owner. The owner was a woman who had lived locally for many years. Her maternal grandfather had been a Dutch diamond merchant who fled from Amsterdam to Britain with his wife and small daughter only hours before Hitler's troops invaded Holland; their only luggage had been a roll of valuable paintings and a pocketful of diamonds, much depleted by the cost of being smuggled out of Holland.

Maltby's had carefully checked the owner's family tree and found it to be genuine; the Dutch diamond merchant was still remembered at his synagogue in Golders Green as a crusty, eccentric man who never learned to speak good English.

But the auction-house had refused to name the woman who had sold the picture.

'One final thing,' Leo said, still polite but firm. 'What prices do seventeenth-century Dutch pictures fetch today, at major auctions?'

Mr Maltby, relieved at the prospect of ending his polite interrogation, said hesitantly, 'Still off-the-record? . . .'

As they left the shop and stepped into the grey depression of a February morning in London, Leo murmured, 'First time anyone's ever taken any notice of my press card.' In silence, they walked towards Piccadilly, where Leo put Plum in a taxi.

Before closing the door, he pulled out his notepad. 'You heard what prices those things fetch.' He read from his notes: 'Jan van Kessel the Elder, from thirty thousand dollars. Balthazar van der Ast and Jacob Hulsdonck, from sixty thousand dollars to around three hundred thousand dollars. Ambrosius Bosschaert the Elder, from a hundred and fifty thousand up to a million dollars for a very good one . . . *Now*, Plum, do you see why I want you to drop this search? People getting that sort of money for fakes aren't going to let *you* expose their game.'

Plum felt a twinge of fear but she also felt triumphant. Leo was not to know that it was only a matter of time before she could prove the forgeries. She certainly wasn't going to give up the hunt now.

At home Plum found a message from Lulu: once again, Mrs Barton could not baby-sit – she had arranged to have her eyes checked – so Lulu would be unable to accompany Plum to Brighton. A minor irritation.

CHAPTER SEVENTEEN

Monday, 17 February 1992

O N THE following morning, just before midday, Plum reached the outskirts of Brighton. She parked her Porsche outside a pub, the Dog and Duck, at one end of a narrow lane of eighteenth-century artisan dwellings, gentrified and painted in pastel shades. The far end of the street was blocked by a large brick building upon which was painted: BORDEN & PLOW: AUCTIONEERS.

Inside the draughty building, furniture was being shuffled along corridors by weary men in baize aprons; the stuffy office seemed well organized in a disorganized way. As no auction was taking place on that day, Plum found the office staff polite and helpful; a plump, purple-cheeked secretary obligingly put down her Mars bar to check the catalogue index for Plum.

The plump girl quickly discovered that in 1988 Borden & Plow had auctioned a Jan van Kessel the Elder (listed but not illustrated in their catalogue) for an anonymous seller. It had been purchased by Mrs Georgina Dodds (no confidentiality requested), of Little Middlington Grange, Little Middlington.

'Mrs Dodds buys and sells here often,' the girl added. 'Her husband was a local bigshot, ever so important.'

In 1989, Borden & Plow had auctioned a Bosschaert. Again, the previous owner had requested anonymity. This time the auction-house had illustrated the painting in their catalogue, and the painting had been purchased by Maltby's, Bond Street, London.

The plump girl was apologetic when Plum questioned her further. 'Can't tell more than that from the index. Better ask the invoice department – that's Greta: third door on the left, along the corridor.' She opened the door, then said, 'Here comes Mr Plow, he'll help you.'

The man who sauntered into the office looked more like a jolly farmer than a businessman. He was big but muscular, not fat, and his weatherbeaten complexion clearly showed that he spent no more time than was necessary in his office; he looked the sort of man who liked to hunt. He wore no tie, and a few curls escaped from the unbuttoned top of his shirt. Beneath his tweed jacket was a canary waistcoat; below it were beige cavalry twill trousers and earth-caked, peanut-butter suede shoes.

Mr Plow half-smiled at Plum, and carefully flicked the ash from what smelled like an expensive cigar. In the slightly arrogant, self-assured voice of a man who has captained school sports teams, he asked Plum how he could help her.

Plum explained that she wanted to check the source of an auctioned painting, and was inquiring on behalf of the present owner, Lady Binger, of Sydney, Australia.

When Mr Plow realized which painting Plum was checking, he laughed ruefully and said he'd let a fortune slip through his fingers. He added that a country auction-house couldn't investigate their lots as closely as a London one, for they hadn't the staff.

Plum nodded. She knew this to be a good reason for distributing fakes from provincial auction-houses, although no guarantee of authenticity was given by any auction-house to any buyer: this stipulation was generally printed (very small) in the catalogue and on the bill of sale.

Mr Plow added that he had been astonished when the Bosschaert fetched such a large sum. 'We get a lot of stuff signed "Gainsborough" or "Constable" – it's not difficult to paint a name on. But naturally, we never believe it. You might see a good imitation bid to a substantial price,' he added, 'if two people think they've spotted a bargain or some unscrupulous dealer reckons he can sell it as genuine. But we're careful what we put in the catalogue.'

Plum was well aware that auction-houses worked with a legal safety net: three different catalogue entries, which Breeze had once cynically interpreted for her. If the Christian name *and* surname of the painter is given – say, 'Augustus John' – then the auctioneer thinks that the picture was painted by Augustus John. If the initial and surname is given – say, 'A. John' – then the auctioneer reckons that this work was produced during the lifetime of Augustus John, possibly by a pupil. If the surname only is given, then the auctioneer thinks only that the picture has been painted in the style of Augustus John: similarly, 'School of Augustus John'.

'Can't tell you any more about the Bosschaert. Confidentiality requested,' said Mr Plow. 'But I *can* tell you that the previous owner met Mr Maltby and we were both satisfied with her explanation of possession.' He gave a brief nod, turned on his heel and left the room.

Following him, Plum watched Mr Plow go down the corridor and enter the third door on the left – no doubt to warn Greta not to answer any inquiries. But at least she knew that the owner previous to Maltby's had been a woman.

As it was nearly one o'clock, Plum decided to walk to the Dog and Duck for a sandwich, a drink and – she hoped – further information.

* * * *

It was the busiest time of day for the pub. Plum pushed her way to the bar, but there was clearly no chance of talking to the barmaid, who snatched her money and thrust a glass of beer at her. Plum fought her way through the crush around the bar, then moved to the back of the noisy, smoke-filled room, where she had spotted two men with baize aprons beneath their jackets, leaning against the wall.

For a few minutes Plum listened to their talk of pigeon-racing, then contrived to drop her glass of beer. One of the men broke off to pick up her glass and the other offered her a grimy handkerchief. ''Ere, love, use this. Shocking waste of bitter.'

Plum dabbed at her coat. 'Oh dear, I'm so small, I'll never fight my way to the bar again. Do you think? . . . Would you mind? . . .' She held out a £10 note. 'Oh, *thank* you . . . Please get a drink for yourself and your friend while you're there.'

Plum soon knew that Bobby Miliner, until recently an invoice clerk at Borden & Plow, had been made redundant six months earlier; the only reason for his dismissal had been the now universal one – lack of work. Times were tough. Greta had been retained because she'd been with the firm since the present Mr Plow was a boy.

Seven Miliners were listed in the telephone directory. Plum's fifth call was answered by a woman who said, 'He's out in the yard. Hang on . . . Bobbbbeeeee!'

Bobby spoke with a whine, and as he swallowed his words, Plum found him difficult to understand. He wanted to know who had given her his number? Why should he help her trace her mum's picture, sold accidentally? Why not ask that bastard Plow? However, he agreed immediately to talk to Plum when she offered to pay him £10 an hour to do so. Bobby named a coffee shop behind the Promenade, where, half an hour later, they met.

The café had a depressed air and few customers; there was a big juke-box, so maybe young people hung out there in the evening. A disinterested waitress directed Plum to a dark booth at the back. Plum sat on a lumpy, red gingham cushion and smiled across at Bobby Miliner.

Bobby was jockey size, and his thin face was suspicious. He smoothed his hair back and said, 'How about you pay upfront for a couple of hours?' Silently, Plum handed him two bank notes. Bobby stuffed them inside his jacket and whined, 'And you can forget the sob stuff about your old mum. Just tell me what you're after and I'll tell you if I know anything.'

'I want to locate the original owners of two pictures.' When she revealed which pictures, Bobby's cunning face looked knowing. 'Cor, there wasn't half a fuss when Old Man Plow realized what he could have made on that Bosh one, if he'd done a deal beforehand!' He looked thoughtfully at Plum. 'That'll cost you an extra two hundred in cash . . .' Keeping his eyes on Plum's face he added, 'Plus expenses . . . plus an extra hundred for Greta . . . plus her expenses.'

'Six hundred's my limit.' Plum realized that if Greta had been with Borden & Plow for years she was probably a trusted employee and certainly would never get the hundred. She was glad she'd removed her diamond ring before setting out.

'OK, OK. What's the matter, don't you trust me? Meet you

here this evening at six. Better move sharp if I'm going to talk to Greta.'

For the next three hours Plum wandered around Brighton, which was as bleakly depressing and windy as any other British seaside town out of season. She needed more cash than she could get on her credit card and finally located a bank willing to cash her cheque.

In a rare, unvandalized telephone box, Plum's finger moved down the pages of the Sussex directory until she located Dodds, G., Little Middlington Grange, Middlington.

A disagreeable female voice answered the telephone. Sharply imperious, it was the voice of a hundred colonels' wives, the voice that had helped Britain lose her Empire. In answer to Plum's nervous request to look at her Jan van Kessel, Mrs Dodds snorted, 'I *do* think this is the most appalling cheek! I don't expect tradesmen to talk to journalists about me! I shall take this up *immediately* with Angus Plow . . . No, young woman, you certainly can't see any of my paintings. If you come here, I warn you I'll set the dogs on you, and call the police! Now fuck orf! And don't phone again – or I'll complain directly to your proprietor!'

At six o'clock Plum returned to the café. Bobby Miliner already sat in the back booth. As Plum slid opposite him, Bobby winked at her; it was a knowing, unpleasant, complicitous gesture that suddenly made Plum feel ashamed of herself. Angrily she told herself that she might be bending the truth a bit, but it was for an honest reason.

'I'll need a bit more cash,' said Bobby airily.

'Sorry. Not possible. I had a problem getting this.' Plum produced the bank envelope, but did not hand it over.

In one swift, eel-like movement, Bobby slid out of the booth. 'You know where to get me if you change your mind.'

'I really did have a problem getting this,' Plum lied, patting the envelope. 'Banks don't just hand over hundreds of pounds if you walk in and ask, you know. I tried at least a dozen local banks before a manager agreed to phone my London bank. This is all I was able to get.'

'How about your watch?'

Plum shot her wrist forward to display her cheap black plastic watch. She stood up, hoping she looked prepared to leave.

'OK, OK. Sit down,' Bobby said sourly. 'Seems like both pictures that interest you was sold by the same person. Here's the address. Now let's see me money.' He pushed a crumpled bit of paper towards Plum, who edged the envelope of cash towards Bobby.

Plum read aloud, 'Mrs Gillian Carteret, The Chantrey, Mallowfield Village.'

'That's right,' Bobby busily counted the bank notes. 'It's up on the Downs. And you got a bonus – the phone number.' He looked up, tucked the notes away and winked again: this time the wink was triumphant and expansive.

He hesitated, then the urge to brag surmounted prudence. He sniggered. 'That old Greta's a pushover. I goes in and tells her Mr Plow says I'm to start work again. Old Greta gives a squawk – she knows there ain't enough work for two – then rushes off to find the guv'nor. Not much chance of *that* in the afternoon! . . . Lucky thing Greta didn't think to take the keys to the filing cabinet before she scampers off to see if I got her job . . . So I unlock the filing cabinet – and Bob's your uncle!'

He winked at Plum again. 'Lucky thing them invoices hadn't been archived yet. I wrote down the reference numbers and straight away I spotted both of 'em showed the same secret code instead of the name. 31A18X195W185B19. Only the guv'nor knows his code for confidentials – he thinks! I cracked it months ago.' He sniggered again. 'He numbers each alphabet letter then sticks an alphabet letter before each double digit, see? . . . So once I've worked out it's Carteret, I checks the confidential address file – and there it is. Tomorrow, I'll say I was pulling Greta's leg, and buy her a box of chocolates. She'll forget the whole thing in five minutes.'

Plum hurried to the back of the café to a telephone booth that smelt unpleasantly of stale cigarettes.

Mrs Carteret's number rang repeatedly without reply. Plum was just about to give up when a man answered and told her Mrs Carteret had moved the previous year. She now lived at the Old Rectory in Bissingthorpe.

Plum telephoned the Old Rectory, but after two rings, she hastily replaced the receiver. Better simply to appear than risk being told again to keep away.

* * * *

Just before seven o'clock, having twice been misdirected, Plum arrived at the Old Rectory. It was too dark to see the house as she stumbled along a winding flagstone path.

A woman answered the doorbell, her tall, wide-hipped, black shape outlined against bright yellow light.

'Mrs Carteret?' Plum inquired. 'I've come from Borden & Plow . . .'

'What is it this time?' the woman said wearily. 'You'd better come in.' She opened the door wider and stepped backwards. She was about thirty-five, and wore a grey, checked tweed jacket over a white silk blouse, a long oatmeal skirt and beautiful tan leather riding boots which matched her belt.

'Looks as if it's going to freeze again tonight . . .' The woman's conventional British chat about the weather stopped abruptly as Plum stepped into the light. 'Good God – aren't you Plum Russell? . . . What are you doing *here*? . . . Come into the sitting room – it's warmer there.'

'How do you know who I am?' Plum asked as she followed the woman into a comfortable, conventionally furnished room, where an open fire burned, flanked by two tasselled, gold velvet Knole couches.

Mrs Carteret hesitated. 'Oh, I've seen your photo in some newspaper.' A slight smile softened her pale face, as she moved to a cupboard. 'Sherry?' Smiling slightly again – it seemed to be a mannerism – she poured Amontillado in two small crystal glasses.

Plum stared at her hostess. Mrs Carteret's straight dark hair fell to her shoulders, and she had bold, dark eyes marred by liverish pouches beneath them.

When in doubt, tell the truth, Plum decided, and explained that she was seeking the origin of a painting by Balthazar van der Ast, which now belonged to her friend, Suzannah Marsh.

Mrs Carteret looked annoyed. 'What *is* the use of asking for anonymity if Borden & Plow cheerfully tell everyone where they can find me?'

Plum looked contrite and said, 'I'm sorry. They never made that clear. Some clerical mistake, I expect.'

'I'll speak to Mr Plow in the morning. He really should be more careful.'

'Why did you sell anonymously?' Plum asked, casually.

'I was short of money after my divorce and I found that embarrassing . . . I didn't want people to know . . .' Mrs Carteret put down her glass. *'But the Balthazar wasn't sold by Borden & Plow! That was bought by Maltby's direct from me!'*

'I expect I'm a bit muddled,' Plum said, apologetically.

Mrs Carteret's dark eyes looked sharply at Plum. Eventually she said, 'You see, I inherited the pictures from my grandfather, a Dutch refugee – Amos Strauss – who brought them to Britain in 1940. I sold three but I've still got the last one – I call it my emergency fund.'

'That's exactly what Suzannah Marsh wants to know to cover the gap in her provenance.' Plum beamed. 'Did your grandfather return to Holland after the war?'

'No. He worked as an interpreter during the war, then afterwards joined a firm of diamond merchants in Hatton Garden. He did well, although he'd never admit it: Mummy told me they always lived frugally. She said he never got over his flight from the Nazis and kept a packed suitcase under his bed until the Japanese surrender.' Again the slight smile lifted the corners of Mrs Carteret's wide mouth. 'But I'm sure your friend doesn't want to know that sort of thing.'

'It's interesting,' Plum said, 'and sad. May I ask what happened to your grandfather after the war?'

'In 1949 after my gran died my mother, then eighteen, married a Gentile. My father was a character actor. Grandad wouldn't see Mummy after that, so I never met him until after she died, which was long after Daddy disappeared – when I was fifteen.'

Mrs Carteret paused as if reluctant to recall painful memories. 'I moved in with Grandad and his housekeeper. I was terrified of this wild-looking, bad-tempered old man who didn't speak English properly. In 1966 he had a stroke and became even more frightening; of course his partner then had to run their business. Grandad died in 1968.'

'And you inherited everything?'

'Yes. By that time the business had dwindled to almost nothing, according to his partner, but at least I inherited the four paintings. Had I realized how valuable they were, I'd have sold them years ago at Sotheby's or Christie's, rather than the local auction-house.'

'That *was* bad luck,' Plum sympathized. 'When did you sell the first one?'

'Shortly after my divorce in 1986 I auctioned the Jan van Kessel, which went for three thousand pounds – *much* more than I'd expected – to a local landowner's wife, Georgina Dodds. I paid my debts, then I auctioned another – the Ambrosius Bosschaert, which was bought by Maltby's, who sold it to some American decorator.'

Mrs Carteret drained her glass. 'That sale enabled me to move in here. Then Maltby's tried to buy Mrs Dodds's picture but I gather she wouldn't consider selling it and was rude to them. Maltby's then tracked me down and bought my third painting last year, the Balthazar van der Ast: that must be the one your friend Suzannah bought . . .'

So clearly Maltby's had faith in the paintings and the provenances, Plum thought. 'Might I ask whether you're interested in selling your remaining painting?'

'I *wish* people would stop asking that! No. As I told you, I'm hanging on to my pension – that's how I think of it – unless somebody makes me a *very* good offer, of course.'

'I think Suzannah is a serious buyer. That's really why I'm here.'

Mrs Carteret hesitated, then gave her faint smile. 'Would you like to see it? I keep it in my bedroom, where I can look at it in the morning as I dress.'

Surely, Plum thought as she climbed the dark, winding stairs behind Mrs Carteret, if this woman were dishonest, she would not volunteer information about her picture and *offer* to show it to Plum?

'Aren't you frightened of thieves, with such a valuable picture in the house?' she asked.

'Yes, especially as Borden & Plow can't keep their collective mouth shut. The painting's going into a bank vault next Monday.'

They entered what was a fairly ordinary country bedroom,

except for the little painting that hung to one side of the pink curtains.

Mrs Carteret walked over to the picture, switched on the brass display light above it, and said, 'Jacob van Hulsdonck.'

The painting showed a small blue and white Oriental bowl of strawberries standing on a wooden table. To the right of the bowl, a blue butterfly perched on a strawberry leaf. To the left lay a few strawberries, dark-red cherries, and a pink carnation with scattered petals. The painting was very similar to the one Plum had seen in Artur Schneider's New York gallery.

Plum's mouth tightened as she reached into her tote bag. As recommended by Stephanie, she had brought with her a cheap, Polaroid camera of the sort carried by antique scouts who want a quick reference record. 'May I?' Plum lifted her camera and quickly snapped the painting, with Gillian Carteret standing beside it.

Mrs Carteret looked astonished, then furious. 'Give that to me!'

'Of course.' Plum's little camera flashed again. 'That one was for Suzannah, so I'll take another for you ... There!' She offered the second picture to Mrs Carteret.

Mrs Carteret hesitated. But what was there to object to? She accepted the second polaroid. 'Should your friend be interested in buying, I'd like Maltby's to act for me.'

'Of course.' Plum moved nearer to the picture and peered at it. 'This really is a beauty ...'

Ten minutes later, she left, convinced that she had just seen another fake, although she dared not remove the picture from the wall and had had no chance to do a pin test. Mrs Carteret had watched her carefully.

As she walked wearily over the flagstone path Plum should have been delighted by the results of her visit. But in a way that she couldn't put her finger on, she felt that Mrs Carteret had made her look a fool.

CHAPTER EIGHTEEN

EXHAUSTED, Plum returned home from Brighton at close to midnight. Breeze, already in bed, was on his new best behaviour: instead of shrieking his usual where-have-you-been-and-why-didn't-you-phone, he asked in a carefully pleasant voice, 'Have you eaten? Can I get you something? There's some hot milk in the thermos on your side of the bed. Plus your phone messages.'

'Toby called, will phone again,' Plum read, then 'Bill Hobbs can see you first thing Thursday,' and 'Enid Soames has your information. Will telephone at 6 a.m. on Tuesday. Repeat 6 a.m. She's catching a plane.'

Plum groaned and set the alarm clock.

She had just fallen asleep when Toby phoned. 'Oh, sorry, Ma, never realized it was so late . . .'

'What did Toby want?' Breeze asked, as Plum settled down to sleep again.

'Toby wants to dump his Industrial Design Engineering course and start a cottage industry toy business in Taiwan.' Plum yawned.

'That means sweated labour,' grunted Breeze disapprovingly. 'I suppose he needs money to finance the astonishing wardrobe of that new girlfriend – what's her name? Satsuma?'

'Mitsuma,' Plum murmured. 'She's a Vivienne Westwood model and buys them all wholesale.'

'I'd better provide start-up money for a small business – provided he finishes his course,' Breeze decided.

'Don't take Toby too seriously. It's probably only this week's ambition.' Plum drifted off to sleep.

Tuesday, 18 February 1992

Dame Enid's clear, ringing voice jolted Plum into consciousness better than the shrill alarm buzz. 'I'm at Heathrow, Plum. Sorry to call you early but I'm leaving for Moscow. Although the Institute can't commit until we examine the actual paintings, it appears from microscopic examination of the brushwork that *all* the paintings you've investigated were painted by the same forger – who also painted the picture that went to Sweden.'

'That's great news!' Plum was now fully awake.

'And we're also fairly certain that this villain's responsible for a Pieter Claesz breakfast still-life, which we examined for a Boston museum in 1989.'

'Could you let me have a transparency?'

'I've already sent it. The Claesz isn't nearly so good as the others – there isn't the same assurance – so perhaps it was one of the forger's early efforts . . . but it's definitely his brushwork.' She broke off, to argue rapidly in a foreign language with someone urging her to hurry. 'Goodness, my Russian's rusty! . . . Plum, are you still there? . . . Listen, both the Pieter Claesz *and* the Swede's picture have been holed, perhaps deliberately, *after* the picture had been painted: they were then repaired.'

Dame Enid paused, to emphasize the importance of what she said. 'So now five of your six fakes might have been deliberately holed and repaired. Perhaps *all* of them have.'

'That may be the forger's speciality?'

'Perhaps. Although of course we can't tell from your transparencies. Incidentally, these fakes are fairly recent: they started coming on the market around 1988 – and they're better than any we've seen for a long time.' Dame Enid again spoke in placatory Russian, then continued, 'Incidentally, we've traced most of the subject-matter back to art books. The rest probably came from museum posters. If he doesn't live in Holland, I expect the forger made a quick trip there to visit the museums.'

Plum heard another roar of angry Russian. Dame Enid spoke even more rapidly. 'I noticed one other thing that might be worth investigating: something's wrong about that big yellow, salmon-tinged tulip in the Binger picture. You might visit the botanist we work with – Will Ashley. He's in the phone book, lives in Barnes.'

Plum felt exultant! She had been right! Breeze, still asleep at her side, would have to eat his words.

Wednesday, 19 February 1992

The front door of the small surburban house in Barnes was opened by a large woman with an old-fashioned white overall wrapped around her cottage-loaf shape. Silently, she led Plum to a conservatory at the rear of the house; it was filled with fleshy, subtropical plants, a dense mass of viridian foliage, jades and spumescent limes; the atmosphere was hot and humid.

Will Ashley was a big-boned, craggy man of about forty, with sandy hair and a knobbly face that was a little too big for his body. He said, 'Can we have some tea, Mother?'

'It's kind of you to see me so quickly,' said Plum.

He smiled, showing uneven yellow teeth. 'I don't get many visitors.' He spoke in a very soft voice and waved Plum towards a pair of battered cane chairs.

From her portfolio, Plum produced the six enlarged transparencies. Will Ashley took them over to a spotless, white plastic tabletop and picked up a magnifying-glass. From time to time he referred to a pile of large books, or scribbled on a notepad. He did not speak.

Half an hour later, Plum, who found it difficult to breathe in the hot, humid air of the conservatory, had drunk three cups of very strong Indian tea and eaten several soggy ginger biscuits. She stifled a yawn: the humidity had made her sleepy.

The horticulturalist glanced up from his notepad. 'I've identified all these flowers. Mother will send you a typed list, with our invoice. There's almost nothing unusual. Of course, they wouldn't all be blooming at the same time but, as I expect you know, this was normal and permissible for those painters. They didn't always paint real flowers, otherwise they would have been limited to painting only in the summer months. They worked from their sketches.'

He lifted Lady Binger's transparency. 'I've noticed a couple of points which might interest you.' He pointed to the large, central flower. 'This big tulip . . . You notice it's a good, strong yellow with a salmon hue on the edges of the petals? That's a Darwin tulip, with a typical Darwin shape: the flower is rectangular and flat across the bottom.' He looked up at Plum. 'The Darwin group was introduced in 1889 by an amateur breeder, Monsieur Lenglard, of Lille, France.'

'So it can't have been painted in 1629?'

Will Ashley shook his head. He picked up Cynthia Bly's transparency. 'And see this black butterfly with big yellow spots on the interiors? It looks a bit like a Monarch, from North America – but these wings are much wider, and the Monarch has brown spots, of course.' He pointed. 'This is really a *big* butterfly, with about a twelve-centimetre wingspan . . . much larger than it's painted here. So I would imagine that it was copied from a book of butterflies by somebody who was a little careless . . . because this is a *Papilio bedoci*, and it was discovered in French Guiana in the nineteen-thirties.'

*   *   *   *

Although it was raining, Plum stood in the road before she slid into the Porsche, and gulped in lungfuls of fresh air. Gratefully, she inhaled the smell of the wet bark from the trees that lined the road, glad to escape from that steamy little suburban jungle.

Thursday, 29 February 1992

On Thursday morning, just after eight o'clock, Plum pushed her way through the busy stalls of the street market at the top end of Armada Road, Islington. Behind displays of fruit and vegetables stood cold but cheerful stall-holders; wearing mittens and old ski clothes, they jumped up and down to get warm, swinging their arms and wrapping them round their chests.

Behind the market stalls, the old rent-controlled terrace houses at the far end of Armada Road were falling to bits, and the street was on the verge of becoming a slum. Plum hurried towards Bill's house, to the left of the far end of the street, which was blocked by a graffiti-spattered wall which hid a railway line.

When Plum was about fifty yards away, Bill's black front door opened and two men appeared on the doorstep. One was clearly a departing visitor, the other was Bill. A tall, stooping figure, his skinny flanks were covered by oversized, stained jeans held up by string. He also wore a once-white open-necked shirt, and an out-at-elbows, shabby jacket of indeterminate colour.

When Bill caught sight of Plum, he grabbed the arm of his departing guest and pointed at her. The second man turned towards Plum and to her surprise she saw that he was Charley Boman. A look of consternation crossed his face – although Charley always looked worried: his straight black eyebrows bent upwards above his nose, so his dark brown eyes always looked anxiously defensive.

Plum was also anxious, as she didn't want her meeting with Bill to get back to Breeze – or anyone else. She decided to brazen it out and behave as if it were normal for her to be in the area. She waved cheerily. 'Hi, Bill. What are *you* doing here, Charley?'

'Bill's restoring one of Dad's pictures.' Charley stared at Plum as if challenging her to dispute this.

'Oh, which picture?' Plum was surprised. She had supposed Bill Hobbs to be a dealer's secret. Plum then remembered that Leo had reported seeing Charley on the cross-Channel ferry. Might Charley and Bill together be responsible for these fakes, Plum wondered? Perhaps Bill produced them and Charley distributed them? If so, that would be a new venture for Bill who had previously worked only on pictures that needed restoring, brought to him by dealers.

'Ain't she the nosey-parker? Hasn't changed in all these years.' Bill's South-London whine still held the obsequious note of an unscrupulous trader. He beamed at Plum and rubbed the pouch under his left eye, in a characteristic gesture that she well remembered: it meant that he was irritated.

'See you next week, Charley,' he said. 'That little tear'll take no time at all, but it'll have to dry before I re-varnish – and this ain't drying weather.'

Bill turned to Plum. 'Come in, darlin'. To what do I owe the honour of this trip down Memory Lane?' He still had the same battered, sexy charm that Plum remembered. His saggy, sallow face wore a mild, favourite-uncle expression, but beneath the overhanging pouches his ferret-bright little eyes were as sharp as ever. Plum noticed that he no longer dyed his remaining strands of hair.

Momentarily, she recalled Bill's bathroom – the only bathroom – in which all his girls washed themselves and their brushes. Always in that grimy bathroom cabinet stood a bottle of Grecian 2000 and a bottle of whisky. The bath was generally filled with some peculiar solution that smelled of laboratory formaldehyde; often, a freshly painted picture was immersed in it, to acquire, chemically and overnight, the bloom of centuries.

She followed Bill into the house. Standing on the bare boards of the hall, she sniffed, but could no longer smell the strong odour of turpentine and varnish that had hung around the ground-floor back kitchen. None of the girls had been allowed to know Bill's special fomulae for varnish, glue and paint solvents; he had mixed them himself, in the kitchen with the door shut. Sometimes he also melted glue in there, after which a disgusting miasma of boiled animal bones hung in the room.

He also used the kitchen stove, to bake his pictures, and thus achieve *craquelure*. All supplies were kept on the kitchen shelves: oils, varnishes, solvents, jars of brushes, cotton wool and Q-tips, and Ajax scourer, invaluable for removing stubborn varnish. On the bottom shelf Bill kept cans of baked beans and boxes of All-Bran (to keep him regular), which he bought in bulk and washed down with whisky.

Plum had met Bill in 1977, while waitressing at the Chelsea Arts Club. Bill had offered to train her as an apprentice restorer, pointing out that at least she'd be painting and acquiring a craft, instead of spilling chicken casserole over customers. He said he preferred to work with girls because they had a better eye for matching colour, and the required patience for the pernickety work. He omitted to add that they meekly accepted his low wages.

So Plum had joined the four mousy young women who toiled with small, sable brushes in the basement at Armada Road. Above the empty fireplace hung a certificate of restoration proficiency from the National Gallery, dated 1947. Bill was very strict – talking was forbidden, for it broke concentration – and a tyrant when he came downstairs late in the morning, red-eyed and hungover. Nevertheless the girls were devoted to him. Plum quickly realized that they had all slept with and been discarded by Bill.

Each girl had her painting speciality. Sally made dull country scenes more saleable by painting in picturesque cows, dogs or kittens. Edna did religious paintings, and was particularly good at thorny crowns and bloody wounds. Joyce did reverse-religious work for Arabs. In the late seventies, London had been a fashionable shopping area for black-swathed ladies in leather masks, who didn't want to buy paintings of the Madonna and baby Jesus. So Joyce touched out the babe-in-arms and substituted a sheaf of flowers.

Mona, the star of the basement, restored portraits, supplying missing eyes and noses or turning a toothless grandmother into a more saleable smiling débutante. An American dealer, who tracked down ancestral portraits, sent Bill recent photographs of existing families, so that Mona could change the features and provide the necessary family resemblance on some job lot of portraits bought at auction by Bill.

If a painting were badly torn and couldn't be patched, it was relined. This was done by the only other male in the establishment – a joint-smoking, genuine left-over sixties hippie who still wore flares and centrally parted long hair. Herb passed his days in an upper room, bent over the big vacuum table, where canvases were relined.

Plum spent her first week with Bill dabbing off old varnish – one tiny area at a time – with solvent on a Q-tip. This delicate, boring task required careful concentration, because different paints needed different strengths of solvent. She spent the second week working on a test piece: a huge seventeenth-century altar piece of the apostles. When Plum managed to clean this satisfactorily, and then paint in the missing bits, she was promoted to seventeenth-century Dutch flowerpieces.

When Bill discovered that she could turn out a tulip, Plum found herself chained to this work, although once she had acquired the technique she found it very dull. If she complained enough, Bill would borrow a cod or a lobster from the Italian restaurant on the corner, and Plum would be allowed to paint a Dutch still-life, with pewter plate, broken bread roll and knife, plus cut lemon with rind peeling off.

To prove he could paint better than any of the girls, Bill always added the final touches to these seventeenth-century Dutch paintings: the crucial fly, caterpillar, or dewdrop on flower petal.

Apart from these finishing touches, Plum had rarely seen Bill paint. His job had been to liaise with the dealers, crack the whip and occasionally visit a client if a dealer wanted a painting cleaned on site. For these trips Bill had purchased an old-fashioned doctor's travelling case, filled with ancient bottles labelled with peculiar formulae – BY385 or VFloGA975 – which deeply impressed the client. In fact, the bottles were filled with white spirit, meths or Flash.

After a few weeks in Armada Road, Plum became uneasy about the borderline between restoration, repainting, and faking. She had never seen a picture forged from scratch, but couldn't help wondering why she and the other girl slaves weren't allowed on the upper floors of Bill's house. And who were the taciturn visitors who delivered and collected paintings to the top floor, so different from the cheery dealers who came down to the basement to specify what expression they wanted on a cow's face?

Bill also became increasingly uneasy – about Plum's questions and uneasiness. After Plum had worked in Armada Road for three months, Bill's resident mistress left. Bill had a bath and reached for the Grecian 2000, then made his regulation pass at Plum, who made it clear she wasn't interested. Shortly afterwards, Bill fired her: he explained that her broad, sweeping style was not really suitable for the precise work that was necessary.

*　*　*　*

Fifteen years later, as she walked slowly into the deserted hall and her footsteps echoed on the bare boards in the hush of the dusty house, Plum remembered the cheerful bustle of the house.

'You still look like the little angel in a Piero della Francesca, you naughty gel,' Bill winked. 'Does your smart husband know you worked for me?'

Plum hesitated.

'Thought not.' He grinned, showing faultless false teeth. 'Ah, well, I'm too old to go looking for trouble. Come 'ere.' He pointed to the room to the left of the front door. This had always been kept shuttered on the street side, because the paintings were stored in it: racks of newly arrived, dingy canvases, those being worked on, and shiny, bright canvases awaiting collection.

Now the racks were almost empty. Bill lit a cheap cigarette. 'What you want done, Plum? I'm not in the business any more. Now I only works to oblige an old friend.' Automatically, he leered again. 'Had a heart bypass, see? Doctor told me, take it easy. I'd been thinkin' of retirement – I'm seventy-two, don't look it, do I? So I packed it in a couple of years back.'

Crisply, Plum said, 'Pull the other one, Bill. I've been looking at some of your work.' She pulled a transparency from her tote bag and thrust it into Bill's hand. 'I recognize your bluebottle, Bill.'

Bill peered at Suzannah's painting, and smiled.

'Remember that dealer from Kensington Church Street,' said Plum, 'the one with the alcoholic husband to support? I remember her asking you to hole your fakes and then mend them, so they wouldn't seem suspiciously undamaged when someone ran an ultra-violet lamp over them.'

Bill looked thoughtful. 'Yeah, Theresa. Nice girl. Told her I'd never get a dealer to pay me extra for ruinin' me work, then repairin' it again . . . Matter o' fact, I tried it a couple o' times – both seascapes, I remember – but it took twice as long to get a picture finished – and no one needed them elaborations.' He threw his cigarette end on a floorboard and carefully stamped it out, then walked back into the hall and held the transparency up to the fanlight, so that he could look at it clearly.

Plum followed him. 'All I want from you, Bill, is written confirmation that this painting came from your workshop. That's all. I understand you'll need to be paid for that. I promise you there won't be any trouble.'

Still peering at the transparency, Bill said, 'Whoever paid a fortune for this painting'll go to the dealer with my confirmation and get his money back, yes? And the dealer'll go to the geezer *he* bought it from and ask for *his* money back, and so on. And you expect nobody to say a word to the cops, because we're all gents in this game, and none of us want the bloody cops nosing around – not that they're any good.'

Plum nodded.

Bill chuckled. 'Well, me little darlin', I'm tempted to do it – write me little confession on a bit of paper and get a thousand pound for it, no doubt. But I'm an honest man.' He winked as he handed the transparency back to Plum. 'Sorry, darlin', this ain't one of mine.'

Plum was chagrined. Her instant reaction was to disbelieve him. But if he'd been rumbled, then he would probably accept money to betray accomplices that he would certainly be unable to work with in future. So he was probably telling the truth.

'Have you any idea who *might* have painted it?' Plum stammered.

'If I had, I wouldn't say, darlin', now would I?'

No, Plum thought, and Bill would make sure he was well paid to keep his mouth shut.

'*None* of these are yours?' She handed him her other transparencies.

'Nope … Nope … Nope … Nice work, though …' Bill paused at the painting that belonged to Lady Binger. 'That big tulip don't look quite right, do it?' He handed the transparencies back to Plum, with a final gesture that indicated the interview was over.

Dispirited, she trudged down the street, towards the market stalls. Then she heard hurried steps behind her, and turned to see Bill, a fresh cigarette hanging from his mouth.

'Cor, you'll give me another heart attack,' he panted, and looked at her with what suddenly seemed sad and lonely old eyes. 'Plum darlin', why not drop this? *You* don't own these paintings. I expect the geezers what own 'em can afford a bob or two.'

He twisted his head to check that no one could hear him, then whispered, 'You don't want to find you got a William Blake by the tail. One o' the reasons I got out of the game … is it ain't what it useter be … There's a lot of dodgy people in it these days. I wasn't going to pay protection money, and I didn't want to find meself being forced to do more work than I wanted. And I didn't want anyone to get into the habit of telling me what to do, see?'

He threw his cigarette in the gutter and put his dirty old hand on Plum's shoulder. 'You got a lot goin' for you, Plum. These geezers could upset you more than you'd credit. Drop it, Plum.'

Plum felt the hairs on the back of her neck prickle. She told herself it was because she didn't want Bill to touch her. But his warning had rekindled the fear she had felt when she first opened the anonymous letter in New York.

She was scared.

* * * *

For the rest of the day she tried unsuccessfully to contact Charley by telephone. When eventually they spoke, she asked him not to mention to Breeze that he'd seen her at Bill Hobbs's. She explained she'd bought a miniature, a gift for Breeze, and had taken it to Bill to repair.

* * * *

The following morning, she woke feeling as if she had a cold combined with a bad hangover. She coughed painfully. Perhaps a hot flannel on her face? But it was too much trouble to lift her throbbing head. She couldn't breathe properly through her swollen, blocked nose. Her bones ached. Her body felt as heavy and unwieldy as a baby elephant.

Plum groaned. Real detectives don't catch flu. And she couldn't afford to be ill in bed for a week because of Victor's end-of-March deadline.

Sunday, 22 March 1992

'Don't get out of bed, Plum. It's much too early for you to be up all day. Viral pneumonia is not to be sneezed at.' Lulu giggled at her weak joke, and rearranged the sheaf of daffodils she had brought.

Jenny, standing by a bedroom window, stared down at the

pistachio green buds scattered over the trees of Regent's Park. 'Breeze'll kill you – and us – if you have another relapse. After all, you've been out of action for a month. He only left for Zurich after you promised to do as the doctor said.'

'And it's treacherous weather,' Lulu added. 'Don't be fooled by the sunshine – it's very cold and windy outside.'

Propped against frilled *crêpe de Chine* pillows, Plum said mutinously, 'I feel fine.'

       *   *   *   *

The previous evening, Plum had telephoned Victor, who said comfortingly that the goddamn painting was the least of his worries: the important thing was for her to get back on her feet.

However, she was determined to go to Paris as soon as possible, to confront Monsieur Monfumat. He could hardly claim that Lady Binger's 'wrong' central tulip was admissible retouching. So perhaps Plum could use that tulip as a lever to force Monfumat to tell her the source of the Artur Schneider fake. If Monfumat had purchased it from Tonon, then Tonon was either the forger that Plum was seeking, or else was selling for that forger.

Three of the forgeries – those of Artur Schneider, Lady Binger and Dame Enid's anonymous Swede – had been traced back to Paris.

Two of the forgeries had been traced back to Britain, to Gillian Carteret: those of Suzannah Marsh and Cynthia Bly. Perhaps four, if Plum counted the painting that Georgina Dobbs had not allowed her to see, plus the little Jan van Kessel hanging on Mrs Carteret's bedroom wall. But without definite proof, Plum couldn't accuse Gillian Carteret of selling forgeries: not without risking a libel and slander suit that might cost half a million pounds in legal fees, let alone damages.

Lying in bed with the gentle spring sunshine warming her face, Plum again went over Mrs Carteret's story. She claimed to have first seen her four Dutch paintings when she was a schoolgirl. The presence of the butterfly discovered in the 1930s proved that Cynthia's picture must have been painted since then. Dame Enid thought that the painter of Cynthia's picture had also painted Suzannah

Marsh's. Therefore two pictures which had originated from Gillian Carteret were fakes.

Had Mrs Carteret's Dutch grandfather carried the pictures to Britain when he fled from Holland? Had he known that they were fakes? Or had he acquired them after reaching Britain? If, as Dame Enid said, the suspect paintings had all come on the market in the previous five years, then two of Mrs Carteret's pictures might have been painted within the past five years – and if so, her whole story fell apart.

Plum wondered how precisely the Institute could date the paintings of Cynthia Bly and Suzannah Marsh.

She also needed to speak to Charley. Perhaps he was smuggling fakes from Tonon into Britain. Perhaps Bill was the British distributor: certainly, he had all the necessary contacts.

However, the only two fake pictures that Plum knew to have surfaced in Britain came from Gillian Carteret, and it seemed unlikely that Bill, if distributing fakes, would have passed them to her instead of using his many dealer outlets. As yet, Plum could see no link to Gillian Carteret. Here she had temporarily come to a dead end. Which was why it was so important that she went to Paris.

* * * *

As she lay in bed and listened to the chatter of her two friends, Plum felt impatient and exasperated by her illness. She felt so sure that she was nearly at the end of her trail; perhaps only one little piece of evidence remained to be slid into place – and then the forger could be trapped.

It would be easy to fly over to Paris for the day and get back before Breeze returned from his business trip the following week – he was flying on to Milan. But first she had to get rid of these two fussing mother hens.

'I thought I'd go to Portsmouth for a few days,' she announced. 'The sea air would be good for me, the doctor said.'

Jenny turned and smiled at Lulu. 'I suppose we can trust her mum to look after her.'

* * * *

Tuesday, 24 March 1992

Standing at the Heathrow check-in counter, Plum jumped as she felt a gloved hand on her shoulder. She turned to see the boyishly handsome face of Richard Stepman.

She was delighted. 'Let's ask to be seated together, then you can update me on the Biennale over breakfast.'

'You're travelling Club class,' Richard said. 'I'm in steerage, and the plane's full, so I can't upgrade.' He shifted a rectangular parcel – clearly a small painting – from under one arm to the other.

'If the plane's full, they won't allow you on with that,' Plum said, pointing at Richard's parcel. 'Let me carry it for you, in Club.'

'No. I can't impose on you.'

'But I'm carrying nothing except a couple of magazines.'

Richard clutched his parcel. 'I'm taking this to . . . a friend of my mother, and I promised Mum I wouldn't let it out of my sight.' He smiled so engagingly that Plum felt sure he'd have no trouble persuading the air hostess to allow him to carry it on board.

❊   ❊   ❊   ❊

When they arrived in Paris, Plum caught up with Richard in the Customs area and offered him a lift. She had booked a car and driver for the entire day.

Richard, although polite, refused. He had expected to be met by his mother's friend. She must have been delayed. He would wait until she arrived.

Plum thought no more of this, and followed her driver to the waiting car. He immediately noticed that an attempt had been made to break into it and as this had to be reported to the airport police, it meant a half-hour delay.

As her car finally slid away from the kerb, Plum leaned forward and stared as she saw Richard Stepman – alone – climbing into a cab.

Plum tapped the glass that separated her from the driver. '*Suivez cette voiture, s'il vous plaît,*' she said, mildly amused. Was that not what Monsieur Poirot would say?

Richard Stepman's taxi did not head for Neuilly, where he had told Plum he was staying. Instead, peering out of the window, she found herself gazing up at Notre Dame. Beyond the cathedral, which stood proudly on the right bank of the River Seine, Richard's taxi headed for the Marais, a once fashionable quarter in the 4th Arrondissement; now the beautiful seventeenth-century buildings included not only the well-preserved houses of the wealthy, but also badly maintained, crumbling rent-controlled apartments of the poor.

Richard Stepman's taxi stopped outside a building that Plum immediately recognized as Lévi-Fontaine. The auction-house was run from the two lower floors of a tall, square building with a large central courtyard. Large green gates (now propped open) separated courtyard from street. The vehicles squeezing in and out of these gates were guided by a fat, grey-haired concierge wearing a heavy coat and carpet slippers. Imperturbable, she ignored the impatient horns of blocked cars in the narrow street outside.

Sitting well back in her car, Plum watched Richard jump out of his taxi, pay the driver, then step into the auction-house. He had lied. He had said he was going to deliver a picture to a friend of his mother – and instead he had taken it to an art auction-house.

She remembered what Leo had said when they lunched at L'Étoile. 'If you're going to suspect everyone who goes to Paris of passing fake pictures, why not ask that rich layabout Charley Boman what he was doing at Lévi-Fontaine?'

Was Richard taking a picture to Lévi-Fontaine to sell? Was it possible that pictures were not being smuggled into Britain – but out of Britain?

Plum told herself that she mustn't be unduly, unfairly suspicious. Were Breeze here, he would certainly tell her that she was being paranoid. He would point out that she had seen Leo, Charley and Richard carry paintings before now. People in their circle carried paintings as casually as tourists carry pocket dictionaries. And why should there be any sinister significance in a trip to Paris? Paris and London were two of the world's three major art centres. No more odd for Leo, Charley or Richard to be going to Paris with paintings than for a fishmonger to be heading for a fishmarket.

But then, why had Leo, Charley and Richard deliberately misled her?

CHAPTER NINETEEN

Monday, 23 March 1992

PLUM'S driver tipped the fat concierge to allow the car to wait in the cobbled inner courtyard. She sat back, unseen, and kept her eyes on the gap between the two dark green gates – the only exit from Lévi-Fontaine. After only forty minutes she saw the big, upright figure of Richard Stepman walk confidently through it – without his parcelled painting.

As soon as he had disappeared, Plum hurried into the auction-house and a warren of passages. Asking repeatedly for *'le bureau'*, she finally found herself in a hall where four rows of secretaries typed as fast as they could, as if in some 1930s typing pool, overseen by a thin woman with frenzied eyes, dressed in a pink Chanel suit. She directed Plum to the main reception office, which was lined with trestle tables covered with paintings lying on their backs, and to a blonde young woman in a long black sweater over red patent thigh-boots, who spoke almost-perfect English in an upper-class accent. Plum explained that she had just seen an old friend, Richard Stepman, enter through the main gate, but had lost sight of him in the maze of passages outside.

The young woman explained that Monsieur Stepman had already left, after delivering a painting for auction. They had only a London address for him. While she scribbled it down, Plum looked around the room, which was far more efficiently organized than she had realized. The languid security guard immediately became alert when Plum strolled over to the trestle tables and examined the paintings.

She walked over to a painting that had a guard all to itself. It was

244

a small Braque gouache sketch, in greys and sand colours, of two seagulls. With a feeling of *déjà vu*, Plum tried to recall where she had seen that Braque. Clearly genuine, it was a far more valuable painting than this second-division auction-house would normally sell. Plum wondered why anyone would sell top-quality art here, where the painting would not fetch nearly such a good price as if sold by one of the leading auctioneers. Possibly the reason was that here, sale details were not publicized around the world, as with top auction-houses. So Lévi-Fontaine was a good place to unload a painting that was, perhaps, too hot to sell in London or New York.

'That Braque's coming up at Wednesday's auction,' said the girl in the red thigh-boots. 'It's easily the best thing in the sale.'

'It's good,' Plum agreed. 'Who's the owner?'

'Anonymous. Are you interested? Would you like a catalogue?'

As she accepted it, Plum asked casually, 'What was Monsieur Stepman selling?'

'An Augustus John drawing, very pretty; it's been taken to our studio to be photographed. It is the first time that Monsieur Stepman sells with us. He is a new client.'

'Why do you think he is selling here instead of in London?'

The girl shrugged her shoulders. 'He was recommended by another Englishman for whom we sell. Perhaps you know Monsieur Boman?'

'I do indeed.'

Plum could get no further information. Nor could she get a sight of the John drawing. As the girl in red thigh-boots had started to look suspicious and wary, Plum withdrew.

She wandered slowly back to the courtyard, wondering why Douglas Boman should be selling pictures anonymously. Perhaps in order to avoid paying tax on the profits? Perhaps Charley had brought them to Paris for his dad, and been spotted by Leo on the ferry. In which case there was nothing sinister about it, so Plum could cross off Charley as a suspect.

But that did not explain Richard's odd behaviour on the trip from London to Paris – or his evasiveness.

Plum wondered whether the John drawing was genuine.

* * * *

Half an hour later, Plum stood in the Rue Jacob, screwing up enough courage to enter Monfumat. She had asked her driver to telephone and ask if Monsieur Monfumat was available to speak to an English buyer, and had been told that he would not be in the shop until late that afternoon.

Eventually she told herself that if she didn't enter soon, she risked the return of Monsieur Monfumat. The sooner she went inside, the sooner her ordeal would be over. So she pushed open the wagon-green door and once again sniffed the smell of beeswax, heard the old-fashioned bell jangle. Again she saw the foolishly pleasant face of the blond young assistant as he hurried towards the front of the shop. As he recognized Plum, the young man smiled, the pleased smile of a favourite cousin who was always willing to put aside whatever he was doing in order to help someone else. 'Is it that your husband appreciated the Jacqueline jug?'

'He loved it,' Plum said truthfully. 'But this time I'm looking for a gift for my aunt.' She would not have time to visit Aunt Harriet, who would be at the Sorbonne all day, but she could arrange for a surprise to be delivered.

As the young man wrapped a yellow Limoges cup and saucer, Plum said, 'A friend of mine has a query about a picture that came from this shop. When will Monsieur Monfumat be available?'

The young man stopped twirling green tartan ribbon around the malachite box. 'A query? What type of query? Monsieur Monfumat will be here after the luncheon. It is only he who concerns himself with the paintings.'

When Plum again produced the Binger transparency, he remembered. 'Ah, the Bosschaert. This picture concerned you on your previous visit, is it not?'

'Yes. This picture came from Monsieur Tonon. Would you please give me his address?'

The young man's pleasantly vapid face looked uncertain. 'I am not allowed to speak of our sources, you understand . . .' He was extremely embarrassed.

'And why should you wish to know this?' The voice came from behind Plum, who had not heard the bell. She spun around and, without being told, knew that she was facing Monsieur Monfumat.

Small sharp black eyes stared through rimless spectacles, from a face the colour of a peeled potato, surrounded by thick grey receding hair.

'I . . . er . . . I want to . . .' she stammered, furious with herself for being nervous. 'There's a tulip in this picture that didn't exist when it was supposed to have been painted.'

'And why does this picture concern you?'

'Lady Binger, the present owner, wishes to know the reason for the discrepancy. Professor Enid Soames of the British Institute of Art has asked me to help her with her investigation. We know that you acquired the picture from Monsieur Tonon, so I want to speak to him.'

Monsieur Monfumat plunged his hands into the pockets of his mink-collared overcoat and stared at Plum. 'These may or may not be facts, but they are certainly not credentials, and no reason for me to discuss my business affairs with a strange young woman.' He spoke deliberately, with pauses between his sentences, clearly not a man who allowed interruptions. 'I am not at liberty to discuss my sources and have no wish to do so, Madame. I would refer you to our conditions of sale – this is not a criminal matter, I assume?'

When Plum shook her head, Monsieur Monfumat seemed to relax slightly. 'Of course, it is possible that the picture was restored – most pictures of that age have been restored. So that would explain a modern tulip, would it not? . . . Good day, Madame.'

Back in her hired car, Plum once again faced a dead end. Tonon was not an unusual name in France, and her driver had already telephoned all the Tonons in the Paris telephone directory without locating a painter or an art dealer. He might be anywhere in France, Belgium, Luxembourg or Switzerland – or somewhere else: people moved around these days, they didn't automatically stay in the country of their birth. Monsieur Tonon might be anywhere in the world.

Saturday, 28 March 1992

Five days after her trip to Paris, Plum, wearing a paint-streaked khaki flying suit, sat cross-legged on the floor of her studio and poured tea for Jenny and Lulu, who had brought Wolf. Wolf had already eaten three buttered crumpets and two rich black slices of rum fruitcake.

'Nice one, Plum.' Jenny jerked her head towards the big canvas propped against the wall.

'Um . . .' Plum screwed her eyes up, cocked her head to one side and peered at the canvas. It was coming along well, but that small brown section, bottom left, was still too dull; perhaps hatch it in turquoise? She didn't want it too busy, didn't want to break the tension between those subtle siennas, and the bottom right slab of earthy orange – an old-fashioned, boot-polish colour. She'd sharpen up the indigo-to-black area, so that the central cream shape receded. At the moment it was too demanding. *And* remove those tomato stripes on magenta: overkill.

'I'm sorry we've missed Breeze . . . put that crumpet *down*, Wolf,' Lulu barked, in the schizophrenic conversational tones used by mothers of young children.

'I almost missed him myself,' Plum said. 'He got back from Milan last Wednesday, then left for New York yesterday – but he'll be back here *next* Tuesday.'

Just before he left, Breeze had reviewed the paintings produced by Plum since her return from Australia. He had paced the studio assessing the three finished canvases, two small and one large. 'Not much, but good,' he acknowledged with relief. 'I'm bloody glad you're concentrating on the Biennale at last. Thank God you've got this new stuff for the British Council. Definitely a new departure for you. The big one's the best: that's your Biennale focal point. It's wonderful.'

The big picture had been painted in pale and delicate colours. Mauves, violets and greens predominated, but, despite the light tones, the sure construction and bold application of paint gave strength to the canvas.

'It's called *Awakening*,' Plum said.

'It looks as if there's more to it than meets the eye – almost as if there's something underneath it,' Breeze said, narrowing his eyes. 'Something similar in feeling – although not in rendering – to that Aboriginal thing you bought in Australia.'

Plum had wondered why, when Breeze could so easily understand what she wanted to convey in a painting, he wouldn't listen to her thoughts and feelings when she put them into words. Perhaps it was because as a painter she slotted into a different category from that of a wife; she was listened to, allowed and encouraged to be herself, and to experiment and grow.

*   *   *   *

'Wolf, come away from that paint table,' shouted Lulu. 'Sorry, Plum, I shouldn't have brought him here. He's as quiet as an angel in my studio.'

'He'll never learn to behave if you leave him at home,' Jenny remonstrated. 'Don't be so strict with him, Lulu. Relax.'

'Wait till you've got one, and you'll realize you can't relax for the next eighteen years.' Lulu jumped up to pull Wolf away from the open tins of paint.

'How's Don?' Plum asked hastily, suddenly recalling the name of Jenny's new boyfriend.

'Don and I broke up last night,' said Jenny tersely. Tears came into her eyes. '*I don't understand what I do wrong.* Why *do* men leave me? I'm so very careful now.' Long ago, after Lulu had reported her mother's advice, Jenny had sworn never again to tell a man she loved him or – worse – that she wanted to have his baby. The biggest compliment she could pay a man had the magic ability to propel him out of bed and down the street before he'd zipped up his pants.

As always, her two friends comforted Jenny as she lamented her misfortune and fretted about her biological clock. Unobserved, Wolf seized the opportunity to finish the muffins.

'Why must *I* pretend I don't care for a man when I do?' wailed Jenny. 'Why should *I* have to fake what I feel?'

'Because that isn't all you fake,' Lulu said bluntly. The three of them had endlessly discussed Jenny's sexual performance anxieties: Jenny's desire to please; Jenny's fear of being unable to climax as fast as the fellow's previous girl-friends; Jenny's fear that her lover would get impatient – and leave her.

'A man can't tell,' Jenny said, as if to reassure herself.

'Maybe he can't tell physically if a woman is faking,' Lulu replied, 'but maybe he knows you well enough to tell when you're lying. And if he spots that but doesn't like to argue about it, what sort of relationship do you have? *A fake one.*'

'And if you fake it and he *doesn't* notice,' Plum pointed out, 'you'll probably be resentful – which'll *definitely* screw up the relationship.'

Lulu leaned forward. 'You know that sex isn't just the physical act – and it isn't confined to bed. Sex affects your whole life, because it affects the way you feel when you get *out* of bed.' Dreamily, she leaned back and stretched her arms. 'A good sexual experience can make a rainy Monday seem wonderful, and an unsatisfactory sexual experience can depress you for days; even if you're in the most wonderful place in the world, with palm trees waving, you feel inferior, cheated and miserable.'

'Especially if the man's clearly had a great time,' Plum added.

'Then your feelings affect all your out-of-bed relationships.' Lulu slapped Wolf's buttery hands off her leggings. 'You feel tearful one moment, aggressive the next, and snap at the children.'

Plum giggled.

'This is no laughing matter for me,' said Jenny crossly. Although she asked for advice, she felt attacked when it was given.

'Of course not,' Lulu said, 'but we're just trying to make you feel less depressed. Wolf, *put that teapot down!*'

'I don't think either of you have any idea how I really feel,' said Jenny bitterly. 'Especially when I listen to your condescending advice.'

'We don't mean to be condescending, do we, Plum?'

'That's what it sounds like to me.' Jenny was still bitter. 'You two don't understand how tired I am of being quiet, reliable old Jenny: the back-up person, charming, cheerful, give-no-trouble, always-willing-to-baby-sit, lend-you-her-last-penny, let-you-sleep-on-her-sofa-for-weeks Jenny. And, of course, Jenny the bridesmaid, never the bride.' Defiantly she tossed her amber hair. 'You two don't know what it feels like always to be the one in the background. How many times have I heard one of you ask, "Can I bring my friend Jenny?" And whoever you're talking to knows by the sound of your voice that Jenny is being slid in, Jenny isn't the flavour of the month, Jenny is available because nobody else wants her! . . . But why?'

She scrambled to her feet and stared at herself in the studio mirror. 'I know I'm too big to wear these yellow leggings with a red sweater, I look like a large court jester. So have a good look! And let's not try to disguise it in future! Jenny is not Amazonian or Junoesque: Jenny is *big*! Jenny is always bigger than the blind dates you fix for her. I don't need anyone to tell *me* that anatomy is destiny.'

Plum caught Lulu's eye; they loved Jenny but they knew better than to interrupt as she strode to the window and stared at the pale light of the setting sun above the green canopy of budding trees. Quietly she said, 'What I yearn for – and somehow feel entitled to – is what you two have: a man and children of my own to love.' She turned to face her friends. 'Can't you look at me for once and *see what I am* – and how little likelihood there is of my ever getting even ten per cent of what you *both* take for granted?'

Wordlessly, Plum dashed over to the window and hugged her friend.

Grabbing Wolf away from the tea-tray with one hand, Lulu cried, 'Jenny, we love you. You're part of our family. You're our special, chosen sister . . .'

'Chosen because *you're* so special.' Plum hugged harder. 'We know you and trust you . . .' She stopped as she heard a knock on the door.

Sandra held out an envelope to Plum. 'A messenger just delivered this. I thought it might be important.'

Her attention still on Jenny, Plum hastily pulled open the envelope and withdrew a single sheet of white paper.

Plum turned white. 'Oh, my God.' She held out the paper. 'It's another threatening letter!'

Jenny's insecurity forgotten, the three women stared at the piece of ordinary white typing paper. On it, spelled in letters of differing sizes, cut from newsprint, were the words:

DROP PIX HUNT OR YOU DIE

The envelope, an ordinary office buff one, had been addressed by hand, in black biro. While the three women stared in silence at the letter, Wolf managed to finish the rum fruitcake.

Plum grabbed the intercom, dialled the kitchen and asked where the messenger came from. Sandra reported signing a receipt for a lad of about eighteen who wore motor-bike leathers and a crash helmet, so she couldn't see much of his face. She had no idea where he came from.

'It's from the same person, using the same method.' Plum's hands trembled as she stared down at the words.

'Are you sure? Where's the other letter – the first one that was sent in New York?' Jenny asked. 'You should compare them.'

Plum couldn't remember whether Breeze had kept the first letter.

'I'm surprised whoever wrote it hasn't used cut-out letters for the envelope,' Jenny said.

'Then the messenger might have remembered it,' Lulu pointed out.

Plum tried to think. 'The words on the New York envelope were written in capital letters, but this is written like any hand-addressed envelope.'

'If the writer wanted to be untraceable, surely he or she would have used a typewriter?' Jenny theorized. 'Of course, they *can* be traced, but the police can't inspect every typewriter in Britain.'

'Not everyone has a typewriter,' Lulu said. 'Whoever it is certainly doesn't work in an office – or the envelope could have been typed on computer, then erased. If he works in an office, then he's too grand or too old to know how to operate a computer.'

'What did the New York letter say?' Jenny asked.

'*Forget Dutch pic or you are dead.*' Plum would never forget those words. 'He's used the word "pix" this time, and spelt it with an "x". That's an American habit. A British person would spell it "pics", wouldn't he?'

'Maybe. Maybe not,' Jenny said.

Plum looked again. 'The only other word in both messages is "or": that doesn't tell us much.'

'Are you going to the police?' Jenny asked.

'Probably not,' Plum said. 'They'll only ask how I can be sure it isn't a prank. I don't know . . . I'll think about it. I'll see what Breeze thinks . . . No, I don't want Breeze to know about this. He's only gone for a few days; he might feel he ought to come back, but I know he's on a tight schedule and some of it'll be impossible to rearrange. And what good could Breeze do? I couldn't be safer than I am in this house . . . I can't decide . . . I don't know . . . I'll sleep on it.'

Lulu squinted again at the envelope. 'Obviously this handwriting is disguised – any idiot knows you can be traced by your own writing. But not everybody knows you can be traced by your *disguised* handwriting.' She turned the envelope over.

Jenny peered over Lulu's shoulder. 'How do you know the letter writer didn't ask someone else to address the envelope?'

'Because then somebody else would know about it, so he'd risk discovery.'

'How do you know it's a male?' Plum asked.

'Maybe it isn't,' Lulu said.

'How can we find out more about this damned letter?' Plum was anxious and impatient.

'What about Clare Stevens, that graphologist I used to type for? She checks people's character from their handwriting, before they're employed. Clare might help us assemble a psychological profile of the letter writer.'

As there was no telephone in Plum's studio, Lulu clattered downstairs to Plum's bedroom, dragging Wolf behind her.

White-faced, Plum turned to Jenny. 'I can't help being frightened. I wish Breeze were back.' She shivered. 'Of course this place is a fortress – the insurance people insist on it because we keep valuable paintings here.' Plum knew that there were steel grilles at all the windows, and an alarm connected to the police station, which was only a step away, in Albany Street. 'But I'm scared, Jenny,' she wailed.

'Maybe it's not as dangerous as you think,' Jenny soothed. 'Maybe someone wants you to give up your search – but I can't believe that anyone's going to kill you if you don't. He or she just wants to frighten you.'

'He or she's succeeded.' For the first time since she had started to search for the forgers, Plum was terrified. Breeze had down-played the first threatening letter in New York, which certainly might have been a stupid prank. But two letters, obviously from the same source and delivered in different countries, were unlikely to have been sent by a prankster.

Maybe Breeze was right, thought Plum. Maybe her search to expose the forgers *was* . . . dangerous.

Wordlessly she turned to Jenny and again the two women hugged, but now Plum was being reassured by Jenny, who had forgotten her previous angry words.

Lulu reappeared in the studio doorway. 'Clare Stevens says she'll do it straight away, but as she's going to the theatre you must get over to her place fast.' She pulled a wry face. 'Plum, I'm sorry. Wolf's been sick over your lace bedspread. I'd better take him home.'

✳   ✳   ✳   ✳

Clare Stevens, small, neat and quiet, lived in a small, neat, quiet terrace house in Chelsea which had obviously cost a fortune.

In a small back sitting-room, Plum and Jenny perched in silence on flowered chairs and stared at the graphologist, who wore a pink satin dressing-gown and large horn-rimmed spectacles. She laid the envelope on a small, lady-like desk and examined each word with a magnifying-glass, which hovered over the words written in black ballpoint pen:

Plum Russell
129 Chester Terrace,
Regent's Park
London NW1 6ED

Eventually Clare Stevens said, 'It's an attractive writing that dances fluidly across the surface. It's probably been written by a man; I can tell from the size of the fingers. It's rapid and free-flowing. It's certainly an intelligent, decisive person who's trying to disguise his handwriting.'

'You mean he *hasn't* disguised it?' Plum asked hopefully.

'No, he's only altered it: the characteristics are still the same – that flourishing T on "terrace" for instance.' She put down the magnifying-glass and pointed at the envelope with a silver paper knife. 'As this script slopes backwards, let's assume for the moment that his normal handwriting is upright or slopes forwards. Now that flourishing T with the base joined to the top on the left hand side *cannot* be written as a forward letter – so we can assume that this is normally an upright hand.'

Mrs Stevens looked at Plum. 'This is a rapid and free-flowing hand, the writing of an agile mind accustomed to quick twists and turns of ideas to serve a manipulative purpose.' Fascinated, Plum watched the pointing tip of the silver paper knife, as Mrs Stevens indicated different letters. 'The letter forms aren't particularly original. These narrow angular letters with daggers and needles have a mean look . . . There's something pretentious about those claws and hooks – particularly the h and the g – that make me suspect an undercurrent of aggression, avidity and danger.'

She handed the envelope back to Plum. 'I'm certain of what I just told you, but I could also speculate a little, if you wish. In view of the circumstances, an informed guess might be useful.'

'You're probably giving me the only help I'm going to get,' said Plum.

Although the room was warm, Clare Stevens pulled her dressing-gown around her as if to protect her from the cold. She looked directly at Plum. 'He's probably compulsive and wilful . . . He appears amiable but he has a big chip on his shoulder.' She hesitated, then said, 'And I think . . . he might . . . be unable to tell wrong from right.'

'What do you mean?' Jenny asked in a quiet voice.

Mrs Stevens's voice was regretful, but carried a clear warning. 'He might be a psychopath.'

*   *   *   *

'That's all I need – a psychopath!' Plum slewed the black Porsche around Sloane Square.

'Slow down or *you'll* kill yourself,' Jenny advised.

'I'd better tell the police.'

'Of course, people in the public eye often get death threats from silly idiots.'

'I'll let the cops decide.'

*   *   *   *

At Albany Street police station, where the smart reception area was walled in dark cedar panelling and a huge silver metropolitan police crest decorated one wall, Plum told the friendly constable on duty far more than she had intended. Eventually, she told her whole story, even including her doubts about Richard Stepman in Paris.

'This sounds a case for the fraud squad,' said the constable. 'No use phoning now – they've all gone home, they keep regular office hours. We'll inform them in the morning and they'll probably pay you a visit. In the meantime, I'll keep your envelope.'

*   *   *   *

Suddenly the house seemed over-large and oppressive, sinisterly quiet. There was no sound from the park outside. Plum had refused Jenny's offer to stay the night, although, after she chained the front door behind her friend, she wished she had accepted it. She wished that Breeze was with her, and was tempted to telephone him. But what good would that do? Her news would only make him worry. And if he dumped his trip and returned to England for nothing – how would Plum feel? Or if he didn't – how would she feel then?

She checked the burglar-alarm in the kitchen, then every grille in front of every window on every floor; they were all drawn and padlocked. Sandra did this every evening at six o'clock.

Plum decided to go up to the studio, where she always felt cosy and safe. Once there, she immediately shifted her attention to the picture in progress. Her eyes slowly followed the line of the picture edge on all four sides, then she stared again at each angle in turn: she liked to come in from the sides and take care of the corners.

She picked up a brush, hesitated, then daubed a patch of purple on a sky-blue area. She jammed the brush into a paint-encrusted pot and scattered bright pink spots, first on a turquoise ground, then on a tangerine area. Yellow spots were then flicked on a crimson background, violent as a close-up of a strawberry.

The picture now looked as if it had caught some form of outer-space measles. Damn! She was definitely jumpy. And she should have known better than to paint by artificial light; when she did so, she always had to rework the picture the next morning.

Plum wandered to her bedroom, where her anxiety increased, for no reason, she told herself, except that she was alone in the house. Yet she'd been alone there many times before without concern.

As she undressed, Plum felt as if she knew that a peeping Tom were watching her, but could do nothing about it. She felt frightened and angry.

Suddenly she sensed that somebody *was* hidden in the room. She could feel a thick, invisible presence, almost hear somebody breathing.

For five minutes, she stood trembling in the centre of the room – but nothing happened.

Plum slowly lay down on the carpet by her bed. She hesitated with one trembling hand on the pleated valance that surrounded the base of the bed. Suppose she lifted it – and found herself gazing into the cruel eyes of a psychopath?

Telling herself she couldn't lie naked on the floor all night, she cautiously lifted the valance and peered beneath the bed.

There was nothing to be seen, except fluff.

She slid between the cool, embroidered linen sheets but could not sleep. Her fears would not leave her: who was this unknown person who wished her harm? Who could possibly want to kill her? Was he a trickster or a killer? It seemed a ridiculous idea . . . until you opened a newspaper: they were filled with stories of lunatic violence.

Where would she feel safe? Where could she hide? She couldn't stand this fear. She couldn't stand feeling that some large cruel giant were watching her from above, as if watching a canary in a cage . . . about to open the cage door so the cat could get in.

She felt vulnerable and exposed. She felt trapped. She sensed an almost tangible, invisible web that was starting to tighten, to close around her, constricting her safety.

At two in the morning, hot, restless and still unable to sleep, she pulled back the bedroom curtains and opened the windows, to allow the chill night air to enter.

As she re-locked the window padlock, then turned her back to it, she suddenly felt vulnerable once more. Suppose the psychopath had a gun, and had climbed up a tree in the park outside her window? . . . She told herself firmly not to have such stupid fears: the park was always locked at dusk. But the man might have hidden in the bushes and *then* climbed a tree . . .

But how could anyone have known that she would open her curtains? Plum tried to pull herself back to reality. Certainly, she had received two anonymous letters, but the police would deal with them in the morning. And until then, it was impossible for anyone to get into this house. All she had to do was jump into bed again, and bury her head beneath the bedclothes.

But still Plum could not sleep. She tried to read but couldn't concentrate on her own bedside book – the latest Iris Murdoch – and when she started to read the Dick Francis thriller from Breeze's side of the bed, she found herself thinking once again of killers on the rampage.

Firmly, she told herself that such things only happened in books, not in real life. And until the police arrived in the morning, she merely had to stay indoors, tell Sandra to let no one in, and keep the chain on the door whenever she opened it.

CHAPTER TWENTY

Monday, 30 March 1992

As the morning sun streamed into her sitting-room, Plum sat nervously on the edge of a sofa, staring at her visitor and feeling as if she were applying for a job. She realized that she had just made a mess of telling her story to the police by introducing too many red herrings. Although Detective-Inspector Grigg of the Fraud Squad (arts and antiques division) had listened patiently, his carefully noncommittal expression must mean that she was over-dramatizing events.

The detective had been a surprise. He didn't look more than thirty years old, and seemed the sort of person that Plum might meet at a smart London party, tall and lean, with crinkly ginger hair, a pale, freckled complexion and eyes of so bright a blue they might have been expensive contact lenses. Politely, swiftly and accurately, in a well-educated accent, he summarized her story, confirmed the spelling of the names of the people involved and then said, 'I assume I don't yet need to check on the technicalities you've given me. At the moment we've received no official complaint from an owner about these forgeries, so we can do nothing, although we'll be very interested to know the final result of your inquiries.'

'Whoever it is clearly realizes that I'm now tracking more than one picture.' Plum shivered. 'It must be someone close to me.'

'Do you have any close American friends?'

Plum shook her head. 'Lots of acquaintances in New York, but no one living in Britain.'

The detective closed his notebook and said carefully, 'There may be nothing sinister here. The letters may be a practical joke in poor taste, or they may have been written by someone who doesn't like you: someone wants to upset and frighten you, but doesn't really want to kill you. Sometimes people write these things for the same reason that people stick pins in wax images – because they hope that heaven or hell will intervene to do as they wish.'

The detective leaned forward. 'But without wishing to alarm you, Mrs Russell, we always take death threats seriously. We can't afford to do otherwise. So please be careful. And don't hesitate to call me if anything else occurs during office hours. Otherwise, ring this number.'

He handed Plum an address card. 'But because of these unpleasant letters, you *may* be inclined to link things that you normally wouldn't, and see as coincidences things that you'd normally take for granted. For instance, you saw Mr Stepman with a painting in Paris; you heard that Mr Charles Boman was seen on a Channel ferry; you discovered that Mr Leo Mann sometimes drives art work to the Continent. These are not necessarily sinister happenings.'

Plum, who had been delighted to find that she was being taken seriously, now changed her mind: he was filing her in the compartment reserved for little old ladies who complained of peeping Toms.

* * * *

After the detective left, Plum dashed upstairs to dress for lunch. She had just wriggled into flame tweed shorts fringed with red raffia and worn over black tights and bovver boots, when Max phoned to ask if she felt like buying lunch for him.

'Sorry, darling, but I can't today. What's up?'

Upon reflection, Max thought that pottery wasn't very exciting, so had definitely decided to become a stage designer. Could he take an extra course in stage lighting? Later than ever, Plum hurled herself into a black lace vest and flame tweed jacket to match the shorts.

Held in the Victorian grandeur of the Reform Club, the buffet luncheon was in honour of Valentina Tereshkova, who wasn't quite as famous as Ivana Trump but who had achieved more than most women: she was the world's first woman astronaut, a scientist, and an elected member of the new Soviet Parliament.

Valentina, a cheerful, motherly woman, radiated charm and enthusiasm as she moved among her guests, although Plum sensed that she would prefer to be in a flying suit rather than her smart black and white outfit. When they spoke, Plum asked on impulse whether she was happy. Valentina looked surprised, then laughed. 'Yes. But not as I expected and planned to be happy: I am divorced.'

'You can't plan happiness.'

'No, but you can steer towards it – you can deliberately increase your chance of happiness.'

'How?'

'A job you enjoy is as important as a job that pays well.' Valentina threw one arm towards the roomful of achievers. 'All the women here today know that.'

Valentina threw her other arm around Plum's shoulders, to oblige a photographer. She added, 'The respect and appreciation of others for your job is also important for the self-esteem, especially if your job is looking after your family.'

'But your job was so dangerous,' Plum pointed out. 'Didn't you feel frightened when your spacecraft first lifted off?'

'Of course. Everyone does.'

'Then how do you overcome fear?' Plum's mind was still focused on her second frightening letter.

'You accept the fear and do it anyway. Otherwise you will achieve nothing.'

* * * *

Wednesday, 1 April 1992

Breeze returned in time for breakfast on Wednesday morning. 'But I have to get back to New York next Monday,' he warned Plum, as she washed his back in the tub. 'Can you scratch lower with the back brush, darling . . . lower . . . Ah, that's better . . . Don't know why a night flight's so much more exhausting than a daytime one – my face feels like a stale bun.'

'I hope you're not turning into a transatlantic commuter.' Plum squeezed the sponge over her husband's head, then reached for the shampoo bottle.

Breeze sighed luxuriantly as she massaged his scalp. 'I might be flying down to Rio quite a bit . . . Want to come? Victor Marsh has a Brazilian friend – a mining tycoon who wants to form an art collection to counteract the philistine image of the insanely rich: he's hinting he may eventually present it to his country. So he needs a European agent.' With lather streaking his face, he twisted round and grinned up at Plum. 'Sounds like a dream assignment, doesn't it? He's flying up from Rio de Janeiro on some other business, so he can see me in New York on the seventh of April. Blast, I've got soap in my eye.'

Plum showered his hair; Breeze twisted round again to face her. 'By the way, I've a message from Victor. He says he's happy to forget your bet about that Dutch flower painting. I was relieved to hear that.'

Plum sat back on her heels. '*You* asked him, didn't you? Because of the Biennale.'

'It isn't only that, darling.' Breeze clambered out of the tub. 'Poor Victor hasn't time for triviality. He's worried about his daughter. As usual, Suzannah's over-dramatizing the situation, prolonging it with publicity.' He wrapped himself in a towelling robe. 'Suzannah's inaugurating a hotline for pre-teen children with suicidal tendencies – which means she has hardly any time for Felicity.'

'That poor child! Of course I won't distract Victor. It was kind of him to offer to forget it.' Plum was tempted for a moment to accept the offer. All she had to do was agree, and she could walk away from the fraudulent picture trail. Breeze would smooth out the situation. She would receive no more frightening letters. She could sleep at night. She could get on with her life.

Slowly, she said, 'That may be the best thing to do.' She told Breeze of the second anonymous letter, and of the graphologist's opinion.

Breeze, a towel wound round his lean waist, was immediately alert and attentive. 'Thank God, at last you realize you've bitten off more than you can chew! You say this police detective is coming here again this afternoon? I'll see him. I'll tell him to deal with me in future. I want you to simply *forget* this unpleasantness and concentrate . . .'

'. . . on the Biennale,' Plum finished, glumly. 'By the way, the detective wants to see the first letter. Where did you put it?'

Breeze reached for his bathrobe. 'I threw it away when I returned from New York and sorted out my post-trip paperwork.' He opened the door to his dressing-room. 'Now I can see I shouldn't have done that. But I really thought it was something mischievous rather than sinister – and I still do.'

Plum was indignant. Breeze had no idea what it felt like when someone threatened to kill you.

* * * *

Later that afternoon, Detective-Inspector Grigg and Breeze discovered over coffee in the drawing-room that their old schools were long-standing cricket rivals. They immediately understood each other, and became friendly male confederates. Plum felt an outsider.

The Inspector explained that little could be deduced by police analysts from the anonymous letter or its envelope, both of which had been purchased from a large chain of office stationery suppliers. It was unfortunate that Breeze had discarded the first letter, as they had no comparison.

The only fingerprints on the second letter were those of Plum, Jenny, Lulu and the graphologist, while the many fingerprints on the accompanying envelope were too smeared to be informative. The police agreed with the graphologist that the envelope was probably written by an intelligent man, but there was no proof that the writer of the envelope also assembled the letter. They did not accept Clare Stevens's graphological guesses, which they felt dramatized the situation unnecessarily.

'Then this psychopath probably doesn't exist?' Breeze asked.

'The graphologist said she was only guessing.'

Breeze, smiling, turned to Plum. 'So you see, darling, you needn't worry about malevolent killers hiding up trees in ambush for you.'

Hesitantly, Plum persisted. 'There's something that puzzles me about those two letters. The writer wants me to stop looking for the forger – right? *But how will he know if I do?*' She bit her lower lip, 'I feel as if he's watching every move I make. That's what's so frightening.'

Breeze looked at her indulgently. '*If* anyone is watching you, darling, they'll be able to see that you're upstairs in the studio, painting, not running around London and Paris with a magnifying-glass.'

'But two threatening letters *were* sent to your wife,' the detective pointed out, 'and neither she nor you know anybody who might bear her a grudge. So can either of you think of anyone who might bear *you* a grudge, Mr Russell?'

Breeze gave a grim smile. 'Dozens of rival dealers, I should imagine. Seriously, I expect any businessman of my age would have collected a few enemies. But I can't think of anyone in particular.'

Plum noticed the guarded look in Breeze's eye and knew that he was lying.

The detective had made inquiries. Charles Boman could not be located, for he was with his father on a cruise in the Caribbean. Lady Stepman had confirmed that she had asked her son to sell, on her behalf, an Augustus John pen-and-ink sketch of a gypsy woman. The painting had been given to Lady Stepman's mother by the artist; there was a pale patch in her drawing-room, where it used to hang. Lady Stepman herself had asked Charles Boman where the drawing should be sold, and had made it clear that she would like this done discreetly, as she did not want people to realize she was short of money. He had recommended Lévi-Fontaine, and their cheque had been made out to Lady Stepman.

The detective had added that if the widow of Major-General Sir

Stephen Stepman was a hardened criminal, and the brains behind a major art-fraud gang, then he reckoned she would not be living frugally at 248 Marlborough Mansions, off the Gloucester Road, where she had resided for the past seventeen years.

After the detective left, Plum looked at Breeze. 'Who has a grudge against you? Who were you thinking of?'

Eventually, Breeze admitted that it had crossed his mind – only for a moment – that the culprit might be Jaimie Lorimer. He might well have been in New York over Christmas, and was in London at the moment.

'I've never understood why you loathe Jaimie so,' Plum said. 'It clearly goes deeper than professional rivalry.'

'Fucking right,' Breeze said grimly. 'That bastard Lorimer told the press about my first wife; he'd heard the story from some pal of his on Ibiza, which is where Geraldine-Ann had gone to live with her girl-friend. As you can imagine, I felt a bit of a fool when I read the story in some gossip column – any husband would – but the person it really hurt was Geraldine-Ann's mother: she didn't know her daughter was a lesbian until she read it in the paper.'

'I can't believe that Jaimie wrote those two letters!'

'For God's sake, let's forget about them,' Breeze said, irritably. 'As you've agreed to drop your search, you won't get any more letters.'

'I haven't decided yet.'

'Oh, for God's sake!' Breeze stamped out of the room.

Plum told herself she should have remembered that the mention of his first wife always upset Breeze, as it upset her, to a certain extent. Surely every second wife suffered to some extent from the Rebecca syndrome, and wondered with wistful jealousy just how much her husband had loved her predecessor, Plum was thinking as the telephone rang.

'Leo! What can I do for you?' As she could hear people talking in the background, she assumed Leo was telephoning from some pub.

'Plum . . . can you hear me? . . . Yes, I'm in the Bunch of Grapes . . . Listen, I think I've discovered something that'll interest you . . . I think I know who's selling these fake paintings. I should've realized it earlier, because I've seen him twice on the ferry, and each time he was travelling alone. Remember I told you the ferry's an obvious route for a smuggler? No, not over the phone . . . No, I can't talk any louder . . . I'm with a bunch of people and I want to keep this quiet. What's that? Can't hear a thing you're saying . . . Jesus, this place is a fucking zoo . . . Look, why don't I come round and see you?'

'Not possible, Leo. We're due to have drinks with some Swiss clients at the Savoy in half an hour. But we should be through around nine – why don't you come round here to supper? No? Then we'll have to make it tomorrow . . . OK, your place, around four o'clock. Longing to hear your news!'

As she dressed, Plum thought excitedly about Leo's intriguing telephone call. She whistled as she pulled a black tulle slip dress over her head, then wriggled into silver tights.

'What's got into you?' Breeze flipped a fresh tie around his neck. 'You seemed a bit downcast a short time ago.'

Almost breathless with excitement, Plum looked appealingly at her husband. 'Darling, I need *just one more day* on my fraud case.'

'*Drop it.*' Breeze scowled. 'One more day couldn't possibly make any difference.'

'Oh, but it could! And you know how exasperating unfinished business is!' As she thrust her feet into silver platform slingbacks, Plum told Breeze of her conversation with Leo.

Thursday, 2 April 1992

Thursday afternoon was a typically dull, British spring day. Understandably the daffodils seemed reluctant to nod their golden heads, thought Plum as she zipped through Regent's Park in her black Porsche.

Leo lived at the south end of Maddox Square, in a perilous-looking small building which was about to be pulled down. It contained a few bohemian offices and some residential apartments which had a dusty, forlorn air; for years nobody had bothered to spend any money on maintenance.

Surprised to find the dirty cream front door swinging open, Plum rang Leo's bell, but there was no response. Perhaps it was out of order, which might be why Leo had left the door ajar.

Swiftly, she climbed the narrow, steep, uncarpeted stairs to Leo's apartment on the second floor. As Leo's own front door was ajar as well, Plum pushed it open and walked in.

Inside, a large, white room was sparsely furnished with two worn black leather Le Corbusier chairs and a black leather couch before the empty fireplace. Beneath the uncurtained window, a large work-table was piled with newspapers and magazines.

A cream wool, hand-woven Greek rug lay between the black couch and the fireplace: upon it lay Leo, face upwards, staring at the ceiling. His fine, blond widow's peak of hair was tousled, his normally cheerful face was set in a rictus of terror, and his hands were flung wide on either side of his chubby naked body, which was the pale, waxy cream of a church candle. Leo was covered in dark, dried blood, and he was dead.

Plum gasped. She screamed. She immediately thought, I shouldn't have done that! Whoever killed Leo might still be hidden in this place! If so, he heard me! He knows I'm here!

She couldn't breathe. She couldn't move. She could feel the blood thumping in her ears and hear her heart pounding against her chest, as if she were running hard. *I must get out of here!*

But she couldn't move. She listened, not hearing the normal city street sounds outside the window, but straining to hear the slightest sound break the silence within. Her face turned red from the effort of holding her breath.

If someone comes out of that bedroom or the bathroom now, she thought, he'll be able to kill me, because I can't budge – even if my life depended on it. She tried to make herself move, but she was rigid with fear, unable to motivate herself to get out of that flat as fast as possible.

Sharply, harshly, the telephone rang.

The shrill, insistent rhythm seemed to release Plum from her frozen terror. She leaped forward to the heaped mess of papers on the table beneath the window, grabbed the telephone, and with both shaking hands held it to her ear.

'Leo?' It was a girl's voice. 'Benny wants you in his office.'

'Leo's been killed,' stuttered Plum. 'He's lying here dead . . . there's blood all over the place . . . Get the police here, quickly . . . Who? . . . Plum Russell, a friend of his.' She burst into tears, dropped the telephone, tore across the room and hurled herself out of the open front door.

She half-stumbled, half-fell down the precipitous, narrow stairs to the safety of the street. On trembling legs, she ran up the road to her neat, sane, shiny little Porsche, tore open the door, slid in, then locked herself inside. Trembling with shock, she could not move, until she heard a knock on the side window.

Beneath a uniform cap, a moon face peered at her. 'I'll have to give you a ticket, madam, if you don't drive on.'

*　*　*　*

Two hours later, the ticketed Porsche was still in Maddox Square, and Plum, who had hailed a taxi to get home, was still trembling.

In the kitchen, Breeze poured her another mug of tea. 'Look darling, it's *over*! You were very good with the police. You answered all their questions. You're going to drink this and then go to bed.' He poured whisky into the mug. 'Don't argue darling – drink!'

'Perhaps somebody overheard Leo talking on the telephone to me,' she persisted, 'when he arranged our meeting. Perhaps one of those noisy people in the background at the Bunch of Grapes was Leo's killer.'

Breeze poured himself a neat whisky. 'You've already said that to the police, darling. There's no reason to think Leo's death was linked to your forger – although I expect the police'll consider that. But a forger isn't necessarily a murderer. And there's *nothing* to link the two crimes.'

Sitting on the edge of the kitchen table, with one leg swinging, he smiled reassuringly at Plum. 'The police said Leo was shot twice in the stomach and once in the chest at close range. They haven't got the gun. The time of death was probably between one and two in the morning. Leo had eaten curry for dinner. That's all they know. They have no leads.' Breeze sipped his drink. 'You say Leo swore that he had nothing to do with the forgeries – why not believe he was telling the truth?'

'But Leo knew who the forger was,' Plum protested. 'That's what he told me. At least . . . that's what I *think* he said . . . I can't remember exactly what he said. I should have written it down . . .'

'Look! Leo's death had nothing to do with the forgeries! So it doesn't bloody matter what Leo said! You're having nothing more to do with this dangerous business!'

'How can you be so sure there's no connection?'

'*Because there's no reason to think that there is!* You're becoming obsessed! You're paranoid!' Breeze looked worried. 'I'd better take you to New York with me on Monday – I can't leave you alone in this state!'

'No, Breeze, I'll be OK.' Plum felt safer in the familiar surroundings of London than she would in New York. Besides, if someone were after her – what was to stop him catching a plane to New York? That's where the first letter had materialized. She said, 'Maybe Jenny can come and stay with me – and you're only going to be away for a few days.'

Obediently, she went to bed and lay in hushed luxury, staring at Emily's carefree pink and ochre painting; again she wondered what mysterious story was half-hidden beneath the pattern of dots.

Monday, 6 April 1992

On Monday, after Breeze had left for the airport, Plum immediately called a cab and directed it to Covent Garden. Fifteen minutes later, she was in the airy, converted warehouse office of *New Perspective*, facing Leo's boss, Benny Smith. As she needed his help, Plum had been obliged to confide in him.

Benny leaned backwards against his layout table. 'I know how tough this must be for you, Plum. I've already been grilled twice by the police.'

As she stared at Benny's small, delicate features and pink and white, china-doll complexion, she wondered whether she should have trusted him.

Behind thick-lensed spectacles, Benny's quietly cynical eyes stared back at Plum. 'I think they suspected *me* at first, but I had a brilliant alibi. We live miles away in Putney. Carol and I were having dinner with neighbours on the night Leo was killed – and got home to find we'd been burgled. Vindictive, us-against-society job, the house was a bloody shambles. They'd shat on everything – maybe they take castor oil before going on a job. They'd peed into Carol's drawers and generally made as much mess as they could. So we were with the police from about midnight. Lucky the bastards didn't catch Carol alone in the house,' he added.

'Yes,' Plum said with fervour. 'I don't think the police suspect me: they reckon I'm a harmless nut. But I don't understand why they think there's no connection between Leo's death and what he was about to tell me.'

'Because they've a pretty good idea why Leo was killed,' Benny said, turning to the table behind him. He opened a cigar box. He picked out a ten by eight inch photograph and offered it to Plum. Plum stared at Leo, wreathed in cigarette smoke, at a party or in some nightclub. He stood in the middle of a line-up of tall, laughing, glamorous girls, who wore elaborate evening dresses.

'They're all guys,' Benny explained. 'Leo kept quiet about it because he didn't want his family to know he was a transvestite. His dad's a respectable bus-driver who lives in Pinner and thinks AIDS is a heaven-sent plague to rid the world of faggots.'

'So the police think it's some sort of sex crime?'

'I'd bet on it. Personally, I think Leo's death may have been linked with drugs, although I saw no reason to tell the fuzz. Leo was a freelance here – we can't afford to employ full-time staff writers – so he didn't have a secure job. And I noticed he was an almost obligatory party-goer.'

'Leo was a pusher?'

'A provider of some sort. Those truck-driving trips to the Continent weren't just because he liked rough trade . . .' Benny hid the photograph in the cigar box. 'So you needn't blame yourself, Plum, for getting Leo involved in your search for the forger.'

'Thanks, Benny.' She was not convinced.

* * * *

After Plum had left Benny's office, she wandered over cobblestones, past old warehouse buildings that now harboured chic boutiques. As she walked, she tried to sort out her thoughts.

Perhaps the two letters *were* written by a mischief-maker and were not linked to the forgeries. Perhaps Leo's death was *not* linked to the forgeries. In which case there was no logical reason for Plum to stop looking for the forger, to whom she seemed so close now.

In a few days Cynthia's painting would arrive at the British Institute of Art. If that was proven a fake, Cynthia could complain officially to the British police. With Plum's evidence, she could approach a newspaper that had the necessary international links required to nail the complete story. Victor could then contact Maltby's with positive proof. Plum could see nothing inherently dangerous in that situation.

On the other hand, if Leo's death, the threatening letters and the forgeries *were* linked, then she was walking into danger, even though the entire affair was now almost out of her hands. If the forger cut her into small pieces and recycled her as cat food, he could not avoid the exposure of his work, if not of himself.

Eventually Plum concluded that she could best protect herself by assuming she *was* in real danger. In which case, she had two alternatives. The first was to expose the forger before he carried out his threat, which seemed unlikely; the second was to hide, until Cynthia's picture was definitely proven a fake by the British Institute of Art.

Suddenly, she realized how vulnerable she was in the crowded streets of Covent Garden. She threw a quick look over her shoulder, then hurried across to the car park where she'd left the Porsche.

Tuesday, 7 April 1992

Well before dawn, Plum woke suddenly, the echo of a scream in her ears. She realized that it was she who had screamed. The darkened room felt suffocatingly close, and once again she felt the menacing presence of a stranger in the room. What had Benny said about those burglars? That it was lucky they hadn't found his wife alone in the house.

Trembling, Plum reached out a hand to turn on the bedside light. Slowly, her breathing returned to normal. She slid from the bed, and dashed to the windows to open the curtains.

As the bleak dawn light crept into the familiar room, Plum knew that she couldn't live like this, feeling unprotected and vulnerable, until the forger was located and arrested.

She knew that it was no use looking to Breeze, Jenny or Lulu for reassurance, because they would only again advise her to give up her search. They could not see, as she could, that if there were real danger, then it was already too late for that.

So she could either stay at home – in which case her enemies would know where she was. Or she could disappear – making sure she wasn't followed – to a place where she could hide until Cynthia's picture had been analysed: somewhere where nobody would think of looking for her.

Suddenly Plum realized where she could safely conceal herself until Breeze returned. She wouldn't even tell Lulu or Jenny where she was going, so they couldn't accidentally inform anyone else. She would only tell Breeze.

CHAPTER TWENTY-ONE

Wednesday, 8 April 1992

P LUM gazed out through the aeroplane window. 'I'm going to Aquitainia,' she thought, and the word sounded mysterious and magical.

In the twelfth century, Eleanor of Aquitaine, one of the world's great heiresses, had married Henry Plantagenet, the future King of England. Eleanor's dowry was Guyenne and almost the entire Atlantic seaboard of France. Despite her enormous wealth, Eleanor was miserably unhappy and disputes over her dowry, which gave England a huge slice of France, had led to the Hundred Years War between the two countries.

Now, far below, Plum could see the green and gold patchwork of Eleanor's dowry slowly taking shape through misty cloud. Down there, from an eastern amphitheatre of hills, the three major rivers of south-west France flowed towards the Atlantic through the blossoming April valleys of Aquitaine, which produced some of the finest wine in the world – the claret of Bordeaux.

Further to the west she could see the spires of that beautiful city – Paris in miniature, and the largest wine-trading port in France: beyond those pale-grey classical buildings lay the rolling breakers of the Atlantic Ocean.

Plum's reason for going to Aquitaine was not only to escape unknown enemies. She had another reason, one that had been in the back of her mind since seeing Aunt Harriet, when, during their long conversation about happiness over the kitchen table, her aunt had asked Plum whether *she* were happy.

'That's a taboo subject, like sex used to be.' Plum had ducked the question defensively, then realized why the Australian punk journalist had asked it.

'Sex was only taboo because some women felt furtively guilty if they didn't function in the way men wrongly expected,' Aunt Harriet said. '*Now* women feel guilty if they don't feel happy in the way they're supposed to.' She poured more wine into Plum's glass. 'Every woman is responsible for her own happiness, as she is for her own sexuality. Other people aren't responsible for your life – you are. This can be a frightening thought, because there's no one to blame.'

'So why aren't women taught to be responsible for themselves?'

'Women haven't been taught how to survive life because their mothers didn't know, and their fathers didn't think it necessary to teach them.' Aunt Harriet poured herself the last of the wine and waited.

After a long silence, Plum confessed, 'No, I'm not happy.'

'At least you recognize that. Some women wouldn't notice happiness if it bit them on the bum, and some women are determined to ignore unhappiness.'

'What can I do about it, Aunt Harriet?'

'Work out what you want and what you don't want – and why.' Aunt Harriet lit a Gitane. 'Then, one by one, eliminate the things on your list you don't need.' She added with a giggle, 'The secret of life is elimination: if only we could buy psychic All-Bran.' She puffed on her Gitane. 'Eventually you'll be left with what you really need most to have a contented relationship with yourself. Then happiness tends to follow, because happiness is also a state of mind.'

'I've already worked out roughly what I want,' Plum said. 'I want to feel as happy in the rest of my life as I do when I'm painting.'

'Now be more specific, dear child. I can't help you, because happiness means different things to different people, so only *you* can decide what you're looking for, and only *you* can find it.'

'But how do I start?'

'When were you last blissfully, carelessly happy? Go back there, and work out why.'

*   *   *   *

As the plane started its descent, Plum saw the accentuated loops of the River Garonne, a flat, glittering curve, bordered by dark trees, that snaked through the golden and green chequered pattern. In those river valleys below grew melons and peaches, apricots and nectarines, apples and grapes, tobacco and sunflowers. Plum remembered the sunflowers that grew in the field across the river at the bottom of her garden. She wondered how Valvert had changed in the past eleven years: perhaps an ugly new housing estate now stood on the opposite river bank.

As the plane descended, Plum could gradually distinguish sleepy grey hamlets and farmhouses. Woods clung to the curves of little hills; she knew that wild strawberries grew in summer beneath those chestnuts and oaks, followed in autumn by truffles and mushrooms. She could almost smell the thick rich layer of loam beneath the trees: damp-wood-scented, yielding beneath her feet, a fertile, decomposing humus of fallen leaves, twigs and rotting bark.

Early April was probably too late for bluebells but the hedgerows were always speckled with wild flowers. Plum remembered picking honeysuckle, sweet peas, dog-roses, cornflowers and poppies. The local housewives despised wild flowers, so they grew roses, lilies and violently coloured dahlias to cut for their own homes. Plum's neighbours had a relentless love-hate relationship with nature: grass, nettles and brambles were constantly hacked back from their smallholdings; starlings and rooks were scared off. In autumn the men of the village shot wild boar, rabbits, game and any wild thing that moved. On Sundays they would take the gun from its hooks over the hearth for a couple of hours' massacre, before going to mass in the twelfth-century church, built by their English enemies, which stood across the road from Plum's cottage.

Valvert – the word meant 'green valley' – was sixty miles southwest of Bordeaux. It could be reached only by a narrow road, which had replaced the dirt track in 1978, three years before town water was piped in. Unlike the industrialized north of France, the southwest was still a rural area, only recently mechanized. Plum could remember the two oxen that her neighbour, grandfather Merlin, had used to draw his plough: he scorned the hire of farm machinery. The old man had never possessed a pair of shoes – they wore out, didn't they – but shuffled in wooden sabots until he died, the year after Plum had bought her cottage. Thrift and economy were much admired in Valvert, and nothing that might conceivably be used again was thrown away: bits of string, worm-eaten chair legs, honey-jar lids and the like were carefully kept in the barn or attic.

Like the rest of Aquitaine, the area around Valvert was still a land of self-sufficient peasant families like the Merlins, who maintained traditions and lived in what they called 'the old way'. They were as fiercely independent as their peasant ancestors – not serfs, as in feudal Russia, but smallholders who prided themselves on their self-sufficiency, and felt themselves rooted to the land. It was hard to make a living locally *unless* you worked on the land, although there were factories in the small industrial town of Miramont, five miles away. In the early morning a few people from Valvert bicycled to work at the shoe factory or the tannery.

The villagers were never idle because, as Breeze had pointed out on his only visit to Valvert, something always needed to be done in the country. The villagers relied as little as possible on outside sources; they made their own living with their own hands from their own soil. Every family grew its own animal fodder and produced its own vegetables, fruit and nuts. Few villagers now kept a cow because, as they said, '*la vacherie, c'est de l'esclavage,*' but pigs weren't slavery and every family kept one. It was an almost sacred tradition, and even little children prided themselves on fattening *le cochon* for its winter slaughter. Chickens, ducks, geese and rabbits were reared in back yards and fields; the wine on every family's table came from its own vines, as did the brandy. There was heated dispute as to who made the best *eau-de-vie* in Valvert.

In the late summer of 1983, when Toby was eleven and Max nine, Plum had taken Breeze to Valvert. He hated the place: he was fidgety, bored, missed his comfort and found it frustrating to be without a telephone. 'Cultural suicide' was how he had later described Plum's rustic dream to his secretary.

Breeze's idea of an idyllic country setting was a luxuriously converted Tuscan monastery or Provençal château. So for eleven years Plum had not visited Valvert; few people knew of her cottage, and even fewer knew where it was.

Surely no murderer would ever think of tracking Plum to the sleepy little place? Valvert was a simple, peaceful place where nothing ever happened, which was why the local children left as soon as they grew old enough to escape to the noisy, neon, juke-boxed excitement of the city.

* * * *

At the crossroads by the schoolhouse Plum turned left and drove her hired white Citroën up the hill. She looked to the left and felt a wave of pleasure as, once again, she looked at the cream walls and lavender shutters of her cottage. The little orchard was a froth of white and pink blossom, and beyond it Plum could see the foot-high tangle of overgrown grass which rolled down to the bottom of her garden, and the olive water of the river. The opposite bank was a ragged line of silvery green willows beneath which cows – some black and white, some creamy Blanc d'Aquitaine – grazed amiably or slept in the shade. Beyond them was a field of wheat, and behind that the other side of the valley rose in a soft, green curve.

Plum pulled off the road and parked under the cherry blossom, by a plum tree she didn't remember, although she recalled planting it once, late in September, just before returning to London; the sapling was now a sturdy tree. She felt a drowsy, relaxed contentment, as though she had returned home – bruised and weary – after a long and arduous trek, and could now undo her boot-laces. Here she could forget her anxieties, sit on the grass, lean her head on her knees and sniff the fragrance of the lavender bushes by the terrace, and the damp scent of the river. For the first time since receiving the second death threat, Plum felt safe.

She gazed happily round her garden. The grass, although overgrown, must have been cut recently, or it would have reached her shoulders. Wistaria – not yet in flower – climbed over the front of the house, above the south-facing terrace that caught all the sun, and was separated from the garden by a low wall of lavender bushes. Beyond these, a large magnolia tree was silhouetted against the pale gold afternoon sky.

As she reached the terrace – some cracked tiles needed replacing – Plum startled a small animal, which shot off through the grass, reminding her of summer sunrises when rabbits hopped over the dewy grass, larks sang, swallows dived and doves cooed, as if directed by Walt Disney.

She turned the key in the kitchen lock, half-expecting it not to open, but the door swung wide. She stepped inside, as if she were moving into a fairy story, where everyone had been asleep for 100 years but was now about to come to life. She walked round the kitchen, half-surprised not to find it covered in cobwebs, although Marie-France from the next village came to clean once a week, while her husband tended the garden. Nevertheless, the cottage had the forlorn feeling of a neglected place; it needed warmth, cooking smells and flowers, firelight and laughter, to bring it to life.

Plum walked to the sink and turned on the hot tap. After a few seconds, warm water flowed. So Madame Merlin had turned on the power and water, as requested – telephones had reached Valvert in 1985. As Plum watched the water splash over her hand as sparkling as the diamond upon it, she knew a moment of luxury, for she remembered when there was no tap water at Valvert and every back-breaking bucketful had to be humped from the Merlin well.

'Welcome back, Madame Russell!' All the villagers addressed each other formally, and rarely used a first name.

Plum turned to see the wispy grey hair, scraggy figure and outstretched arms of Madame Merlin.

They cheek-pecked in the Gallic fashion, then Madame Merlin peered at Plum's diamond ring. 'You shouldn't wear that around here – some fool might think it's real. Sadly, the countryside is no longer safe. There are thieves everywhere. That ring is an invitation.' She pointed to the shelf above the fireplace. 'Hide it in your soup tureen.'

Five minutes later, the kitchen fire smouldered (Madame Merlin had forgotten to have the chimneys swept) and on either side of it the two women sat in armchairs, catching up on eleven years of gossip, in a way that was not possible on Christmas cards. Plum's side was easy: yes, she was still amusing herself with the painting; her husband, the businessman, was indeed prosperous, thanks be to the good Lord; no, no more children, such was the will of the Lord;

her sons had left school and were both at art college; yes, steady jobs were indeed difficult to find today.

Madame Merlin's idea of news was a long list of the local people who had died during the past eleven years. Her husband had now retired; her daughter Solange now ran the family farm; her other daughter was a corporal in the air force; Paul . . . poor Paul . . . yes, still a schoolmaster – in fact he was in charge of the infants' school at the crossroads. Paul had come home after his tragedy . . .

Three years earlier, while visiting her parents, Paul's wife, Annie, had been killed in a car crash near Toulouse. A drunken driver coming round a bend on the wrong side of the road . . . a monster, a fiend, a depraved one . . . Paul's two-year-old twins, Marie and Rose, had been strapped in the back of the car and were unhurt, blessed be the saints. The other driver got off with a suspended two-year sentence – didn't even go to prison – because he was a rich and important local man, and such types knew how to protect themselves, more was the pity.

'But you never told me of this tragedy!' Plum exclaimed.

Some things could not be written briefly on a greetings card, Madame Merlin sighed, and she wiped her eyes with the corner of her apron. She told of the sad change in her son. He hadn't been to church since the other driver had been sentenced, he was now bitter and resentful and no longer had a schoolmaster's belief in justice and authority. But at least he had come home. She had not slept one wink during the two years he taught in Paris. Now Madame Merlin could keep an eye on the twins, although Paul would not allow them to live permanently with her: they all three lived in the schoolmaster's house, at the bottom of the hill by the schoolhouse.

Plum remembered Paul as a cheerful scrawny lad of fourteen; he must be about twenty-seven by now. He had been mercilessly teased by his schoolmates because he couldn't swim, which was why she had taught him. To distract him from his anxiety, Plum had asked him what his favourite poem was. He didn't have one. Then his favourite song? No. Then did he know the Lord's Prayer? Good! He was to recite it when she shouted. After his first three tentative strokes, Plum had shouted, *'Allez oup!'* Spluttering the Lord's

Prayer, which distracted his attention from his fear, Paul had reached the far side of the river. Then he swam back. The Lord, rather than Plum, had been credited for this minor miracle.

* * * *

After Madame Merlin left, Plum wandered through the rest of her cottage, which did not take long. A door at the rear of the kitchen led to a small pink bedroom with a black wrought-iron lace-covered bed; beyond it was the only bathroom. Like the kitchen, the living-room and the other two bedrooms faced the terrace.

Outside in the barn attached to the back of the house, where animals once had been stabled, Plum spotted the three bicycles, among empty tea-chests and cobweb-covered wine-crates. Plum saw that the wheel rims were a bit rusty, which was only to be expected after so many years of neglect. She wiped the dust from her old green bike, then tested the brake; she rummaged in the dusty toolbag and oiled it; as the pump worked, she cautiously pumped up the tyres, which stayed hard.

Plum wheeled her bicycle through the unruly grass to the road. Slowly – it had been years since she had ridden a bike – she turned left and wobbled up the empty road through the village. In her navy jeans, blue checked shirt and canary yellow ballerina pumps, she felt young and girlish, as she stood on the pedals and jerkily exerted maximum foot-pressure to force the bicycle up the steep incline beyond the village. Quickly she regained her confidence and equilibrium, enjoyed the caress of the warm breeze against her face, and sniffed the pungent earthy odours of the countryside.

When she reached the crest of the rise behind the village, Plum stopped to pick some buttercups. She put them in the wicker basket, then turned back, downhill. Effortlessly she whizzed through the village, where nothing impeded her progress: there were no cars, cats or dogs in the sleepy street, the women were inside preparing the evening meal, and the men had not yet returned from the fields.

As she sniffed the grass-scented air, she wondered why it had taken her so long to return to this delightful place. Somehow there had always been other priorities, but who would have expected life to have flashed past so fast? In future, nothing would stop her coming to Valvert at least once a year. Perhaps she could turn a part of the barn into a studio; then she could paint seriously here and Breeze would not be able to complain that she was neglecting her work.

Having almost reached her cottage, Plum braked hard, preparing to turn off to the right, into her garden.

Nothing happened.

Plum yanked repeatedly at the useless brakes, as the bicycle's speed increased under its own momentum. She had nearly reached the chestnut trees that lined the crossroads. She had to decide quickly whether to fling herself into the ditch, which might be dangerous, or – and this seemed the better idea – to keep her head, keep her balance, and let the bicycle continue its momentum until it reached the next uphill incline, beyond the crossroads, which would slowly bring the machine to a halt. She decided on the latter course; the chances were a thousand to one against a collision with another vehicle at the sleepy crossroads.

The bicycle flashed towards the crossroads, faster and faster. Plum glanced left to the schoolhouse and the playground merry-go-round; nobody was visible, and beyond, the road was clear. Plum looked to her right . . . and to her horror, spotted a little red van approaching the crossing.

She remembered the van: it was a travelling shop that came to Valvert once a week and sold basic kitchen necessities: brooms and washing powder. Now the red van trundled, at what probably seemed a slow speed to the driver, towards the crossroads, while Plum approached at what seemed to her the speed of light. She felt a ghastly inevitability. The impending accident seemed as predetermined as that of a Keystone Kops car approaching a railway line.

Once more, Plum pulled at the brakes, but the bicycle tore onwards.

Just before reaching the crossroads, Plum decided. She yanked at the left handlebar, guiding her bike towards the ditch. The front wheel responded, but the back wheel skidded to the right. As the bike's left pedal hit the road, sparks flew off the tarmac; Plum's right shoe flew off and landed twenty yards along the road before her. She was hurled from the machine and towards the ditch. Pain flashed through her head and her body as she crashed. Who would have thought soft grass could feel so hard? . . . She blacked out.

* * * *

Bright green worms writhed across a lurid yellow background, then the area behind Plum's closed eyes turned scarlet. Slowly she regained consciousness. Instinctively she jerked her arm to her forehead, and felt sharp, throbbing pain, as though her skull were being squeezed, rhythmically. She yielded herself up to the pain. Briefly, it reminded her of childbirth: to be able to bear it you had to surrender to it.

'Don't try to get up. I'll take you back to your place then call the doctor. You're the English woman, aren't you?' A deep male voice spoke.

Plum groaned. With what seemed like an enormous effort, she opened her eyes. Above her, silhouetted black against the sun, stood a tall man holding a yellow ballerina pump in one hand.

Plum groaned again and closed her eyes. As the man picked her up in his arms, she yelped with pain.

She heard the click of steel boot-studs against the tarmac. The man moved his body in a jerky, angular fashion, although perhaps he moved more smoothly without a body in his arms.

But something was wrong . . . Sensing that she was being carried away from the village, rather than towards it, Plum opened her eyes with an effort, and looked up at her rescuer.

She saw a wind-tanned face, hair black and glossy as a raven's wing; black, straight eyebrows crossed a thick, straight nose above a strong, square jaw.

The man looked down at Plum with dark-lashed brilliant blue eyes. 'I'm carrying you to my car; it's too far to carry you to your place.' He wasn't a peasant: he spoke in English.

'You must live in Valvert.' How did he know where she lived?

His wide, sensuous mouth stretched in a smile. 'Yes. I'm Paul Merlin. You taught me to swim, remember?'

Thursday, 9 April 1992

'How're you feeling?'

Plum recognized Paul's silhouette in the kitchen doorway, open to the terrace. He wore espadrilles, faded jeans, and a navy V-neck pullover with no shirt beneath; Plum could see dark chest hair as he slipped his hand inside the neck-line and rubbed his collar-bone: was that a nervous gesture? It was a lean hand with long fingers and short, well-kept nails – a novelty in Valvert, where work-worn hands were ingrained with dirt.

Plum, who had been lying on the couch before the fire, started to scramble to her feet, then winced. Her left elbow, upper arm and hip bone had been skinned and her left knee had been ripped open; her scratched and bruised face still looked like a De Kooning bicycle woman.

'Don't get up. Doctor Combray told you to take it easy,' Paul reminded. 'I've straightened the wheels and the handlebars, and fitted new front brake cables: the old ones had rusted and probably snapped when you braked hard.'

Although his words were friendly, there was something remote and abrupt about Paul Merlin. Plum remembered his mother saying that Annie's death had completely changed him, so that sometimes she felt she was not speaking to her son, but to a stranger.

'You speak very good English.' Plum stared, thinking what a daft observation that was. She found it hard to stop looking at those brilliant blue eyes, surrounded by those thick, dark curling lashes. Unfair.

'I teach English. I specialized in modern languages ... No, I won't come in. I've put your bike in the barn.' Paul disappeared.

Plum stared beyond the dark doorway to the pale green serenity of the garden. It emphasized the turmoil of her body, which was shaking like a spin-drier in its second cycle. She had never felt such lust for a man. In the course of ten years with Breeze, she had naturally been attracted by other men, and had flirted with some of them, but had never allowed her erotic feelings to sweep her into bed with any of them. She associated casual lust with treachery, upheaval and disaster. She dreaded the guilt that she would undoubtedly feel if ever she tried it.

She tried to switch her feelings away from Paul. As she had nothing to do, think about, or worry about, naturally she felt horny. That was what was supposed to happen on holiday. Fleetingly she wondered whether she would feel as weak at the knees, as languid in the groin, as warmly willing to yield, if Breeze were with her.

No. Plum had never felt so sensually hungry as she did for this big, dark Frenchman.

* * * *

She saw her rescuer only for a few, maddeningly brief moments each day: this she managed by working out exactly when to borrow a little sugar, flour or coffee from Madame Merlin.

When afternoon school ended, Paul's two little girls walked hand-in-hand up the quiet country road with their father, to be with their grandmother until supper-time. Although both daughters had inherited their father's gleaming black hair and blue eyes, they were not identical twins. Rose, slim and silent, was already a beauty; she loved clothes, and whenever possible she wore silver dancing pumps, a birthday gift. Marie, an adorable, chubby little extrovert, who was taller than the other five-year-olds in her class and wore her hair in bunches, was never still and rarely quiet. She never minded what she wore or whether it was clean; her Aunt Solange had been exactly the same, said Madame Merlin.

Plum, who could not force Paul from her mind, always tried to lead his mother's conversation to her adored only son, so she heard stories of Paul's boyhood and gazed at innumerable graduation photographs (Paul had been the first of the family to attend university) and wedding photographs (Annie had indeed been very pretty), as well as all the snapshots of the twins as babies, in Paris. Madame Merlin, who had never had such a receptive audience, did not realize that each time Plum saw her son, she felt such an erotic magnetism towards him that she feared the older woman would sense it.

Monday, 13 April 1992

By Saturday, Plum had recovered enough to remount her bicycle, and by Monday she felt able to cycle the five miles to Miramont. There, she wandered around the town, enjoying feeling part of a small community. Monday was market day, and country people had arrived early by car, lorry, or on foot if they were pushing a hand cart. They brought with them everything that was surplus to their own needs, even if it were merely a few carrots.

The food market consisted of simple stalls – planks on brick supports – lined up beneath the medieval arches of the town hall. These gave protection from the wind and rain to the women who sat on stools behind their produce: perhaps a few leeks, pulled from the garden just two hours earlier; perhaps a tray of pungent, round cheeses. Live chickens, ducks, turkeys and quivering rabbits lay with tied feet by the stools of the women who had raised them, or stared from wooden cages. Until fairly recently, country people rarely went to the butcher but raised their own meat, and killed it.

Plum purchased some local delicacies that never appeared in shops: rare mushrooms, walnuts, chestnuts, walnut oil for salads, goat cheeses, fresh herbs, home-made cakes for Paul's daughters, and country-baked bread. Then she left the food market and wandered through the streets of the little walled town, which had been planned in a square pattern in medieval times to withstand attack. Now these streets were lined with stalls displaying goods for sale: old carpets, antique linen and furniture.

Within an hour Plum had bought a Khelim carpet, a big old-fashioned oil lamp, a small armchair and two pairs of antique embroidered sheets, made by country girls who used to have nothing else to do in the evening but work on their trousseaux and dream of marriage. Now, they watched TV and demanded easy-care polyester sheets.

Plum piled her purchases beside an outdoor table at the local café and regretted having come to market by bicycle. She would have to cycle home and then drive back, she thought, as she squeezed through the crowd in the central square, where clothing, cheap boots, tools and household utensils were being peddled from the small vans that travelled from market to market with their wares.

As she reached the far side of the market place, where she had left her bike, the midday siren rang, a signal for everything to stop for three hours while everyone ate, then slept. The peasants and their wives drifted towards the café, to exchange local gossip over a glass of *pastis* before setting off for home – and the enormous midday meal. Of all the French regional cuisines, that of the south-west was the most respected. As every Frenchman knows, 'Near Bordeaux, they eat well.'

Plum heard a voice call her name, and turned to see Paul waving from a small café table as he beamed his slow, erotic smile. Her heart lifted, her body felt lighter, as she hurriedly crossed the cobblestones towards the table.

As they drank coffee, she was relieved that he couldn't read her mind: all she could think about was what Paul looked like without his clothes. She longed to see his strong, long legs; she longed to stroke his dark, down-covered muscular brown arms, check how much hair there was on his chest and whether it reached all the way down from his navel to his ... Hastily, she pointed to the small packets on the table in front of Paul. 'What did you buy?'

'I came into town to pick up some school stationery, but I also bought *cèpes*, and honey,' Paul said. 'Nothing my mother makes – I wouldn't dare.' He told her that the dishes of the south-west had recently become chic: delicacies such as he had just purchased, home-cured hams, pâtés, jars of preserved duck or goose, garlic sausage and other sturdy aromatic dishes were now sent straight to Paris. The family cheeses of Valvert, once sold only in the Miramont market place, were now available in London, New York and Tokyo.

'Partly because this food drew attention to the south-west, something amusing has happened,' Paul added as he signalled the waiter for the bill. 'The countryman's unwillingness to change, our obstinate nature, the way we cling to old customs – all the things city people used to laugh at – have suddenly become a national asset. Now people who live in dirty, dangerous cities no longer despise our way of life, but long for it.' He pointed to her purchases, and smiled that erotic smile. 'Want a lift? I've a Renault Espace – I need something that takes lots of kids. There'll be enough room for your bike.'

Was that slow, sensual smile meant to be an invitation? Maybe he flashed that smile at everyone. Or was that particular expression a particular come-hither invitation meant only for her? Was his mother the only woman in the district who thought Paul still pined for his lost wife? Was Plum sitting with the local Don Juan?

*　*　*　*

During the five-mile drive, Plum said quietly, 'I was sorry to hear about your wife's death.'

Paul's face immediately became taut. 'I suppose my mother's been talking to you. She understands unhappiness, but she can't seem to understand that Annie's death completely altered my view of life, and what I want from it.'

'Your mother only said that you're sad and disillusioned,' Plum said timidly. She regretted her impulse, but surely to have ignored his wife's tragic death would have seemed equally thoughtless?

They drove in silence. When Paul spoke again, he spoke slowly, almost as if explaining something to himself. 'When Annie and I left the country for Paris, we loved that life: we were out on the town every night, and bought a lot of smart stuff that we didn't really need. Then, when Annie was killed, I lost not only her but our home; without Annie's earnings I couldn't meet the mortgage payments on our Paris apartment.'

Paul braked sharply as a tractor slowly jerked out from a side track. 'Suddenly, I was overwhelmed by troubles – until I realized most of them were unnecessary. Suddenly, the way Annie and I had lived seemed stupidly expensive and childish – perhaps a little greedy.' He drew out to pass the tractor, then added, 'Behind the glamorous veil of Paris I saw restlessness, dissatisfaction and insecurity. I felt I didn't belong there – I felt alien.'

'I often feel that way at smart parties in big cities,' Plum said, 'especially when we're with the glitterati, the staple-diet-of-paparazzi-crowd.'

'Who are they?'

'Rich people who spend their entire life on holiday. I wonder where they go when they can't stand one more *day* of jet-lag – how *can* you take a holiday from a permanent holiday? The women swoop from Geneva to Portofino to Milan to Paris for clothes; the winter is spent skiing in St Moritz then Aspen. They all meet in Monaco in May for the Grand Prix then hop to London for the Season, after which they descend on St-Tropez to jetski or ride in their powerboats, followed by the Costa Smeralda for yachting. By August 12th they're in Scotland to shoot and fish, after which it's back to Monaco for the Red Cross ball, then New York for more shopping ... Anyway, Paul, I never know what to say to these people. I don't feel I belong with them.'

'I only felt at peace when I came back here, to the self-sufficient sanity of Valvert. Although we don't take self-sufficiency to extremes.'

'It's certainly convenient to heave your bike in the back of a station wagon.'

Paul laughed. 'Even Thoreau would agree with you.'

'Who's Thoreau?'

'My poor little savage, what do they teach you in British schools?' He grinned at her, and suddenly his dark, remote mood disappeared. 'Thoreau was a practical, nineteenth-century Yankee naturalist and writer. If you want to lead a self-sufficient life, you have to be self-sufficient in the head, as he was.'

'How did *he* live?'

'In a hut in the woods that he built by himself. He simplified his life as much as possible and reduced his needs to bare necessities, to leave more time for living.' Paul braked as he approached the crossroads by the schoolhouse. 'He also anticipated the tensions of modern America. It was Thoreau who said most people lead lives of quiet desperation.'

'I don't suppose he was very popular.'

'Reading Thoreau helped me a lot when Annie died. I reconsidered the reasons for everything I believed in and did. I tried to work out what I was supposed to do with my life.' He turned to Plum and grinned. 'The easiest way to enjoy life is to make it as simple as possible: so many people's lives are spent preparing to live, instead of living.'

'My Aunt Harriet once said something like that. She also said that happiness is a state of mind.'

'The things we value in Valvert are states of mind, not *things*.' Paul almost spat the word. 'The way children should feel when they wake up in the morning: happy, loved, secure, at peace with the world. Adults should also feel like that.'

'What do you mean by *things*?' Plum mimicked his violent delivery.

'The things that people are told will make them happy – a car, a house, a holiday, a ticket to somewhere else: material possessions.'

'Thoreau may have got along fine without a car, a video or indoor plumbing, but I'm not prepared to.'

'Oh, I'm not against those things; I'm only against thinking that they'll bring happiness: watch any TV commercial to see what I mean.'

'Come on, life isn't all gloom and doom,' Plum teased.

Paul still sounded sad. 'And *things* aren't the only kinds of false happiness. You expect a work promotion or a love affair to make you happy – but suppose the love affair leads to misery and promotion leads to a heart attack?'

'Work can be great so long as you don't let it take over your life. And I've heard that a love affair can even be pleasant.' She smiled at him. 'You need time for fun.'

As the car drove past the children's playground, they heard happy screeches and yells. Paul jerked his head towards the noise. 'I decided to come back to the country, to lead a gentler life at a slower pace, watch my children grow in a healthy, natural setting.'

'A good choice.'

'Not everyone thinks so. Teaching young children in a village school is considered a dead-end job. But you don't need much money to live this sort of simple, rural life. And anyway, I've found that security isn't having a lot of money – it's knowing how to live without much. And in Valvert, we are expert at this; here, prosperity is a state of mind, and life is as simple as you care to make it.'

'Surely teaching is rewarding,' Plum said, as the car stopped outside her barn.

'Yes. I shape fifteen new young minds a year; if I live for forty more years, that's six hundred minds in my lifetime.' He turned to Plum and smiled. 'Children never forget a good teacher, so that teacher lives on for another lifetime. Six hundred heads is enough immortality for me.'

'Will you have lunch at my place?'

Paul shook his head. 'I have to get back to school.' He smiled his slow smile and added, 'And if I stepped inside your door, the entire village would immediately assume we were having a passionate affair.'

If only, Plum thought, as she stared after the Renault Espace.

It stopped, then backed to where she stood. Paul stuck out his head. 'So it's up to you.' He shot off.

As Plum ate a cheese omelette on the terrace, she wondered what time the twins went to bed. Because it was clear to her that if she wanted to be alone with Paul, she had to go to his place. Wasn't that what he had been telling her? Or was she hoping for too much, reading too much into a few casual words?

*   *   *   *

At eight o'clock, Plum stood in the pink bedroom and stared at herself in the mirrored wardrobe door. She looked rested and healthy; the dark rings below her eyes had disappeared, and her skin looked luminously pale against her dark red hair. Over a pair of navy leggings she wore a loose hyacinth sweater that matched her eyes.

In the kitchen, she picked up a flower basket and a pair of secateurs, and set off towards the crossroads. It was an odd time to go for a walk to pick wild flowers, but it was still light, and the English were notoriously eccentric; and she did not want to leave a giveaway bicycle or Citroën outside the schoolhouse.

As she walked down the hill towards the chestnut trees, Plum felt nervous: small wonder, she told herself. Did she feel guilty? You bet. Once again, she firmly reminded herself of the hours she had waited for Breeze when he was with that Argentinian bitch at Claridges. She tried not to remember her distress and pain when she discovered his infidelity; she reminded herself only of the easy excuses with which he had shrugged off his adulteries. Plum could now apply these to her own behaviour.

But perhaps Paul was not interested in what he called a half-educated little English savage. Perhaps he *was* still sorrowing for his wife. Madame Merlin had spoken of Annie's beauty: in her wedding photograph she looked a little like the young Princess Grace of Monaco, dammit. According to Madame Merlin, Annie's charm was *légendaire*, as was her goodness; she was a veritable saint; and of course, Annie was of an intellectual stature *incroyable*. It was unfair: how could Plum compete with a woman who had more or less been canonized?

In the suddenly cool evening, as Plum walked beneath the chestnut trees towards the grey door of the schoolmaster's stone house, she repeated to herself that old-fashioned morality no longer applied to the present world. If Breeze judged her by his own standards, he probably didn't believe that she had never made love to another man since they married.

As she hesitantly lifted her hand towards the brass knocker, the door suddenly opened and Paul's deep blue eyes looked into hers. With the smile that rendered Plum helpless and reduced her IQ by eighty points Paul took the basket from her hand. 'I was beginning to wonder whether you'd come.'

Each took a hesitant step towards the other and then they lunged into each other's arms. In the doorway, in full sight of the road, they clung together, bonded as if by some magnetic force, now both helpless in their yearning; body pressed to body, wreathed by their arms, unable to move or to speak. Then Plum felt his warm, generous lips on her throat, the line of her jaw, her cheek.

Eventually, Paul muttered, 'The door.' He shuffled backwards into the hall, and her body moved with him, like a lifesized doll attached to the feet of a Pierrot dancer; except that her body was not an obedient, yielding stuffed doll, but felt vibrantly alive, as it had not done for years. As Paul moved, she felt the pressure of his body against hers, felt an enormous cock hard against her stomach.

She couldn't move. She'd fall down if she tried to walk a step. She could feel Paul's legs, also trembling. She felt strong hands run sensuously over her back, as if he were a sculptor, moulding it. His firm chest rubbed against her breasts, and she felt a fierce stab of pleasure in her groin. She shifted her grip, and her hands felt his hard, muscular buttocks. She smelled Paul's animal excitement – no expensive after-shave but the unmistakably sensual odour of a strong, husky male in a state of high arousal.

He shifted his position and slid one hand between her legs, feeling beneath the tight woollen leggings for her cleft. Plum jumped, and gasped.

Alarmed, he whispered, 'Did I hurt you?'

'No, no,' she groaned with pleasure, 'don't stop. Please *don't* stop.' She felt his hand reach for her again, thrust herself towards it, trembled violently at his touch. 'I can't . . .'

Fiercely, he whispered, 'Yes, you can.'

'No, I can't stand up.' Her legs were buckling.

They did not want to separate their bodies, but they wanted to be naked, so reluctantly they drew apart. With trembling fingers, Plum tore at his shirt, almost hissing the words, 'Off! Off!'

Still trembling, she fumbled with his buttons, but could not undo them, so he pulled off his shirt. As he did so, she smelled the moist fresh odour of his armpits, sniffed the pungent warmth, and felt her head swim with excitement. She touched the damp, curled hair with the tip of her tongue: it tasted acrid and forbidden.

Paul's long fingers felt beneath the thin wool of her sweater. He pressed her breasts slowly, rubbing hard, in a sensuous, circular movement, then gently squeezed her nipples. Plum gave a low animal sigh of pleasure, and pulled off her sweater. She heard a warning growl of mounting passion.

'I can't stand much more of this,' Paul muttered, pulling her hips to his body. She thrust against him with equal ferocity. 'I want to kiss every inch of you,' he whispered as he picked her up in his arms. 'I want to smell your secret places, explore every crevice, lick every inch of you. I want to know every part of your body: what it feels like, what it smells like, what it tastes like.'

He moved along the dark passage, kicked a door open, and lowered Plum to his bed. He raised her hips and ripped off her leggings. 'I want to feel your naked body against mine.' He shucked off his jeans and flung his body on hers.

Then they tore at each other. There was no foreplay. Plum didn't care whether she came or not – she only wanted to feel him hard inside her as fast as possible, their bodies joined together as he thrust deep inside her.

Lying beneath him, she clutched at the taut shoulder muscles, then her hands slid lower down his back until her fingers felt the dip at the base of his spine which divided hard, muscular buttocks. As she felt him enter her body, Plum gasped with pleasure; whoever said that size didn't matter must have been a man. She whimpered as she felt his thick cock slowly surge inside her, then thrust deep. As his body slammed against hers, she sensed that he no longer controlled it. She thrust back just as hard. She felt joined to this male body, as if they were Siamese twins, as if one could make no move in life without the other.

Bodies slippery with sweat and totally out of control, they hurled each other on waves of passion as fiercely relentless as Atlantic breakers. Bucking and thrusting, they performed the strange and thrilling horizontal dance; each knew what move the other was about to make, and followed it, as if they had been making love for years. Plum heard herself shrieking and realized she was about to climax.

Paul came with a low howl, which excited her afresh.

Afterwards, spent, they lay side by side on the white crochet bedcover, under the gentle moonlight.

*   *   *   *

'What's this?' Plum picked up a small battered calf-bound book that lay in the soft puddle of light below the bedside lamp.

'The poems of Ausonius of Bordeaux, written in the fourth century.'

Plum opened the book at random and slowly translated, ' "Let no passage of time change our ages at all; I will remain your young lover, you my new bride." '

'He adored his wife Sabina, who died young. Ausonius mourned her for forty years.'

Plum looked up and stared at Paul. White-faced, he stared back at her.

Sad and cross, she wondered whether it was possible to compete for love with a beautiful young bride who had died so tragically.

CHAPTER TWENTY-TWO

Sunday, 19 April 1992

O N EASTER Sunday, before the elaborate midday meal, the
Merlin men sat with Plum before their six-foot-wide kitchen
fireplace – the centre of peasant family life – to drink the
traditional home-made *apéritif*. Solange's husband, Roland, also
worked on the Merlin farm; it was understood that the farm would
belong to them after her father's death. They would borrow the
money to pay off Solange's brother and sister, who under Napoleonic
law were equally entitled to inherit.

Plum wore a melon silk mini-dress, demurely buttoned from
neck to thigh. She hoped no one would realize the erotic tension that
stretched, taut as violin strings, between herself and Paul; then she
wondered how it was possible not to spot it. Should his mother not
notice it, then surely Solange – accustomed to wordlessly sensing the
moods of animals – would sense her brother's sexual tension?

Although the weather was warm and the door stood ajar, a fire
burned as usual in the huge kitchen, and a cauldron of stock
simmered above pungent, slow-burning logs. On long winter evenings, the family gathered around this fire to roast chestnuts and
gossip or tell stories, over a glass of wine or *eau-de-vie*.

As the group around the fire finished their drinks, Madame
Merlin and her two daughters bustled around the stove at the back
of the kitchen and darted in and out of the dark storeroom beyond
it, a fantasy beyond the wildest dreams of Julia Child. Blackened oak
barrels of salted pork, pickled cucumbers, cabbage and onions stood
on the quarry-tiled floor; on shelves above were mysteriously

colourful glass jars, containing preserved fruits or vegetables, the star turn being plums preserved in brandy; from the blackened rafters of the larder hung strings of preserved mushrooms, gargantuan sausages and home-cured hams; at the far end of this treasure cave, floor-to-ceiling racks held home-made wine, cognac and colourless, treacherous *eau-de-vie*.

Paul's sister Mireille, a corporal in the air force, had temporarily discarded her uniform for yellow leggings and a tight sweater, which her father grumbled was an invitation to rape: these days one knew not whether a young woman was attired for the street or in her underwear.

Paul's father had been Mayor of the district ever since Plum had known him. Although a Mayor was supposed to hold office for only seven years, nobody else in Valvert had wanted to take on the job which Monsieur Merlin – a greying, weatherbeaten version of Paul – performed so conscientiously.

From the back of the kitchen, Mireille called softly to the twins, who ignored her and continued to loll against their grandfather's knee. So she barked an order, at which everyone in the kitchen jumped, and the twins ran obediently to wash their hands before the meal.

Valvert had taken its second great leap into the twentieth century when town water arrived in 1981. In 1982 Madame Merlin had insisted on a modern, pink-tiled bathroom. This set a trend, and all the wives plagued their menfolk until, by 1990, every home possessed one.

As the church clock chimed midday, the Merlin family sat down to a meal which was entirely home-made; they started with *pâté de foie gras* and fresh baked bread, followed by green salad with walnuts, dressed with walnut oil; then poached salmon with mayonnaise was served, followed by roast duck with new potatoes, tiny turnips and onions. Next, Madame Merlin produced a selection of home-made cheeses. Finally – as is the French custom – came a brandy-flavoured mirabelle tart served with a pot of thick cream to pour over the golden pastry.

Afterwards, Monsieur Merlin ceremoniously poured a cognac laid down by his ancestors 100 years before, a tradition that still continued: every year, Monsieur Merlin put aside a dozen bottles of his own *eau-de-vie* for the future generation.

The meal finally ended at five o'clock.

Outside in the sunshine, Paul's twin daughters rushed up to Plum and pulled her aside.

'You taught Papa to swim, didn't you?' Marie whispered.

Slowly a smile spread over Plum's face as she remembered teaching Paul to overcome his fear of the water.

'Why are you smiling?' Marie demanded.

'Because it was such fun when I taught your papa to swim.'

'Will you teach us?' Rose asked shyly.

'Of course, then we'll all be able to play water polo in the river.'

The twins beamed.

Plum knelt down on the grass and gratefully put her arms around both little girls. She had never expected or hoped that it would be so easy for them to accept her.

* * * *

As soon as it was dark, Plum hurried down to the schoolmaster's house, as usual.

Silently, Paul took her in his arms, lifting and crushing her against his chest. She kicked off her shoes, slithered down his firm body, and stood on tiptoe, on his feet. In what had become their custom, without releasing her, Paul walked in slow, rocking steps, down the passage that led to his bedroom.

'I think your sister Solange guesses,' Plum breathed in his ear.

'Who cares?' He nuzzled her neck. 'Shall I tell you what I wanted to do at that meal? I wanted to lay you on that table, pour that hundred-year-old cognac into your navel, watch it spill over your little white hips, then lick it up.'

'And what would your father have said?'

'That it was a waste of good brandy. That I should not mix my pleasures.'

Slowly and drowsily they made love.

Plum drifted towards sleep, blissfully aware that when she woke up, their arms would still be entwined. With Paul, she did not feel psychologically or physically threatened; she did not feel under pressure to perform, to get out there and strut her stuff, to play a part that she didn't enjoy in order to be a success. In whose eyes, she now asked herself? Was Paul successful? Did she care? No!

Neither did Plum care whether or not Paul's ideas were practical; she only knew that they felt right and they seemed to work. She wanted to follow his back-to-nature lead. She sensed that she was on the right road, although she still did not know where it led. Plum had felt at peace ever since she had arrived at Valvert.

She snuggled against Paul's big naked body, as her consciousness floated into a dream world.

* * * *

She woke suddenly. She was lying on her back. Soft moonlight, falling gently through the lace curtains, cast a pale grey flowered pattern across her naked body. The curtains moved slightly, in the cool breeze of the night.

Plum knew that somebody else was in the room.

Lying beside her, also naked, Paul stirred. In his sleep, he reached for her, muttering under his breath. Plum, lying rigidly alert, felt his long fingers on her breast, sleepily groping for her nipple. As he touched it, she felt the erotic response that ran through her body mix with simple terror. She felt her heart thump against Paul's warm hand. She could feel her blood pounding in her ears. She tried to breathe lightly.

Paul mumbled some endearment. Sleepily, his warm hand stroked her ribs and belly, each stroke reaching lower until the palm of his hand covered and lightly massaged her pudendum.

Plum lay rigid with terror.

'Papa . . .'

Instantly, Paul was wide awake. In one movement he slipped from the bed towards the door, swept the small figure into his arms. Whispering soothing words of comfort to the child in his arms, he disappeared down the corridor.

Plum relaxed. Then she started to cry softly.

Paul padded silently back into the bedroom, then slid back on to the bed. 'Rose only wanted a drink of water. They often wake me in the night – maybe to reassure themselves that *I'm* still here.' He took

Plum in his arms. 'There's no need to cry. I should have remembered to lock the door, but thank God she didn't see you.'

'Would that have been so terrible?'

'Of course. Rose might have been frightened, bewildered, resentful: they both remember their mother very clearly.' For a moment, his voice saddened, then became carefully matter-of-fact. 'And then it would have got back to my mother; or perhaps via the school playground to the rest of the village. This isn't St-Tropez, you know: the village schoolmaster isn't supposed to have a fling with a married woman.'

Plum, ashamed and humiliated, felt as if she were in bed with someone else's husband, deliberately seduced. But she wasn't, she reminded herself, there was no need to feel guilty on Paul's account, but this little episode had underlined his true feelings for her. They were having a fling, and she dared not allow herself to think otherwise.

Saturday, 25 April 1992

The bay of Arcachon is an area of sand dunes, wind and pine forest, protected from the occasional fury of the Atlantic Ocean by long spits of sand.

Paul parked the Espace in the shade of the forest and they headed for the beach. Plum carried the picnic basket, Paul his bed quilt, a cassette player and two wine-bottles in a string bag, to be submerged at the water's edge, so that the wine chilled before lunch. They walked slowly over a carpet of dry, slippery brown pine needles, which released a sharp fragrance that mingled with the salty smell of sea and wet sand.

They stopped just beyond the ragged line of pines, at the edge of a steep, sandy slope. Below them a wide, flat beach of silver-white sand wrinkled by the wind stretched for miles in both directions.

'Until recently, this area was virtually inaccessible,' Paul said. 'Even now, for most of the year, the only visitors are seabirds.'

Laughing, they slid down the steep slope, moving in decelerating, jerky movements, as though each foot were ploughing not through sand, but snow. When they reached the beach, Paul dumped the quilt in a nest formed by three sand dunes. This shelter cut the flutter of wind, and provided privacy.

Paul waved to the only person in sight – a distant figure at the water's edge, perched on a beached craft that looked like two canoes joined by a canvas mat. 'That's Robert. We're borrowing his Hobie cat. Get your swimsuit on, it's a wet and energetic sport.'

'But I can't sail.'

'You soon will.'

Half an hour later, Plum leaned away from the hull of the Hobie cat and hung on to a rope as hard as she could, while the little craft slid over the waves.

'This is more like swimming than boating!' she yelled. 'Much more exciting than sitting on the deck of something slow and sedate.' She felt erotically out of control, and laughed with excitement as the boat started to plane, skimming over the surface of the water at what seemed a great speed.

'Fun, eh?' Paul grinned at her.

In that split second when his attention was diverted, the boat lurched, and Plum's rear was soaked. Quickly, Paul hauled in the sail and pushed over the tiller, to correct his course. 'Never give the sea a chance,' Paul muttered, 'or she'll get you, the treacherous bitch.'

After half an hour, he encouraged Plum to take the tiller. 'Just watch ahead and keep your back to the wind; you can go anywhere ahead – so long as the wind's behind you. To go left, you push the tiller to the right, and vice versa . . . Gently . . . Now I'll show you how to tack. You need to get up speed before tacking, or she'll wallow and nothing will happen . . .'

By lunchtime Plum felt wolfishly hungry, as she hadn't done since childhood. Paul beached the boat, shucked his jeans, retrieved the wine-bottles from the water, and walked naked up the beach towards Plum, who was bending over the picnic basket, her back towards him. Plum screeched with alarm as she felt Paul's unseen hand slip into her wet pants.

Both naked, they slowly moved back to the dunes and collapsed on to the quilt. Paul pulled her on to his cock; she sat astride him, leaning forwards, her hands on his chest, feeling him deep within her. They moved rhythmically together, rocking in joyous frenzy until Plum felt as she had when the boat was planing: at one with the endless ocean and the soaring blue sky.

* * * *

Hungrily, they ate the cold lobster that Paul had bought in Arcachon, then tomato salad with a yard-long, crusty loaf of bread and goat's milk cheese. Then they fed grapes to each other and drained the bottle of *Pouilly-Fumé*.

Afterwards they walked along the beach. Feeling the dry sand slip between her bare toes, Plum threw her arms up to the cloudless sky. 'I feel *so* happy!' Suddenly serious and surprised, she turned to Paul. 'With you I feel as happy as I do when I'm painting.' Until that point Plum had deliberately not mentioned her painting: she had wanted to forget the pressures of work until the last possible moment.

'Then why haven't you painted in the last fortnight? Didn't you bring your paint-box to France?'

Plum laughed. 'I can't paint just anywhere. I work with *buckets* of paint, not little tubes, on big canvases, in a high studio with ladders and masses of plastic sheeting over the floor, to limit the mess.'

'What are these pictures? Portraits?'

'No. I'm an abstract painter.' Plum hesitated. She could not put it off any longer. She turned and looked up into the brilliant blue eyes. She tried to say it gently. 'Paul, I have to prepare for an exhibition, in June, so I have to return to Britain . . . tomorrow.'

Abruptly, Paul stopped walking. 'Why can't you stay *here* until June?'

'Because I must meet critics, be interviewed and photographed.'

'You mean, you're *famous*?'

'Not exactly . . . Well, a bit . . . Painters have heard of me.'

'I didn't realize I was in bed with a celebrity.'

'Will it make any difference?'

Paul considered. He looked down at the sand; with his big toe, he drew a letter P in it. Eventually he said, 'Of course it will make a difference. Because it means you're leaving and I had not allowed myself to think about that.' He held Plum's bare shoulders and looked into her eyes. 'Maybe you say your marriage is none of my business, but I'm starting to think it is.' Gently, he added, 'Plum, what is the situation between you and your husband?'

Plum was silent. Had they reached my-husband-doesn't-understand-me time? She felt guilty and disloyal at the thought of discussing her marriage with her lover.

She wondered what Paul had meant by saying that her marriage was his business. *No, she wouldn't allow herself to hope that!* She must retain a little mental self-protection. She must remember that Paul was an unbelievably sexy, drop-dead-gorgeous, Frenchman-of-the-world.

'Breeze and I don't live our lives, we act them,' she said slowly. 'Breeze treats me like a child and there's a part of me that loves feeling protected. But now I want to be treated like a woman, and I know I can't be both.'

'So your husband doesn't treat you like a woman?'

Plum considered. 'He doesn't treat me like a mate. Grey geese mate for life, whether or not the other dies: that's how I'd like to be married.'

'Ah, so he is unfaithful, your husband?'

Plum nodded. 'Although I didn't know about his women, I'd slowly sensed our relationship alter: I don't think Breeze realized that. He thought his love affairs were no problem, provided I never found out.'

She looked down and with her toe traced a second P on the wet sand. 'Discovering his liaisons finally made me realize there was a carefully guarded area in Breeze's life that was forbidden territory to me.'

'It had never been a grey geese marriage?'

Plum shook her head. 'Our life together has always been very busy, very social, very smart: there's never been time to think. But it's always been a good working relationship.'

'And now you will not settle for that alone?'

Plum tried to be honest with herself, as well as Paul. 'Until I found him with this other woman, I really loved Breeze, although I didn't always like him. But there is no emotional superglue. I really wanted to forgive him – but something had changed.'

'What?'

'I was always a bit in awe of him: he's sophisticated and self-assured, very confident, very much respected in the art world. But now I'm no longer in awe of him.'

Sensing that she had more to say, Paul waited.

'Something else had also changed,' Plum said sadly. 'True love – the sort that everyone wants – is when someone cares for you, no matter what you do, even when they know what you're really like. I no longer care for Breeze like that.' Her feelings for him had dissolved like morning mist in sunlight. 'When I tried to discuss it, he said that passion only lasts a couple of years or so; and then romantic love slowly changes into a loving, mutual regard.'

Paul said slowly, 'All relationships alter constantly; two people in a relationship may grow at different speeds at different times. There is no permanent one-and-only: *you* are your only permanent relationship.' He bent and tenderly kissed the top of Plum's nose. 'Tell me, was that why you came alone to Valvert? To think about all this?'

'That was one reason.' Plum was suddenly serious. She would tell Paul about the death threats later.

'And the other reasons?'

'When I was staying with Aunt Harriet I realized something was missing from my life, but I didn't know what.'

'And do you know now?'

'I want to find *myself*. I want to work out who I really am – the person who seems to be submerged by my roles of wife, mother, daughter, painter. I hoped that in Valvert I might work out who I am and why I'm here. I want to *do* something with my life – not just play my roles and make money.'

'Maybe you came to find one thing, but have found another. Shall I tell you what I hope you have found?'

Plum nodded.

Paul hesitated, 'I will not disguise from you how deep was – is – my love for Annie.'

'I'm glad you don't try. That's a private part of your life, and I respect your privacy.' They walked on in silence for half an hour. Then Paul stopped abruptly. He caught Plum's hand. With his big toe, Paul traced another two Ps in the sand, and drew a heart around them. He took both Plum's hands and looked into her hyacinth eyes. He said quietly, 'I hope you have found your grey goose. Will you stay with me, Plum? For ever. Will you marry me?'

Plum felt as though he were asking her to jump from a bridge, but not to worry because he'd catch her. She trusted Paul but she did not trust her own muddled feelings. She did not know whether she loved Paul. What people thought was love was often lust, dependence, possessiveness, or simply the urge to fill the aching void in a lonely life. So Plum deliberately forced herself to see what lay before her in the terms that Breeze might use. She couldn't dump her life for an itch in the groin, he would tell her, not for a holiday romance.

* * * *

They returned to Valvert after dusk. They finished the last few minutes of the journey in unhappy silence, knowing they were to separate on the following morning.

Plum turned to Paul. 'I can't help wondering if . . .'

'Oh, I'm sure my parents know. And if they don't – I want to tell them.'

'But what will your parents think of me? What will they think about Breeze?'

'They are French, they are not idiots, and they realize that customs have changed since they married . . . By the way, did you ever marry in church?'

'No.'

'Then you are not married in the eyes of God. So for them there will be no problem.'

'Don't rush me. I can't give you my answer yet. Please don't tell them yet, Paul. Let them think what they please, for the time being.'

After Paul had collected his daughters, Plum slipped next door; she reddened as she asked Madame Merlin if she might use her telephone. Plum knew that she knew. The French woman's manner was stiffer than before.

As Plum told Breeze she was going to stay at Valvert for another week, she heard a yell of rage. 'Have you lost your mind, Plum? There's only five weeks to go before the Biennale. *Seriously*, Plum, I want to know if you're feeling ill? . . . NO? *Then, what the hell is happening?* Have you taken leave of your fucking senses? Have you forgotten it's an honour to be chosen to represent your country? . . . Pushing aside the fact that this is the most important moment – the make-or-break point – of your career, *do you realize you're letting me down?*' With an effort he lowered his voice. 'I can do a lot for you, Plum, but I can't give your damned interviews for you, and they don't want to see *me* on TV!'

'I know. I'm still staying another week!'

After a further ten minutes of argument, persuasion and threat, Breeze finally growled, 'Do you *promise* you'll be back next Sunday? Because I warn you, if you're not – I'm coming out to get you.'

'I promise, Breeze. I'll be in London next Sunday.' Plum carefully replaced the receiver, then burst into tears. She ran past the astonished Madame Merlin and into the kind, black night. As she stumbled towards her kitchen door, she wondered how the happiness she had known all day could so quickly turn to black misery and fear. Being forced to give that promise to Breeze made her realize what she would leave behind her when she left Valvert and returned to London. Could she do that? How many chances did a person get in one lifetime to be really happy? And would returning to London also mean risking her future happiness in another way – by putting her life in danger?

CHAPTER TWENTY-THREE

Wednesday, 29 April 1992

O UTSIDE the schoolmaster's house, a sudden thunderstorm growled. Paul hastily ran to close all the windows and shutters, then returned to his kitchen.

'What's that you're cooking? It smells delicious!' Plum shuffled some purple wild iris in a cream jug, which she placed in the centre of Paul's kitchen tablecloth under the hanging oil lamp. Often the electricity supply was deliberately cut off during a storm, to lessen the risk of fire.

'You smell garlic potatoes.' Paul shook the heavy-bottomed casserole on the stove.

Plum sniffed the enticing aroma. 'It smells so good, even *I* want to know how to cook it.'

'You fry half a dozen cloves of garlic in bacon fat, add finely sliced potatoes dried on a cloth, then cook for half an hour on a low heat.'

'I can cook but I hate it. So you're indeed the man of my dreams.' Plum looked up and smiled. Outside, the thunder, low and ominous, emphasized the security of the lamplit room.

Paul waved a wooden spoon. 'Don't let the potatoes stick to the pan; they shouldn't brown. Season them just before serving.' He ground fresh, black pepper and sprinkled salt over the casserole, then triumphantly carried it to the table, where he lifted the bottle of red wine and refilled their glasses. Plum drank from a chainstore wineglass, Paul's was an antique.

'Shall I tell you why I bought that glass for you?' Plum asked.

'Because it's the metaphor of a perfect relationship. I think two lovers should be as independent as the spiralling threads in that glass stem: see how the twin white threads swirl upwards and around each other, always together but never touching, never getting in each other's way.'

For one swift moment Plum thought of Breeze's probable reaction to her metaphor. He would scoff: 'Poetic, pretentious crap.'

Paul leaned across the narrow table, pulled Plum's hand to his lips and kissed the fingertips. 'Why shouldn't our lives be like that?'

'I often imagine it,' Plum said dreamily. 'We sleep entwined and wake to the sound of the wind rustling the chestnut trees. During the day we lead our own lives: I paint and you don't resent it. You eat your midday meal with the children at school – that's important because I have no time to prepare a midday meal, and I'm a lousy cook . . . Then, when our work is finished, in the summer evenings we swim in the river, or go for a walk among the wild flowers, then we drink a glass of wine on the terrace, talking, or quietly listening to music.'

'After Marie and Rose have gone to bed, of course,' Paul reminded.

'I've always wanted a little girl. Twins are a bonus.'

'Then in winter we sit reading on either side of the fire, hypnotized by the glow and the sparks, each enjoying the silence, country and the comfort of the other.'

'We enjoy our intimacy,' added Plum dreamily, 'but we don't feel possessive. We respect each other's privacy. We don't hope or demand too much from each other.'

'We move to the same rhythm, in bed and out of it.' Paul leaned across the table and stroked her feathery red curls. His hand fell to her neck and started to caress it.

Plum gazed at him. 'You promised not to excite me until we've finished your delicious potatoes, and this wonderful bottle of claret. Don't tell me it's one of your dad's.'

Paul laughed. 'My father cannot produce wine like this. The parents of a pupil gave it to me at Easter. It is from one of our best local vineyards – Château Margaux.'

They heard a tremendous crash.

Plum turned white and dropped her glass. Red wine splattered over the tablecloth, and dripped on to the floor. In a high, agitated voice, she stuttered, 'Was th – th – that an explosion?'

Paul had jumped to his feet. 'No, of course it wasn't. But it *was* close to the house. Maybe lightning hit one of the chestnut trees. I'll check.'

Five minutes later, he returned drenched, and started to towel his hair dry. 'It's the big chestnut. A bough fell on the schoolgate, and smashed it; it's too heavy for me to lift. I'll get the tractor in the morning.' He moved towards Plum. 'What's the matter? You've turned white. Surely you weren't frightened by the storm?'

'No. I thought it was . . . something else. Silly of me.'

Paul threw his towel on a chair. 'You thought it was an explosion. That is what you said.' He looked sharply at her. 'Now why should you expect an explosion in the middle of the peaceful French countryside? I can see you are frightened of *something* . . . Is it terrorists? What *is* it that you seek to hide from me?' As his anxiety grew, Paul's English became more stilted.

'Yes, there's something that frightens me, Paul. I've tried to put it out of my mind, and I've almost forgotten it since coming to Valvert.' She quickly told Paul of her search for the forger of the Dutch paintings, of the anonymous threatening letters, and of Leo's death.

'The death of your friend might not be connected to your search,' Paul said, 'but those letters certainly are.' He took her in his arms. Crushed against his rain-spattered sweater, Plum felt safer.

'Who knew you were coming here?' Paul asked.

'Only Breeze.'

He looked thoughtful. 'Modern husbands do not get rid of their wives by killing them in cold blood. They divorce them.'

Plum didn't like to think of herself as an easily discarded encumbrance. Stiffly she said, 'I don't think Breeze wants a divorce.'

'You produce a large income, so you are a valuable asset to this fake marriage. You paint and paint – and he has affairs. But that is no reason for him to kill you.'

'Oh, how mercenary you French are! *Of course Breeze doesn't want to kill me!*' Encircled by Paul's strong, muscular arms, she felt safe. He had become her psychological bullet-proof waistcoat.

'Of course not. But *somebody* wants you to *think* you might be killed.'

'I know. I can't help being scared.'

Paul kissed the top of her head. 'The quickest way to get rid of your fear is to find this forger. So how can we do that?'

'By finding Tonon.'

'Are you convinced that all the paintings come from this one source – Tonon?'

'I don't know. If so, I'll be at the end of my search. If not, I'll still have to pursue it: but either way I won't know – until I locate Tonon.'

'How can you be so sure there's only one forger, not a gang?'

'The British Institute of Art believes there's only one forger – although he may have more than one accomplice to distribute the paintings.'

'And Monfumat is definitely a suspect?'

'Yes. So many links connect through him. He sells to Maltby's, he sold the picture to Artur Schneider in New York, and he sold the Binger picture – with the tulip that hadn't yet been invented – to Forrestière.'

'Then why don't you go to the French police?'

'I only have circumstantial evidence. The police will only consider hard evidence – something tangible that they can see – and I haven't got that yet. If I went to the police with my transparencies, they'd say, "Very interesting, come back when you have hard evidence."' Plum gave an exaggerated, philosophical Gallic shrug. 'So I must wait until Cynthia's picture has been analysed by the British Institute of Art, who then can compare it to their report on the Swedish picture.'

'So at that point the police will take over?'

'No, the British Institute of Art may feel they've conclusively proved that both pictures were painted by the same person – but the police won't understand *why*. The cops are out of their depth in the area of brushstroke comparison, it isn't as easy to spot as fingerprint matching.'

'Would I spot it?'

'No, Paul.' Plum sighed. 'And anyway, a British Institute of Art *opinion* won't be accepted by the police as *positive proof*. If only there was something more visually obvious – say an orange-spotted bluebottle in all the pictures – the police would accept a clear visual link.'

'So you can't make any formal accusation?'

'Not yet – especially as I'm not the owner of any of these fakes. Monfumat's lawyer would say . . .'

'. . . You're a meddling foreigner trying to link a few coincidences to cause trouble.'

'Exactly. And I've come to a dead end because I've no idea where to find Tonon. I telephoned Cotton's of Bury Street, who refused to buy the Binger picture from Tonon after getting unfavourable expert opinions, but they said they had no record of Tonon's Paris address or his London hotel.'

'Where did the anonymous Swedish businessman meet Tonon?'

'Dame Enid said the Swede always stays at the *Plaza Athenée* on his buying trips to Paris. Tonon heard he was in town, telephoned, then called at the hotel with the painting.'

Paul held up the wine-bottle. 'Forget your troubles while we finish this wonderful wine.'

Plum nodded and raised her glass. 'Tell me, how do you choose good wine? I've always wanted to know.'

'Foreigners think every Frenchman has the palette of a connoisseur, but the truth is that most of us drink *vin ordinaire* most of the time,' Paul said, as he carefully poured the last of the claret. 'But there's an easy way to choose a good wine, without knowing anything about it.' He pointed to the wine label on the empty bottle. 'You simply look at the bottom of the label, for the words *"mise en bouteille au château"*. Those words mean that the owner bottled it on his estate: no one bothers to label a wine he's not proud to have produced.'

'You mean, to bottle your own wine then stick your label on the bottle is to show you're proud of your work? Just as an artist signs his painting.'

'Exactly.'

'My forger must be proud of his work – because it's very good.' Thoughtfully, Plum put down her glass. 'A detective I met in Australia told me that good forgers are always contemptuous of experts and proud of having fooled them.' She pulled back her chair. 'If my forger is proud and contemptuous, then perhaps he uses a visual signature!'

'What's that?'

'Some small object that the painter paints in his picture as well as – or instead of – his own signature. Genuine old Dutch pictures often have a visual signature: a snail, a fly or a seashell.' Plum flung her blue-checked napkin on the table and stood up. 'Paul, *let's get back to my place, and look in my file!*'

'I can't leave the children.'

Plum sighed and sat down again. 'Well, I couldn't check those transparencies with a magnifying-glass by candlelight, blast it!'

As she spoke, the electric lights flickered on again.

Paul said, 'I had intended to end this evening in a different way . . .'

'Time for that later, darling. I'll get the transparencies.'

Wearing Paul's overcoat and gumboots, Plum shuffled up the hill to her cottage, grabbed the magnifying-glass, her box of notes, photostats and transparencies, then splashed back to the school-house.

'I'm brewing coffee,' said Paul. He had cleared the dishes and brought an angled reading lamp from his desk to the table.

Plum spread out the contents of her box file. 'I'm interested in eight pictures.'

'But you only have *seven* photographs here: six transparencies and a polaroid.'

'That polaroid is the painting in Mrs Carteret's bedroom. I haven't even *seen* the eighth painting. It belongs to that rude bitch in Suffolk – Georgina Dobbs – but it's linked to the rest, by supplier.'

'I don't understand.' Paul lifted the kettle and poured hot water over the freshly ground coffee in the pot.

'All these pictures are linked to each other, but not always directly.'

Paul paused, the steaming kettle in one hand. 'How?'

Plum did not reply, but scribbled a list which read:

LINKS
Style
Repaired holes
Anachronisms
Identical content
Suppliers

'What is the most important link?' Paul poured coffee into yellow-striped mugs.

'The style link established by the Institute is the one that most people can't spot; it's been established that the pictures in the six transparencies were probably painted by the same person.'

'Can the British Institute of Art *prove* this from transparencies?'

'Not conclusively. That's why it's so important to compare Cynthia's painting to the picture owned by the Swede. And once we've proved that, it should be easier to get all the other actual paintings to the Institute for comparison. Although I feel Georgina Dobbs will be too bloody-minded to cooperate, and Gillian Carteret might refuse because it's against her interests to prove her remaining picture – her pension – is a fake.'

'And the other links?'

'There's one area where coincidence is stretched to implausibility: the number of these forgeries that have been holed and repaired. Forgers rarely bother to paint a picture on repaired canvas.'

'So if those repairs are similar, that would be further circumstantial evidence?'

'Yes. The Institute spotted repairs in the Swede's picture, the Cotton picture that ended up with Lady Binger, and the Pieter Claesz in the Boston museum. And a repaired hole is mentioned in the provenances of Suzannah's picture and Cynthia's picture.'

'But you say that's still not hard proof.' Paul sat down at the table and sipped his coffee.

'No,' Plum agreed, 'but there's another area of circumstantial evidence – items that didn't exist when they were supposedly painted.'

'Something such as a telephone in a portrait of Napoleon?'

Plum handed two transparencies to Paul. 'See that black butterfly with the yellow spots in Cynthia's picture? . . . And this bright yellow tulip with the strong salmon hue on the edge of the petals in Lady Binger's picture? . . . That butterfly and that tulip weren't discovered until the twentieth century.'

She lifted her mug of coffee. 'Any anachronisms can be explained as careless restoration work; but if further evidence of fraud is produced, then that defence is less acceptable.'

Paul lifted his eyebrows. 'Too many coincidences are too much to swallow.'

Plum handed him the relevant transparencies, then pointed out the bluebottle in Suzannah's painting, and the identical bluebottle in the Artur Schneider one. 'Here's another type of visual link.'

'Give me the magnifying-glass, please.'

'Paul, look at the yellow lizard in Suzannah's picture. The green lizard in Cynthia's picture is identical, although it's a different colour. So those three pictures are visually connected . . .'

Paul peered at the transparencies. 'Yes, anyone can see that.'

'Now look at the caterpillar in Lady Binger's picture: it's identical to the caterpillar in the Swede's picture.'

'Yes!' As he saw the visual links, Paul started to get excited.

Quietly, Plum said, 'But I can see nothing that's immediately and obviously identical in all eight of the pictures – and that's what I'm looking for tonight.'

She pointed at the transparencies upon the table. 'Four of those pictures – including that of Georgina Dobbs – came from Gillian Carteret, but I can't get beyond Mrs Carteret, and at this stage there's not much point in trying. If I prove her pictures are fake, she'll blame it on whoever supposedly sold them to her grandad.'

'And she might be telling the truth?'

'Not if any of that paint existed only *after* 1973, when her grandad died.' Plum pushed three transparencies towards Paul. 'These three came from Paris. The Artur Schneider and the Binger both came from Monfumat, and if they came from Tonon, then that links to the picture Tonon sold to the Swede – which would supplier-link the three pictures from Paris. *That's* the proof I need! At some point I need to force or trick Monfumat into admitting it – if it's true, of course.'

'What you propose we look for now is something that is identical in all these paintings?' Paul asked. 'Something that visually links these two groups of pictures – the French and the British?'

'Yes. If I can find a visual signature – that'll kill two birds with one stone. It'll tie all the pictures, and it'll put Monfumat in a tricky position, and eventually, he'll have to answer police questions.'

'So what do we do now?'

'We search each picture to find a common denominator. Hell, I wish we had a light-box.'

Together, they started to check the contents of the five transparencies. Plum held each of the enlarged transparencies against the reading lamp and put the magnifying-glass to it. Paul made notes.

Although many of the six transparencies shared similar or identical components, none of the pictures contained one item that was clearly identical to all of them. The polaroid of Mrs Carteret's painting was not large or clear enough to accurately check the content.

After an hour, Paul put the magnifying-glass on the table and rubbed his eyes. 'We've examined them all, and found nothing.'

Plum rotated her aching shoulders. 'We must be more systematic, more methodical.'

They decided to list the entire contents of each picture, one longitudinal inch at a time, blocking off the rest of the transparency with paper. They worked from the top to the bottom of each picture. It was difficult work that demanded close attention, so they took it in turns to hold the magnifying-glass and dictate to the other the contents of each area.

After working for an hour, Paul fetched eyedrops from his bathroom, while Plum slowly rotated her stiff neck.

At midnight, for one glorious moment, she thought she had spotted a certain wrinkled leaf that was common to each picture, but this proved a false alarm.

At two in the morning, Paul rubbed his tired eyes. 'My darling, I have to occupy myself with twenty-seven children at eight-thirty. Before that, I have to dress and feed my own two . . .'

'Just let me finish this section . . .' Plum murmured, knowing that she could not continue by herself. Slowly, she finished crossing off the contents of the seventh column, marked G. Now only the final column, H, remained.

Paul stretched his arms. 'Plum, I know we've only about an hour's more work, but it's just too much for tonight; I'm not concentrating well enough to be of any use . . .'

He stopped in mid-sentence as Plum gasped, and pointed to his list. Without speaking, they both realized that the same item was in the three G columns they had so far examined: in the bottom left-hand section of each painting was – a fallen flower petal.

Feverishly, they worked on. At three-fifteen, Plum looked at Paul, her eyes shining. 'Look – here it is! The sixth fallen flower petal! And I'll bet there's one on Mrs Carteret's pension picture!'

'And the Mrs Dobbs.'

Plum nodded.

Triumphant, she flung her arms around Paul. 'With the modern tulip in Lady Binger's picture – that's all the proof I need to put the pressure on Monfumat.'

Paul pulled away. 'Shhh, the children,' he cautioned, 'they mustn't know you're here so late . . . How can you put pressure on Monfumat?'

'I'll tell him that unless he reveals his source I'll go to the police.'

Paul took her by the shoulders and said earnestly, 'I think you should go to the police now – the French police.'

'No. My French isn't good enough to explain such a complicated story. I'm having enough trouble with the British cops.'

'So we go to the Paris police together,' Paul said firmly. 'I cannot miss school, but the South of France express to Paris passes our local station at five in the morning: if we catch that train on Saturday, I can return on the Sunday night train, in time for Monday school.'

'You're a darling,' Plum said gratefully, 'but let's visit Monfumat before the police: we've nothing to lose, and we might have much to gain. We'd better check the shop's open on Saturday. Will you phone?'

'If they close on Saturday, I shall tempt them to remain open by pretending to be a rich, Bordeaux wine wholesaler – which will explain my regional accent . . .'

'I love your country accent.' Plum threw her arms around him and whispered, 'I love everything about you. *I love you.*'

Paul tilted her chin upwards. 'At last you said it.'

'I didn't mean to . . .' She had been avoiding the committal and the consequent guilt.

Paul's exhaustion was forgotten in the adrenalin rush of excitement that followed not so much their discovery as at hearing Plum say that she loved him. Tenderly he lifted her into his arms and carried her down the corridor.

She inhaled the rough, male smell of blankets and the sharp tang of starched sheets; she felt the old-fashioned mattress sag beneath them as she welcomed the weight of Paul's body on hers. She was sharply aware of the exciting hardness of his strong cock against her naked stomach, the crisp dark curls from which it reared up, and she revelled in the masculine odour.

The few men that Plum had known between husbands had whipped as fast as possible through the three Fs of modern courtship: free meals, flattery and foreplay. But Plum had sensed that they were not really interested in affection, they hadn't wanted to touch or kiss without fucking, they had merely wanted to stick it in; they saw traditional foreplay as both an exasperating delay and a necessary inconvenience.

Paul touched her nipples, hardened by excitement, and fondled them until Plum could no longer lie without moving, but bucked up against his body as she pulled him down against her. She stroked the hard cheeks of his buttocks as if memorizing their contours, pulling him even closer against her body. She wanted them to be joined as close as stamp and envelope, as quickly as possible, before her body exploded from the frenzy of her desire to feel him inside her. She wanted only to feel the sensual reassurance of him moving inside her.

He entered her slowly, easing himself gradually into her. When fully joined, they paused by unspoken consent, to savour the joining of their flesh. Plum rubbed her breasts against his hairy chest, luxuriating in the tactile difference.

As Paul started slowly to move with her, each of them simultaneously pushing against the other, she fleetingly thought of the way he moved when he walked, the grace of his big, athlete's body and his sure-footed stride. He had this same bodily grace when making love. Plum felt the strong grace of a dancer, as he pushed against her and they moved as one being.

Faster and faster, their hips gyrated more and more urgently, until she sensed the simultaneous building-up of intense pleasure, the gnawing that was almost a physical pain deep inside her body and the impatient yearning to be filled. She wanted to kick and shriek and howl.

Reaching her peak, she was aware of pleasure that was almost exaltation. It seemed a love that exceeded her personal feelings for Paul; a boundless emotion that spilled out of her mind to embrace the entire universe. Intertwined and united with Paul, she quivered joyfully to her climax.

Afterwards, fulfilled, she lay beneath him, feeling his heart beat against hers. Her own heart felt swollen with joy but she trembled close to tears, with a lump in her throat that threatened to swell and spread until it consumed her entire body with sadness: for she was about to leave him. Moonlight again delicately painted their bodies with the flowered pattern of the lace curtains, as they clung to each other.

'In the two years since Annie died,' Paul whispered, 'there have been others. But not love. I did not want to love.'

'Paul, has your mother said anything?'

'Yes,' Paul said shortly, remembering his mother's indignation when he had collected the twins after their sailing trip to Arcachon. She had hustled him into her bedroom and pointed to the crucifix on the wall above her old mahogany bed. 'This is no time for hints.' She had crossed herself. 'This affair with the Englishwoman has clearly gone too far! I ask you to respect our religion, my son. She is a married woman. And she is almost old enough to be your mother.'

'Maman, I am only ten years younger than Plum. I don't care and neither does she.'

'That is not the only problem.'

'I know, Maman.' At first, Paul had told himself that he was merely Plum's holiday pastime, it was just a flirtation. Then he had told himself that he was only going to have her on his terms. He had made sacrifices, taken risks to establish his way of life, and he was determined that nothing and nobody was going to upset it.

But when Plum seemed to agree with his principles and accepted his way of life with relief, Paul had found himself wondering what life would be like for her, should they marry. The main problem was not that she was a foreigner or married, but that she was as different from the Valvert concept of a wife as if she had a green bulbous head with two antennae sticking out of the top. Although in Valvert everyone understood that women worked, a woman did not have a career: it upset the natural order of life. Plum would always be considered a freak in Valvert. But did that matter?

Paul's mother clearly thought so. 'It will *never* work! She is a nice little neighbour but she doesn't fit our way of life. She is a foreigner. A *mad* foreigner – she comes here once every ten years for a holiday. This is not normal behaviour, this is madness, my son . . . And have you seen her crazy paintings? I remember them well . . . She is an eccentric; she is not *une femme sérieuse*! So I hope this episode is not serious . . .' Again, she crossed herself.

'It is *very* serious, Maman.'

'No! You, my son, have the natural urges of a man and need a wife . . . the twins need a mother . . . Of course we all hope that one day . . . But this one . . . she cannot even cook!'

'She *can* cook, but she doesn't enjoy it. I do.' Gently, Paul had told his mother that he was not prepared to discuss further so personal a matter with her at this stage.

But on the way home, as the twins skipped hand-in-hand down the hill ahead, Paul had wondered whether marriage to Plum would be as difficult as his mother feared.

Now, in the milky light of the moon, he asked himself the same question. Propping his dark head on one elbow, he gazed down at Plum, curled up beside him. He heard a stifled sob.

'What's the matter?' He stretched out a hand to turn her face towards his. In the moonlight, she appeared even more fragile than usual. 'I can't bear to think I must leave you, Paul.'

'You needn't leave. You could stay here. We could be married.'

Plum sat up. In the moonlight, she wrapped her arms around her naked shoulders, as if to protect herself. She spoke slowly. 'Paul, I've thought very carefully about living with you – married or not.'

'I know. So have I.'

'I'm scared of doing something foolishly female and rash – giving up all that I have and perhaps causing much misery – for a romantic illusion. I've seen so many women gamble their entire life on a man.'

'Men also take this gamble.'

'Not such an absolute, all-embracing one. And I've already done that twice. Why *do* women risk it?'

'Because they hope for magic,' Paul whispered.

'I don't know *any* married woman who still thinks she's living with the great love of her life: it's all settled down to whose turn it is to put out the cat.' Plum put out her hand and lightly touched his forehead. 'It's too big a gamble.'

In the moonlight, she saw Paul stiffen. 'I'm not offering you a romantic illusion, I'm offering you reality.'

'Paul, please understand why I'm nervous,' Plum pleaded. 'Two divorces . . .'

'Then let's try an alternative to marriage. Perhaps some form of renewable lease: maybe five years, maybe twenty, if we want children. A lease is clearly not a permanent situation – which means that nobody expects it to be.'

'Sounds like planning for divorce.'

'On the contrary, marriage leases would cut down bitter divorces: you merely wait until the end of your lease.'

'A lease is not what your mother sees as marriage.'

Paul sat up, leaned forward and took Plum into his arms. 'Don't let her unrealistic old-fashioned view of marriage obstruct our happiness. Why spend the rest of your life with someone else – when you love me?'

'Any moment now, you'll tell me that I only have one life, so I owe it to myself to behave badly. Was Thoreau non-judgemental?'

'Far from it. But why not separate your anxieties? Separate leaving your husband and joining me: these are three separate issues.'

'Surely two issues?'

'No, three. Because I think you also need to resolve your relationship with yourself: you not only search for fakes, you also want to discover how much of your life is fake.'

'Is it so obvious?'

'No, but I love you, so I can feel that you are not happy with yourself – *bien dans sa peau*, as we say in France. You do not fit contentedly into your skin.'

'Certainly I don't want to run from one marriage to another, when I might be carrying my problem inside me, and so take it with me.'

Lightly, Paul traced the line of her eyebrows. 'Which is why I want to help you with both of your searches.'

Saturday, 2 May 1992

It was a beautiful spring afternoon, and the hyacinth blue of the sky was the colour of Plum's eyes, Paul said. The sun in the Rue Jacob was so dazzling that the interior of Monsieur Monfumat's shop seemed even darker than usual.

As the doorbell jangled, Monsieur Monfumat surged forward, hands in the pockets of a navy cardigan, worn over a dark-blue shirt with navy knitted tie: the off-duty uniform of a middle-aged French intellectual.

'How can I help you?' His shrewd, intelligent eyes looked sharply at Plum from behind rimless, hexagonal spectacles; the small, self-confident mouth would never say anything imprudent.

Paul stepped forward. He wore what he called his meet-the-school-governors uniform: a navy blazer. His voice sounded wearily neutral; he sounded as if he might be some sort of government official. He behaved as a detective making routine inquiries would behave, Plum thought, as from his brisk-looking briefcase he pulled out the file of transparencies. 'We wish to discuss certain Dutch paintings with you.'

Then Monfumat recognized Plum. His mouth tightened and his eyes sharpened. Behind him the young assistant with the limp hair and the cheerfully foolish expression looked alarmed.

Monfumat listened carefully to what Paul said. Then, in a politely insolent voice, he asked him what business it was of his.

Sounding faintly bored, Paul said that in a private capacity he was making inquiries on behalf of Lady Binger in Australia, Miss Cynthia Bly and Mrs Suzannah Marsh in America, the Grant Museum in Boston and the British Institute of Art in London.

Paul's expressionless speech certainly sounded both authentic and potentially ominous, Plum thought. If she were Monfumat, she'd be nervous.

Monfumat looked disdainful, but asked to see Paul's credentials.

In the same politely neutral voice, Paul replied that at this stage, Monfumat might regard the inquiry as unofficial.

Monfumat rubbed his nose and looked thoughtful: an unofficial inquiry implied the possibility of averting an official inquiry. He pointed out that his conditions of sale were on all his bills and clearly stated that he could not be responsible for authenticity of description.

Paul slightly inclined his head, and said that was clearly understood. Had Monfumat been deceived, there was no reason why he should be dragged into the imminent exposure. Would Monfumat have the goodness to examine Paul's transparencies, and say whether there was a possibility that he had handled any of those paintings?

Monfumat called for a magnifying-glass, and when the blond assistant had rushed forward, he carefully examined the transparencies.

After ten minutes had passed, when Plum knew that it should take him only about two minutes to identify goods that had so recently passed through his shop, she guessed that he must be deciding what he should do.

Paul again unclipped his briefcase, produced the sheaf of provenances and held them out to the antique-shop owner, who glanced through them and immediately realized that this matter would not end with his denial of having seen these paintings. Mildly, Monfumat said that he *thought* he recognized the paintings that now belonged to Lady Binger and Artur Schneider, but to be certain, he would need to consult his records.

Paul flipped open a notebook, which Plum knew contained only ideas for future children's classes. Politely, he asked Monfumat to observe the suspect tulip in the Binger picture – which indeed might be due to restoration – and to look equally carefully at the caterpillar – *lackey caterpillar malacosoma neustria*. Would Monsieur please note that a similar caterpillar also appeared in this painting, sold to a Swede. Finally would Monsieur please note the fallen flower petal in the bottom left-hand corner of the pictures.

Wordlessly, the antique dealer did so. Paul then asked him to observe the bluebottle in the painting purchased by Artur Schneider, which also appeared in the painting sold to Suzannah Marsh of New York. Finally would Monfumat examine the important fallen petal in the bottom left-hand corner of the Artur Schneider painting, because a flower petal similarly placed appeared in each of the six transparencies: no doubt Monfumat recognized a visual signature?

Monfumat nodded.

Paul said quietly, 'But these six pictures were supposedly painted by five different artists over a period of about one hundred years.'

Monfumat's mouth tightened until it was only about two centimetres wide. 'What do you wish me to do?'

'Only tell us the name of your supplier.'

'Regrettably that is impossible. We never divulge the name of a supplier where someone wishes to remain anonymous.'

'Then you do not know Monsieur Tonon?'

For the first time, the antique dealer was caught off guard. Eventually, he growled that he would not continue the conversation unless his solicitor was present.

Paul scribbled in his notebook. 'You understand that this matter will not disappear, Monsieur Monfumat? Your cooperation now will make things easier for us – and so for you in the future. Because there would then be no reason for you to be involved.'

'Why bother with me, then?'

'We require the address of Monsieur Tonon and we would like you to telephone him.' Paul did not intend to risk being given a false address and telephone number.

'Nothing more?' Monfumat's face cleared, as he saw the possibility of a deal.

'That is all.'

'Then let's go to my office.'

They all trooped into the office at the rear of the shop, a small, stuffy room heaped with fabric samples, files, reference books and wire trays of letters.

Monfumat moved to a telephone on the table. Paul came up behind him and picked up the second earpiece of the old-fashioned instrument, as he checked that Monfumat was indeed dialling the number that he had scribbled down for Paul.

The telephone was answered by a harassed-sounding woman. 'I'll see if he's here . . .' She yelled shrilly, 'Monsieur Tonon! . . . Monsieur Tonon . . . Yes, he's coming.'

'Who's that?' asked a sharp nasal voice with the flat vowels of the Toulon area.

After exchanging a few platitudes, Monfumat explained (as Paul had requested) that he had a client who wanted a seventeenth-century Dutch flower painting.

The nasal voice said cautiously, 'It could take months to get one.'

'Ask him if he has a Dutch contact that he might telephone,' Paul said.

In an expressionless voice, Monfumat relayed the question.

After a long, suspicious silence, Tonon said, 'I'm surprised you ask questions about my sources.'

'My client is with me and would like to discuss the matter with you. May I give him your address? . . . Then you will need to give it to me.'

Tonon gave an address, then added, 'But my friend, tell whoever is standing by your elbow that I cannot help him.' Paul heard a derisive snort, then a click as the line went dead.

Monfumat looked quietly triumphant and his mouth relaxed a fraction. 'I cannot do more.'

Outside, blinking in the sunlight of the Rue Jacob, Paul hailed a cab and gave Tonon's address. Once in the cab, Plum flung her arms around him jubilantly. 'You were *great*, my darling.'

Paul was not so cheerfully triumphant. 'We're heading for a

fairly sordid area: a tough part of town, with lots of immigrants. Perhaps I should go alone.'

'Not on your life!'

The cab finally stopped before a grimy office building on the curve of two streets. Plum peered out. Peeling advertisements were pasted across dilapidated walls; filthy windows clearly hadn't been opened for years; two mangy cats rooted among garbage sacks in the gutter.

'*Merde!*' Paul growled. 'Tonon gave a false address to Monfumat! He turned to Plum. 'I'm sorry, darling . . . I vaguely sensed at the time that something wasn't right, but didn't pay enough attention to the warning bell in my head. I was so pleased with myself for getting the address, so pleased with my performance as an amateur Arsène Lupin!'

'Don't kick yourself too hard.' But Plum was equally vexed.

'I should have realized Monfumat was tricking me when he asked Tonon for permission to give us his address, *and then also asked for the address*. He would have *known* the address of someone he dealt with. So by asking for it, he deliberately alerted Tonon.'

'Let's try Tonon's telephone number: that was clearly genuine.'

Paul directed the taxi driver to take them to the nearest respectable bistro, where they ordered coffee then rushed to the communal telephone.

After a quick conversation, Paul replaced the receiver and turned to Plum. 'Yes, that's the same number. I recognized the woman's voice – she's probably a waitress. It's a bistro called Le Rouge, in a very rough part of that area we just left. She says Tonon isn't there, and she has no idea where he lives. He's a regular customer, but she knows nothing about him. Or else she's not talking.'

'If Tonon uses their telephone, surely he must work near by?'

'Maybe he conducts his business at a table in the bistro. I doubt anyone there will admit it: I expect he tips them well.'

'Couldn't we offer someone more money?'

'Counter-bribe? Not a hope. If Tonon's paying them, then they'll simply use our offer to get more money from him. The only way for us to get information out of a shady bistro is by going to the police on Monday.'

'But Tonon might have done a flit by then!'

Paul shrugged his shoulders. 'You can do nothing until Monday. No French detective is going to give up his weekend to investigate your story of fallen flower petals on paintings, or a deserted office building that's supposed to be the workplace of some man you never met and cannot accuse of anything. So you'll have to wait until Monday.'

'I can't do that! I promised Breeze I'd be home tomorrow night. I'm booked on the last plane to London. Damn! I'll have to fly back to Paris some time next week. I'll book a translator: I can't risk misunderstanding something.'

Sunday, 3 May 1992

Paul refused to tell Plum where they were to eat lunch. 'It's somewhere you have assuredly never been.' Laughing, he shook his head at each of Plum's guesses, until the taxi halted.

Plum peered through the window. A crowd of foreign tourists jostled against each other at the base of the Eiffel Tower.

'On top of the Eiffel Tower is a very good restaurant – one of the few tourist restaurants patronized by Parisians,' Paul promised.

Squeezed into the great metal elevator, they hissed up to the sky ... up ... up ... passing the enormous iron girders, so delicate when seen from a distance.

Plum, seated in the restaurant, gazed out at an astonishing view. She was sitting in a cloudless blue sky and below her was – the whole of Paris. This aerial view differed from an aeroplane view because it was comparatively near to the ground, the detail was distinct, and so the view became more intimate. She felt as if the doll-like people, bicycles, cars and tiny buildings were her toys. Fascinated, she gazed down at the River Seine, the Cathedral of Notre Dame and the Île St-Louis; all around her, Haussman's grand plan of Paris was clearly visible – broad avenues which ended in splendid *places* to form a magnificent geometric design unequalled in the world. How many gardens and parks there still were, even among those distant, pale, modern apartment blocks!

Paul ordered champagne, fresh asparagus with Hollandaise sauce, lobster and salad; then they ate *meringues glaçées*, stuffed with chestnut purée and topped with whipped cream. Afterwards, with other lovers similarly hand in hand, they strolled along old, cobbled quays on the edge of the Seine. A storm had swept the city earlier that morning, but now only a gentle breeze rustled the dark leaves of trees which gleamed as if freshly waxed.

'I wish you could have met my Aunt Harriet,' Plum said, 'but she's away – a wedding in Burgundy.' She ducked as a poplar swayed in the breeze, and a shower of raindrops fell on the cobblestones.

'I don't want to be with anyone but you on our last day.'

'Neither do I,' said Plum, dreamily. 'I'm so happy.' She stopped and stared in a puddle at her lover's reflection.

Paul squeezed her hand. 'Being happy is much simpler than most people realize. It doesn't mean that everything's perfect – because life never is. And it doesn't mean you never make mistakes, have problems or aggravation.'

'No,' she agreed. 'About thirty per cent of normal life is beyond anyone's control: someone snaps at you because he's had a row with his wife, the breakfast milk's sour, or the cat's sick over your shoes.'

Paul swung their clasped hands in rhythm with their strides. 'Happiness is enjoyment and contentment . . .'

'Appreciating what already exists, refusing to be negative.' Plum grinned at him. 'Looking on the bright side. We call that being a Pollyanna.'

'Nothing wrong with that. Happiness often depends on whether you decide to be happy: happiness is a state of mind.'

'Is it that simple?' Plum hopped over a puddle.

Paul ruffled her hair, and she ducked away. He said, 'Of course you can't be happy if your mother's just dropped dead, or your business collapses, but few people live in a permanent state of tragedy.'

'The problem is that we've become so *confused*,' Plum thought aloud. 'We follow what we're told is the path to happiness – then find we're trapped by some expensive life-style that we don't really enjoy.'

'Or trapped by a mortgage that we can't afford – as I was.'

'But how can you change your life?' Plum thought of herself.

'In your biggest area of discomfort – because often everything else stems from that. That's why I left Paris and went back to Valvert.' He stopped, placed both hands on her shoulders, looked earnestly into her hyacinth eyes, and said, 'Please will you join me there, Plum?'

'It's such a tempting offer – to live with you. But I can't promise you . . . yet.' They both knew that she had to talk to Breeze. Paul stuck his hands in his pockets and marched on in silence.

Paul stopped, and caught her by the wrists. 'Let's go back to the hotel . . .'

* * * *

On Sunday evening Paul, his arms around Plum, stood by the sleek navy train to Bordeaux. As departure time drew near, Plum found it difficult to hold back tears. When the loudspeaker crackled its final warning, she held him even tighter. 'Don't be angry with me, Paul, because I won't agree to what we both want.'

'Just promise you'll come back?' The drabness of the station enhanced Paul's vivid blue eyes.

'I don't know,' Plum whispered unhappily. 'I can't say yet.'

'Why are we whispering in the middle of this din?' Paul prised her fingers from his neck, one at a time, as gently as if he were picking flowers. 'Plum, d'you remember Doctor Combray, who treated you after your bicycle accident? He once told me that he'd tried to comfort a rich woman who was dying; in tears, she said to him, "You don't understand – I'm not crying because I'm going to die. I'm crying because I have never lived."'

The train let out a shriek.

'À la prochaine,' Paul whispered encouragingly.

Plum wondered if there would be a next time. She managed a trembling smile, but her eyes brimmed with tears.

Swiftly and finally, Paul kissed her cheek. He swung himself on the high step of the train, turned and waved, then disappeared into the carriage as the train jerked slowly away.

Plum's heart felt pinched and shrivelled. She felt as if a part of her had been amputated. She felt as if she were walking along the path of her future life, and now it stretched grey, grim and cheerless before her.

Feeling solitary and sad, she listened to the rumble of the train wheels gathering speed. Paul, now leaning out of the window, grew smaller and smaller. He was waving something strange . . .

Despite her misery, Plum laughed as she recognized the canary yellow shoe that she had lost during her bicycle accident.

And then he was gone.

CHAPTER TWENTY-FOUR

Monday, 4 May 1992

'SO YOU'VE finally decided to come back!' Breeze, who had been stuffing papers into a briefcase, turned from the desk between the windows of their bedroom. Plum saw that his face was thinner and paler than usual; he looked tired and under strain. His dark winter overcoat made him look even taller and leaner, and his streaky blond hair needed cutting and stood up like a cockatoo's crest. His coat needed brushing, his crumpled tie didn't match his shirt and his shoes needed cleaning. What had happened to Sandra?

'Her mother's ill,' Breeze said, wearily, 'and I've more important things than laundry to worry about. My secretary phoned Harrods for some socks and underpants – so you see I've just about survived without you.' He made no attempt to kiss Plum. They stared at each other in silence.

He glared at her, then telephoned his office. 'Amanda, you can cancel my flight to Bordeaux . . . Yes, she's back. Yes, looking very rested . . . Yes, I'm glad, too . . . Yes, I'll tell her . . . Thank you.' He put the phone down.

'Is everything OK at the office?' Plum asked cautiously. She hoped that Sandra's absence was his only problem.

'Everything's fine, now that you're back,' Breeze said in a tightly controlled voice. 'Although I can't pretend business is booming: market confidence in art is depressingly low.' He crammed more papers into his briefcase and snapped the locks. 'As you know, we've seen a bit of pyramiding – over-leveraging; so the art market's now in the same sort of trouble as the property market.'

Plum instantly realized what he meant: any art dealer's wife, no matter how disinterested in maths, knew the equation. Supposing a dealer had a Matisse sketch worth 200,000 dollars, he could use it as collateral to borrow 100,000 dollars to buy another picture – say a Matthew Smith – so that he was able to offer customers not 200,000 but 300,000 dollars' worth of stock.

Then came the world recession. Paintings crashed to almost half their value, but customers had no money to buy the bargains. Without normal sales to pay bank interest on loans, a gallery might be forced to sell its stock for what it could get – which might mean selling 300,000 dollars' worth of paintings for only 100,000. If so, when the bank was repaid, the dealer would be left with only a quarter of his original investment – if he was lucky. If he'd only been able to sell those paintings for 100,000 dollars, then after repaying the bank loan the dealer would be left with – nothing.

Plum looked frightened. '*Surely – you haven't been pyramiding?*' A pyramider was a dealer who then raised money on the second painting, to buy a third. And so on, going deeper into bank debt.

'No, thank God. There's nothing to worry about. I'm only in the same sort of shit as everyone else in the game – but I *am* a bit stretched. You've no idea how much it costs to run the gallery and this place.'

'I'll help in any way I can.'

'The best way you can help is to put on a good show at the Biennale.'

'My new paintings are nearly all finished.' Plum tried to look firmly supportive. 'I'll be in Venice on time *and* in the right frame of mind. I'm fit and rested – ready to take on the press: I'll do all the interviews you want.'

'That's just as well, because the art press of the world has been phoning and faxing non-stop . . . Oh by the way, I hope you don't mind – I've told Nicholas Herring he can interview you here, after lunch. He was insistent and I was running short of excuses, so I crossed my fingers and just hoped I wouldn't have to cancel.'

'No, that's fine. Don't worry, Breeze, I won't let you down. For the first time in my life – I'm not frightened of the press.'

Breeze laughed. 'I'll believe that when I see it. Seriously, you know how important the media is to us at this point. Journalists need to see you looking confident: they're all going to ask you what you think your chances are . . .'

'Breeze, I was lucky to get chosen! You *know* I haven't a chance of winning a prize. Unrealistic hopes just make me more nervous! You *know* they won't let the British win again!' The Golden Lion painting award had gone to Howard Hodgkin in 1984, Frank Auerbach in 1986 and Tony Cragg in 1988. And at the previous Biennale, the Premio 2000, for artists under thirty-five, had been won by Anish Kapoor.

'And *you* know these things don't only rest on merit, Plum. Remember you're the British choice, even if you are the token woman.' They both knew that Plum had been nominated because the theme of the 1992 Biennale was 'A View of Woman' and because the British had nominated only one other woman in the past hundred years – Bridget Riley.

'But let's not have unrealistic expectations, Breeze.'

Breeze knew his salesman's optimism occasionally soared to targets beyond the attainable. 'Look,' he said apologetically, 'I hope I haven't pushed you too hard.'

'I'm glad you did. You've always told me that a person can have a flexi-time job but a flexi-time career only happens in beach-read books.'

'You don't need me to tell you that you can't half-paint. I know you have to put everything you've got into it, or else you're unhappy to some degree.'

They stood silent, yards apart, at opposite sides of the bedroom. Plum wondered how much longer they were going to talk about the damned Biennale. How much longer were they going to postpone the conversation that they both knew had to take place?

Nervously, she gabbled, 'I'll always be grateful to you, Breeze, for the way you encouraged my painting – as well as building my career.'

'That little speech sounds as if you're about to dump me, and walk out.'

They stared at each other, Breeze in hurt and angry silence, Plum nervous but with determined defiance. She hadn't meant to walk straight into a showdown – but perhaps it was the best way to handle this situation.

Finally, Breeze said, 'You'd better tell me about him.'

'So you guessed.'

'Not difficult. One look at your face.'

Plum felt relieved and less defensive. She also felt guilty. She had expected an outburst of furious temper when she had the showdown with Breeze, rather than despondency and resignation.

Briefly, she told Breeze about Paul. On the flight back to London Plum had repeatedly rehearsed this in her mind, but hearing herself speak, she realized that her description sounded like an over-emotional story in a True Romance magazine.

Breeze attacked with angry wit. 'I suppose he's one of those sensitive, hairy Iron Johns in muddy boots, a plaid shirt and dungarees with longjohns beneath. I expect he spends his weekends running around naked in some forest, or chopping down the goddamn trees for his wood-burning stove. Does he drive a pick-up truck or a dirt bike? . . . Or is this bloody Frenchman more of an intellectual wimp – some Jean-Jacques Rousseau update? Does the pokerwork text above the bed read, "Man is born free but every-where is in chains"?'

Plum's face showed Breeze that he had scored a bullseye. He pushed his advantage. 'Sounds as if you've caught a touch of the Gauguins – remember that Tahitian canvas, *Where Do We Come From? What Are We? Where Are We Going?* For God's sake don't get didactic, Plum, it'll ruin your market . . .' Abruptly, Breeze stopped sneering as he remembered he was trying to placate Plum, not goad her. He said in a tight voice, 'I suppose it was only to be expected.'

Indignantly, Plum cried, 'Paul isn't my childish revenge!'

'Perhaps not consciously. If not – explain the big attraction. What do you see in this bastard?'

Breeze was hurt by the dreamy look that appeared in Plum's eyes and the softening of her voice, as she repeated, 'What do I see in Paul? Simplicity, straightforwardness, gentleness. Paul isn't fright-ened of the world. He's not temperamental, or judgemental: he doesn't find faults and he doesn't seem to mind the ones he notices.'

'Sounds more like a monk than a man,' Breeze sneered. 'Are you *sure* he's passionately in love with you?'

'Paul's passionate about a lot of things, but most of all about living a simple life. He says simplicity brings happiness.'

'Simplicity as in no central heating?' Breeze asked nastily.

Since saying goodbye to Paul, Plum had tried to decide on her options and responsibilities. Breeze's aggression now provided the two grains of sand which tipped the balance in Paul's favour. She told Breeze that she wanted to leave him and live in Valvert. She told him why. She finished by saying that Breeze could remain her dealer but in future she wouldn't produce nearly so many paintings: her days as a picture factory were over.

Breeze exploded. 'I hope he's a wonderful lover,' he screamed, 'because you'll have precious little else to do in that godforsaken place! You're making the biggest mistake of your life!'

'Maybe the biggest mistake would be to stay here.'

'What's suddenly so wrong with our marriage?'

'Our marriage has become nothing more than a habit.'

'What's wrong with that? It's a *comfortable* habit. That's what I like about it. Our marriage reminds me of that bit of Thomas Hardy where Gabriel tells Bathsheba, 'Whenever you look up, there I shall be, and whenever I look up, there will be you.'

'You can't look up if you're not at home, Breeze.'

'You don't miss me when I need to socialize,' Breeze pointed out. 'You prefer to have your girl-friends round for a chat. Or you like to go to bed early, with supper on a tray, and watch a video.'

'But not every night.'

'For God's sake, Plum! You only have to lift the fucking phone and you can go to every party in town! And you have plenty of friends to go with. I'm your husband, not your walker.'

'Perhaps that's why I never seem to get your full attention.'

Breeze glared, astonished by this new, spirited Plum.

Eventually, he grunted, 'I admit I haven't been perfect, but on the whole our marriage seems to have worked very well for the last ten years. I gave you what you said you wanted. I gave you what I could. But I can't turn myself into a New Age bliss-ninny because that's what you've decided you want this year.'

'Please don't try.'

With difficulty, Breeze lowered his voice. 'For God's sake, reconsider,' he implored. 'Some women have affairs on cruises, some prefer the Hamptons. Wherever it happens, a holiday love affair is only part of the change from normal routine life, that's all.' He threw out his hands. 'For God's sake, don't throw our life away just because you've spent three weeks in some bucolic paradise with a Young Thoreau update.'

Another bullseye. Plum cried, 'You never saw the point of Valvert!'

'Because I know too much about that sort of life! My grandfather was a tenant farmer, remember? Our holidays were spent helping him, because he needed us and we couldn't afford to go anywhere else. So I know that country life isn't simple; country life is damn complicated: there's never a spare moment and it takes all your time to stay dry, warm and clean – and those are your constant priorities. I *know* that being down on the farm isn't like the margarine commercials on TV.'

In silence they glared at each other.

Eventually, Breeze burst out, 'Haven't you got *enough* in your life here? God, you're so bloody selfish! God, you're so controlling!'

Plum remembered what Aunt Harriet had said about accusations of selfishness. Sharply she retorted, 'Only controlling men accuse women of being controlling. Breeze, I haven't got the things I want, but the things *you* want. And I've been doing what *you* want for years; if our wishes didn't coincide, you *never* gave way to me; women are supposed to be so manipulative, but men are ten times craftier at getting their own way indirectly.'

'OK, out with it! Tell me *what it is you want.*'

'What I want most at the moment, Breeze, is more time to think.'

'You don't want to *think* – you want to hop into bed with this bloody Frenchman!' With an effort, Breeze again lowered his voice. 'OK. Why not? How about a couple of months sailing around the South Sea Islands?' He looked pleadingly at her. 'After the Biennale, of course. For God's sake, let's delay this discussion of your – our – future until after that, because your whole future depends on it.'

Plum shook her head. 'I don't need a holiday. I'm going to give the Biennale my best shot. Then I want to nail whoever's forging these paintings . . .'

'Oh, God, are you *still* obsessed by that?'

'Yes, I am! So why can't *you* do what *I* want, for once? Why not *help* me? I've asked you often enough! Help me find these forgers?'

Breeze hesitated. Picking his words with care, he said wearily, 'I didn't help you because I didn't think you'd really go through with it. And I still think it's none of your business.'

'But I'm about to crack it!' Briefly, Plum told of her progress in tracking the forger.

Breeze looked horrified. Eventually he said, 'You say you want to simplify your life and then you proceed to complicate it in this *dangerous* manner!'

'You're deliberately misunderstanding me!'

Breeze looked at Plum and slowly shook his head in disbelief. 'I don't understand what's got into you this year. You suddenly seem prepared to risk so much . . . do you realize you've not only been risking your chance of the Biennale, but also your fucking life, if those threatening letters are to be taken seriously?'

'Leo may have sent the letters,' Plum suggested.

'Leo had nothing to do with those forged pictures,' Breeze said with brusque finality.

'*How can you be so sure?*'

'Because Leo was killed for . . . a different reason.'

'*How can you be so sure?* I know the police think it's some sort of gay killing, but remember the cops never lose a chance to blacken gays.'

They stood glaring at each other, until the temporary maid knocked at the door and asked if she could clean the bedroom now?

*   *   *   *

Depressed, Plum flung out of the house for a bracing walk in the park. She tramped over miles of grass, she circumnavigated the duck lake, she watched some small boys muddy themselves on a football pitch. Then she found herself at the entrance to the zoo, and upon impulse, she clicked through the turnstile.

Plum hadn't been in the zoo since her sons grew up, so she had forgotten the decrepit concrete, the apathetic plants and trees that simulated a natural environment for the trapped animals. She walked the dusty paths, growing increasingly depressed. Finally she stopped before the tiger compound. On the far side of a concrete moat filled with brackish water, a lean and supple tiger paced restlessly back and forth, as if in an invisible cage. Plum watched the powerful muscles move beneath the beautifully kept black and tan stripes: back and forth – swing round – back and forth – swing round . . .

Suddenly the tiger paused; the powerful head turned slowly. Huge yellow eyes stared at Plum, and in them she saw sadness and resignation. This tiger was trapped for life in its own depression. Suddenly Plum understood the message being beamed to her by those topaz eyes: *You know what I was. You see what I am. I remember what I was. I know what I am. I can't change my life. But you can, you can. Look at me and leap away!*

＊　＊　＊　＊

As Plum returned to her doorstep, a Range-Rover drew up, with Jenny at the wheel; Lulu and Wolf were waving from the back seat.

'Like it?' Jenny shouted, as they all jumped down.

'You *must* be doing well,' Plum said admiringly.

Jenny's face clouded. 'Daddy left more than we expected.'

As they clattered into the kitchen (Lulu now refused to let Wolf into any other part of Plum's elegant house), the telephone shrilled. It was an excited Toby, who had just been voted treasurer of the students' union after a brilliantly bizarre publicity campaign run by his new girlfriend, Venetia, whose father ran a rare bookshop near the British Museum. The thing is, there wasn't much money in the kitty and Toby wondered whether Breeze could help him reorganize the union finances . . .

After Jenny and Lulu had congratulated the mother of the new treasurer, Plum fixed chocolate milkshakes and dolloped peanut ice-cream into a bowl for Wolf.

'So tell us the rest of your news! *What happened in France?*' Lulu asked eagerly.

Plum's eyes lit up. She needed no further prompting.

For the next half hour she talked non-stop about Paul. Her two friends were intrigued and giggly, but they both liked Breeze, and neither of them knew this beautiful French yokel with whom Plum had been so deliciously sinful, although Jenny thought she remembered Paul . . .

'Wasn't he the kid with bandy legs and acne – the one you taught to swim? . . . Ow, stop it, Plum! . . . OK, I take it back!'

Spattering her story with 'Paul says' and 'Paul thinks', Plum then told of the flower petal visual signature, and her progress towards Tonon.

'At least you haven't been worrying about those threatening letters,' Lulu pointed out, as she pulled Wolf away from a carton of raspberry ripple.

'Paul said the best way to deal with the letters was to find the forger.'

'Surely Breeze must now be impressed by what you've discovered?' Lulu asked, yanking Wolf away from the freezer.

'We're not exactly on chatty terms at the moment. I told Breeze, of course, but he seemed exasperated and impatient. He said that as the forger had been feeding the market with fakes for years, he could wait another few weeks until after the bloody Biennale.' Plum turned to Jenny. 'By the way, you *are* still coming?'

'You bet. What're you planning to wear in Italy?'

Lulu broke in, 'Hey! Where's your diamond ring, Plum? Hocked it?'

'No, it's in the wall safe in my bedroom. I feel unfaithful if I wear it.'

'Unfaithful to whom?' Lulu grinned. As she spoke, the telephone rang.

Plum answered it. 'Enid? Yes, it's me . . .'

When Plum replaced the receiver, Lulu cried, 'Come on, tell! We could see something terrific's happened . . . Put that *down*, Wolf! It's cat food.'

Plum glowed. 'Terrific indeed! Enid's just confirmed that Cynthia's picture *was* painted by the same guy who painted the Swede's picture. But Ambrosius Bosschaert the Elder, who supposedly painted Cynthia's picture, lived from 1573 to 1621; and the Swede's picture was supposedly painted by Jan van Kessel the Elder, who wasn't born until 1626. So we now have definite proof of forgery!'

'And I suppose you'll soon have two official complaints: Cynthia and the Swede?' Jenny asked.

Plum's face clouded. 'There's a complication, because Cynthia's picture was purchased in Britain, and the Swede bought his in Paris: so police coordination must be arranged, and that's likely to take time. But the net *is* tightening! Enid won't tell me who the Swede is, but she reckons he'll agree to relinquish anonymity to nab the forger . . .'

'So you're about to pounce on the forger?' Lulu asked.

'No, dammit,' Plum said crossly, 'I've still no idea who he is . . . Lulu, is Wolf allowed to drink cooking sherry?'

Thursday, 7 May 1992

Three days after Plum's return, Detective-Inspector Grigg called. Wearing an expensive Burberry raincoat, he sat with Plum in the drawing-room, where she talked excitedly, pushing notes and transparencies over the coffee table. When she had finished, she looked up expectantly, expecting a few words of approval.

Reflectively, he tapped his pen against his teeth. 'You've done quite well . . .'

Plum beamed. She felt close to trapping the forger. She also felt less vulnerable to a potential killer. Paul had pointed out that Leo might have written the two threatening letters, for he had been in New York when the first one arrived, and his death implied that he was certainly involved with a dodgy crowd. The more Plum thought about it, the more plausible this theory seemed.

The detective continued, 'I can now pursue this with the French police, but I expect you realize that Tonon may be just another link. You have no hard evidence that he's a fence or a forger. If he is, he'd probably have been much more difficult to trace.'

'I've done more to trace this forger than anyone else!' cried Plum indignantly.

'True, but your mistake was getting Monfumat to phone Tonon. If you'd alerted the French police, they'd have tracked Tonon's telephone number and been waiting at that bistro – at the *exact* moment when Monfumat telephoned him: that would have been a neat and easy trap.'

'D'you think Monfumat would have meekly given some *gendarme* the telephone number – and not immediately warned Tonon?'

'Monfumat would have done exactly what the French police told him to do. They're a tough bunch. They'd have stuck with him – if they didn't keep him at some *gendarmerie* – until they'd tracked down that bistro and ordered him to call Tonon.'

Grigg looked into Plum's eager face. 'But instead of setting a trap, you warned Tonon that he'd been rumbled. By now the forger will also have been warned. He'll have gone to ground, so we may *never* catch him ...' Although he did not say them, the words 'Thanks to your amateur ignorance and impatience' hung in the air between him and the crestfallen Plum.

Relenting, the detective added, 'But you certainly seem to have established that crimes have been committed, Mrs Russell. When do you suppose Cynthia Bly will lodge a formal complaint?'

'There's been a slight hitch. We may need another month as the anonymous Swedish owner won't go public. Dame Enid suspects it's for some tax reason. So Victor Marsh is sending over his wife's painting to be analysed – which will take at least three weeks. Both Americans will use our lawyer to make a formal complaint to Maltby's, and to the British police.'

The detective scribbled the address of Breeze's lawyer, then stood up. 'From now on, Mrs Russell, please leave this matter to the police. Remember those threatening letters.'

'I haven't received any more since Leo Mann died. So I'm inclined to think he sent them. He tried to warn me in a friendly way that I was getting into something dangerous, but I wouldn't take any notice. So maybe that's how he tried to stop me – by sending the letters.'

'Don't count on it.'

*　*　*　*

That night, Plum woke drowsily to find she was lying on her side, with Breeze's arms around her. He had crept into her bedroom, quietly pulled back the sheets, and pushed up her Victorian lace nightdress, chosen by Plum because it covered her body and she didn't want him to see her in anything translucent. Now he was skilfully fondling her breasts, and Plum could feel the warm flesh of his rampant penis hard against her stomach.

'*Stop that, Breeze!*' Plum raised her arm and fumbled for the light-switch.

In the soft yellow glow, Breeze's eyes were determined; wordlessly he grabbed Plum's naked buttocks and pulled her body against his.

Panting, Plum tried to wriggle free and pull down her nightdress. 'Breeze, acquaintance rape *won't work*! Nobody wants to fall out of love but once it's gone, it's *gone!*'

In answer, Breeze thrust his hands up under her nightgown and again grasped her breasts. As he touched her nipples, Plum felt a jolt of sexual excitement. As he tried to kiss her, she jerked her head backwards. 'Breeze, for God's sake, understand how I feel. *It's over!* If you cared for me you'd understand that!' She looked into his unhappy eyes. '*Can't you understand?*'

Huskily, Breeze muttered, 'How can you be so sure, if you don't put it to the test?'

Plum remembered how exciting, how passionate, how loving Breeze had once been in bed, before sex became more or less a habit. Was that the reason Breeze had started to have other women? Or was it the result? He had always been a skilful but emotionally uninvolved lover, although she had only realized it after she'd caught him with that Argentine bitch.

After their reconciliation, Plum had consciously looked for an emotional union in their love-making, rather than just the physical joining of two bodies in sexual gratification. It was then that she noticed that Breeze withheld himself; without has invisible emotional armour, he seemed afraid of his vulnerability.

Breeze, sensing Plum's sudden sadness, wrongly thought she was weakening. Urgently, he whispered, 'Surely ten years together counts for something? And surely there's *something* to be said for me?'

'Of course there is.' Fleetingly, Plum remembered how well Breeze got on with the boys; he had been distraught when Max ran away from school. He had argued with her until two in the morning before she'd agreed that Toby could have a motor-bike for his sixteenth birthday. Breeze was generous and kind, encouraging and supportive.

As if reading her thoughts, he said, 'How do you think the boys will take this? They're as fond of me as I am of them. If that hadn't been so, I'd have wanted children of my own.' This was a sneaky dig.

As Plum looked hesitant, he added, 'Just because they're practically adult doesn't mean the boys won't be upset if their family splits apart, and their home disappears.'

'The boys both *chose* to leave home – I'd have been worried if they hadn't. You and I aren't going to disappear. Motherhood isn't a full-time occupation. And it's as quick to get to Bordeaux from here as it is to get to Edinburgh.'

'Darling, please give me *one* more chance.' Breeze pulled her towards him. Plum suddenly felt a giddy, physical impulse to thrust back, to grasp his flesh, to enjoy sensual pleasure in each other.

Realizing her arousal, Breeze coaxed gently. 'Let's try to make it work again, darling?' His fingertips flicked down between her thighs. 'Let's forget what I've done and what I haven't done?' His hand reached the silky pubic hair, and knowingly pressed it in a soothing, circular motion. His index finger slid towards her cleft and gently rubbed her clitoris in the steady rhythm that he knew excited her. She knew a dizzy yearning.

'I can feel your wetness. I can smell that musky odour. You know I want you.' He pulled her hand down to his penis.

With difficulty, Plum yanked her hand away and scrambled off the bed. 'I'm sorry, Breeze, but that's *not* what I want.'

'You can't fool me! You want it just as much as I do!'

'No! One sexy romp won't mend our relationship. Why can't you admit that we've grown apart?'

'Because I don't believe we have!'

'You mean you don't want to admit it! Can't you see we don't even seem to be friends any more?' Plum glared. 'Maybe it started when you bedded other women – I don't know; but I *do* know that after going off with someone else, *I* don't feel the same way about you, Breeze. *You* think that the odd fuck doesn't matter if you don't get caught – but I've found out that it does.'

Breeze tried to interrupt her, but Plum was determined to finish. 'Some people have dozens of affairs and still seem to lead a happy married life – but do they, Breeze? How can you have a trusting, truthful relationship with a person if you're lying to her about it? And if an intimate relationship isn't a truthful relationship – then it's a fake relationship!'

'Men feel differently about these things.'

'Do they? Only when it suits them. I've met some very possessive men.'

'Look – will you please tell me what's suddenly so repulsive about me? What's this fucking Frenchman got that I can't give you?'

'*Himself!* It's because you won't share *all* of yourself with me that you and I don't have a real relationship – as I do with Paul . . . It was after I caught you with that Argentinian cow that I noticed you withhold yourself from me,' she added sadly. 'Perhaps this guardedness, this holding back, was always there. Perhaps you *never* trusted me enough to really share yourself entirely with me. And I never noticed because I loved you, so I only saw what I wanted to see.'

'I'm not saying I'm perfect, Plum . . .'

'On the outside, Breeze, you're as near perfect as possible. But on the inside – what *is* inside, Breeze?' Plum clasped her hands together. '*I don't know!* What fears, doubts, anger does your defensiveness hide?'

Breeze, now detumescent, slid off the bed and grabbed his Paisley dressing-gown from the floor. Plum could see that he was very angry.

'Has that fucking Frenchman bewitched you?'

'Paul isn't the reason we're breaking up. Paul happened because we'd already broken up, although we couldn't see it.'

'Just how long do you think your idyllic, irresponsible interlude with him will last?' Roughly, Breeze yanked the ends of the belt together. '*I'll* tell you how long it will last. Two years at worst and seven years at best! And then what?'

'Then I'll decide.'

'I'm warning you,' Breeze growled, 'once you cut apart from me – that's it, Plum. Game over. Divorce. You can't come back and ask or expect forgiveness. You're not twelve years old any more.'

CHAPTER TWENTY-FIVE

Friday, 29 May 1992

A WARM breeze lifted Plum's red curls. She stared ahead as the Hotel Cipriani's private motor launch cut across the lagoon towards the Campanile di San Marco – the landmark of Venice, which reared up from the Piazza San Marco. In the Piazza's columned arcades, European knights had once haggled over provisions before setting out for the Crusades; now, twenty thousand sunburned tourists, hung with cameras, shopped there.

It was hard to believe that Venice was not a fantasy, a setting for some opera, Plum thought, as the motor launch spumed towards the landing stage, and the romantically beautiful buildings of central Venice came into focus. The canals were lined with decaying but exquisite palaces, coloured dusky pink, russet and every shade of warm brown from Marie-biscuit to dark ginger; the doors and windows were elaborately framed in white marble, which was also used for the arcaded private landing stages, marked by striped mooring poles stuck in the canals.

Plum remembered how surprised she had been on her first visit to find that Venice was *not* built on water: the city was a group of over a hundred tiny islands inside a sheltering lagoon, huddled closely together. Small bridges linked one island to the other, over narrow waterways which acted as roads. These canals – not always fragrant – were now crowded with public water buses, humble rowing boats, luxurious private motor launches and sleek black gondolas punted by knowingly picturesque *gondolieri* wearing ribboned straw hats.

Plum left the landing stage and strolled towards the Piazza, once again feeling as if she had been miniaturized and was moving through a Canaletto or a Guardi.

She and Breeze were staying at the Cipriani, in a suite with separate bedrooms. The atmosphere between them, friendly on the surface, was tense beneath. Breeze was doing his best to be supportive, but he wasn't made of stone, as he would point out whenever he broke their promise to call a truce and not mention to each other the possibility of a divorce until after the Biennale. He could not resist making waspish references to the hick in the haystack, and other bitter taunts, but Plum firmly banished them from her mind, as is the female custom, in order to keep the peace.

Plum had also promised herself that, with one exception, for the week of the Biennale she would concentrate on the Olympics of the art world and ban all thoughts of seventeenth-century Dutch paintings and her search for the forger. The French police had been unable to trace Tonon in Paris, so she had not needed to return; they thought it likely that Tonon was circulating forged art in several countries, probably under several names. Alas, having been clearly warned, Tonon had now gone to ground and they could find no trace of him.

But before Plum postponed her quest, she intended to take the opportunity to question the one person who had so far eluded her – Charley Boman. Charley's father was consultant to a Cubist exhibition in Buenos Aires, and he and Charley had been there for some months, but they had returned briefly to Europe, expressly to attend the greatest spree of the contemporary art calendar. For the events which the Biennale generates throughout Venice excite as much attention from the international art mob as the World Cup does among football fans. Consequently, Venice is part carnival, part museum, part market place and part art trade fair, where everyone in the business catches up with what everyone else is doing.

*   *   *   *

As Britain's main entry, Plum's time and energy was consumed by the people that Breeze brought to meet her. As her picture dealer, he was working overtime, and her life threatened to be one continuous, exhausting cocktail party for the hectic four days of the official opening – the wheeler-dealer period before the public is allowed in, when collectors are anxious to buy at advantageous prices, art dealers are eager to sign up new stars, contracts are drawn up or renewed, shows arranged, books planned, exhibitions and careers orchestrated. During these four days, exhibiting artists got immediate reaction to experimental new work, and the press interviewed anyone important.

As Plum turned left into the Piazza, out of the blazing sunlight, she quickened her pace through the crowded Piazza towards the Café Florian, which was in the shade until late afternoon – one reason for its being the gossip centre of the Biennale. Over the elaborately mirrored interior, and the crowded tables outside, hovers a constant sparkle of rumours and suspicions. Over iced coffee or *Bellinis* – fresh peach juice mixed with champagne – the choice of selection committees, artists, juries and prizewinners is unscrupulously dissected; everyone's worst opinions are cheerfully confirmed, and vague allegations of jury-tampering are whispered. But although normal lobbying and horse-trading take place, conspiracy theories and pay-off rumours are unlikely to be true, especially those concerning the always distinguished jurors.

In fact, as Breeze well knew, the best and cheapest way to influence the jury was via the media. This year, publicity campaigns kicked off by elaborate press parties had been organized by many dealers, and by all the countries taking part. The Americans had flown in celebrities by the jet load, President Mitterrand was, as usual, attending the French party, and the British had invited over 1,000 people to their candlelit masked ball on Tuesday night, to be held in a Gothic *palazzo* on the Grand Canal, furnished as it was when first purchased in the late eighteenth century by the family who still owned it. Plum – a guest of honour – planned to wear strapless white tulle spangled with black plastic stars and cut just above the knee, with white kid bovver boots.

She reached Florian's and scanned the tables for Charley. Hearing her name called, she spotted Jenny waving from a crowded table. Jenny was the paying guest of an impoverished Contessa, in an old and crumbling *palazzo* on a not-very-smart canal.

Plum waved back, then picked her way through the crowded tables towards Charley, who sat alone; whispers followed her.

'That's Plum Russell, chosen instead of Richard Hamilton, can you believe it?'

'I hear she's already slept with the Spanish juror . . .'

'I heard it was with the American juror . . .'

'But isn't that a woman?'

'Exactly.'

'I heard Breeze offered her to all of them . . .'

'He wouldn't dare; Plum's been the mistress of the British juror for years . . .'

'God, save me from bitches!' Plum flopped into her chair.

'And bad jokes.' Charley grinned. The Biennale theme – 'A View of Woman' – had already launched lewd witticisms in many languages.

Charley ordered iced coffee, then held his thumb and forefinger together in a gesture of approval. 'Nice outfit, Plum.' She wore a butter silk backless halter-neck jumpsuit with apricot silk sandals.

'You too, Charley.' Plum smiled into Charley's dark eyes, which for once were not contracted in a worried frown. His pink shirt was from Christian Dior, his double-breasted cream silk suit from Armani: Charley always wore wonderful casual clothes, and everything he put on his back was carefully coordinated. Only his small petulant mouth – inherited from his father – prevented him from being really good-looking.

Plum pushed a thin magenta book across the table. 'I brought you my catalogue, Charley. Like it?' A frenzy of colour, it had been produced by the British Council. It contained an account of Plum's evolution as an artist, two interviews by distinguished British critics, and photographs of the paintings she was showing – six produced since her nomination of the previous year.

'They've done a beautiful job . . .' After exchanging leisurely gossip, Charley asked casually, 'Heard the news from London about Jaimie Lorimer? . . . He's just been arrested.'

'*What?*' Plum had wondered why she hadn't yet seen Jaimie, who always stayed at the Cipriani.

'It's true,' Charley said. Plum learned that during the golden years of the late eighties, Jaimie Lorimer had persuaded businessmen to invest in his gallery by promising a large resale profit on pictures he claimed to have pre-sold to collectors and museums. At first, all investors were paid the promised profits, and the recent drop in art market prices had not seemed to affect them: their confidence remained high.

In fact, these payments were made by Jaimie not from art sale profits, but from capital provided by new investors, led to believe their money was buying bargain paintings in a cheap market. But these paintings listed in Jaimie's inventory either did not exist, or belonged to somebody else. When the art market continued to plunge, Jaimie had panicked, then tried to recoup his losses by gambling on the Future Commodities market. He lost.

'Apparently,' said Charley, 'when the police broke into Jaimie's secret office they found a labyrinth of cables and electrical equipment: a computer to check his market dealings, direct teletype connections to trade his eight commodity accounts, a financial news wire and closed circuit TV.'

'Are you *sure*?' Plum's mind was whirling with possibilities. 'This isn't just Biennale gossip?'

'Afraid not. Depressing, isn't it? Although,' Charley added, 'I don't suppose Breeze'll be sorry to hear that one of his biggest rivals is out of the way.'

'Breeze doesn't like to hear of anyone being in trouble,' Plum said shortly. She liked Jaimie and had always regretted that they never met because of Breeze's aversion to him. But this news enabled Plum to cross Jaimie off her list of suspects: were he the forger, Jaimie wouldn't have invented fictitious paintings for his inventory; he would have used forgeries.

She realized that here was a natural opportunity to introduce the reason for this meeting. 'Right now, lots of people are bending the law in desperate attempts to save their business. Do you think what Jaimie did was basically dishonest, Charley?' she asked casually.

'Of course. That's why he's been arrested – for fraud.'

'For tricking people.' Plum leaned across the table and looked into Charley's eyes. 'That's what fraud is, isn't it, Charley? Getting money out of people by false pretences.'

Under Plum's stare, Charley's face started to redden. 'Look, let's forget this, Plum,' he said. 'I never realized you'd be so upset about Jaimie.'

'Not only about Jaimie.' Plum continued to stare coldly across the table. 'There are lots of ways to defraud people in the art game, aren't there, Charley?'

Charley slowly dropped his eyes to his coffee cup.

Plum had never expected Charley to crumble so easily – or so quickly. Nice guys don't make good crooks, she told herself, as she pressed her advantage. 'I know what you're doing, Charley. I've already told the British police, who are working with the French police on it.'

Charley looked up with frightened eyes. '*What do you know?*'

'I'll swap information,' Plum offered. She saw from the hesitancy on Charley's face that this inducement might persuade him.

With visible effort, Charley tried to talk normally, but his voice was higher and more rapid than usual. 'Plum, I don't know what the hell you're talking about. If you're implying I'm involved in Jaimie's scam – '

'No, Charley, I'm talking about *your* scam.'

'I don't have to stay here and be insulted!' Charley thrust banknotes on the table, pushed his chair back, and left.

Plum jumped up and dodged after him as he circumnavigated the tables. Just beyond the outdoor restaurant she tugged at his cream silk sleeve. 'Charley, nothing was ever solved by walking away from a problem.'

Charley quickened his pace.

'Charley,' she hissed, 'if you don't stop and talk to me – I'm going *straight* to your father, to tell him what I know.'

Charley stopped. He turned and grabbed Plum's arm. 'If you go near my dad, I'll . . . I'll . . . I'll kill you!'

Plum gazed into his dark brown eyes, now so terrified and determined. 'So it was *you*, Charley!'

'What the hell do you mean?'

'*You* sent me those threatening letters, you bastard!' Angrily, Plum pulled away from his grasp. 'I'm going straight to Breeze.' She turned away from Charley, towards the Bacino di San Marco and the hotel motor-launch.

Charley looked astonished. He hurried after Plum. 'I never wrote any threatening letters! Threatening to do what?'

Plum stopped. 'To kill me!' She turned and glared.

Astonishment showed in Charley's eyes. 'Plum, I don't understand . . . Stop talking bloody nonsense!'

'Don't waste your time trying to fool me!' snapped Plum. 'You won't fool the police!'

'For Christ's sake, Plum, don't go to the police! *Or* my dad! . . . Look, I'll tell you about it.' He looked around the crowd of tourists. 'Where can we talk alone without being overheard?'

'In the Basilica?' Plum jerked her head towards the most renowned church in Venice. She had no intention of going anywhere alone with Charley. After what he had just threatened, her old fears had resurfaced. She wanted plenty of people within screaming distance.

They hurried across the Piazzetta, through a splendidly arched doorway, and into hushed magnificence. In quiet, incense-perfumed gloom, small groups of tourists listened to their guides. At the rear of the church, half-hidden in a dark, elaborately carved embrasure, Plum listened to Charley.

'You must understand how it started,' he whispered. 'You know – everyone knows – I have to look after Dad. As a matter of fact I'm really fond of the old boy: he's a tiresome, tough old skinflint because he's never recovered from when he was young, and hungry. Of course that was before he inherited Aunt Polly's money, and was able to marry my mother. I don't know whether he really loved her – he certainly didn't behave as if he did – but he was a snob and she was well-connected. She protected me from his temper but she died when I was fourteen, which was when Daddy started to cling to *me*; now, of course, he's permanently on my back, like the Old Man of the Sea.'

Plum hissed. 'How does this tear-jerking story of upper-class deprivation lead to fraud?'

'Be patient,' Charley pleaded. 'My big problem started when I went to university. Dad kept me really short of cash – still does – because he's afraid I might leave him; which is why he still gets jealous if I get too close to a woman.'

'Is *that* why your affairs always fizzle out?'

'They don't fizzle out. First there's a bloody great explosion at home.'

'I thought you *liked* to be with your father. I thought you were the clinging one.'

'God, no!' After disapproving looks from pious visitors, Charley lowered his voice and resumed his story. 'At Cambridge, everyone knew that Dad was rich and nobody believed he gave me no cash. They assumed *I* was the skinflint. So I felt obliged to prove I wasn't. Before long I was badly in debt. Dad had to bail me out. He was furious, said if it ever happened again, he'd cut me out of his will – and I knew he meant it.' Charley shrugged. 'Naturally, like any normal student, I didn't give a damn, at that point. I knew Dad couldn't control me once I'd got a degree and a job. But I was wrong.'

'What went wrong?'

'When I came down from Cambridge, Dad wouldn't let me train for a job . . . He was fairly ill at that point, he'd had a minor stroke and it was important to keep his blood pressure down. He said *he* needed me more than anyone else. Just until he was on his feet again, he said.'

'So that's how you became his unpaid secretary?'

Charley nodded. 'Whenever I asked for a salary, Dad screamed that he paid my bills, and I lived rent-free in one of the loveliest manor houses of Kent. He always followed this with a bit of bribery: I was his sole heir, and one day his priceless collection of paintings would be mine, so I'd better learn to look after his business affairs.' He looked directly at Plum. 'Naturally, I was delighted to be his sole heir, although I realized Dad might live for years, and there was no guarantee that I'd ever get anything . . . He's got a nasty spiteful streak, you know, especially if he thinks people are plotting against him.'

'Why didn't you just – leave?'

'Whenever I said to myself, "Sod his money, I'll make a break to free myself," Dad *didn't* cut me out of his will – but he did something I still find completely unnerving.'

'What?'

'He starts to sob. Then his body shakes, he goes completely to pieces and gets hysterical, so then I worry about his blood pressure. So I call his doctor. After Dad's been calmed down and put to bed, he quietly tells me that he'll kill himself if I abandon him, then asks me what I think Mummy would want me to do . . . He knows how to press every bloody guilt button I possess! Then he promises me *anything* to stay – so I ask for a salary, and he assures me I'll get it.'

'What happens then?'

'He'll prevaricate about it for weeks until his confidence returns – because I didn't leave, as I'd threatened, did I? – and once again he feels omnipotent and safe. Gradually he reasserts himself until again I feel I can't stand his bullying any longer, so I tell him I'm getting out – and then we go through the whole business again.'

'Couldn't you leave without telling him?'

'I tried it, when I went to live with Jenny. You remember, Plum – it didn't last very long. One night Dad turned up in his Rolls, parked outside Jenny's flat, and for the next hour he either hit the horn, rang the door bell or bellowed for his *son*. When the neighbours called the police, Dad convinced them that he'd been locked out of his own flat. So the cops made us open up. Dad then collapsed in the living-room. We didn't get everyone out until five in the morning . . . So I saw that, with Dad around, marriage would be an impossible strain.'

Charley hesitated. 'And to be honest, there was something else. After living with Jenny for about a month, I slowly realized that – in an odd way – she reminded me of Dad: I had the uneasy feeling that I might be exchanging one clinging burden on my back for another.'

Plum sighed. 'The same old problem.'

Mistakenly thinking she was referring to him, Charley nodded, 'Dad's always been an irascible old boy. Then, about four years ago, his doctor quietly told me that Dad was losing his faculties – eyesight, hearing, marbles – the lot were wearing out. He warned me Dad was no longer entirely responsible for his own behaviour.'

'Alzheimer's?'

'The onset. It's not too bad yet, but he gets a bit paranoid, yells, claims I'm plotting to get rid of him so I can inherit his bloody art collection.' Charley shook his head. 'As I've already told you, I might not inherit anything . . . Dad's last spiteful revenge might be to punish me by leaving the lot to Masters.'

'*Who?*'

'Stanley Masters,' Charley said contemptuously, 'Dad's driver for the last twenty years. Shrill, bossy little bugger who loves being in uniform. Dad'll never hear a word against the smug bastard.'

Plum remembered the over-officious little figure with a ginger moustache. 'But why should your dad leave all his money to his chauffeur . . . unless . . .' Plum looked at Charley.

Charley grimaced. 'I've often wondered . . . No doubt poor Mummy wondered . . . Masters arrived a couple of years before she died, and from that moment he went everywhere with Dad – still does.' Resentful, he raised his voice, 'Whatever he does, I bet Masters gets bloody well paid for it.'

'Shhhh! We don't want to be thrown out of here,' Plum cautioned, as tourists turned to stare. 'Charley, I still don't understand why you're telling me this.'

'Because that's why I don't consider it dishonest, you see.'

'No, I don't see, Charley. Selling forged paintings *is* dishonest.'

'But those paintings *aren't* forged!'

A praying woman turned to glare at Charley, who again lowered his voice. 'All the paintings I've sold have been genuine, Plum.'

Suddenly, Plum realized what Charley had been doing. 'How did you manage to swap them, Charley?'

'I'd remove a small painting from the wall – never one of Dad's favourites – and take it to Bill Hobbs. So that Bill had plenty of time to copy it, I always did this just before we left on some trip. I'd say I'd forgotten a suitcase and dash back into the house. I'd stuff the painting in the suitcase, replace it with one I kept in my bedroom, so the staff never reported a missing painting – Dad's always re-hanging them. I had plenty of other excuses in reserve. If anyone asked, I planned to say the missing painting was being cleaned – but no one ever asked.'

'So you replaced the original with Bill's fake – then sold the original in Paris?'

'I thought you knew that, Plum. Of course I only sell Dad's lesser-known paintings, which won't be recognized.'

'But aren't they ever photographed for the Lévi-Fontaine catalogue?'

Charley shook his head. 'I always ask for a back-room deal – a private collector, a quiet offer and cash. So the picture never actually comes up for auction.' He added defiantly, 'I hoped I wouldn't be exposed before Dad's death. If he leaves everything to Ginger Masters or some obscure charity for one-eyed cats, then I'll be glad I got some sort of pay for my miserable job. If he *does* leave everything to me – well then, I've only borrowed from my future inheritance, haven't I?'

Plum stared at his pleading face. She felt sorry for Charley, but surely theft was theft, whether or not you stole from someone in your family.

Plum also realized that she had just lost another suspect.

Friday, 5 June 1992

To arrange an event as ambitious as the Venice Biennale needs efficiency on an international scale, which is unfortunately absent. The notorious disorganization of the Biennale is blamed on lack of funds, administrative tangles and the normal institutional power struggles. Because this art festival is world-famous and always controversial, it is closely – some think too closely – controlled by the Italian government; some of the political stooges who supposedly organize the event seem to have little experience of organization, and none of modern art. The authorities decide nothing until the last minute; the officer with whom arrangements had been made in March may have disappeared by June, and his replacement may deny their existence. In 1974 the Biennale was actually *cancelled* after a quarrel among Italian politicians.

Consequently, by the first Monday in June, tempers are frayed, everybody is exhausted and there are few signs of *entente cordiale*. But everyone has recovered by Wednesday, Thursday and Friday, which are private viewing days, when water-buses jostle with gondolas and private craft to reach the tree-filled public gardens of the Giardini di Castello.

A central pavilion houses the main international exhibition. Scattered around it are three dozen national pavilions: the British building looks like an Italianate English country mansion; the German pavilion is an Albert Speer-type 1930s block; the Russian pavilion is a tiny minareted gem from the Russian Steppes, and so on. Seventy-five young artists exhibit – by invitation only – in the long, columned walks of the Aperto, an old rope factory, and it is here that you see what is new, vital and controversial: a significantly placed rotting cow's head, luxurious colour photographs of the heads of corpses, or a fire hose stuffed with litter culled from the streets of New York – that sort of thing.

The group of distinguished international jurors has a last look at the exhibits on Friday afternoon, then meets to judge on Friday evening: after a break for dinner, the final voting takes place. Rumours whizz around Venice on Friday evening, and by Saturday morning everybody thinks they know who has won. The winners are told on Saturday night, before the prize-giving ceremony on Sunday morning.

* * * *

Despite Plum's repeatedly telling herself that she had no hope of winning a prize, by Friday – judgement day – she was nervous and edgy. She could not concentrate on a book, or even a magazine. She avoided the Giardini, she avoided other people, and she snapped at Breeze when he said that was understandable. Sympathetically, he suggested that she visit the Galeria dell' Accademia – 'Those Carpaccios and the Titians'll make you forget everything else, Plum.'

But Plum could not concentrate even on paintings. Instead, she decided to go for a long walk; she loved the unexpected little snapshots that the streets of Venice offered around each bend of the walls.

Wearing big sunglasses, a scarf tied around her hair, blue jeans and a T-shirt, Plum felt comfortably anonymous as she sniffed the unique smell of the city: a dank, stagnant water smell tinged with rotten cabbages and sewage. Soothed by her stroll, she rounded a bend in a narrow lane and unexpectedly found herself on a hump-backed bridge, where a woman fed pigeons. Birds were clustered on the woman's shoulders and her outstretched arms, and perched on her grey, straggling hair. '*Sono mei amici.*'

The woman laughed at Plum, who strolled on. Around the next bend lay a delicate Renaissance church; around the next, a busy Piazza; beyond were wrought-iron gates behind which two small girls in white dresses played in a tiny rose garden. Next, Plum found herself at a deserted landing stage. An empty black gondola tied to a turquoise-and-gold-striped mooring pole seemed mysteriously inviting, as if Fate had placed it there for her. For a moment she was tempted to climb into it. Then, from the opposite direction, a self-engrossed couple appeared, arm-in-arm. The man climbed aboard the gondola, gallantly turned to help the woman, then kissed her. The gondolier jumped aboard, and gracefully poled off. Laughing, the man opened a bottle of champagne.

Plum jammed her sunglasses more firmly on her nose, and held her hand over the bottom of her face. She was sure that Victor Marsh would not want to be recognized with Betsy – Suzannah's chief assistant.

✶   ✶   ✶   ✶

Meanwhile the panel of jurors had filed into the conference room. Were these seven distinguished jurors biased? Most certainly: where over forty countries compete, seven judges may well push their favourite forward; and national pride may lead each to award his national contender the highest possible marks – as is obvious at international ice-skating competitions.

Other factors may also influence the Biennale judges: two traditionally rival countries may detest each other enough not to vote for each other's entry, and there is often bitter prejudice against America, perceived as having an extra advantage as the richest and most powerful participant with a huge population from which to pick her entries.

The private rivalries, bitter jealousies and antagonisms of the art world also influence decisions, as do shared past problems and successes. The Italian juror is particularly susceptible to political considerations. And all of them are susceptible to flattery.

Finally, the physical presence of an artist carries bonus points: all jurors know that it is anticlimactic to announce, to the sound of trumpets, an absent winner. And an absent winner cannot give interviews that publicize the Venice Biennale to the waiting press of the world.

All these considerations were in the minds of the seven people who took their seats around the long leather-topped table in the conference room. At the head sat the President of the Jury – Renato Dotelli, a civil servant from the Italian government's advisory committee on arts funding, and a personal friend of the Italian Prime Minister. In his late fifties, an urbane figure in an immaculate cream linen suit, Dotelli was known to be a good chairman, efficient and imperturbable. He was notoriously susceptible to the influence of pretty women, and equally notoriously anti-gay.

Discussion started amicably enough. As always, it was agreed that a winner from an underprivileged nation or race – such as the Australian Aborigines – would offer worthwhile encouragement. As always, this decision was not to be reflected in the final choice.

Swiftly the contenders were whittled down to ten in each category – the Golden Lion awards for the best painter and best sculptor, the prize for the pavilion with the best national presence, and the Premio 2000, given to the best artist under thirty-five, in any category in the Biennale.

The American juror, a gaunt, supremely self-confident breakfast heiress, was a director of one of the most powerful American museums. It soon became apparent that she had already decided who should win the Premio 2000 prize: Saul Abraham Jacob, a loudly political, gay, young Jewish sculptor whose enormous, painted phallic groups had powerful impact. Ms Elderdale's calm and tactless assumption fast irritated her fellow judges.

The British juror – an orthodox Jew – immediately started to argue. The editor of *Global Review* magazine, had a heavy, olive-skinned, smoothly Byzantine face; a slow, smooth talker, he was quietly determined to see that the Premio 2000 did not go to the strident Jacob, who attracted as much anti-semitic publicity as possible, in order loudly to deprecate this.

The Spanish juror jumped into the argument. He was a powerful, self-made, opinionated man with a magnificent collection of modern sculpture; swarthy and overweight, he came originally from a poor village in Andalucía, but now owned a nationwide chain of cut-price *farmacias*. Unfortunately his bullying aggression often aroused antagonism, where he should have found support. Now, he supported Saul Abraham Jacob.

The volatile French juror interrupted. Sharply articulate, with an eye to the main chance and any others he happened to spot, the Frenchman normally enjoyed anything controversial; but as a guest on his arts round-up programme, Saul Abraham Jacob had been openly contemptuous, and such lack of fawning deference was unforgivable.

As mild argument grew into noisy altercation, the most persuasive suggestions for a peaceful solution came from the Japanese juror. Tall for a Japanese, he wore a dark city suit and an air of authority. The eminent director of the Tokyo Museum of Modern Art and Design, he was an administrator of extraordinary flair, cunning and tenacity, known invariably to achieve his own aim, firstly by disguising it, and secondly by efficiently using his fluent wit and persuasive charm.

The bony German juror also tried unsuccessfully to keep the peace. A Principal Director of the Dietrich Arts Foundation, established by his industrialist grandfather (a Nazi supporter) with profits from huge steel factories in the Ruhr, and a brilliant art scholar, he was unfortunately shy and reticent, so his efforts were ineffectual.

Jurors began to shout at each other. Old grudges surfaced and old quarrels were revived. Eventually, the President, as hungry as he was bored, decided to announce that the first-round vote for the Premio 2000 would now take place, immediately followed by the break for dinner. The ballot was secret, and the room fell silent as the jurors scribbled their choice on slips of paper.

Predictably, the President voted for an Italian woman mystic painter, who worked in misty colours, combining alchemical forms such as retorts, pentagrams, and other traditional New Age symbols.

The British and French jurors both voted for an Indian who painted very small, cool abstracts from a ghostly palette. The Japanese juror voted for the youngest entrant, a twenty-four-year-old Swedish sculptor who used wood and other natural materials in surprising juxtapositions, with an inventive wit and grace.

The German, the Spaniard and the American all voted for Saul Abraham Jacob. The protesting uproar that followed the President's announcement of the first vote continued through dinner.

For the second vote, everyone understood that they should be prepared to compromise on their first choice, or the jury would never reach a final decision. But no one was in a cooperative mood.

'The penis man will undoubtedly get good media coverage,' asserted the Frenchman, 'but he'll take advantage of the publicity platform that we provide to shriek political protest about insufficient US government funding for AIDS research.'

What was wrong with that, the American asked. She intended to vote as her conscience dictated – for Saul Abraham Jacob.

The Italian President knew that a blatantly pornographic element might be used to trivialize the Biennale. Furthermore, the Prime Minister's wife was to present the prizes, and might not appreciate being photographed with an enormous arrangement of penises. He decided that, having shown bias for an Italian entry who was clearly not going to win, he could switch his vote to the British entrant, Plum Russell; her work was not so blatantly sexual as that of Jacob – and she was a pretty woman who photographed well.

The Japanese stood to lose face if the American won. His museum contained no example of work by Saul Abraham Jacob; but the previous year the Tokyo museum had acquired one of Plum Russell's paintings, and they also had two good examples of the work of the Italian woman painter. Seeing no point in throwing his vote away upon the Swede, the Japanese decided to vote with the President, for the Italian woman painter. He had no means of knowing that the President had switched his vote to Plum.

Insults were still being hurled across the battered leather tabletop as the President announced the second and decisive vote.

Having previously demonstrated his lack of national bias, the British juror now changed his vote to back the British entry, Plum Russell.

The German juror quietly reminded them that this year's event purportedly celebrated women. Nobody took any notice. Influenced by her superb gift for colour, he finally decided to vote for Plum, knowing that this was what the British juror would do.

The Frenchman and the Spaniard stubbornly stuck to their original choices: the Frenchman voted for the Indian and the Spaniard for Saul Abraham Jacob.

In the final voting, Plum received three votes, Saul Abraham Jacob received two; the Indian abstract painter and the Italian woman mystic painter each received one vote.

It is not unusual for the favourite of the first round to get knocked out in the second round, perhaps unfairly. And once again, despite the French judge's growl of 'Why should the British win *again?*', it was decided just after midnight that Plum Russell was the winner of the Premio 2000 for the 1992 Venice Biennale.

*   *   *   *

Breeze shook Plum awake. His voice was hoarse, trembling. '*You've won!*' He had never really expected this. It was like winning a national lottery: naturally, you wouldn't enter unless you had a chance of winning, but deep down, however much you hoped, you knew that the odds were so great that to win was scarcely possible. Nevertheless . . .

'Eh?' Plum woke from a deep sleep, confused by her unfamiliar surroundings. Why was Breeze shaking her shoulder so hard?

'*Darling, you've won!*'

Plum jerked upright. She was in Venice, it was early on Saturday morning, and she had just won the Biennale . . . No, she was not dreaming . . . No, Breeze would not be so unkind as to joke about it – would he? She'd kill him if . . .

Breeze saw the uncertainty in her eyes and shook his head. 'No, it isn't a joke!' Tenderly he kissed the tip of her nose. 'I'm *so* proud of you, darling!'

'How do you know?'

'Everyone knows. The reporters and photographers'll pick it up within an hour, so get ready to face them. You'll be told officially tonight.'

Plum did not hear the joyous peals of bells in her head that she thought she ought to hear. She felt no exultation. Instead, she felt dazed and surprised. Then she felt sick. She flung back the bedcovers and ran to the bathroom.

She returned wrapped in a broderie anglaise négligée, a froth of frills to the floor. 'I'm OK now, Breeze, I just couldn't believe it. I didn't know there was a knot in my stomach, until it dissolved.' She laughed, but she was trembling, exhausted, and every bone in her body felt ninety years old.

'You'll feel better if you eat something.' Breeze looked at her with tender pride and moved to the lavish breakfast table that had been wheeled in and set before the open window. Champagne waited in a silver bucket.

Plum managed to eat some dry toast and drink a little milk, as she listened to the birdsong outside. She too felt joyously triumphant; she felt as if she weighed no more than those birds, could soar through the window and join them, could glide high above Venice and look down on the cluster of islands, and all the pink palaces, all the charming little hump-backed bridges . . .

'Be careful what you say to the press,' Breeze warned, 'because it will be reported worldwide. So decide now what you want to say, then keep repeating it: don't be side-tracked. And avoid anything that might sound political, especially with the Italian press. Of course I'll record everything – but they'll still invent stuff.'

'I'm going to thank my mum for giving me my chance – and you, of course . . .'

'No, leave me out of it. We don't want anyone to start a Svengali story, and that'll give more weight to thanking your mother.'

'Breeze . . .'

'Yes?'

'Why did I get it? Tell me the truth.'

'The truth is, I don't know,' Breeze admitted. 'I'll find out later. But just remember – *you're the winner!*' He pushed back his chair, lifted Plum's arm by the wrist, and imitated a boxing referee. 'Ladies and gentlemen, I give you the winner of the Premio 2000 . . .'

Plum twisted around and looked at him in astonishment. 'Breeze . . . Haven't I won the Golden Lion?'

Breeze laughed. 'No, darling – the Premio.'

'But that's for artists under thirty-five years old!'

'Sure.'

'But I'm thirty-seven!'

They stared at each other in silence.

Breeze said quietly, 'Oh, Christ.' He sat down heavily, threw his napkin on the table and gazed through the open window at the boundless blue sky. 'How did it happen? Why didn't they realize? Why didn't I remember, fuck it?'

'I *was* thirty-five when I was chosen,' Plum said slowly, as she realized what had happened, 'but that was over a year ago, at the beginning of May 1991 – just before my thirty-sixth birthday.'

'And your thirty-seventh birthday was two weeks go, on May the twenty-fourth. *Shit!*'

Plum could see Breeze trying to figure how she could keep the prize.

'It's no good, Breeze. That's the primary rule. They'll disqualify me when they find out.'

Breeze looked determined. 'But not *until* they find out!'

Plum instantly realized what he meant. She shook her head, 'No!'

'Why not? We won't conceal it. We'll just keep quiet about it for a bit – OK? Then you'll get worldwide publicity – and perhaps even more when they disqualify you.'

'No! Apart from the moral issue, I'd never be able to hide it. Everyone would see from my face that something was wrong.'

'That won't matter, provided nobody knows what it is.' Breeze caught her hand. 'Plum . . . if I've ever meant anything to you . . . If you think you owe anything to me, *please be guided by me now.*'

'No!'

'I'm not asking you to tell a lie – I'm only asking you to wait a bit before telling the truth,' Breeze urged. 'And surely you deserve that for being landed with this disappointment – and this muddle – because I put your correct date of birth on the entry form. They just haven't bothered to check. And of course you look so much younger.'

'Stupid *idiots!*'

'So let's cash in on that now, Plum! Let's retrieve *something* from this mess.'

She hesitated. She had not only herself to consider: much of the credit for this award went to Breeze, who had worked towards this moment for ten years. From a tough, commercial viewpoint, she knew that Breeze's suggested line of action made sense.

'Breeze, I can't think now. I'm *really* going to be sick.'

CHAPTER TWENTY-SIX

Saturday, 6 June 1992

THE DAY still felt fresh as Plum, wearing white jeans and a mango silk T-shirt, paused outside the crumbling palazzo where Jenny was staying. Outside at street level was a sidewalk café: under the scalloped candy-pink awning, people ate a leisurely breakfast or drank small cups of bitter black coffee before going to work. Above the café, dark red paint peeled around elaborately arched windows, some framed by cracked marble pillars, some with rickety, wrought-iron balconies before them.

Inside the once beautiful oval hall, coloured light fell down from a stained-glass skylight and splashed Plum with amber and red as she trudged up steep flights of cracked marble towards Jenny's bedroom on the fifth floor.

Extravagantly ecstatic telegrams of congratulation had arrived at the Cipriani from Max and Toby, whom Breeze had secretly telephoned before he told Plum that she'd won. But had she? Unsuccessfully she had furtively tried to telephone Paul, to discuss her moral dilemma. Was Breeze correct in his thinking? What should she do? Should she truthfully and immediately inform the British Council that she was over the qualifying age for the prize she had just won? Or was she an unworldly, unrealistic, uncommercial idiot, as Breeze said, to think of ditching a Biennale prize because of a minor technical matter?

Supposing she agreed to what Breeze suggested? Supposing she said nothing about it – but then somebody spotted she was over age, before Breeze decided to announce it? Then she would lose both ways: she would have a bad conscience, as well as being publicly branded a cheat.

Out of breath, she knocked on Jenny's door.

Jenny wore only a black satin slip; long wet hair fell over her bare shoulders, and she carried a hairbrush.

'Tried to phone but got no reply,' Plum puffed.

'It's out of order. So's my hairdrier . . . Ah, well, we didn't travel all the way to Venice for an efficient electrical system. Come in darling.'

Plum stood in the doorway of Jenny's once splendid but now bare room. At ceiling height, a frieze of ivy leaves had been painted around the crumbling *eau de Nil* walls. Opposite the door was a large, opened high-arched window, through which cheerful chatter from the café below could be heard faintly.

On her right, Plum could see an old-fashioned chest-of-drawers and beyond it an empty fireplace; beyond that hung a large, elaborately framed mirror, above a table littered with make-up, curlers, and other hairdressing impedimenta.

Jenny moved back to the mirror and picked up a brush. 'I'm going to try it parted in the middle – what d'you think?' Absorbed, she peered at herself in the mirror. When she arched her eyebrows and pointed her chin towards the mirror, Jenny saw her face as it might be, but for the unfortunately high bridge of her nose, which made her look arrogant. 'Think it'll suit me?' Jenny twisted her hair and considered.

To Plum's left she saw a black, curlicued bedstead; the sheets had been thrown back, and a sketchbook lay open upon them. Clearly, Jenny still obeyed Professor Davis' dictum to produce a sketch a day, even if that meant missing breakfast.

As there was nowhere else to sit, Plum plonked herself on the end of the bed. She flung her arms over the black whorls of the bed-end, scuffed her white bovver boots against the amber-stained floorboards, and said nothing.

Jenny murmured, 'Want to go downstairs for a coffee as soon as my hair's dry? . . . Hey, why are you round here so early, Plum?'

Diffidently, Plum said, 'I've won the Premio 2000.'

Reflected in the mirror, Plum saw unexpected emotions cross her friend's face: astonishment was followed by consternation, and then fury. Jenny slowly lowered her arms. Wet strands of amber hair fell around her face as she put the hairbrush on the table, her face the yellow-white colour of a church candle. '*It can't be true!*' she gulped.

Plum was puzzled. 'What's the matter? Aren't you glad I've won?'

Jenny gave a shaky laugh. 'Of course . . . What a wonderful surprise . . . Congratulations.' She twisted to face Plum. 'I'm *thrilled* for you!'

Swiftly Jenny turned back to the mirror and picked up the hairbrush, not realizing that Plum could still see her pale face in the mirror, as it contorted in the anguish of silent pain.

Plum stared in surprise at her friend. 'Jenny, are you feeling OK?'

'Just a bit tired, that's all.' Jenny started to brush her wet hair fiercely.

'There's a catch to the prize. Let me tell you.' Plum flung herself backwards across the crumpled bedclothes, her hands clasped behind her head. As she moved, Plum's change of position dislodged Jenny's sketchbook, which slid off the bed to the floor.

'So what do you think I should do?' Finishing her story, Plum sat up wearily. She bent to retrieve the sketchbook, shifted her position, and, sitting with one knee propped up on the bed, idly flipped through it, only half-conscious of the drawings: people sitting in a gondola, some studies of a cat's head, a pencilled sketch of Jenny's landlady, after which the pages were clean – except for the back one, on which was a carefully detailed pencil drawing. The little pencilled reptile half-reminded Plum of something, but her conscious thoughts were focused only on her problem.

'So what would you do, Jenny?' Plum finished. 'Confess or keep quiet? . . . I *don't* want to keep quiet about it – but Breeze says we should make a unanimous decision, which means, of course, that he wants me to keep quiet.'

In a high, tight voice, Jenny advised, 'You must do what you think best.' She shook her head, as if to clear it, took a deep breath and added, in her normal steady voice, 'Personally, I wouldn't be able to sleep at night if I had something like that on my conscience.'

She stared firmly at her reflection in the mirror, then looked beyond it to Plum, and the open sketchbook on her knee.

Jenny dropped her hairbrush. '*Put that book down, you bitch!*' she shrieked.

Plum looked up astonished.

Jenny twisted round and yelled, 'You've no right to come here, spying on me!'

Immediately Plum realized where she had previously seen the pencilled lizard: in the Dutch flower paintings of Suzannah and Cynthia. She gasped, '*You're* the forger!'

Jenny hurled herself across the room, tore the book from Plum's hands, rushed to the heavy chest by the door, and shoved the sketchbook in the top drawer. 'Now, get *out* of here, you bitch! *Get out!*'

Frozen in disbelief, Plum stared at Jenny's red face and threatening attitude.

Jenny leaped towards her. 'Get *out*, you interfering cow! *Get out!*'

Plum grasped the wrought-iron bed-end and hung on, as Jenny tried with all the strength behind her large frame to yank Plum away from it.

Plum clung tenaciously to the black whorls as Jenny shook her shoulders. The bedsprings wheezed beneath Plum. She hunched her shoulders against the attack and pleaded, 'Jenny, *let go!*' She twisted her head to look into the angry amber eyes. 'What's got into you, Jenny? You're one of my closest friends . . .'

'Since *when*?' Jenny gave a hysterical laugh.

Jenny's true feelings for Plum now poured out in a monologue that was the accumulation and culmination of twenty years of suppressed resentment and anger, hatred and jealousy . . . *You* never had to live on a permanent diet, Plum . . . *You* were the pretty one . . . All the men went after *you* . . . *You* got reviews and I didn't . . . You as good as earned them on your back . . . *And then I had your bloody fame shoved down my throat!* As Jenny finished, she banged Plum's head painfully against the black swirls of the footboard.

As Plum clung tenaciously to the iron bedstead and dodged

Jenny's blows, she realised from the pain in Jenny's angry voice that that was what Jenny most resented: her hunger for fame must be as desperate as her well-known hunger for love. Perhaps Jenny confused the far-flung, diffuse approval of fame with the close, indulgent approval of love, but over and above that confusion was Jenny's fear of failure to get either fame or love.

Nevertheless, Plum was bewildered. She could understand that another painter might be jealous of her success, but why had Jenny continued to be friendly? Plum instantly realized the answer: because Jenny was playing the Gallery Game. Breeze was Jenny's best contact in the art world, and Breeze was influenced by Plum. If Jenny didn't get an invitation to some big opening – why, she had only to mention it to Plum, and Breeze always wangled one for her.

But that did not explain why Jenny should have hated Plum *before* her success as a painter. From what she said, Jenny had *never* genuinely been fond of Plum, had been secretly envious of her since their college days. Jenny's friendship had been fake from the beginning. Why, she asked Jenny.

'Why should *I* want to be friends with you?' snarled Jenny. She emphasized her words with sharp punches between Plum's shoulder-blades. '*I* should have had your success! *I* won more prizes at college than you ever did! When we first showed, why did *you* get good reviews when I didn't? . . . Because those critics were biased! And why did they ignore me and fawn on you? . . . Because *you* were being fucked by an influential dealer! That was bloody clever, of course!'

'Jenny, stop it! You're hurting me!'

'What did *you* do that I didn't – apart from fucking Breeze? Lucky for you Breeze liked small girls! That was *really* tough on me!' Another shake threatened to dislocate Plum's neck, as Jenny growled, 'Well, eventually, I realized I had to make my *own* luck, if I was to beat you!'

'Why *beat me*, Jenny?'

'Because we started out level. Then you schemed and you manipulated . . .' Jenny's face reddened as her voice rose. 'And finally, the only man I ever loved, loved you – you bitch!' With her left fist, Jenny took a handful of Plum's hair and yanked her head backwards. 'I had no money but *you* were rolling in it. *You've* had two husbands and *I've* had none! *You've* had two children and *I've* had none! I had to live in a near-slum in a bloody basement when you were queening it in an all-white palace in Regent's Park! *How do you think that felt?*' With her right fist, Jenny cracked Plum across the ear.

Plum screamed in pain. But despite her dazed head, she realised one simple fact: if she left this room with that sketchbook, she could prove the identity of the forger; and if she left without it, then Jenny would immediately destroy it, together with any other incriminating evidence. And then Plum might never be able to prove the identity of the forger.

Plum had to play for time. So long as she was in that room, something might happen. She might get a chance. But she would never have an opportunity if she let Jenny throw her out.

'Stop being pathetic!' Jenny hit her again then wrenched Plum's head backwards. 'D'you remember what a pathetic sight you were after Jim left you – with two brats and no time to paint – before you so cleverly fucked Breeze?' Jenny spat pent-up venom. 'How do you suppose I feel, knowing I've as much talent as you, Plum? I won't claim to be a better painter – but by God I'm just as good! And now I've proved it! You must admit *that*!'

'You certainly fooled me,' Plum gasped.

'*And* all those *phoney* experts!' said Jenny triumphantly. '*My* paintings have been described as minor masterpieces!'

'And so they are,' Plum hastily agreed. Jenny's grip slowly eased. Realizing that flattery helped, Plum added, 'Dame Enid Soames told me the Dutch forg – painter . . . was a genius.'

'She did? When?'

Plum felt the blood pounding in her head. 'I can't talk like this – bent backwards.'

Jenny slowly released her grasp.

Plum sat up and rubbed her aching neck. She saw the room through a red haze, oddly two-dimensional, as her blood pressure returned to normal. Desperately, she tried to think. *As Jenny had been lying all these years – how did Plum know she was telling the truth now?*

She laid a trap. Quietly, she said, 'But Enid said that if you'd been *really* clever, you'd have restored your own fakes.'

Jenny looked startled. 'But I did! After I finished a picture, I pushed a broom handle through the front. Then I patched and restored the damage, so it'd show up dark under ultraviolet!'

Plum needed no further proof.

And it was obvious to Plum that Jenny had restored her fakes in exactly the way that had once been suggested to Bill Hobbs. Surely that was unlikely to be a coincidence?

Softly, Plum said, 'So Bill Hobbs taught you?'

Jenny's truculent glare told Plum that she had guessed correctly.

Plum breathed, 'So that was how Charley met Bill Hobbs – through you!'

'It was *my* idea to substitute his dad's pictures with fakes,' Jenny said defiantly, 'but Charley was too gutless to do it until after we split up. Then his moral scruples suddenly subsided; maybe his next girl was more expensive than me.'

'How did you meet Bill? I can't remember ever meeting you there . . . except once.'

'Once was enough,' Jenny said triumphantly. 'At least *Bill* preferred me to you!'

Plum realized what had happened. She remembered the painful early months of 1977, when Max and Toby were living with her mother in Portsmouth. Slowly Plum said 'Of course – I wouldn't sleep with Bill, but you would! So *that's* why he fired me! I could never understand it, because my restoration work was good! And Bill said he hadn't enough work to keep me on – but we could all see that wasn't true: the front room was stacked to the ceiling with canvases.'

'Sexual discrimination! Tough!' Jenny jeered. 'Well, things were tough for me, too!'

Another piece of the puzzle fell into place. Plum said, 'It must have happened after your grant was cancelled.' Jenny's grant had been rescinded because of changed tax regulations, which meant that her father no longer qualified for government assistance. He had been unable to afford to keep his daughter at one of the most prestigious art schools in one of the most expensive cities in the world.

Jenny snarled defiantly, 'I don't have to justify anything to *you*! I can sleep with anyone I please!'

'Of course you can, Jenny.' Plum stood and slowly rotated her aching shoulders. Somehow, she had to tempt Jenny towards the window. Away from the door. And Jenny wouldn't be suspicious if Plum moved *away* from the chest-of-drawers which contained the sketchbook.

Plum started to cough. She moved slowly towards the dressing-table by the window, and her hand reached for a box of tissues.

She blew her nose. 'What . . . I . . . can't . . . understand . . . is . . .' As she spoke, Plum drifted between the bed and the window, then spun round and faced Jenny. 'How you could sleep with that disgusting old man?'

Goaded, Jenny took two steps towards Plum. 'I *like* older men,' she spat defensively, 'and he liked me. Bill was kind and protective.' She took two more steps towards Plum. 'Sure, at first I needed the job. But as a matter of fact, Bill was a terrific lover.' She gave a reminiscent smile. 'He certainly knew more about anatomy than a lot of younger men I've fucked.'

'But you couldn't be seen with him, could you, Jenny?' Plum taunted.

Jenny took two more steps towards her. 'Bill didn't fit the upmarket image you were trying to project, did he? That's why you kept your affair a secret.'

Plum wondered how much longer Jenny would allow her to continue this conversation. After keeping her secret for such a long time, Jenny clearly wanted to brag of her cleverness; but for how long?

'It was clever of you to keep your secret all these years.' As she spoke, Plum casually picked up a heavy glass ashtray from the bedside table.

Jenny sprang forward. 'Put that down!'

Plum looked surprised and replaced it. Jenny was now on the window side of the bed. Mission half accomplished.

Plum sat down on the window side of the bed, and turned round towards Jenny. 'When did you start faking on your own, Jenny?'

Jenny gave a short laugh. 'After suggesting the substitutions to Charley I thought, Why should I get work for Bill? I could do it myself. Why should Bill get all the profit from my work? He only loses it at the dog track.' Jenny wandered across the room to face Plum. 'And by then Bill had a heart problem and was talking of packing it in.'

'So *that's* how you got enough money to buy the flat in Craven Hill Gardens! Your dad and your grandmother didn't leave you money, you . . .'

'. . . Earned it! Every penny!' Jenny was triumphant. 'I always thought Bill could have charged more than he did.'

'And the pictures were worth it,' Plum said sincerely. 'Your Dutch work's really good, Jenny.'

Jenny launched into a tirade against the so-called experts of the art world: what Jenny called her simulated paintings – those which she could not openly acknowledge – were highly praised and fetched high prices, whereas her 'own' paintings were dismissed by critics, and did not sell.

Plum needed to know the name of Jenny's accomplice. Was Jenny working with one partner or an organization? Who distributed the forged pictures? Plum dared not ask outright: she needed a more subtle way to discover who linked Jenny to Tonon.

'What surprises me is that you've managed to pursue two careers at once,' Plum said admiringly. 'That couldn't have left you much time to distribute those Dutch paintings. I suppose Charley was your partner?'

The pleased smile left Jenny's face. 'None of your bloody business. Get out of here!'

As Plum stood up, she realized something else. 'Jenny, *you must have written those two death threats that frightened me so!*' Plum was stunned: she could no longer think clearly.

Jenny gave a pleased, reminiscent smile, 'If you were scared, you might have given up.'

'*And was that why you told me Breeze was having an affair?*'

Jenny smiled maliciously. 'I wanted to distract you. You were getting too close. All's fair in love and war,' she added defensively.

Plum trembled with fury. She forgot her clever strategy. She forgot how successful her tactics had been until that moment. She blew it.

Plum made a dash for the door. Jenny leaped forward to stop her, but caught her left hip on the metal bed-end, and yelped in pain.

These few seconds of delay gave Plum enough time to dodge past Jenny, yank open the top drawer and grab the sketchbook. But as her left hand pulled the sketchbook out, Jenny leaped forward and slammed the drawer shut.

Plum screamed as violent pain shot up her left arm. 'You've broken my fingers!' She kicked backwards.

Jenny grunted in pain, swung her right arm round Plum's neck and yanked her backwards. They struggled together, staggering back towards the bed. Although Jenny was far bigger and stronger, the diminutive Plum was quicker and more agile.

Plum dropped the sketchbook.

Jenny yelled again, as she banged into the black bed frame and a metal whorl dug into her kidneys.

Despite the pain in her arm, Plum managed to bend at the knees and slip from Jenny's grasp. She looked at the floor, but could not see the sketchbook. It must have slid beneath the bed. Plum dived beneath the bed, saw the book, and grabbed it.

Jenny staggered upright, yanked up the end of the bed and slammed the entire frame against the back wall. Plum, defenceless and on all fours, twisted around with her back to the window; her right arm clutched the sketchbook to her chest, her left arm was lifted to ward off the expected blow.

Slowly, arms outstretched, Jenny advanced towards Plum.

Slowly Plum back away from her adversary, towards the window. Realising her danger, she jerked her head round and glimpsed, five floors below her, the paved sidewalk and beyond it the brown water of the canal.

Plum screamed as Jenny lunged forward and her hands shot out towards Plum's throat. Together, the two women swayed in the open embrasure.

Jenny's hands were around Plum's throat, and her weight slowly forced the top of Plum's body backwards, over the low window frame.

Plum tried to scream, but her constricted throat could make no noise. Bent backwards, there was little she could do. She could not knee Jenny, whose body thrust against that of Plum too close for Plum to bring her leg up.

Then Plum realized that although her body was trapped, her arms were free from the elbow downwards. She groped until her fingers curled around the open windows and, with all her strength, yanked them towards her.

The windows hit Jenny from behind and shoved her forward. Astonished, Jenny released her grasp on Plum's throat, Plum slithered beneath her to the floor; with all her remaining strength, she pushed upwards at Jenny's body.

Trembling and panting, Plum heard screams from the café below.

CHAPTER TWENTY-SEVEN

Thursday, 11 June 1992

ON THE flight back to London, cumuli were drifting in a cerulean sky outside the window: only the cupids were missing. Plum finished reading about Ivana Trump's latest escort and turned to the transformation of prince into frog in the fairytale marriage of the Princess of Wales. When she looked up from her newspaper, she wondered whether *anybody* who seemed to have everything was really happy.

Plum yawned and fingered the lemon chiffon scarf around her neck, which hid ugly gamboge bruises. A sore throat, she had explained to anyone who asked. Nobody except Breeze and the doctor had seen her shoulders, arms and breasts, which were also badly bruised. Feeling suddenly tearful, Plum told herself once more that this was what the doctor had predicted: she was apparently one of the 5 per cent of people involved in an accident who suffered the same sort of traumatic stress disorder as many victims.

Certainly, in the five days since the accident, Plum had found that she could not get it out of her mind and kept reliving the experience. She felt surges of anxiety that actually made her gasp for air, as Jenny's violently malevolent expression of final triumph again flashed across the internal screen of her mind. She shuddered as once more she felt Jenny's fingers squeezing her throat, tighter and tighter, as Jenny forced Plum's body backwards, through that open window.

She had never experienced anything like Jenny's treachery. Had she discovered that one of her sons secretly hated her, she could not be more shocked or more emotionally disoriented. Bewildered, she no longer knew whom she could trust. Certainly she could no longer trust her own judgement. She had trusted Jenny completely, and still found it difficult to believe that her friend – seemingly so gentle and kind, patient and understanding – had really felt only envious hatred.

Breeze could not understand that the shock of discovering Jenny's treachery and hatred had been like that of burglary or rape – a violation of Plum's feelings that she could not banish from her mind.

He simply said that he had never felt at ease with Jenny, partly because he had *never* totally trusted her, which Plum knew to be true. But why had Plum not been able to spot whatever had made Breeze feel this? She glanced at the next seat, where Breeze was writing in his jumbo-sized Filofax. Absent-mindedly, she watched the rapid, upright, free-flowing scribble, the tail letters elaborately hooked.

Paul, whom Plum had expected to understand her misery and confusion, had seemed more interested to hear that she had identified the forger. 'What's happened has happened – it's over,' he had said on the telephone. 'Of course you're upset about Jenny's treachery – but that is now your *past* and you can't change it, so put it behind you. What should still concern you is that Jenny couldn't have been working alone.' Paul deliberately did not voice his fear that Plum was still in danger.

So she had tried to call Lulu, possibly the only person who could truly understand her chaotic feelings – and share them, because Jenny had also deceived Lulu. Plum longed to speak to Lulu, face to face, rather than briefly on the telephone. Only by talking it out with her could Plum banish those terrifying scenes from her head.

* * * *

Jenny had fallen forward, arms outstretched. Forty feet below, the pink, candy-striped, canvas canopy of the restaurant had broken her fall and saved her life. The man upon whom Jenny had fallen was not so lucky: he had been smashed forward into his breakfast on the metal table; his nose had been broken, and his face badly cut by broken crockery and burned by scalding coffee.

The ambulance launch had arrived seven minutes later. The

wounded man, the unconscious Jenny, and Plum had been taken to the main Venice hospital, next to the Church of Saints Giovanni and Paolo. Breeze had quickly arrived there and taken control of the situation. Plum's hand had been examined and X-rayed – there was no serious damage, although her upper knuckles were badly bruised and bleeding. Together, she and Breeze had waited to hear news of Jenny, who had been wheeled into the operating theatre.

'Is she going to live?' Breeze anxiously asked the Italian surgeon, after Jenny's operation.

The surgeon looked surprised. 'Of course. Two broken arms and two broken ribs are not fatal – although she would almost certainly have been killed had her fall not been broken. And of course she also has mild concussion and shock.'

Much to her subsequent disgust, Plum fainted.

* * * *

In the motor-launch on their way back to the Cipriani, Breeze had exclaimed through gritted teeth, 'I've been a bloody fool! I should have realized this might happen! I should have warned you, Plum.'

'How could you possibly have known?'

'I've seen it happen so many times before.' He had run his hand through his hair in a gesture of exasperation. 'Someone hits the jackpot, and it's wrist-slitting time for everyone in the same game: they can't help wistfully wondering, "Why him, why not me?" So they copy what the successful person has done, and they try hard. But no matter what they do, they still can't make exactly the same thing happen to them.' Breeze shook his head. 'Which is when envy and resentment start to grow, like a worm in an apple.'

'Eventually you have a rotten, poisonous apple.'

Breeze took Plum's hand, which was cold despite the heat. 'We must handle this cleverly, Plum,' he said gently. 'We don't want scandal. We want to avoid linking your name to Jenny's in what might be made to sound like a fight between a couple of alley-cats. We don't want you to face an attempted manslaughter charge in an Italian court, and we don't want a libel case – which is what you risk if you say anything against Jenny that you can't actually prove . . . And don't think she might not do it.'

Neither did he want the British police involved ('Now that we know who wrote those letters . . .') until Plum had further proof of forgery, not merely Jenny's sketchbook, and until he and Plum had discussed the allegations with Jenny.

'But that will give her accomplices time to cover their tracks,' Plum objected.

Breeze thought the British police could be relied upon to persuade Jenny to name her partners. Remembering Jenny's tenacity, Plum doubted it.

Breeze then told Plum what to do. Still in shock and mourning the loss of her friendship, Plum obeyed him, and subsequently everything had worked out as Breeze had planned.

He refused to allow her to see Jenny until they were both back in Britain. Instead, he spoke to Jenny as soon as she regained consciousness. Afterwards, he told Plum that Jenny was immobilized and could do nothing for herself; she could not even feed herself or wipe herself, because both arms were in plaster. He arranged for Jenny's mother to fly out to Venice, and promised to pay all hotel and hospital bills, collect the necessary documentation for Jenny's medical insurance claim, and organize her return to Britain. Jenny was to worry about nothing. And neither was Plum.

When she was interviewed, through an interpreter, by the *carabinieri*, Jenny, as coached by Breeze, confirmed Plum's description of the accident. She had leaned too far out of a window with a low edge. She had over-balanced and fallen. She was extremely distressed to hear of the injuries to the man upon whom she fell.

After the police had questioned her, Jenny was kept very quiet because of her head injuries. She was allowed no telephone, and no visitors, except for her mother.

* * * *

As the chirpy air stewardess took their drinks order, Plum wondered yet again how Jenny had managed to distribute the fakes and procure the forged provenances. She *must* have had at least one accomplice – but who?

Plum now had no remaining suspects. Jaimie and Charley were both guilty of crimes, but not the one that interested Plum. The

British police had cleared Richard Stepman, who had been very helpful and supportive after the Biennale, when the press were clustering round her. And poor Leo was dead.

As the stewardess bent to serve champagne, Plum turned, perplexed, to Breeze. 'Why were you so *sure* that Leo had nothing to do with the forged pictures?'

Breeze waited until the stewardess had departed, then whispered, 'Because Leo was a pusher. He supplied me occasionally – just a little coke for parties. He may have pretended to do some truck-driving on the side – but that was a cover. He wasn't exporting art, he was importing speed, shit and dope.'

Suddenly Plum understood other things that had puzzled her about Leo. His involvement with criminals not only explained his death, it explained why he knew such a surprising amount about crime.

'Breeze, there's something I still find puzzling. On New Year's Eve – when I first saw Suzannah's flower painting – why were you so strongly against my search for the forger? You gave me a lot of reasons – but I sense there's something more to it.'

Breeze turned his head to the window. He turned back to Plum. He looked sheepish. 'When Suzannah first asked Victor to buy that van der Ast, Victor phoned to ask me if the Maltby outfit was kosher. So I phoned Maltby's and . . . they agreed to pay me a hidden commission.'

Plum wished that her instincts hadn't been right. 'So *that* was the reason you didn't want the painting going back to Maltby's! You'd have had to refund the commission!'

'I didn't want to lose Victor's respect for my judgement – which is just what *has* happened.' On the previous Monday, Breeze had told Victor the identity of the forger. Victor had immediately made it clear that he no longer had great regard for Breeze as an evaluator of what he called antique paintings, or for Breeze's ability to deal with the subsequent problems.

'But he's pleased we've found the forger,' Plum pointed out. Miss Ohrbach had already air-freighted Suzannah's van der Ast to London, for evaluation by the Institute.

Breeze sipped his champagne. 'Incidentally, did I tell you that Victor's leg-over situation with Betsy looks permanent?'

'I expect Victor's tired of coming home every evening to a *Good Housekeeping* photographic set. How do you know?'

'He said he's building a new house in Westbury, Long Island. Totally modern – the whole building will be an ideal art gallery for his collection.'

'He owns enough of my paintings alone to stock a gallery,' Plum remembered. 'He was leading me around Venice like an owner with his winning racehorse . . . Incidentally, did you ever tell him about the hitch to my award?'

'Hell, no, I never tell a client anything negative.' The smile dropped from Breeze's face as he remembered the hours of anxiety on the previous Saturday afternoon.

Breeze had talked to the British Council representative, and together they had suggested to the Italian President of the jury that perhaps the qualifying rule should be . . . retrospectively amended. Otherwise the Biennale organizers would look even more incompetent than usual, they would lose a popular winner of the Premio 2000, the subsequent winner would be made to feel he had received the award by default, and the international public would be confused.

The British Council rep then reminded the President that there was a precedent for this: Anish Kapoor had been thirty-six years old when he won the under-thirty-five award in 1990.

So the qualifying rule had been quietly amended and included in all official press releases: entrants for the Premio 2000 were required to be under thirty-five years of age at the date of selection.

Remembering, Breeze turned to smile at Plum. 'I'm truly proud of you – for lots of reasons.' He squeezed her hand. Plum tried to suppress a wince as the diamond ring bit into her flesh.

'*Please* give our marriage another chance, Plum,' he whispered earnestly.

Plum realized the truce was over, and that she was trapped in persuasive argument for the next two hours. She felt wretched. No one could have been more supportive than Breeze during the past few days. It was going to be hard to be tough.

Breeze said softly, 'I realize things must change, and I must adjust to a new partnership.'

Plum put down her champagne-glass. She looked uncertain.

Breeze spoke with casual care. 'Look, if you *must* have this affair with . . . Paul . . .' He spoke the name as if it threatened to choke him, 'then I'm prepared to look the other way until it's over.' As if he were laying a deal on the table, he offered magnanimously, 'I'm willing to try and do whatever you want.' He leaned towards her and whispered, 'Surely, Plum, you don't believe that the way to solve a relationship problem is to hop out of the relationship? I love you, Plum, I swear I do. And I want to stay married to you. I want things to be like they were when we first married.'

Plum shook her head. 'We aren't the same people any more.'

'Have I altered so much?'

'Over ten years of marriage, we were both bound to change.' Plum suddenly realized that as she had struck out on her own in her search for the forger, she had gradually allowed the self-confidence that she felt in her work to extend into the rest of her life. Assertiveness worked. Now self-worth was balancing out self-doubt. At least now, instead of wondering if she was good enough for someone, Plum wondered if someone was good enough for her. Gently Plum added, 'Breeze, you aren't the man I thought you were, that's all.'

'That's hardly my fault!' Breeze was immediately defensive. 'That's just the tragedy of marriage: the woman wants the man to change in certain ways – and he never does. The man wants the woman to stay exactly the same – but she never does.'

'I certainly have changed,' Plum said thoughtfully, wondering why it was that Paul understood the reasons so easily, but Breeze – no matter how hard he tried – could not.

'OK, if *you* can change – what makes you think I can't. If you think *you* deserve another chance – what about me?'

Plum knew Breeze to be sincere. She remembered all the years they had been together. With guilt, she thought of Paul. Was she really in love with him? And would she be contemplating leaving Breeze if she didn't have Paul to go to? Was she subconsciously *using* Paul as a stepping-stone to freedom?

Breeze looked more cheerful as he suddenly thought he saw the reason behind Plum's recent unpredictable behaviour. 'Perhaps you're having an early mid-life crisis!'

'No, I'm having a normal female identity crisis,' Plum said crossly. She tried to explain that her life felt out of balance: the scales seemed to be tilted too much towards the big pile that was career and money; but the little pile on the other scale was the living part of her life.

She finished by saying, 'Our values are different; you want money and success . . .'

'And I suppose you *don't*?' Breeze snapped. 'Can't you remember what it felt like to be poor and unsuccessful? Bloody uncomfortable, depressing and tiring.' With an effort, he lowered his voice, 'So you've just discovered that money doesn't bring happiness. What do you think *does*, Plum?'

'Relationships. No rushing. Rewarding work – but not too much of it.'

'Am I hearing that you want to stop painting? But you *love* your work!'

'I'm a person as well as a painter, and I want to feel fulfilled as a person.'

'Everyone does,' Breeze said comfortingly. That was why a lot of women wanted a career rather than a job – they didn't only want better pay, they wanted acknowledgement, identity and respect.' Breeze looked complacent. It was as he had suspected: a search for the Real Me. And only to be expected when every pop magazine and TV chat show now preached the all-important need for personal growth. He had noticed that lots of narcissistic women with a bit of education now wanted *more* out of life. They wanted eternal youth and beauty. They wanted freedom as well as a family. They wanted a satisfying sex life but also the right to remain tired. And now the nineties woman wanted to find her bloody purpose in life and fulfil it.

'*And* I'd like to feel independent,' Plum quietly added.

Breeze became exasperated. 'But you *are* independent, Plum. You're one of the few truly independent women in the Western world. Hardly *any* women have their own capital.'

'Sure, I earn a fortune, but I don't have time to spend it. I've found that time is more precious than money. I want enough time and energy to enjoy the simple things of life without pressure.'

'Don't we all?' She's just tired, thought Breeze. Post-natal problems after the huge effort of the Biennale, plus the shock of this business with Jenny. She needs a rest, then she'll soon be back to normal. He patted her arm. 'I'll arrange for you to go to a health farm for a fortnight.'

Plum said angrily, 'From now on, *I* want to decide what's good for me. *I'll* decide if I want to go to a health farm – which I don't. I simply want to be by myself and think without distractions for a day or two. I feel that my career has me by the throat. I'm depressed that a part of me *still* feels empty, and I won't be happy until I find out why. Because if self-fulfilment isn't nest-building at home, and isn't being successful at work – where have they hidden it?'

'You've got everything most women want to make them happy . . .'

Plum thought of Ivana Trump, the Princess of Wales and other women who appeared to have everything: children, looks, wealth and position – but who did not look happy.

With an effort, Breeze lowered his voice. 'What you *really* mean is that you want some high-minded excuse to fly off to your French lover – and then you want plenty of time in bed with the bastard. This quest for the Real You is just an excuse to get back to that Nouveau Rousseau and fuck your brains out.'

'This isn't about choosing Paul,' Plum said, 'it's about looking for *me*. I'm looking for a happy relationship with myself.'

'Fasten seat-belts,' trilled the air hostess.

CHAPTER TWENTY-EIGHT

Thursday, 11 June 1992 – London

AT SUPPER that evening – hamburgers in the kitchen – Max and Toby were unnaturally subdued, having heard media reports of Jenny's accident and then been told by Breeze of Jenny's treachery and what had really happened. Both Plum's sons also quickly picked up the tense atmosphere between Plum and Breeze. Over his hamburger Max's eyes looked warily from one elaborately over-polite adult to the other; Toby never took his eyes off his plate and never said a word.

The next morning, when Plum wandered down to the kitchen for a cup of tea, she found Max, who had stayed overnight, making toast. In words that had clearly been well rehearsed, he said in a slightly embarrassed voice, 'Toby and I . . . well, we want you to know that we think Breeze is a great guy and you've got to understand that, Ma. After what he's done for us, our feelings for Breeze aren't going to change. But we're your sons, Ma, and whatever's going on, we want you to know that we're right behind you.'

Silently, Plum hugged her son.

*　　*　　*　　*

Later, from her black marble bath, Plum stretched out a sudsy arm to answer the telephone. 'Hello, Mum . . . no, it's not too early, I'm awake – it's nearly nine, after all. Yes, Mum, I still feel the same as last night . . . Yes, tired but happy . . . Yes, it's nice to be home . . . Yes, I know the boys are proud of me . . .' Plum listened to her mother giving her opinion of the latest royal scandal. Her mother's voice hesitated, then sharpened. 'You seem quiet today, dear. Are you bilious? That oily foreign food upset your bowels? *What is it, dear?* Tell your mum . . .'

Plum burst into tears. 'It's n – nothing, really Mum,' she stammered.

'Don't be silly, dear. Tell your old mum what's the matter, there's a good girl.'

At the sound of her mother's let-me-kiss-it-better voice, Plum remembered that she was speaking to the one person in the world who she would always trust. In broken, half-finished sentences, she told of Jenny's treachery.

The supportive flow from Portsmouth was immediate. 'Serpent . . . viper in the bosom . . . my poor girlie . . . I never *did* like her . . . something about her eyes reminded me of my Uncle Albert, who skipped with his mother's savings . . .'

'I never realized you'd understand what I feel like, Mum.'

'Course I do! You've been bereaved. You're mourning your friendship. You feel angry, and indignant. You're sad and lonely. Loss is loss. It's always painful, always hard to accept.'

Half an hour later, as Plum shuffled through a basket of post, Jim rang unexpectedly, to discuss his summer holiday with Max and Toby. The three of them always did something strenuous and manly; this August it was to be white-water canoeing in the Gorges de Verdon, France's mini-version of Colorado's Grand Canyon.

'Jim, why don't you sort out these details direct with the boys?' Plum asked, vexed. 'Surely that'd be easier than doing it through me? How can you expect me to buy stuff for you from the army surplus shop when I know nothing about this sort of equipment? Why can't the boys damn well go to Laurence Corner and buy it?' Jim might have congratulated her on her Biennale award, especially if he intended to dump this tedious job on her.

'Plum, you're practically next door to the shop, so it'll only take you half an hour, and naturally I'll pay for everything,' Jim pleaded. 'Otherwise it means my wasting a whole day on a trip to London.'

Tersely, Plum said, 'OK. Read the list again.'

Jim hesitated. 'Did you get my flowers?'

'*You* sent *me* flowers?' Plum could not disguise her surprise.

'And congratulations, of course. We're all *very* proud of you. You're already a legend down here – our most famous pupil. You must be thrilled to pieces, and so must Jenny and Lulu.'

'Oh, Jim . . . You don't know what's happened . . . I feel so awful about Jenny . . .' Jim, once their fellow-student, would understand the pain of Jenny's treachery.

As Plum told him the story of Jenny's duplicity, his disbelief turned to indignation, then anger, when he realized that Toby and Max might have lost their mother. He asked the occasional question as Plum told him of her search, her discovery that Jenny was the forger, Jenny's jealousy of Plum, and finally the accident in Venice. 'I *can't* seem to stop thinking about that frightening incident in Venice,' she concluded.

'Trying to kill you is hardly an incident! Jenny bloody well deserved to end up in hospital. How long'll she be there?'

'Her mother's flying back with her on Saturday evening,' Plum added morosely. 'After that I don't suppose I've much chance of getting positive proof of forgery.'

'And then what? The police?'

'I suppose so. Although I need positive proof of forgery by Jenny before I go to the cops.'

'Surely you've got enough to go on?'

'Not enough hard evidence. I need to locate Jenny's secret studio – not the studio at her flat, the place where she did this secret work. And I *must* discover it before Jenny gets back, on Saturday.'

'How are you going to do that?'

'I'm going to her flat, to look for clues. It was careless of Jenny to draw that lizard study in an everyday sketchbook. So if she's been careless once – she might have been careless twice.'

'One sketchbook looks much like another,' said Jim reflectively. 'Perhaps Jenny snatched it up when she was packing, without realizing she'd already started to use it for studies. But are you *sure* she has a second studio?'

'I've never seen anything like a Dutch flower painting in that little studio in her flat.'

Hesitantly, Jim said, 'Look, I know it's none of my business, but

384

I don't think you should go there alone. It might be dangerous. You've just told me Jenny must have partners. Can't Breeze go with you?'

'I told you – Breeze hits the roof if I mention this business. He'd do all he could to stop me.'

'I could come up to London for the day, if you like,' Jim offered. 'I could go to Jenny's flat with you, then buy the camping equipment. I don't feel I can burden you with that when you're so distressed.'

'I was going to ask Lulu to come to Jenny's flat with me.'

'You need a man for this, Plum . . . You might need protection. Let me think . . . I've got a class this morning, then I'm having lunch with our new lecturer . . . I can catch the two twenty train, it gets to Waterloo at four . . . So I'll be with you at four thirty. Let's meet at your place.'

'I could meet you at Waterloo,' Plum suggested, touched that Jim should offer to do this. Ruefully, Plum had noticed how much more even-tempered and mellow Jim had become since marrying Sally.

'No, don't meet me. The train might be late and it's hell to park at Waterloo.'

'I'm not sure it's necessary to involve you.'

'Plum, if this trip *isn't* dangerous, then we merely look idiots; but if it *is* dangerous . . . the boys would want me to go with you.'

'You won't tell Toby or Max? I don't want them to worry . . . And you won't go behind my back to Breeze?'

'I won't tell anyone,' Jim promised.

* * * *

Half an hour later, Lulu telephoned; she had just returned from taking Wolf to his playgroup. Hearing her cheerful voice, Plum again burst into tears, then snuffled through a disjointed explanation of what had happened to Jenny. She finished, 'It's like having a constant nightmare – only during the day! Post-traumatic stress disorder, they call it.'

'Poor baby,' Lulu said, and the loving sympathy in her voice made Plum cry harder. 'Listen, are you *sure* of this? I simply can't believe it of Jenny! Thank God her mother's flying out . . . I can't bear to think of Jenny so broken, alone in some foreign hospital where she can't even understand the nurses . . .'

'What about *me*, Lulu? What have *I* done to deserve this? If you're on Jenny's side, *I'll never want to see you again!*'

'I'm on both your sides,' Lulu said unhappily. 'Plum, darling, *please* stop crying . . . Oh blast, I can't come round to you. A new baby-sitter's coming for an interview some time this morning . . . Why don't you come here, Plum? Bring those Dutch transparencies with you – I've had an idea about them. I suppose you still need circumstantial evidence?'

'As much as possible. I'll drive round straight away.'

'Incidentally, while you were in Venice, the police arrested some coke head who's confessed to killing Leo. One of Leo's customers. Apparently he thought Leo might have a stash hidden in his home, but Leo woke up and surprised him.'

'Poor Leo. What a waste!'

※　※　※　※

Like Aunt Harriet, Lulu lived in her kitchen, but not so elegantly. The window looked over a depressed Bayswater back street, and the jungle scene that Lulu had painted on the walls no longer looked witty and cheerful (as it had when there was nothing else in the room) but as forlorn and depressing as a nightclub in daylight. Her kitchen table-top was not antique pearwood but white, easy-wipe plastic: on it lay the remains of breakfast, an open sketchbook, a tortoiseshell cat, a motorcycle helmet and some battered toys that included the eyeless, aged teddy that Wolf took to bed with him.

'Got an aspirin, Lulu?' Plum threw her purse and burgundy suede tote bag into the muddle on the table, sat down, leaned her elbows on the table and rested her chin on her hands. Lulu noticed that Plum's fingernails were gnawed, red stubs.

'Sorry. Nothing addictive here. Have a mug of Red Zinger . . . Wow, you look terrible, darling!' She peered at Plum's hyacinth eyes, now swollen and red-rimmed.

Once again, Plum started to sob. 'Lulu, *you* understand how I feel, don't you? In the back of your mind you know a man might double-cross you – but you don't expect treachery from women friends.'

'So much for sisterhood,' Lulu said sourly, 'I'm *also* confused about Jenny. If Jenny was faking her friendship with you – what do you suppose she really feels for me? If *you* can't trust her – how can I? For years Jenny's apparently acted a part with us and hidden her true feelings . . . I feel I don't know this woman. I'm not sure I want to.'

'How *could* a friend do such a thing?'

'Because she never was a friend,' said Lulu sadly. 'She's proved that.'

Plum blew her nose, drank some herbal tea, and felt slightly better. 'Lulu, have you any idea where Jenny painted these flower pictures?'

After a few minutes of thought, Lulu suggested, 'Maybe she still used her old place in Westbourne Grove.'

Surprised, Plum said, 'I thought she'd let that place go when she moved to the new place in Craven Hill Gardens.'

'No. I asked her if I could quietly use her old basement studio – it was rent-controlled and cost next to nothing – but Jenny said she was keeping it for storage.'

Plum stared at Lulu. '*Where can I get the key?*'

'No idea. Maybe Jenny left it with a neighbour; if so, you could try and con your way in, I suppose.' But they both knew that Plum, in her beige silk, flared pants suit, would be seen as an outsider and potential enemy by the West Indians and out-of-work Irish who lived on welfare among the decaying, rat-infested buildings of Westbourne Grove.

'No, Jenny wouldn't trust anyone else with the key to a forgery studio. I think the key must be somewhere in her flat.' Plum glanced at her watch. Eleven o'clock. She felt the need for action. It seemed ridiculous to wait another five-and-a-half hours for Jim to arrive, when she might be using that precious time to search Jenny's flat. Plum could ask the caretaker to let her into the flat – the man had seen her dozens of times, and she could make some excuse to get him to go up with her so she wouldn't have to go in by herself. If some villain *were* already in the apartment, then he would think twice before attacking the burly caretaker.

Again Plum looked at her watch. Five past eleven. She couldn't hang around in this nervous state when she might be doing something positive about it.

'Listen, Lulu.' Plum explained her change of plan.

Lulu stared. 'I don't think you should go alone. I can't come with you – I have to collect Wolf from his playgroup in half an hour. Can't you get Jim to catch the eleven twenty?'

'No, he's got a class, and then lunch with a visiting lecturer. And I've only got until tomorrow evening. As soon as Jenny's back, she can get to a telephone. She'll alert her partners and they'll destroy all the evidence. She may already have found some way to alert them. So every hour means I have less chance of finding anything left at her secret studio; every hour gives them more time to destroy evidence.'

'For God's sake be careful.'

Plum hugged Lulu, grabbed her purse and rushed off.

Three minutes later, Lulu hurled herself down the stairs with Plum's forgotten burgundy tote bag, but as she rushed out from the front door, she saw the black Porsche disappear around the corner.

'Hi, Lulu.'

Lulu spun round. 'Hallo, Mandy. What're you doing back in London? Thought you were bumming round the world.'

'Ran out of money in Istanbul – so it's back to baby-sitting till I can afford to take off again. You're the first interview the agency gave me.'

'Thank heaven it's you. Now I can leave Wolf to you!'

'When?'

'Today. You know where everything is – still in the same mess.'

'Fine. I'll ring the agency. Lunch money still in the teapot?'

*　*　*　*

By eleven thirty, Plum stood in Jenny's sunny yellow living-room, wondering where to start her search for the key.

By twelve thirty, she had searched the sitting-room, bedroom, bathroom, kitchen and the second bedroom that served as a studio but contained no trace of fake paintings: no materials, no books or posters to copy. Nothing.

Exasperated, Plum realized that she would have to sort through the beige concertina file of book-keeping documentation by Jenny's desk, in the sitting-room; it might provide some evidence of a landlord. Jenny wasn't paying the Westbourne Grove rent in cash, or it wouldn't be a controlled tenancy; so as it was official, there must be cheque payments somewhere, and some record of them.

Plum gazed with distaste at the bulging concertina. Hopefully she need only look in the used cheque books section, to find a scribbled cheque stub for the rent. Or maybe there were receipts? But there were none.

Then something else. But what? And how would Plum recognize it? And once Plum had located a landlord, how could she persuade him to allow her access? A landlord was unlikely to be so easy to con as the Craven Hill Gardens caretaker, who had immediately unlocked Jenny's flat for Plum. Perhaps Plum could tell the landlord of Jenny's accident, and spin him some lie about getting a few of Jenny's things to send to the hospital.

As she tried to decide on her next course of action, the door-bell rang. Plum's taut nerves contracted, and she jumped in fright. Then, furious with herself for being so feeble, she headed for the door. When she reached it, she peeped anxiously through the spyhole.

She opened the door to the amiable caretaker. He wanted to know when Jenny would return from hospital, because she was Secretary of the Tenants' Association, and the communal gardener had just complained he hadn't been paid for the previous month.

After the caretaker left, Plum chained the front door, then leaned against it. She felt weak as the surge of adrenalin drained from her body: she was getting as jumpy as a cat, she thought, as she stared at the coats which hung on the old-fashioned hall stand . . .

She jumped forward, and thrust her hands into the pockets of each coat: Jenny's big winter greatcoat, the scarlet lunch-in-smart-restaurants Kenzo coat that Plum had bought her, a black velvet evening cloak, a checked Burberry left by some equally forgotten lover, and an old beige raincoat. In the pocket of the raincoat, Plum felt something hard.

Triumphant, she stared at the key in her hand. It was not a small, shining key of complicated modern cut, but an old, large, heavy one. Plum could not remember ever having seen the key to Jenny's Westbourne Grove studio, but the key that Plum now held in her hand – dark and battered, cold and tangible – was certainly an old key to an old house.

Exultant, she dashed to the phone to report her triumph to Lulu. She finished, 'So I'm going round to Westbourne Grove now.'

'Get a cab. You don't want the Porsche duffed up while you're inside.' Lulu added, 'Listen, you left your tote bag here.'

'Blast. The trannies are in it. I'll collect it later.'

*   *   *   *

Shortly after one o'clock, Plum reached the dingy lodging house where Jenny had lived when she first came to London. It had once been a prosperous businessman's residence, but now was overstuffed with impoverished families. The imposing steps which led up to the portico were used as a communal porch.

On these steps, surrounded by children, sat a tired, orange-haired, pale woman next to a fat black granny, bulging in a bright turquoise pants suit; behind them, a thin Indian in a too-large brown lounge suit lolled against a peeling grey column.

Two big-eyed pretty little black girls with braided hair jumped down the steps. 'You got cigarettes, lady?' They clutched at Plum's purse and pulled at her silk shirt.

'Sorry, no.' Plum stared nervously at the people blocking her way to the front door. She told herself that it was stupid to be afraid of them.

The hall inside the house contained a row of battered sour-smelling litter bins, a ruptured mattress that stank of urine, and several bent bits of what might once have been a bicycle. Plum edged past these to a door beneath the stairs which led to the basement. Nervously, she produced the key.

It slid easily into the lock.

Plum jumped through the door and locked it from the reverse side, shaking with relief. In the darkness she unsuccessfully groped for a light-switch.

Trembling, Plum inched her way down the stone stairs, wishing she was not wearing the dangerous high-heeled pumps that added to her height. When her groping foot reached the last tread, she shuffled forward and with both hands fumbled for the door to the front room. She felt for the door knob. The door was not locked, as she had feared it might be.

With relief, she found herself standing in dim daylight, which came from a grimy barred window high up against the ceiling.

Plum stared around the room; formerly a kitchen, it must once have produced enormous meals for some Victorian family. Surprisingly, the room was immaculately clean, and almost bare – except for a wooden table, higher than normal, with a silvery metal top and machinery beneath it; an on/off button was set into the side of the frame.

Who would need a vacuum table – used to bond an old damaged canvas to an undamaged one – except a restorer of paintings . . . or a forger?

Plum backed into the corridor, where she could now see the light-switch and hurried to the back room, which Jenny had used as her studio. Hopefully she flung open the door, and looked into blackness. Again, she groped for the light-switch.

Plum was standing in the cleanest studio she had ever seen. In fact, she had never seen a clean studio: they were generally unavoidably grubby places. Against the wall to her right stood a metal shelving unit, upon which tins and tubes of paint were neatly ranged; on a lower shelf stood a kettle and coffee equipment; beneath this was a row of art books, the covers tatty from use; on the bottom shelf, rags and newspapers were neatly piled.

Opposite Plum, wooden shutters had been fitted across the windows of the room. In front of the window stood an easel, with a canvas propped upon it, facing the window. To the left of the easel was a high stool, a table with a clean palette upon it, and a tin jug of brushes.

Holding her breath in excitement, Plum sped across the room to the canvas. She saw a small still-life. From a central basket of fruit spilled cherries and peaches. Flowers were strewn around the base of the basket, and in the right-hand corner was a half-eaten peach. The picture had been drawn in, and the painting work had started, but only the brown-green background and strong yellow tones had been applied.

Plum was looking at the early stages of a Balthazar van der Ast.

* * * *

Just before two o'clock, Lulu pulled Plum's file from the burgundy tote bag. She found the envelope of transparencies, upended it and shook them out. As well as the transparencies, a Polaroid photograph fell upon the table.

Lulu picked up the Polaroid and glanced at it. She frowned in puzzlement, trying to remember something. She groped in Plum's bag for the magnifying-glass, then peered again at the Polaroid.

Lulu instantly realized that Plum was in danger. She jumped to the red wall telephone and quickly dialled long-distance.

* * * *

Plum realized that she had now linked the studio that produced the forgeries to Jenny, but still had not found anything that clearly established Jenny as the painter of the forged paintings. Nor had she found any indication of Jenny's partners. She hurried over to the bookcase: those books might provide a clue.

Suddenly, she heard a noise behind her.

She turned, illogically expecting to see one of the little girls who had been playing on the steps outside.

To her astonishment, she found herself facing Jim.

'Jim! You came on an early train . . .' She stopped abruptly and her welcoming smile faded as she stared at her ex-husband. His handsome face was pale and taut, his thin lips sucked between his teeth; his grey eyes looked coldly at Plum as if she were a stranger. He looked determined and dangerous.

Plum gasped. *'How do you know about this place?'*

Jim shut the door quietly behind him. He wore black jeans and a bomber jacket, and carried a large suitcase in his gloved hands.

'Well, now you know . . .' Jim said defiantly.

Plum realized that he must have caught the eleven twenty train and come straight from Waterloo to Westbourne Grove, expecting to have three hours to remove any evidence.

'What are you going to do about it?' Jim asked roughly. 'How do you suppose the boys will feel if you send me to gaol?'

He must be nervous to play his ace of spades so quickly, Plum told herself, and the thought gave her confidence. She held the winning cards – if only she kept her head and remembered to play them correctly. She forced herself to think clearly, to remember what she needed to discover: the missing link between Jim and Tonon. Jenny would never divulge that – why should she? But now Plum had an opportunity to worm it out of Jim.

'Jim, of course I don't want you to go to gaol.'

'When I phoned, you said you hadn't been to the police?' Jim's face showed how anxious he was for confirmation.

Plum hesitated, remembering Breeze's suggestion that she wait to tell the police who had sent the threatening letters. 'Once you go to the police,' he had said, 'that's irrevocable. So before you do – make sure you want to see Jenny in gaol.' He had almost managed to make Plum feel guilty as he added, 'Why not wait till she's back in London. There's no hurry to put the poor creature behind bars.'

But should Plum admit to Jim that she hadn't been to the police? She wished she could remember what she'd already told him. She'd better not contradict herself; she didn't want to make him more aggressive than he clearly was.

But she knew that she would have told Jim the truth, which was that, swayed by Breeze's arguments, she had *not* been to the police.

Her back to the metal shelving unit, she shook her head. 'No, the police don't know that Jenny's a forger.'

'You certainly believe in calling a spade a bloody shovel, don't you?' Jim's snarl immediately reminded her of their old, bitter marital squabbles. Don't respond, she told herself. Don't get personal. Get back to the paintings. Use your old tactics: placate Jim by praising him. Get to a praise-position fast.

'How did you get involved in this, Jim? I thought you couldn't stand Jenny.' Plum remembered Jim's waspish references to her two friends; when they were still married, his antipathy had certainly not been assumed.

Jim smiled complacently. 'Although you were too self-absorbed to notice, Jenny's been in love with me since we were all at college.'

So the only man that Jenny ever loved wasn't Breeze after all! The reason for Jenny's long-rooted jealousy of Plum was . . . Jim.

'You *don't* mean . . .'

'No, we've never fucked. But I only had to lift my finger, and your precious friend would have been down on her knees.'

Plum bit back the antagonism that welled up as she saw Jim's self-satisfied smirk. 'So Jenny trusted you.'

'You always trust the one you love. After realizing I had no great urge to get into her knickers, Jenny decided I was her ideal elder brother.'

'Jenny needed a partner to organize the forged provenances, and you're a graphic designer.' To Plum this seemed a far more likely reason than infatuation for Jenny to link up with Jim. Or was she being naïve again?

Jim nodded. 'And Jenny knew I needed the money.'

'How did she know that?'

'Any teacher with young kids needs money.'

'So you two have been operating together right from the time Jenny left Bill?'

'In 1988, with a list of Bill's clients – the ones that purchased fakes.' Jim laughed.

Remember to flatter, Plum told herself. 'You were brilliantly successful, Jim, but you can't have been the brains behind this operation – who was the boss, the leader?' As she talked, Plum edged inch by inch over towards the easel.

'I organized every bloody thing!' Jim said, clearly rattled, as Plum intended. '*I* organized the distribution routes. *I* organized the provenances and *I* found the old artist's materials, in antique shops, or on junk stalls.'

'And the distribution route led through Gillian Carteret?' Plum moved almost imperceptibly to her right.

Jim looked astonished then fearful. 'Leave her out of this!'

'Jim, three trails lead straight back to her. And she still has a fake hanging on her bedroom wall.'

Jim spat, 'How could Jilly be so *stupid*?'

'Jilly?'

Sullenly he said, 'She was Jilly Thompson before she married that pompous prick.'

Inching further towards the easel, Plum remembered. 'Of course – Jilly Thompson was in Lulu's year at art college.'

Plum itched to wipe the smirk from Jim's face.

Jim said, 'I'm damned if I'm going to give you any more details, Plum . . . *What are you trying to do, you bitch?*'

She had moved too quickly.

As Jim jumped towards her, Plum leaped behind the easel, grabbed the half-finished canvas, and held it behind her back.

Jim lunged towards her, determined to retrieve the canvas.

Plum shoved the six-foot-tall easel at him. The main upright hit Jim in the face. He yelled in pain, and clapped both hands to his face.

Plum dashed towards the door.

Jim thrust the easel aside and, panting, charged towards her.

As Plum yanked the door open, Jim grabbed at her shoulders and spun her round to face him. 'You haven't changed, you little bitch!' She saw blood running from his forehead as he grabbed behind her for the painting.

Plum staggered backwards into the hall, then felt Jim's weight thrust her against the wall. This struggle was not like her fight with Jenny: against the man's strength, Plum was almost helpless.

'You smug, arrogant little bitch,' Jim grunted. Closely locked in combat, their bodily contact seemed to release Jim's resentment and jealousy of Plum's success, which underlined his failure and fuelled his hatred of her.

As Jim slammed her head against the wall, Plum saw an orange-red haze. He shook her like a furious child shaking a rag doll. Then, with one hand, he caught hold of the pink chiffon scarf around Plum's throat and twisted it. She screamed at the reactivated pain of her bruises.

As she felt Jim's hands tighten around her throat, Plum dropped the precious canvas, and her hands flew to her neck.

Jim continued to squeeze. Plum could not scream but only gurgle, as she tried unsuccessfully to prise his hands from her neck. They swayed together, trampling on the ignored canvas.

As Plum felt herself losing consciousness, she forced herself to make one last effort. As hard as she could, she jabbed her right thumb into Jim's left eye-socket.

Jim screamed in pain, and clapped his left hand to his eye.

Feeling his grasp weaken, Plum corkscrewed downwards. Freeing herself from his grasp, she staggered along the passage towards the stairs.

Jim reached her as she started up the stairs. With one frightened glance over her shoulder, Plum saw his face – white with anger and determined.

Her instincts screamed at her to get up the stairs, but her intelligence told her that Jim would undoubtedly catch her before she reached the top. Fleetingly, Plum thought of screaming, but knew it would be useless: screams – assumed to be marital arguments – would scarcely raise an eyebrow in this building.

With a great mental effort, she twisted round to face Jim, then kicked out at his face.

Jim howled again in pain, and fell back. Furious, he charged up the stairs again.

Every time Jim lunged forward to grab her, Plum bent her knee and kicked again – and her legs were longer than his arms.

One step at a time, she backed her way up the stairs: each time she retreated, she kicked out with her high stiletto heel. Once her heel slashed his cheek and Jim yelped in pain.

Each time Jim backed away, Plum looked into his shrewd, calculating eyes and knew that Jim was trying to think of some clever, unexpected move.

Plum only realized that she had reached the top of the stairs when she suddenly felt the hard frame of the door behind her. Momentarily disconcerted, she stumbled.

Jim saw his chance. He crouched, then lunged upwards, head bent well down and both arms outstretched, as he grabbed her legs in a rugger tackle.

Plum screamed, as together they fell down the stone stairs.

She felt her head bang against the iron railing, felt their entwined bodies crash into the wall that faced the stairs and carom off it. She felt Jim's heavy body on top of her. Terrified, she knew that he had trapped her.

On the periphery of consciousness, Plum heard banging and shouting from the other side of the door at the top of the stairs, then sounds of splitting wood . . . a sharp thud . . . a splintering door. A stream of dark uniforms flowed hastily down the stairs towards Plum's body. And from behind them, Plum heard Lulu's high-pitched yell, '*Hurry*, you stupid bastards!'

CHAPTER TWENTY-NINE

Friday, 12 June 1992

HUDDLED in the back of the police car, Plum asked Lulu, 'How did you know I was in trouble?'

'When I opened the folder in your tote bag and the picture of Jilly Thompson fell out. I recognized her immediately. You couldn't mistake that querulous expression, the long witch hair and the eyebags. As Jilly was standing next to a Dutch flower painting, I realized it must be the Polaroid you'd talked about – of Gillian Carteret in her bedroom. And then I realized Jilly Thompson and Gillian Carteret were the same person. So I guessed her connection to the forger was Jim.' Lulu looked slightly embarrassed. In order to avoid distressing Plum, Lulu had never told her of Jim's affair with Jilly Thompson, but the signs had been clear: the two were once 'accidentally' locked together in a classroom for over an hour, and there was ample evidence of Jim's favouritism. Furthermore, Jilly openly bragged of having the best-looking tutor at college under her thumb. Theirs had been a public secret.

So when Lulu saw the Polaroid of Jilly, she had immediately guessed that Jim was not travelling up from Portsmouth to help Plum, but to harm her.

Lulu phoned Hampshire Art College and asked to speak to Jim. She was told that Jim was not due in that day, as he had no classes scheduled. The secretary added, 'I already checked after Plum Russell phoned.' The fact that Jim had lied to Plum confirmed Lulu's suspicions.

Plum lowered her voice so that the cops in the front of the squad car couldn't hear. 'But how come I was rescued by the *drug squad*?'

Lulu looked embarrassed. 'I didn't know which police department you were dealing with. I knew I probably couldn't locate it – and if I did, I wouldn't be able to explain why I was worried. It would all take too long. By the time I'd convinced the cops you were in danger, you might have been shot, sawn up into bite-sized chunks, neatly packed in a suitcase and dumped in the left-luggage department at Paddington station.'

Lulu giggled. 'So I told the cops what I knew would get them off their asses in a flash. I said you were a pusher going to meet your supplier. I said you could get anything – coke, ecstasy, crack, acid, smack – but you wouldn't let me have any more on credit . . . I tried to sound vengeful, and it must have worked because they asked if I'd be prepared to come along with them, and make the identification.'

From the front seat the drug squad detective turned round and grinned. 'She was very convincing, Mrs Russell. You were facing fourteen years in prison – maximum penalty under the Misuse of Drugs Act for possession of Class A drugs with intent to supply.'

'Thanks for saving me, Lulu.' Plum put her left arm round Lulu and hugged her; as she did so, her diamond ring glinted in the sun. Without removing her arm from Lulu's shoulders, Plum tugged off her ring. 'Here, give me your hand.'

She placed the ring in Lulu's palm and closed Lulu's fingers over it. 'That should pay off your mortgage, Lulu.'

Lulu gasped, 'Oh my God . . . I can't . . . yes, I can . . . You don't know what this will mean to me, Plum.'

'Oh, yes, I do. Freedom,' Plum said firmly. 'I've had enough of diamonds. They're a nuisance to look after and expensive to insure. They attract envy, violence and muggers. They're a lousy investment that earns no interest, and loses half of its value five minutes after you've paid for it. I'll be delighted if that useless thing pays your mortgage, Lulu.'

Lulu slipped the ring on her little finger. 'I can't believe it! I *long* to get rid of that bloody mortgage – Ben still uses it as an excuse for saying no to everything.' She quirked her finger and the diamond flashed light. 'D'you mind if I keep this for a couple of days, before selling it? Just for fun?'

Sunday, 14 June 1992

When she visited Jim, Plum found him contrite and chastened. He was in a cell at the police station, prior to going to the Magistrates' Court on the following morning to face charges of forgery and actual bodily harm.

Thinking of their sons, Plum tried to persuade the police to drop the ABH charges, but a detective said, 'We can see your neck. We caught him doing it. We can't turn a blind eye to attempted strangulation.' Had they still been married it would have been termed a marital dispute, and therefore not illegal.

Because of the ABH charge, the police would not allow Plum into Jim's white-tiled cell, but she was allowed to peer at him through a small wicker window at head height. Fully dressed, he was lying on a rubber mattress on a fixed bench that ran the length of his cell and incorporated an open toilet seat at the far end. The small window beyond was barred.

'Thanks for trying to get the assault charge dropped,' he said.

'That's OK. We also tried to get you released on bail.'

'I'm sorry about the kids. I expect they'll kick me out of college.' Jim knew that he was heading for prison, and that his wife and family were ashamed of him. He didn't want to talk.

Just before she left, Plum asked Jim if he'd really only phoned to talk about the summer holidays. She remembered that something in his voice had made it seem unlikely. She had forgotten it until now.

'Your mum telephoned and told me something useful, for the first time ever.' Jim gave a rueful grin. 'She said you were in tears because Jenny had attacked you because you'd found her forging flower paintings. So I immediately phoned you – to find out what the hell had happened.'

※　※　※　※

Around Plum's bruised neck was an orange scarf; she wore a yellow cotton dress and thick, cork-soled sandals that made no noise upon the rubber floor as she entered Jenny's pea-soup-coloured hospital room.

Plum stopped abruptly in the doorway and stared at Jenny; it was difficult to see a part of her that was not bandaged or encased in plaster, but she saw no remorse upon what was visible of Jenny's face, only accusation.

From her black-barred hospital bed, Jenny glared at Plum.

'I suppose you realize I'll end up in gaol,' Jenny snarled, 'thanks to you!'

'What did you expect if you were caught?'

Jenny grunted. 'I hope you also realize it's *your* fault that Jim's in gaol. How do you suppose your kids feel about *that*?'

Plum, who had thought about this for hours, was silent. She hoped the boys would not blame her, and that she could help them through the ordeal that lay ahead of them.

Plum said, 'I never realized you loved Jim.'

'Typical of your bloody insensitivity! *I*, on the other hand, realized that he loved you – even before you did.' In a dreamy, reminiscent voice, Jenny added, 'And that's when my hatred of you started, Plum . . . D'you remember driving back from that first New Year's Eve ball, jammed in Jim's old Ford, with about ten other sleepy people? I was the last one to get out – except for you. I remember bunching up that net dress and stumbling through the snow to the front door. Then I turned to wave goodnight.'

A hard edge crept into Jenny's voice. 'But you had both forgotten me. I saw Jim stroke your face with one finger, as if your bloody face were the most fragile and wonderful thing on earth. You weren't even necking, he was just gazing at you . . . and I realized that what he felt for you – was what I felt for him.'

'That was a long, long time ago,' Plum said gently. 'Let's forget it, Jenny.'

'I'll *never* forget it! I stood in the shadow of the doorway, outside the yellow lamplight that encircled you both, and I felt an outcast.'

'That was hardly my fault,' Plum protested.

'You must have led him on!' Jenny said heavily. 'Anyway, I avoided you until spring term started, by when I reckoned I'd get over it. But then I felt that misery again – as if a band of pain was tightening around my chest – and this time it had nothing to do with Jim.'

Jenny's voice took on a dreamy quality. 'Remember the day we first used oil-paint? My easel was opposite yours, because I was painting you and you were painting me. At the end of the afternoon Old Davis wandered round as usual, gave my work a two-second glance, then stopped at your easel. He called his buddy – Briggs, the life-class master – and they both stood looking at your painting and muttering to each other, as if neither of us were present.'

'Jenny, you can hardly blame me – '

'Why not? *You* were the cause of my pain!' Jenny looked coldly at Plum. 'At first I told myself that I might as well be jealous of Picasso or Jane Fonda: but *they* weren't there, beside me, making my life miserable.'

Plum wished she could say she was sorry that she'd made Jenny feel miserable. But she could only remember the two threatening letters and Jenny's hands around her throat.

'One of the best moments of my life,' Jenny sniggered, 'was when you burst into tears in the toilets and told me you were pregnant. You couldn't face your parents. You didn't know how to tell Jim. I knew so well what wretchedness felt like. I was exultant! I thought you'd have an abortion, you see. But you didn't. And my tight band of misery squeezed harder whenever I imagined Jim's child growing in *my* body.'

Jenny's smile broadened. 'I knew as soon as Jim was unfaithful – not only by the way he looked at the girl, but by the way he looked at *you*. You were obstructing him! I watched Jim's boredom turn to resentment, then hatred. And then at last Jim and I were bound together – not by love but by hate: hatred of you, Plum!'

Plum felt anger rise. How could Jenny – who hated her so – have concealed her true feelings so cleverly for so many years! 'Jenny, I'll never understand why . . .'

'Oh, fuck off!'

* * * *

402

Driving back from the hospital, Plum automatically slipped the Porsche in and out of traffic as she agonized over her other dilemma: she was no nearer choosing between Breeze and Paul.

Breeze was not making her decision easy. Anything she said to him was twisted into an argument against her leaving him. Plum had never expected Breeze to be so upset at the thought of losing her: she'd found it touching, while resenting the guilt it aroused in her. Then she would crossly ask herself whether her husband's feelings concerned the loss of Plum the woman, Plum the wife, Plum the painter – or Plum the possession. Would Breeze still feel the same if Paul did not exist? Was his resentment of Paul that stiff-legged, keep-off-my-territory confrontation that you saw in dogs?

What about responsibility? Plum remembered that once she had promised to love and cherish Breeze until death, not lust, separated them. It was no excuse to say that Breeze had broken his promise, therefore releasing her from her promise – she should perhaps remember that bit about for better or for worse? Had *that* promise meant anything? If not, why not?

Perhaps because the woman who made that promise no longer existed? Perhaps it was a promise no woman can truthfully make, for no woman can look into the future, she told herself.

Logic and duty told Plum to stay with Breeze; but her feelings tugged her gently and insistently towards Paul, and they would not be denied or smothered. Those emotions existed, and would continue to exist, whatever choice she finally made.

How long was she prepared to be unhappy, Plum wondered. Should she not join Paul, how long would it take for thoughts of him to fade – as Breeze assured her that they would?

She had only one life to lead. Should Plum's future be dictated by guilt or joy?

Did Plum really want a future that meant taking on the difficult task of speaking a foreign language, learning foreign customs, living in a foreign country and bringing up two small foreign children?

Aunt Harriet would probably suggest that, at this point, Plum might live by herself for a bit, and learn to stand on her own feet before leaping into matrimony for the third time.

Wistfully, Plum remembered Aunt Harriet saying that every woman is responsible for her own happiness. And conversely, for her own unhappiness, Plum supposed.

Only one thing was clear to her: she had a choice between remaining in a life which had not brought her happiness, and choosing a life in which she felt happy, simply because she existed.

But supposing Paul *did* turn out to be a passing infatuation, as Breeze insisted?

* * * *

Just before midday, Plum parked outside her front door. She felt relieved that Breeze would not return from Zurich until Friday; hopefully, that gave her time to disentangle her feelings, and come to a decision.

As she pushed her key into the front door lock, she felt a firm hand on her shoulder.

Startled, she jumped, and yelped. She spun round, and found herself looking up into black-fringed, brilliant blue eyes. She shivered with desire.

'I didn't mean to frighten you.'

Plum threw herself into his arms. 'Paul, darling! What a wonderful surprise!'

'I thought it simplest to come and get you. I've booked us on the two thirty flight back to Bordeaux.'

'To Aquitainia,' Plum murmured against his chest.

'Yes. You have half an hour to pack.'

Plum glanced towards the front door. She ran to the Porsche and pulled out the ignition key. She snapped open her purse, fished out her front door keys, and pushed them all through the letter-box.

Then she ran down the marble steps, and into her future.

ACKNOWLEDGEMENTS

U NTIL now all my books have been written by hand: this is the first book I've typed. So I'd like to thank Queen's College Secretarial School, London, England, for their excellent seven-day typing and word-processing course (cost: £200 in 1992), after which I typed at twenty-two words a minute, with the rest of the class.

I am particularly grateful to Suzanne Baboneau of Pan Macmillan, who was kind enough to travel out to Monaco for three hectic and enjoyable days of editorial criticism. Geraldine Cooke and Cyra McFadden also visited Monte Carlo and fearlessly criticized my manuscript. And as always, I am indebted to my agents, Morton Janklow and Anne Sibbald, for their interest, kindness and protection.

I'm also grateful to the people who ran the rest of my life while I wrote this book: in Monaco, Richard MacLellan and David Solomon; also Roselyn Haudberg, who could not be persuaded to cook without cream and wine.

For reading the manuscript from the point of view of their special knowledge, I am grateful to Nicola Jacobs; to the necessarily anonymous art detective, who kindly gave me the benefit of her worldwide knowledge and experience; and to Charlotte Abrahams, who managed to do an astonishing amount of research in one day in London.

Soviet astronaut Valentina Tereshkova, Joan Whiffen, the Dinosaur Lady of New Zealand, and Ivana Trump were kind enough to talk to me about what women *really* want: except for these three, and Aunt Harriet (who got a 2:1 in her Finals), all the characters in this novel are imaginary and are in no way intended to depict real people: any resemblance to anyone living is accidental.

For supplementing my own experience of what it feels like to be a painter, I'm grateful to painters Gillian Ayres, Deryck Healey and Mary Lee-Woolf.

For their specialized information, support and constructive help I would like to thank my family: my daughter-in-law Georgina Godley Conran, the family forger, my graphologist sister Isabel Carr, my aunt Dorothy Spittle, my sons Jasper Conran and Sebastian Conran.

For supplying or checking esoteric detail in odd places I'm also grateful to the following people:

In France: William Waterfield for his knowledge of historical botany; François Marat, Nice fishmonger and lepidopterist; Alexander Mosley for his knowledge of the seedier parts of Paris; Charlotte Mosley for her knowledge of the grander parts; Roger Batt for his knowledge of my word-processor.

In Australia: I was lucky enough to have Ita Buttrose's advice and Susanna de Vries-Evans's art expertise. Kate Halfpenny discussed the theme, and I also appreciated James Fraser's geographical knowledge (where the best beaches are).

In Britain: The Fine Arts and Antiques Fraud Squad at Scotland Yard generously helped me, as did Patrick Grayson of the Jules Kroll Agency, and Walter Whyte, formerly of the CID. Phillip Saunders of *Trace* magazine and Robin Townley of Sotheby's were also generous with their time and expertise. Dr Dennis Friedman taught me how to break arms and legs. Angela Lambert sent me fascinating notes on Cleo's progress. The Duchess of Bedford supplied jokes, Baroness Brigstocke lent erudition and the Marchioness of Lothian provided the Russian Connection.

For their expertise and patience, I would also like to thank Leslie Waddington and Tim Taylor of Waddington Galleries and Tim Hilton. Henry Meyric Hughes, Director of Exhibitions at the Hayward Gallery, told me a great deal about the history of the Biennale (much of it too scandalous to include), as did Sandy Nairn of the British Council, Isobel Johnston, Andrew Rose, Muriel Wilson and Mary Oppenheim.

I enjoyed discussing diamonds with Christopher Macdonald of Tiffany. For locating out-of-print books I am indebted to Douglas Matthews and Edward Preedy of the London Library, Geoffrey Bailey of Harrods bookshop, Rob Cassy of Hatchards and Joe Saumaurez Smith of the Heywood Hill bookshop, London.

In Monaco: I enjoyed discussing my theme with Carson Churchill Pratt, Jacqui Graham, Margaret Frazer and Julia de Biere, who also has an Eye *sans pareil.*

In New York: I would like to thank Sandi Mendelson for her advice; designer Kenneth Jay Lane for making beautiful jewellery available to normal women; fashion designer Anna Sui, who designed Plum's touring wardrobe; and Avril Giacobbi for her insider's knowledge of SoHo galleries.

In Los Angeles: I am, as always, indebted to Joanne Brough, and I shall never forget the pleasure of being stuck in gridlocked traffic for days on end with Judy Hilsinger.

I'm particularly grateful to Elizabeth Chatwin, not only for her knowledge of forgery but also for giving me a privately printed book by her husband, Bruce Chatwin. *The Morality of Things* arrived after I had finished my manuscript, but reminded me of how this story began.

Bruce knew that I collected West African tribal sculpture, among other things. After lectures on the dangers of acquisition and the treacherous nature of possessions, one day he brought me an elegant sculpture from Paris: the size and shape of a small watermelon, it was hollow and made of heavy bronze with a slit down one side. I could not guess what it was. 'It's the ankle bracelet of a Benin chief's favourite wife,' Bruce said. 'And it's so heavy that she couldn't move when she wore it.'

I stopped collecting.